HOMINID

Other Books *by* John C. Boland

NOVELS

Out of Her Depth
Last Island South
The Margin
Death in Jerusalem
The Seventh Bearer
Rich Man's Blood
Brokered Death
Easy Money

SHORT STORIES

30 Years in the Pulps

NONFICTION

Wall Street's Insiders

HOMINID

a novel

JOHN C. BOLAND

PERFECT CRIME BOOKS

Library of Congress Cataloging-in-Publication Data
Boland, John C.
Hominid / John C. Boland
ISBN: 978-1-935797-16-6

First Edition: October 2011

For John Isaac Boland

Biz hundert un tsvantsig.

Flesh perishes. I live on . . . .

Thomas Hardy

One: The Tomb

A crypt excavation may occasionally cause . . . considerable distress to some members of the workforce. Any crypt excavation team should include members with either a forensic or medical professional background.

Appropriate working practices should be adopted to minimize stress to the workforce. Psychologists should monitor this area of staff health during the project. . . .

Given the small but significant risk of exposure to pathogens as a result of crypt excavation, it is recommended that . . . the work-force have had primary vaccinations. . . .

Margaret Cox
School of Conservation Sciences,
Bournemouth University

1

WIND ROCKED THE HELICOPTER, SPRAYING THE WINDOW WITH snow and frozen rain. *Airborne slush*, David Isaac thought, leaning closer to the glass. They had been flying south, passing frayed barrier islands as they met the storm front. The pilot, who was two seats forward, had announced their altitude a minute ago but otherwise hadn't said much during the two-hour journey. Neither had the big man next to David, who leaned forward now and tapped a down-pointing finger against the glass. Eight hundred feet below, gray waves were rolling into a wide bay, just beyond the mouth of which lay an island. The island was small and narrow, its snow-spackled flatness broken by clusters of trees and buildings. As the helicopter descended, David saw details. Less than half the roofs showed heat markers; maybe fifty occupied dwellings. There were a few streets, hard to identify because they hadn't gotten much use since the last snowfall.

"This is it?"

Paolo Becker looked out the opposite window. "Ewell Island.

Right below us, that's the only village, Tyler. We're going further south."

They were near the treetops. Bands of water sliced through snowy marshes, reflecting the torn sky. Trees leaned into the tide that flooded the low ground.

"There," Becker said.

A scar of activity came into view, a tarp-covered truck, frost-backed automobiles, rivers of ice surrounding large tents. David sat straighter. Why couldn't the project have waited for spring?

"How many crew?" David asked.

"If you stay, seven professionals."

"Students?"

"None. Dr. Sprague is keeping this close. He hired a couple of locals as laborers."

On the phone thirty hours ago, Noel Sprague hadn't asked after David's family, hadn't voiced regret that they hadn't spoken in five years. He'd said, "I need your experience." Refused to say more, except that if David was available Becker would pick him up the next day.

They landed in a small clearing, crossed a no-man's-land of brush and trash to the edge of the camp. The pockmarked landing pad surrounded by rotting trees had a rushed feel to it. Not like Sprague's usual, meticulously planned projects.

Icy rain was falling.

"When do you tell me what we have?" David said.

"Better you see for yourself."

There were eight tents of varied sizes. All were mounted on wooden frames, supported by platforms held a few feet off the ground by blocks. Electrical generators rumbled in the dusk, feeding cables to the shelters. Becker led the way to the nearest structure, climbed a step and opened a door. Cots and cluttered belongings took up most of a muddy plywood floor. Becker tossed David's bag onto a cot that was already loaded with gear. "Sprague and his wife camp here. We'll move you later."

"Where are they?"

"Other end of the island. They should be back by dark." He glanced at his watch. His manner was brusque. He had been a Sprague loyalist for as long as David had known him, nervous about any slight to the man's reputation. "They'll fill you in. I'm supposed to show you the excavation from above ground—you can't go down till we check it out. We've got visuals and GPR logs. You get to review everything."

"Looking for what?"

"We may have a water problem."

David didn't answer.

"A little one," Becker said. "Come on."

They stepped outside. Becker set off toward a large canvas dome at the opposite edge of the camp. From a distance David could see it was different. It had twice the footprint and was half again as high as the other tents. Inside there would be direct access to the earth, half-dug trenches, maybe a few trails of duck boards, every kind of digging equipment from a toothbrush to a backhoe, probably no heat. The excavation itself shouldn't be more than a few feet deep. Nothing found on these coastal islands was really subterranean. So what was Becker talking about—viewing the excavation from above ground? They had crossed half the distance when light flared in the doorway and a man came out.

He saw them and began running. Rain washed mud from his face and clothes.

"Dr. Gerson—" he cried, *"—in the pit!"*

The man grabbed Becker's arm. David continued through the door of the excavation tent. What he saw was not what he had expected. There were no shallow trenches, no catwalk of duck boards. In the middle of the tent, lit by overhead floods, a six-legged metal hoist loomed at least a dozen feet tall. The machine made him think of an insect, its angular shoulders hunched, its head nodding. David stepped past a rope enclosure and found himself staring into a hole. The opening was stone, roughly circular, no more than three feet across. A torrent of foul-smelling air blew from the opening into his face. The top couple of feet of a metal ladder rattled against the stonework.

David bent forward. The ladder was empty. It stretched down some distance—ten feet?—into a roaring blackness.

Fast-moving water.

He stared.

The water was flowing with the power of an explosive, sudden flood. One of the unpredictable horrors of underground work. And someone named Gerson was down there, either in trouble or dead depending on whether he had air.

David tried not to think about what he did next. He reached for the ladder.

Six steps down, fast, took him past stone and mud, put him knee deep in the torrent. Two more steps and his lower body entered the water, and the icy shock took his breath away. He could see that there was more than a vertical shaft. A tunnel ran in two directions, no higher than his chest. Water poured in hard against him from the left. It was six inches from reaching the tunnel ceiling.

He scanned the surface for a bobbing head. Anyone caught by the flood's impact could have been carried to the end of the passageway, however far that was. He swept a hand out, hoping to touch clothing or flesh.

A voice shouted down. "Get out of there!"

David looked up.

Paolo Becker stretched a leg to the ladder.

David called, "No! Stay up there. Send down a rope." He turned, keeping a grip on the ladder. He had to duck to get his eyes to the level of the tunnels. He needed a flashlight, but there wasn't time to tell Becker to drop one. Once he ran out of air . . .

A backwash struck his chin, curled over his shoulders and churned behind him, like hands massaging his body, squeezing and pulling.

The backwash complicated things. It could have carried an unconscious person to the other side of the shaft.

David felt his numbed fingers loosen from the ladder and pushed himself forward. He was scrunched to two-thirds his normal six feet, balancing on bent knees, hair brushing the overhead roughness, right hand guiding him along the wall. Backwash splashed his mouth. He tilted his head back to call out.

Nobody answered.

A current spun him. He shifted his weight just as the next surge caught him. He stumbled backward and went under.

Total blackness.

He felt himself being rolled. Thrashing, his arm found a wall and he pushed himself back toward the ladder. When he got his head clear of the water, there was still blackness. The lights had shorted out. He reached the shaft, and its dim light drew him.

He was halfway up the ladder when he noticed the water following him, clutching, dragging, refusing to let go. It had filled the underground passages, and pressure was forcing it up the shaft. In an instant froth passed his shoulders, swept over his head.

He held his breath and climbed, broke into the air, and Becker pulled him off the ladder.

"You missed the fucking rope," Becker said.

"Couldn't see it."

"What about Bobby?"

David rolled off the stone lip and spat out brackish water. He was shaking.

"Did you see her?" Becker pressed. "Michaels said she was right behind him."

"Her?"

"Gerson."

David forced his eyes open and stared into the pit. The vortex had climbed almost to the rim, a giant black tentacle, twisting and oily.

He hated water.

"I didn't see anyone," David said.

2

THEY GATHERED IN THE DINING TENT.

The man who had run from the excavation tent, Luther Michaels, was shivering under blankets, dried mud on his face, thick hands trembling as they clutched a mug of coffee that his wife had made. Paolo Becker was on a satellite phone, trying to raise Sprague or his wife.

The water in the excavation had fallen several feet, withdrawing toward the level of its apparent source in the bay. David had changed to dry clothes, but the cold of the pit stayed with him.

I need your experience. Sprague's exact words. David appreciated them now. The son of a bitch had known there was water trouble, so he had called on someone who knew archaeological flooding first hand.

There was a depressed mood in the tent. The young scientist trapped underground, Roberta Gerson, had been well-liked. She had come over to this project from the Institute of the

Americas, where she was developing a specialty in Colonial village life.

Two scientists were conferring outside his hearing. David had gotten perfunctory introductions to them. Loren Fane, anthropologist. John Walters, forensic pathologist. Both men glanced at David, then away. He told himself that whatever they thought, whatever they knew about his past, didn't matter. Becker came over, bringing coffee.

"We're working too close to the bay," Becker said. "We may have to abandon the tunnels."

David set the coffee mug down carefully. He wished there was a culpable face to punch. "Did Noel know the danger?"

"Nothing like this. He hoped you could prevent an accident. We started getting a little water two days ago. That's why he called you in. No one was supposed to be working underground until you had made your assessment. Bobby got the same orders as the rest of us. As for Michaels—"

David followed his glance to the man huddled under the blankets. "Who is he?"

"Local labor. His wife Etta cooks—"

Becker's voice broke off, and he stood up.

David looked past him. Charlene Sprague had come through the doorway and was bearing down on them, jacket open, hood pushed back, rusty-brown hair damp and tangled.

"What happened?" she demanded.

Becker answered. "Bobby was in the west passage, according to Michaels. David tried to reach her, but—"

"Could she be alive?" There was a plea in her voice. "Air pockets?"

Air trapped in the chambers would have been compressed by the pressure of the invading flood into quart-sized bubbles, or forced into the porous earth itself. Her glance shifted the question to David, who told her what she already knew. "There wouldn't be any air pockets," he said.

She took the information in silence. She tugged off gloves under which her fingers had broken nails and abrasions. Five years since he had seen her, and she still could pass for a twenty-year-old tomboy instead of an accomplished woman in her thirties. He wondered if she still got carded in saloons. In graduate school, however young she looked, she had been able to browbeat a line of reluctant, superstitious African diggers while clearing as much rock as any of them. It was easy to make mistakes about her. David had made his share.

She dug a tissue out of her jacket, wiped her eyes. "Roberta's twenty-five. She was planning—"

David knew the appropriate banalities by heart: life cut short, promising career ended—as though in the normal course of things people lived until they had had enough. He wondered how long that would be.

"I'm sorry," he said lamely.

Noel Sprague came in, limped across the room and hugged his young wife. He pounded David on the shoulder. "Good to see you. Better circumstances, next time. There's no hope for Dr. Gerson?"

"Not from what I saw down there."

"I don't understand what happened."

Sprague didn't have to call the staff to gather round. Red-bearded and stocky, he dominated the tent, and they drew in close without a word. He had commanded lecture halls at Columbia that way, rolling along on force of personality, glaring at colleagues and students, daring challenge, sometimes mocking his own image. A teaching assistant had photoshopped a caricature of Sprague as a squat Viking warrior with doctoral candidates' skulls on his belt, one of them marked "D. Isaac." Nobody had felt the portrait was unfair—least of all apparently Sprague, who had hung a printout beside the diplomas and photographs in his office. Even Becker, who was six inches taller, lacked the man's presence.

Sprague's gaze swept them all. "What were they doing underground?" He focused on Becker. "Did you authorize them?"

If Becker was offended, he hid it. "No, sir."

Fane, the anthropologist, stood a few steps back, short and sharp-faced, with a bristle mustache. A quilted vest hung open over a military-style sweater. His answer to Sprague was a brusque head shake.

The man beside him, the pathologist, could have been an aging biker, if David judged by the bandana on his head and his denim jacket. When Sprague looked at him, Walters said, "I don't give orders. And no one asked me."

"Who then?"

"Apparently Bobby was underground on her own," Becker said.

"With Luther Michaels."

Becker nodded.

"What does Michaels say happened?"

"Just that the tunnels flooded. He's in shock, not very helpful."

Sprague drew a ragged breath. "This is terrible. I should have been down there. . . ." He looked down at his stiff right leg. "I'll have to notify her family."

There was a moment's silence. Nobody in the tent doubted Sprague's sincerity. The woman's death was a tragedy, and he would have done anything he could to prevent it. But David wondered if Fane or Walters really understood the extent of Sprague's ambition. He got his answer when Fane asked if they should begin packing up.

Sprague ignored the question. "Did we reach the authorities?"

"I contacted the state police," Becker said. "They'll bring a medical examiner."

Sprague told David, "There isn't an elected official or policeman on the island. The honorary mayor is also the Methodist preacher and village drunk." He glanced at Fane, said, "I'm going to keep our options open for a little bit, Loren."

Fane looked surprised.

Sprague turned to David. He said grimly, "Well, let's see if we still have a project. You can give us the answer to that."

"I'll need to see the maps."

Sprague nodded.

They crossed the icy ground to the high tent. Inside, David took in details that he hadn't noticed before. Half the floor was crowded with work tables that supported electronic gear, including video displays from which Sprague presumably could monitor his team's activity underground. A separate wooden table held boxes of mud-encrusted artifacts recovered from the excavation. Wire-bound crates stood against the tent's side walls. Sprague paced over to the mouth of the shaft while his wife sat at a table and began opening computer files. David sat beside her.

"Has Paolo told you what we've got?" she asked.

"Not enough."

"It's a crypt. Most of the mapping was done with ground penetrating radar. But we also ran fiberoptic cameras along the tunnels. There are more than three thousand images. You can see those if you want."

"Let's see the schematics."

She switched screens. David looked at the image and understood it was an annotated three-dimensional GPR rendering of the stone-walled shaft. From ground level to the floor of the pit was a descent of thirteen point two feet. Only two passageways had been found leading from the shaft. Both tunnels were rough and constricted. They had been dug by hand with no thought of providing comfort to whoever came later because no one was supposed to come later. Charl opened a window of photographs that reinforced the GPR images. Raw earth was shored intermittently with what looked like creosoted timbers. David studied the 3-D soundings. The tunnel height ranged from four feet down to less than thirty inches. Average width was two and a half feet. He felt sweat prickle his neck. It was a miracle he and Michaels had gotten out of the hole.

Sprague had come over. He pointed to the diagram of the eastern passage. "We mapped twenty feet in that direction until the tunnel reached a dead end. It was close to the bay. We knew there was a potential for flooding and stayed clear. In the other direction, here, you can go fourteen feet before running into a place the roof collapsed. Unfortunately, what we want is on the other side of the collapse."

The radar image showed that the tunnel continued about ten feet beyond the collapse, to a small cul-de-sac.

"The area we can't reach is the burial vault," Sprague said. "We had planned to drill through the rubble and run a camera inside."

David concentrated on the vault. It didn't belong here. There was a superficial resemblance to ancient sites, in Egypt and Central America, but it didn't belong *here*.

"How old?" he said.

"About three hundred years." Charl tapped a key twice, and the picture became three-dimensional, like a hologram.

"Impossible."

"My initial thought," she agreed. "But here it is."

He searched his mind for an answer. Viking? The Northmen's ships had gotten this far south, but that would mean Sprague had gotten the dates all wrong. The tunnel would be at least a thousand years old.

Charl seemed to read his mind. "It's pre-Revolutionary, David. An English colony. There are records that make the timeline pretty tight."

He nodded, didn't answer.

"The GPR shows the vault is about six feet wide, five deep, two feet high," Sprague said. He pointed to three hazy rectangular objects. "There's little doubt these are coffins. From their density, I think there's a good chance they're encased in lead."

It was one more factoid that made little sense. But David grasped its immediate importance.

"They might be watertight," he said.

"And airtight." Sprague planted both hands on his wife's shoulders. "Show the tidal patterns, dear."

The graphic on the computer screen had been overlayed with the high and low tide readings in this part of the bay. The tide patterns removed any doubt as to whether Sprague had understood the risk of flooding. The tunnel floor had been dug more than two feet below the level the water reached at mean high tide. Two feet equaled additional pressure of hundreds of pounds per square inch on any surface.

But the tides were also the basis of Sprague's hope the excavation could be rescued.

Twice a day the level would fall. When it did, water would recede from the underground passages for hours.

Sprague folded his arms. "If we close off the flood source,

David, we can pump the tunnel dry. Then throw everything into getting past the cave-in. Is there any reason it can't be done? I read your paper on the Yucatan. I'm surprised you didn't bring in pumps after your accident."

"There was nothing left to recover." He didn't want to think about the death that had lain in wait there for centuries. "Here . . . I don't know. The rest of the roof could come down. You're going to have to decide if going back in is worth the risk."

"We'll try to control the risk," Sprague said. He had put his mourning of Gerson aside. For all his professional life, he had strived to see his name up beside Champollion's and Woolley's in archaeology's pantheon. His generation's bad luck was being born after the great discoveries, to careers writing footnotes to famous men's journals.

This project wouldn't rescue Sprague's dreams, but it could end his career on a respectable note—perhaps even, depending on what they found, on a high one.

"We've got other studies," Charl said. She clicked screens, and diagrams flashed by.

"I'll look them over," David said. "Then I'd like to go below."

3

DAVID CROUCHED AT THE EDGE OF THE SHAFT. BELOW HIM, patches of shiny black stone marked the water's retreat. At the bottom of the pit, a man would be chest-deep in a fast-ebbing stream.

In the abstract, he admired the engineering fcat of the long-dead builders. A burial crypt more than a dozen feet deep, at the end of a tunnel twenty feet long. The effort must have commanded months of a colonial settlement's labor.

Why had they bothered?

"Why does this place exist?" he asked over his shoulder.

"We don't know." Charl stood behind him.

He stood up, walked back to the work tables. He glanced in the boxes of relics, lifted a thickly corroded scrap of base metal, most likely iron and tin. It retained its basic shape, which was a cross. If it had ever been beautiful, or had conveyed a sense of an artisan's devotion, those qualities had vanished a long time ago. He said, "Were the colonists Catholic?"

"Mainly. They were from Cornwall."

"This was found in the tunnels?"

"Yes. We're guessing it was left deliberately. An afterthought, perhaps, to make up for the fact this wasn't hallowed ground."

"Which begs the question why they were buried here."

Charl took the object from him, dropped it back in the box. "There was an excavation a few miles up the coast, in St. Marys City, fifteen years ago. That family was buried in lead-shrouded coffins a few feet deep, in a church. This would date from about the same time, early seventeen hundreds."

"Was there ever a church on this spot?"

"No. The settlement has always been at the island's north end. There are a few houses down here, nothing sanctified. You're going through the same process Noel and I did."

"The colonists dug the crypt in unhallowed ground, as far from the village as they could. Any indication why?"

"Disease?"

"Who's in the coffins?"

"We think it's members of a family named Wakelyn. The records up at the village list their deaths from cholera. That could be a reason to move the bodies."

"Cholera was common," David said. "Nobody went to these lengths."

Before Charl could answer, her husband responded. "Well, whatever the reason, we could have something of value down there. The bodies recovered at St. Marys City were preserved better than modern embalming would have done. You realize those coffins held uncontaminated air from a pre-industrial age? Big day for environmental shamans. Then pathologists like Walters catalogued diseases. Anthropologists got to dig through stomach contents. Geneticists tracked DNA back to ancestral homes. Something for everyone. I wouldn't mind seeing that here."

"I don't know much about this area," David said.

"Ewell Islanders were cutthroats," Sprague said. "I think I'd have liked them. They got driven out of a mainland settlement, part of the Maryland Colony, around 1670. Something political. Did a little piracy and fishing over here but never made much of the place. Charl and I have seen the records for the year the Wakelyns died. Bitter winter. A third of the population was killed off by one thing or another—cholera, dysentery, starvation. What have I left out?"

"Scurvy, frostbite, gangrene," she suggested.

"But only the Wakelyns are buried here?" David said.

Sprague said, "They're the only ones we've found. We're guessing that's who's down there. The records aren't a hundred percent. Whoever they are, they're an outlier. Most of the corpses would have been dumped at the edge of the village for bears and wolves to tidy up. No choice, with that much of the population wiped out. Are you sure you want to take a look below?"

"You shouldn't risk it," said Charl.

"When is low tide?"

"Just after midnight," Sprague said: "If you're going down, you should get some sleep."

David looked at his watch. It was barely six p.m., but he felt as if night had fallen many hours ago. He was physically tired but his mind was busy.

"Let's see what your cameras got this afternoon."

The cameras wouldn't have survived the flood, but they might have recorded part of it. David followed Charl to the row of monitors, where she began opening files.

"I'll go back a half-hour before the incident," she said.

"Good," said Sprague. "We need to know what Gerson and Michaels were up to."

A slide show of stored images jumped into the middle screen. The cameras were stationary. There was no color underground, no sense of the tunnel's dimensions. David found the scene claustrophobic as images clicked past, nothing changing, no sign of Gerson or Michaels.

"Speed it up, dear."

Flick, flick.

Half a minute later the screen went dark.

Charl backed up the images. The final seconds showed nobody in the tunnel. She turned. "We lost the picture before the water broke through."

"Also before Dr. Gerson and Michaels went below," Sprague pointed out.

David asked, "Were you getting the feed by radio?"

"Too much interference," said Sprague. "We have a cable."

Charl stood up, groped behind the server. "It's disconnected."

Sprague stared at her.

"Michaels?"

The suggestion hung there.

"If he wanted to be alone with her," Sprague said.

"Luther is as harmless as a kitten," his wife said. "I hooked the system up. Maybe I was careless."

They reconnected the monitor, but there was no signal. Either the cameras had been disabled by someone, or the flood had knocked them out. If he wanted a glimpse of tunnel conditions, David knew, he would have to make a descent.

"I want to talk to Michaels," he said.

Luther Michaels was no longer sitting in the food tent. His wife Etta waved them off. "I couldn't keep him, sir. He said he'd feel better at home."

"Walking through sleet?"

She sniffed. "I told the fool he'd freeze."

4

LOREN FANE ACCOMPANIED DAVID, DRIVING A ROVER ALONG the narrow leg of land at the island's south tip. "Michaels and his wife have a trailer out this way," he said. "He had a long walk home."

The headlights picked out marsh on both sides of the road. No houses yet. Fane drove slowly, flicking the high beams on and off. He was a talker. He was with the University of Rhode Island. He had published papers and books on island subcultures. "You won't see many people on Ewell younger than forty. They can't make a living. Only choice is go on welfare or move to the mainland."

David glanced at him.

"You know why people live here?" Fane said.

"No."

"They can't imagine being anywhere else. Parents lived here, grandparents. Not everyone emigrates. The place is dying. It's got an interesting culture, a product of the isolation. If you've got an ear, you can pick up an accent, a sort of monophthong in vowels. Unusual food, too. Etta Michaels makes us what she calls rockfish pasty that isn't bad."

There were lights ahead, and Fane slowed the vehicle. A half-dozen trailers and shacks stood on concrete blocks along a shallow hillside. As the road ended, the headlights showed lines of mud on building walls that marked flood crests.

"If Luther is awake he may be drunk," Fane said. "You'll get the picture if you know that four of the families down here are named Michaels. Family trees on Ewell are a briar patch. Michaels and his wife are first cousins. Until our little band of grave robbers arrived, people didn't have anything to talk about. Now Etta tells people we're raising the dead." He lifted an eyebrow. "I think she means it literally. This one is Luther's."

They got out into a light rain and mounted several cement steps. Fane knocked, the door opened, and Fane said, "Luther, this is Dr. Isaac. He wants to ask you about what happened in the excavation."

Luther Michaels was large and soft-shouldered. He had changed to dry clothes without doing more than a perfunctory face-washing. His thin, colorless hair was speckled with mud. He wore two heavy sweaters over a plaid flannel shirt, which was buttoned at the throat. The sweater cuffs were pulled down so only his fingers were visible.

The room they entered was choked with shabby furniture—frayed chairs, a buckled sofa, a chrome-legged kitchen table. Cardboard boxes behind the chairs spilled tangled clothes, threaded pipe, rags, newspapers. The floor shook as a furnace pushed dry hot air through the room. It had to be ninety degrees in the trailer, David thought, as he unbuttoned his coat.

"I don't remember much," Michaels said. His voice was high and thin. He lowered himself onto a vinyl-covered chair.

David forced himself not to look away. Even if Fane hadn't made the point, the evidence of inbreeding was there: a round, infantile face, heavy gray teeth, a flattened nose with elongated nostrils. The island man looked unfinished, as if a sculptor working in clay had given up. David couldn't guess his age: thirty and fifty were equally plausible.

David sat on a vinyl chair across from the man. "Luther, where were you and Dr. Gerson when the tunnel flooded?"

"There's a place the ceiling fell down. . . ."

"You were there?"

Michaels nodded. "Yes sir."

"What were you doing?"

"Dr. Gerson was trying to figure out how much rubble we had to move. There's a lot of rock and dirt."

"Did you disturb anything?"

"No, sir. It wasn't safe. 'Fessor Sprague said we had to shore up the roof first. He had some expert coming to take a look."

Watching the small, dull eyes, David said, "Did Gerson disable the cameras?"

"Why would she do that?"

"I don't know her reason. Did you do it?"

Michaels shook his head slowly. "That stuff I don't even know about. I just do what I'm told."

David couldn't read the man at all. His limited intelligence made all his answers sound guileless.

"What happened when the water came?"

"It knocked me down. Came swoosh! Like a valve blowed off a sink!"

"And Dr. Gerson?"

"Her, too. You couldn't stand at first."

"How did you get up the tunnel?"

Michaels ducked his head. "It wasn't too bad once the first rush was over. We both could manage, Dr. Gerson and me. She was right behind me. . . . None of us like that hole. Dr. Fane can tell you. Gives me bad dreams every night."

"How are you doing now, Luther?"

"Freezing cold, all the way in my bones." He sent a pleading look at Fane. "I wanna go to bed now. I'm cold."

David said, "If Dr. Gerson was right behind you, Luther, why didn't she get out?"

The island man shook his head silently.

□□□

They stepped out of the trailer into sleet that felt like sandpaper on David's sweaty face.

"He seemed less stupid a month ago," Fane said. "We should abandon this place to geneticists. They would have fun. Fifteen generations to make Luther. How long before you get only idiots?"

"Let's get back to the camp," David said.

"Luther's right, you know," Fane said. "When you go down into the excavation, you won't like it."

"I didn't the first time."

They climbed into the truck and Fane set the defroster and wipers to clear ice from the windshield. "It's got a rotten feel to it. Becker doesn't talk about it. Gerson hated being down there."

"But she went."

"Yeah. I wouldn't have expected that." He was silent. The wipers scraped. "I don't like this island. Didn't even before today. Professionally I'm interested. Sorry to see distinctive places give in to uniformity. All that stuff." Fane shrugged. "And I've done stints in worse places. I can walk out my office door and find parts of Providence that are more depressing than this. How would you like to be an archaeologist a hundred years from now piecing together life in a high-rise housing project? But from my first trip down this rabbit hole, I've been as superstitious as the locals."

"They're superstitious?"

"They call it religious. Pessimistic, resigned to fate. Maybe I'm a cousin of Luther's."

"You analyze your feelings," David pointed out.

"I still succumb to them."

"Okay, you're Luther's cousin. At least you're not married to him."

The sleet made the drive back slow. "How did you get roped into this project?" Fane asked.

"I was one of Sprague's students."

"Not recently?"

"No."

"You and Becker and Mrs. Sprague were all there at the same time? At Columbia?"

"Right."

"What have you been doing since then?"

There was nothing below the surface in Fane's question, so David answered, "I studied genetics for a while at MIT."

"Thought about switching careers?"

"Not exactly." He thought it was time to change the subject. "How did you come aboard?"

"I worked on the St. Marys excavation. Sprague wanted experience. Gerson didn't have enough."

5

THEY DROVE BACK TO THE CAMP. IN THE DINING TENT, DAVID tried to filter out the murmur of an informal wake for Gerson while he watched Etta Michaels. She looked more like a twin sister or a clone of her husband than a cousin, soft and half-formed. She was having trouble keeping her mind on her work. Twice she yanked the brew drawer out of the coffee maker, stared at used grounds, put the drawer back and made another undrinkable pot.

The table conversation had changed. Noel Sprague was describing an accident in Thebes, near the Valley of Kings in Egypt, more than forty years earlier. It was something else for them to think about, a distraction. "There were defenses against tomb desecrators," Sprague said, "and one of our people, Henri Gassion's son, got caught. Clumsy trap but it smashed his arm."

"I read Gassion's notebooks," Fane said. "Sepsis finally got the boy. You were there?"

"I was a post-doc. That was my fourth field experience. Henri was in charge."

"Most sites aren't booby-trapped," Fane said.

"Most sites aren't viewed as sites by the people who build them," Sprague pointed out. "They're taverns and whorehouses. Henri hadn't made much of a find—a distant royal buried with his wine vessels. So the builders put in a burglar alarm. If it had been somebody important, we might have gotten the full treatment." He laughed harshly. "Henri wouldn't have missed most of us."

"I prefer early Christian and Muslim sites," Fane said. "The big guys in both movements ascended, so there were no divine tombs that had to be rigged."

Becker approached, told Fane, "It would be worth your life to claim you'd found Jesus or Mohammad's bones."

"I'd keep the secret," Fane said. "No point in upsetting everyone."

David spoke into a lull. "Who discovered this site?"

"Splendid question," said Fane. "We're all in the dark. It's a secret."

Sprague raised a silencing hand. "Quit whining, Loren. You signed on knowing the terms. Everyone did—except my young friend David, who didn't think to ask."

"All right, I'll ask," David said. "What's the secret?"

"It isn't just a secret, it's a formal confidentiality agreement with a commercial motive. We're spending a great deal of money. Our backers hope to get a return on it. We may have something worth exploiting. A book or two, perhaps television."

"Who are the backers?"

"They'll remain anonymous for the time being."

David watched the flickering smile on Sprague's face. The man had what he wanted—a project and financing. The money wasn't coming from a university, or he wouldn't have been coy. For too many years he had taken sadistic pleasure debunking other people's work, and too many of the people he had wounded had risen to committees that allocated funding. Sprague had been marginalized at Columbia. So he had gone outside university circles.

David said, "What could we find here that would interest television?"

"It depends what's in the crypt, doesn't it?"

"My guess," said Fane, "we'll find some gnawed bones. Long winter, starvation—a little cannibalism wouldn't have been out of the question. Not something you write down in the church log."

Sprague changed the subject. "David, what did you expect to find in the Yucatan?"

It had been inevitable. Someone would have gotten around to it. David answered quietly. "The Mayans practiced human sacrifice. I knew we might find relics of that. If we got lucky, we might have learned something about the decay of the empire. Evidence of climate change, disease."

Fane wore an odd expression. "You worked in the Yucatan?"

"Yes."

"South of Tulum, near the coast? I should have remembered."

John Walters, the pathologist, had followed the discussion. His interest awakened at the mention of human relics. He sat with his arms crossed over a bright red sweater, thin hands tucked out of sight. "What's the significance of Tulum?"

"They have lagoons fed by underground channels from the sea," Fane said. "Not that different from here. Isaac's group was excavating a temple. They had bad luck with flooding."

Walters looked mildly curious. "How bad?"

David didn't answer.

Fane couldn't resist. "Three or four people were killed." Fane glanced at David for confirmation, then went on. "The Mexicans put him in jail for a few months. Tried to build a murder case, which was difficult as their own ancestors had rigged the place. Bloody little bastards, those Indians."

Walters looked suitably horrified, which seemed to satisfy Fane. He shrugged and was quiet.

Sprague pushed away his coffee mug. "David, you look exhausted. Try to get a few hours' sleep. Use our tent if you like. Neither Charl nor I will be able to sleep until we're sure about Dr. Gerson. Will you show him the way, dear?"

He knew the way. It was where Becker had left his bag. But he let her show him. They didn't talk on the way across the camp. But he watched her, two steps ahead of him. Couldn't *not* do that. The couple's tent was so crammed with gear as to be almost uninhabitable. Two cots, on opposite sides of a narrow aisle, were half-buried in ropes and pulleys, ring binders, video equipment.

"Take your pick," she said.

He reached to the left cot, removed his bag and dumped pulleys and rope onto the floor. He tossed his jacket and bag on top of the gear, then sat on the cot and unlaced his boots.

It was the first time they had been alone together since his arrival. He had yearned for the moment and dreaded it. He couldn't think of anything to say. He didn't want a conversation about old times.

"I'm glad you're here," Charl said. "The project is important to Noel and to me."

He tugged at a boot.

"You shouldn't have cut us off." It sounded like regret rather than chiding.

"I didn't cut anyone off." He knew it was lame. When their affair was over, he had run like a whipped dog. But what had she expected him to do? Send her and Sprague a punch bowl for a wedding gift?

She walked around the cot as far as she could, adjusted a heater. Came back and avoided eye contact. "The first thing we heard from Tulum, I thought you'd been killed. The people in Quintana Roo weren't helpful. Noel raised hell with the embassy and got some answers."

"I owe him, then."

Quintana Roo was the Mexican state that had let the Americans come in to help on an excavation. They'd also set the budget that didn't include GPR equipment for soundings. The skimping hadn't made a difference, but the Mexicans had thought it had. So they wanted the disaster to belong to somebody else.

"I wanted to be there," Charl said.

"Be glad you weren't. Everyone who was with me died."

"They were your friends."

"Yes."

"Including a special friend?"

"Not the way you mean. But friends, and I miss them."

"You couldn't have seen it coming."

"You don't have to convince me." He reached out and grasped her wrist. Her skin was warm. He'd heard a pianist say the knowledge was in the fingers. It couldn't be literally true, but he understood the point. He had known every contour of her face and body. Had been well on the way to knowing the contours of her temperament—so he'd thought. Now he wanted to pull her down with him onto the cot.

She took her hand away, ducked quickly and kissed his cheek and pulled back.

"I'm glad you're here," she said again.

The door closed behind her, and David tugged off his sweater and lay back on the cot. She was the last person he should want to think about.

Winter break they'd stayed on Isla Mujeres, off the Yucatan coast, scuba diving on good reefs and poor ones, not caring much. Mornings reef-diving, afternoons muff-diving. Evenings of rum and dancing. Start over again the next day. They'd known each other six months, had been lovers from the first few days. Impetuous, hungry, inevitable when they talked about it.

Four months after they got back, she told him she was marrying Sprague.

If he'd thought he had a rival, he would have guessed Becker. The three of them, close in age and interests, were more than casual friends. They were thick as thieves. Becker said you couldn't be sure you were incompatible with a woman until you had slept with her a few times. He carried out his research cheerfully, and claimed to have a natural gift for being incompatible.

But it hadn't been Becker.

David pulled the camp blanket across his legs, put an arm across his eyes. It was dark and silent.

He never dreamt, as far as he knew, but in the dreary in-between state he went through the rituals all over again, imagining conversations in which his dead friends were not overly critical about what had happened, accepting his explanations; revisiting practical discussions about who got whose iPod, assuming belongings would be shipped home rather than stolen, about whose life-affirming memorial ritual should be held first, and whether David Isaac was excused from attendance by being in jail. He would have preferred in that murky few minutes bumping into Charlene Weir as she'd been when they were lovers, when their skin was so slippery he could barely hold her. He would have settled for her presence, for small talk, if that was all she had for him. Settled for any part of her—at least in his half-sleep, when his judgment was turned off.

Becker's voice intruded, telling him it was quarter to twelve. Low tide in half an hour.

Time to see what was in the pit.

David wore hip waders, a harness snapped to a featherlight line, and a helmet equipped with a powerful lamp and radio. He looked down the vertical shaft's thirteen feet. Licked by his helmet light, a black unreflecting pool trembled at the bottom.

Becker, who wore gear identical to David's, tugged at a harness strap. "The water is less than twenty inches deep. It should fall for the next few minutes, then remain at ebb for almost an hour. We'll have plenty of time."

"You don't have to come," David said.

"Two of us will work quicker."

Behind them the compressor whirred as it drove fresh air into the hole.

Sprague stood some distance away, clipping on a headphone. "Let's check the communications. Can you hear me?"

"You're clear," Becker said.

"Same," said David.

"Recover Roberta's body if you can," Sprague said. "But assess the tunnels. Can we make them watertight, and can we reach the burial room?" He glanced at a handheld monitor. "The cameras on your helmets are sending good visuals now, but that won't last."

"We could wire up," David suggested.

Beneath the beard, the older man's face was drawn. "No. I don't want you encumbered if you have to evacuate."

Five minutes later David swung a rubber-clad foot onto the ladder.

And started down.

6

HELEN CALDER STARED AT THE MAN SITTING ACROSS FROM her and read his mind. It wasn't difficult. He was thinking:

This fat lesbian is trying to put one over on me.

She snapped shut her briefcase. She didn't care if she had won his respect. She didn't care what he thought of her figure. She didn't care what he imagined about her sex life. She wanted only one thing from Roger Staley: that was compliance. In the end, she would get it.

He had a high patrician forehead, on which right now his pale eyebrows were raised skeptically. It had the look of a familiar pose: the private school rector examining a student who didn't belong among the social elite. The rector's manners being perfect, he expected the student to understand this without being told.

"The St. Leger Foundation receives no government funding," Staley said. His voice was high and precise. "Our operations are supported by an endowment. Therefore I don't see the legal basis of your submission that we must open our books to the National Institutes of Science."

Even Roger Staley's choice of words annoyed her. He called her demand *a submission*. They taught people to speak that way at New England schools where spoiled boys blew farts through keyholes so other wealthy boys could light them.

She made no attempt to hide her rural Kentucky accent. "I'm here, Mr. Staley, because the Institutes received a complaint that your foundation is supporting illegal genetic manipulation. That is a matter of statute law. So your sources of funding are not material."

She had made a tactical mistake, she realized, in not jumping on the matter of funding, about which she wanted to know more, much more. But it could wait.

Wearing a look of strained patience, Roger Staley started to object, but Helen offered a truce. "Our interest is limited to that single matter, and if we can lay it to rest, we're done." Her silent internal voice chuckled. *The hell they were.*

"Perhaps I can satisfy you," Staley said. "The St. Leger Foundation has never provided funds for any sort of genetic research. Whoever your informant is, he's misled you." He had the glossy booklet in front of him, as if the moves of this encounter had been scripted far in advance, and he slid the booklet toward Calder. "Our annual report describes our activities in some detail. You will see there is nothing about genetic research, or medical or biological research. We have been accused of favoring the soft sciences, particularly sociology. I'm afraid this is true. Our founder believed humans know too little of themselves."

Helen glanced at the cover photograph, which showed a particularly grim urban apartment building, its balconies enclosed in metal fencing. Rising behind the brick walls were distant skyscrapers and a skyline she recognized as Manhattan. ST. LEGER FOUNDATION, the cover said, and in smaller script, *3 Alternatives to Warehousing the Poor.* She set the report on top of her briefcase. She had copies of a half dozen years' reports in her files. Like most charities, the foundation painted a rainbow of public spiritedness across its tax-exempt expenditures. The latest report boasted of new insights into urban debilitation, alternatives to prison sentencing, research into drug recovery therapies. She could read until her eyes were bloodshot and never find a mention of genetics, let alone eugenics, and no accounting of the millions of dollars she knew the St. Leger Foundation funneled into illicit biomedical research in defiance of Congress and the NIS. Nor would she find any mention of Roger Staley's salary, which was generous even by the standards of nonprofit organizations. Officially he received one and a quarter million dollars a year, plus a travel and expense allowance that would shame a Cabinet Secretary. She had gleaned those details from a friend at the IRS who had access to St. Leger's tax filings. She didn't care about Staley's salary, or the perks, or his penthouse apartment at the Watergate that was owned by a shell corporation that seemed to do nothing but rent to Staley. She didn't even care that the shell pretended to do contract research into learning disorders in the inner city. Its sole purpose was to enrich its single stockholder, Roger Staley. She didn't care personally about any of that, but she had a professional use for the evidence she had collected. If Staley decided to play hardball with her, Helen would promise to send his pinched ass to jail. That might be the abracadabra that finally opened the foundation's books.

"If you glance through the report," Staley said, "you will see what I've said is true. No gene splicing, no cloning. Those just aren't our angles of attack. St. Leger believes the human animal is more than a biological phenomenon. We look for truths that can be expressed in public policy, not those determined by a genetic code."

He was a pretentious man, but he wasn't good at hiding his surface thoughts. Beneath arched brows, his pale brown eyes wandered, and Helen knew he was asking himself questions. What had brought her here? Someone had complained. If that was all . . .

We've known for years that you run black accounts, she answered silently. *Now we're going to learn what you're doing with them.*

She had gotten far enough in her investigation to know the secret accounts were the foundation's *raison d'être*. What she didn't know was which laboratories were getting the hidden subsidies—or for what purpose. The possibilities kept her awake at night. Some of the things she imagined would give a Pentagon general nightmares.

She tossed the annual report back at Staley. "I've already seen the sales brochures. They're not sufficient for NIS. You're going to have to show us what we want. Talk to your lawyers, Mr. Staley. You've got twenty-four hours before I deliver a subpoena and search the place."

"I don't think that will be necessary."

"It's your choice."

"You're welcome to tour our offices now if you would like," he said.

A tour would be a sham. She made a point of consulting her watch. "Sorry. I have an appointment at the Watergate."

She had no appointment. Ahead lay an evening of cold pasta and whatever fare the old movie channels offered. Until Judy came home, that was life at chez Calder. But the mention of the downtown Washington apartment complex might worry the bastard.

It's us against them, she thought, knowing the categories of "us" and "them" had a deeper meaning than "short and fat" versus "patrician."

She wished she had brought along a subpoena and federal marshals this afternoon. It was a mistake to warn him what was coming. Staley had the legal resources to bury evidence for years. By the time she got the answers she needed—if she ever got them—the damage could be beyond repair. She imagined Roger Staley emerging at a press conference, suddenly welcoming the bright lights, and introducing a fair-haired, pink-cheeked little boy. *"This is Timmy, the first genetically perfect human being. His g-factor intelligence quotient is 190. At age four he has mastered Barrow's calculus. He is free of all inherited disease. During Timmy's long life, his contribution to the advancement of human knowledge will be incalculable. We also want you to meet his nine identical twins."* And onto the stage they troop, the improved human model for the next thousand years. She couldn't let that happen. She couldn't let the human race become a homogenized army of pre-selected, perfect, beautiful specimens. She knew what would happen afterwards to the fat and ugly ones. As she drove across Chain Bridge into the District of Columbia, her hand jabbed the car's cigarette lighter. She wondered if her imagination was working too hard. Her informant had not specifically mentioned a eugenics program. He had spoken of outlawed biological research, and she had taken it from there. The manipulation of the genetic heritage to improve the species was her own particular horror. It had such a monstrous history. A eugenics movement had flowered in the United States in the early Twentieth Century, barring "inferior" immigrants, justifying compulsory sterilization of the retarded. . . .

"It could be eugenics," the informant said coyly. "It could also be human cloning for medical parts. Would you care about that?"

Oh yes, she would care. And she would care if it was any of a half-dozen other research areas that fell under the National Institutes of Science jurisdiction. The Omnibus Medical Science Research Advancement Act had made that jurisdiction wide. Besides cloning, the act had banned research employing human embryonic material. But a lab with an eye for the financial jackpot might still be harvesting stem cells from blastocysts. Probably collecting them from poor black women at some urban storefront clinic in exchange for free abortions. It would revolutionize medicine if those primordial cells from the early-stage embryo could be grown to mature into heart muscle, or lung tissue, or brain cells. Instead of growing perfect babies, rogue scientists would grow anencephalic trees of spare human parts. Then let the bidding begin.

Helen Calder shuddered.

Whatever it was, she was going to get the smug shit.

Geronimo Bix waited five minutes after the woman left before entering Staley's office. He had wanted the foundation's executive director to have time to worry because Staley was easier to deal with when his mind was unsettled.

Stuffing his small clay pipe with the desert herbs of his Apache grandfather, Bix spent a minute facing the window, beyond which the tops of the tallest trees cut the dusky sky.

From here he could imagine cold-minded predators scouring the darkening hills and streets. He was short, with a round head of tightly bound black hair and a broad pockmarked face. He wore an expensive striped suit that drew attention to the brutality of the face. His eyes were dark and steady.

"She said the NIS had gotten a complaint," Staley said. "When I used the term 'informant,' she didn't correct me."

Bix didn't answer. They both knew she could have played along; if you didn't have an informant in the enemy's camp, it was useful to encourage him to think you had. But Bix had an uncomfortable feeling that she had let the truth go unchallenged. Her interest was too specific for the information to have come from outside the foundation. The thought made him uneasy because it implied a failure of the foundation's internal security office. That made it Bix's failure.

"If we have a problem, it's a recent one," he said.

"Otherwise we would know."

"I would know."

"Let's see if we can limit the damage."

Bix retreated to his operations room two floors down. He felt confident that Staley had decided there was no advantage in looking to Bix for a scapegoat. If there was a problem, they both were at risk.

What did the Anglo cow have? *Who* did she have?

There was nothing unusual in a wealthy foundation's having a security department. But the extent to which the St. Leger Foundation guarded the confidentiality of its work would have startled executives of a mainstream charity. The foundation published its annual report of good deeds, but beyond that it volunteered nothing and—always apologetically—gave few answers to questions. The work wouldn't benefit from self-aggrandizing publicity, Staley said with practiced sincerity. The trustees were listed each year, as required by law: well-pedigreed names accompanied by academic credentials and distinguished cultural and charitable affiliations. But the trustees were generously paid to limit their interest in the foundation's affairs to the memoranda Staley presented at the quarterly board meetings. The memoranda were elaborate. The goals admirable.

The means beyond reproach. As each trustee had other affiliations that demanded considerable attention, they were happy to put their trust in Staley. The collegiality of the St. Leger Foundation was a relief from the conflicts of academic, business and government life.

Outsiders who got nosy encountered a maze of blank walls. A few turns into the maze, they met—without realizing it—an obstacle named Bix. Since Bix had taken over security six years ago, no journalist had published more than a paragraph or two mentioning the St. Leger Foundation. The only person who had come close to delivering a full-length article had been a young social activist in a decaying District of Columbia neighborhood, who wrote occasionally for a leftwing monthly magazine. He had come across the St. Leger Foundation and decided its commitment to urban research deserved wider recognition. His interview with Roger Staley, while extremely cordial, left the writer feeling there was more to be learned. He began digging. Early in that process, Bix tossed a lucrative opportunity the writer's way. Calling out of the blue, a travel magazine asked for a series of articles on several impoverished islands in the Mediterranean, a project requiring at least six months abroad. Expenses paid. When the writer said no, Bix made a different kind of phone call. It helped that the young activist was African-American. His military service had been exemplary. His devotion to his wife was unmistakable. He lived modestly. He was known as a man who cared deeply about his crime-ridden neighborhood. But cops, even black cops, are cynics. Two very cynical detectives heard credible rumors about the writer's less savory interests. Two days later, a no-knock raid revealed that the young man was trading child pornography by computer with a network of hundreds of pedophiles. His denials failed to convince anyone, including his humiliated wife. He couldn't explain what had been found in lightly disguised files on his computer. Neither the writer nor his family could raise bail before trial. The project for the leftwing magazine was forgotten.

Sitting at a terminal, Bix called up the video record maintained by the building's dozens of security cameras. Helen Calder had parked in a small, tended lot beside the south entrance. Bix tracked her boarding an elevator, he watched her smirking at herself in the burnished doors as the car descended. Fat lady on a power trip.

Her burgundy sedan didn't look official. Enlarging the picture of a D.C. license tag, he captured the image, then switched to the Metro DMV database and found Helen Ruth Calder's home address in Cleveland Park.

He spent an hour performing complicated searches of the foundation's personnel files, matching names with records on building access and internal computer use. His own comings and goings were the most erratic, and his wanderings in the internal data network were by far the most suspicious. A logarithmic analysis failed to identify a second suspect, after himself. If an informant was gathering information, it wasn't from the foundation's own system. Bix was disappointed. He had hoped his quarry was stupid.

Helen Calder's apartment building was two blocks north of the zoo in a pleasant neighborhood on Connecticut Avenue. Bix parked his car on a back street and walked down to Connecticut. He wore a pure cashmere topcoat and a fedora that sat low on his head. From a glimpse of his dark face, he could be taken for one of the Asian doctors whose offices filled the neighborhood.

He liked the look of the apartment building. Ivy crawled across the dark bricks. Potted junipers guarded the entrance. Many of the windows were lighted. Bix entered the vestibule and lifted the telephone receiver for the benefit of the man who sat behind a polished wood desk in the lobby. The building management was doing its best to make the place look upscale and secure. There were brass sconces on the walls, parquet flooring protected by Aubusson rugs, Chinese floor vases supporting large tropical plants, wingback chairs and a leather sofa.

He held the telephone's disconnect lever down as he memorized the locations of elevators and a stairway door. While he waited, two people buzzed themselves into the lobby. Bix made no attempt to follow them in. After a minute he hung up the phone, turned and walked outside.

He had learned one thing. He could penetrate Calder's sanctuary any time he wanted.

The winter evening was numbingly cold. Cars speeding along the avenue rode swirling carpets of exhaust. Pedestrians in coats and gloves hurried hand-in-hand. The cold didn't bother Bix. He had grown up in the Arizona desert, and the hundred twenty degree summers hadn't bothered him; nor had the mountain nights. He was a spirit, a hunter's spirit, and the shell he inhabited existed merely to be used, not to be protected from discomfort or excited by pleasure. Neither of those sensations mattered. Usually, he barely noticed them. He spotted an awning and crossed the street and ate dinner in a small Northern Italian restaurant. When he came out, life on the avenue had slowed. He brought his car around and sat watching Calder's apartment building until after midnight.

Helen stayed up late, exchanging emails with Judy, whom she missed terribly. Soaking in a warm tub, she planned her next meeting with the informant who would help her put Staley and some of his colleagues in a wringer that she would twist. Her mood was pessimistic. All biological research had at its heart a kind of eugenics, a determination to improve every species that wasn't marked for eradication. It had been only a matter of time before the tinkers turned from crop yields to human yields. In the long run there was no chance of stopping either improvement. In the long run humans would all be perfect, according to somebody's definition of perfection. Looking down at her large sallow thighs, she knew she didn't have much of a future in biological terms. Her DNA would end when she ended.

She could try artificial insemination, there might still be time for that. It would be a close thing at her age. No telling what could go wrong.

If Judy had wanted a child, she would go ahead and try, but Judy didn't want a child and for that Helen felt grateful because her secret fear was that the pretty, younger woman she loved would feel a need for children, which might lead her toward a conventional family in which there would be no place for Helen.

She turned on the hot water tap and settled back, refusing to think gloomy thoughts. She summoned a happier image—Judy at the other end of the tub, or Roger Staley in his office, cowering and blubbering as Helen bitch-slapped him with a search warrant.

She settled on Judy, with the petite breasts and elfin smile, and thought how fortunate she was to have someone like Judy to love.

7

THEY FOUND GERSON ALMOST IMMEDIATELY. WATER LAPPING at his calves, David Isaac stooped in the confines of the tunnel and played the lamp's beam on a muddy sweater, strands of wet hair, the bright twisted temple of wire glasses. The woman's body was mostly grounded as the tide receded, but its right hand waved languidly on eddies stirred by the men's boots. Their lights alarmed a small crab, which plunged out of a tangle of hair into the water.

Becker reported their position. They were a dozen feet east of the entrance shaft. Not far at all, but to David, access to the surface felt remote.

He forced himself to look at the body. The sweater had ridden up to expose several inches of pale belly. Living flesh would have flinched at the cold. He wondered if the people above were getting the visuals from the cameras on his and Becker's helmets.

The body's location told him nothing about where Gerson

had been when water erupted into the tunnel. She could have been swept along the full length of the passageway in both directions as the flood rushed in and retreated.

"We'll come back for her," Becker said. He told Sprague, "You can send down the harness."

As David looked away, the light beam from his helmet bounced along slimy walls. There were occasional passages of stone, but most of the tunnel appeared to have been hewn from the raw earth. It couldn't be stable. Walls and ceiling were shored at wide intervals with timbers. The wood was thick, well preserved.

"We're reversing course, to inspect the blockage," Becker reported to Sprague.

"Okay."

David turned slowly. Even with compressed air being forced down the shaft, the tunnel smelled rotten. *Earth and sea were cauldrons of decomposition.* He remembered the phrase, couldn't remember where he had heard it. He directed the light forward.

Becker nudged his back. "Get moving."

Now that he looked ahead the light traveled without obstruction for a seemingly long distance, but he could not see a collapsed area. It should be less than thirty feet ahead.

He felt fuzzy-minded, and the dullness worried him. A concentration of gases could overcome a man with no warning.

"Did you test the air recently?"

"Don't you feel well?"

"Not very clear-headed."

"A man with a clear head wouldn't be down here," Becker said. "There were traces of methane and carbon monoxide. Not much. The pump is a precaution."

David concentrated on wading ahead. On the fourth step his helmet scraped the roof and a rattle of mud hit his shoulders and neck. Two more steps. The walls were close. Both elbows brushed stone or mud. The swaying light conjured an illusion that ahead the passageway squeezed to nothing.

Becker said matter-of-factly, "You know what happens when the roof comes down. They find landslide victims with mud in their stomachs."

"Did you say something?" Sprague demanded. Becker had spoken away from the microphone.

"We've passed the halfway mark," Becker said.

As David put a heel down, something rose from the water and slapped the wall.

"What was that?"

"I stepped on something."

He reached down and felt roundness slathered in mud. He pulled gingerly. A concave blade spilled water.

"A shovel."

"They had a shovel down here? What were they doing?"

"Michaels might have been clearing debris."

The rubble was thick under the water, clumps of mud and stone that made moving awkward.

"Let's see if we can reach the obstruction," Becker said. "If we're not there in a minute, we turn back."

Too soon to worry about the tide, David thought. He dropped the shovel and crept forward. Mud clung to his boots. Behind him Becker struggled and cursed. The wall of rubble was visible now. The ceiling dipped, and David sank to his hands and knees. Three feet from the collapsed area, he stopped. The ceiling was a few inches higher here, and balanced on his knees he could hold the rest of his body upright. Tilting his head, he examined the ceiling. Shoring would be in order before they proceeded. Lots of shoring. The rough-cut surface ran overhead straight into the obstruction. It struck him odd that no weakness in the roof was visible despite the apparent collapse just ahead. Moving the light a few inches, he realized that not all the blackness in front of him was solid.

Some was void.

He spoke into his microphone. "Sprague. Can you hear this? I can see past the top of the obstruction."

It took Sprague a moment to respond. "Tell me again?"

"I can see an inch or two of clearance above the obstruction."

"You had better withdraw. The next collapse could be worse."

The man didn't understand.

Tilting his head, David squinted to get a better view of the top of the rubble mound. He could see a continuation of the ceiling above the debris.

"It isn't a collapse," David said. "I think the obstruction was placed here . . . mounded up and left here, material from the original excavation. If we didn't have echo-mapping, we would assume the tunnel ended here."

He played the light over the small gap but could see nothing but darkness. The crypt itself lay some yards beyond.

They want out.

He shook his head, wondering where the thought had come from.

They were three centuries dead, beyond all wanting. The truth was more prosaic. *He* wanted *in.*

Becker gripped his shoulder. "Time to head back," he said. "We've still got work to do."

The returning tide was coming in faster than David had expected. The water already was ten or eleven inches deep. As he crawled into the frigid current, he felt his body heat being sapped. Exertion was keeping thermal shock at bay, but he was beginning to tremble. At the bottom of the shaft, they collected rope and a tarpaulin that Sprague lowered.

The dead woman floated toward them. She had rolled face down. Before the head bumped his chest, David grabbed her jacket collar. Becker unfurled the canvas they intended to use to wrap the body. With the tunnel largely dry, it would have worked, but now the fabric absorbed water, and Becker's struggles couldn't keep it from sinking. He cursed. "We should have done this right away."

"Never mind," David said. "Feed me line."

He tied the woman's wrists together. He wriggled past the body, looped a coil of rope around an ankle, pulled it tight, then stretched and got a rope end around the other ankle. He drew the feet together, doubled the knots.

"Okay," Becker said. "We get out of here."

As they headed for the shaft, the tide helped, a shallow river hurrying in, floating their burden, pushing them along.

Becker ran two harness belts between the body's wrists,

cinched them through square buckles, stood back and told Sprague, "We're ready."

Someone overhead activated the electric winch. Slowly the dead woman sat up, head bouncing against her chest, face hidden. Small mercies. David looked up the shaft, saw that none of them had been thinking ahead. "Noel, stop the winch. She could hang up on the ladder."

They were reacting, not planning.

Someone on the top—he thought he glimpsed Fane—hauled the ladder hand over hand to the surface. The winching resumed. David turned away as the body stood up, stretched. He remembered seeing something like that once with his parents, a dancer on her toes, lifting her arms, performing the "Rose Adagio." He remembered the name, because he had thought the movement was beautiful. He didn't want to see it again.

He gestured down the tunnel. "Let's take a quick look."

The flood was a lamplit river pushing against them. It churned over fallen stone, dragged at them with deep snaking arms. Ten yards. There was only one explanation for the tunnel having been dug toward a water source. It made a trap.

He saw phosphorescence ahead.

A tight opening, framed in ragged stone, revealed the heaving oily surface of the bay. Snow swept through the light beam cast by his helmet. The incoming flood pushed his chest.

"Why did it give way now?" Becker said.

"Gerson or Michaels tampered with it."

"Bobby wasn't an idiot."

"She was down here."

Dipping his hands below the surface, David groped for the touch of something other than mud and stone. Rope would have rotted away. Chain would have rusted solid.

"In Tulum, we walked right into it," he said. He covered the microphone as he spoke. This was only for Becker's ears. "We were sticking numbers on baby skulls when the water came in."

"I read your paper. You want to know what I think?"

"No."

"You tried too hard to blame yourself. Anyone with a brain would have found a scapegoat."

David shined his helmet light around the opening, looking for anything that could have triggered the break. Centuries of slowly shifting earth would have undone any system of levers or weights.

Why had these bastards bothered?

"Come up here!"

Sprague's voice filled his ear. David ignored the summons as Becker lifted an object from the water, a five-foot bar of rusted, cratered iron. Useless, whatever it was.

Becker was reaching shoulder deep in the water.

"There are other sections," Becker said. "Perhaps a grave robber missteps, these links pull loose a keystone. But it wouldn't have worked for a long time."

"So something else happened."

"Michaels knows, I'll bet."

Sprague's voice came again, impatient.

"Come up here, gentlemen!"

Gentlemen, David thought.

8

"SHE WAS MURDERED," WALTERS SAID. THE BODY LAY FACE UP on a tarp-covered table. A cold overhead light exposed details David had managed not to notice underground: thin slits of marbled eyes, puffy gray skin, muddy nostrils. Brown water had puddled on the table. Walters extended a rubber-gloved hand, gripped the dead woman's jaw and tilted the head back. A ragged, bloodless tear gaped in the middle of the throat.

"The esophagus and carotids are cut," he said. "Tendons and the spinal column kept the head attached. The back of the skull is crushed. The body is largely exsanguinated."

His tone was clinical, but his hand shook.

"She was murdered," he repeated. "God damn that simpleton."

Fane said, "If he did this . . ."

"No one else was down there," Becker said.

"Isaac was."

"For Christ sake."

Fane smiled faintly at David. "No offense. Just pointing out that the simpleton isn't the only possible answer."

"None taken," David said. He shifted his glance to Sprague. "We may have seen the weapon. There's a shovel that could have done the damage."

Sprague nodded, hand covering his mouth, looking ill.

Fane offered another thought. "You're going to catch hell for moving her."

"So we catch hell," Becker said. "The tunnel is open to the bay. She might not have been there in twelve hours."

In his tent David stripped off his sodden clothes. Hot air from a space heater blasted past his legs as he toweled off and pulled on dry clothing. He added a second sweater and sat near the heater, bending his face into the air flow. His lips still felt numb. He was exhausted, but his mind felt clear for the first time in an hour. He couldn't explain the vague sluggishness that had overtaken him underground. Toxic gases, the cold . . . *They want out.* The thought had jumped into his head, almost as clear as spoken words. It wasn't just absurd but out of character. He'd always been too literal-minded to be afraid of dark rooms.

He turned off the heater and pulled on his jacket.

He helped carry Gerson's body, wrapped in clear plastic, to an equipment storage tent where the temperature was being allowed to fall below freezing. Then he retraced his steps across the camp. All the lights remained on at the excavation tent, but only Sprague was present, standing at the mouth of the shaft, hands behind his back, staring down. Like a man tottering, though he wasn't moving. David heard water swishing softly through the tunnels as the tide rose.

Sprague seemed to have pushed the horror of Gerson's death out of his mind. He said, "If we seal off the bay, can we reach the crypt?"

"Probably," David replied.

"Just probably?"

"If there are no more traps."

"Dr. Gerson didn't spring a trap. Luther attacked her and then broke open the wall to the bay to conceal his crime."

"It looks that way," David agreed.

"She may have rejected his advances. That would explain the attack." Sprague stopped, considered. "But how did Luther know about the stonework? He didn't have access to our mapping. Couldn't have read it if he did. I suppose Roberta might have talked about it."

"She might have. Were they friends?"

"Lord, no. She was a young, pretty woman. Barely noticed Luther's existence."

"But she ignored your instructions and went below with him."

"Yes. . . ."

David tried to imagine the Michaels trailer as the night deepened, furnace hammering, heat swelling the rooms. He wondered if Luther sat awake as brutal images cavorted in his mind.

David dropped his voice. They were standing close. "Becker and I both saw the opening. Regardless of what Michaels knew, the tunnel was built with a water trap. I want to see the village records."

"They're not very informative," Sprague said. "But of course, we'll ride up to the village in the morning. Why don't you get some sleep? I'm going to post a guard. We have to assume Luther is dangerous."

David stopped at the dining tent, found Charl alone, head resting on her arms. She had bolted from the excavation area upon seeing Gerson's wounds. Her glance followed him as he found a carton of milk in the refrigerator, filled the bottom of a sauce pan and set the pan on the propane range.

"Are we shutting down?" she asked.

"Furthest thing from your husband's mind. Should we?"

"You tell me."

"We can probably close off the water source. Reinforce the tunnels. The risk from here isn't that great. What happened was Luther's fault, not Noel's."

"You sound like you hope we succeed."

"I do."

"Despite everything?"

He didn't have to ask what she meant by "everything." It was an interesting question, he admitted, whether he wished either of them—she or her husband—well. He'd told himself he didn't miss them. It was an absurd lie. She had never been far from his thoughts. Even about Noel, his claim of indifference was only half true. He'd liked the older man for as long as he could, until their conflict of interest made fondness impossible on both sides. He said, "You could have told Noel not to call me in."

"I did. He said your professionalism would take over."

"There you go."

"So why did you come?"

"I haven't had a field job in two years. Got tired of reviewing research papers."

"That's what you've been doing? In archaeology?"

"And genetics. A classmate at MIT edits a journal. He likes people who work cheap. When the paperwork thins, I take my dad rowing." His father had loved Charl almost as intensely as David had. *Nice young lady*, he'd say, leaving unsaid that there was something more that he couldn't explain.

She smiled. "How is Bernie?"

"Unsure about being retired. He volunteers at the hospital three days a week."

"Give him a kiss for me."

"I will." He thought about it, then admitted: "There's another reason I came. I hoped you'd gotten fat, maybe had hairs sprouting from your nose."

"Really?"

"Yes."

She laughed. "I'm glad you don't hold a grudge."

"I'm glad I'm disappointed."

How many times had he heard it said that someone hadn't aged a day. It was never true. With her, it came close. And that thing his dad couldn't put a name to was still there. Sexual attraction was part of it, in her case the suggestion that sex would be a rough, down-in-the-mud wrestling match, but sex didn't cover it. "Vitality" was the only word he could think of, and he wasn't sure what it meant.

He drank his milk and left the tent. It was two-thirty in the morning, and the camp was brightly lighted like a fortress expecting a siege.

9

DAVID HAD A BRIEF MEETING IN THE MORNING WITH TWO state policemen, who interviewed each of the scientists and then continued south to talk to the Michaelses. Sprague and David left in the camp's Rover to inspect the village records. There were no outskirts to Tyler. Waist-high hurricane fences marked the settled area, defining cramped yards around one-story cottages with bent eaves and discolored siding. The yards formed passages off the main road too narrow for the vehicle to enter. They passed a single crossroad, from which an alley-wide track led toward the water. It was snowing heavily. Nothing had been plowed.

"Quaint isn't the word that comes to mind, is it?" said Sprague. "This is one of the earliest English settlements on the East Coast. Yet you won't find a building much more than a hundred years old."

"Why not?"

"Dreadful weather, and nobody bothers to fix things. Walters spent a while digging through the registry of births. The island has one of the most inbred populations in North America, worse than the Chicoutimi or Amish. You know the literature? Of course you do. Luther Michaels is a poster boy for why island people need to kidnap fresh women."

"He can't be typical?"

"Pretty damn close."

David stared out at the village. In closed societies, the small gene pool increased the likelihood that peculiar traits would survive and multiply. Amish children showed high incidences of polydactyly and dwarfism. In northern Quebec, appalling numbers of the French-descended Chicoutimi died in infancy of a rare liver disease, tyrosinemia. If the Michaels family was representative, Ewell was paying a grim price for inbreeding.

David hadn't switched interests, as Fane had put it. He'd recognized that the human sciences were converging—archaeology, anthropology and genetics all contributing to the complex picture of humankind. If you wanted to understand migrations, it was no longer enough to compare cultural artifacts. Tracking the spread of genetic traits was far more reliable. As a boy he'd loved Thor Heyerdahl's romantic assertion that South Americans on primitive rafts had colonized the Pacific, recounted in his book *Kon-Tiki*. But the theory was wrong, and the genetic trail of a rare blood disorder proved it wrong. The disorder, alpha thalassaemia, survived and spread because it strengthened the human immune system's response against malaria. The blood trait didn't exist in South America. It *did* exist in Indonesia. When the trait was discovered in Polynesia, where there was no malaria, a strong case emerged that people had migrated east into the Pacific from malaria-ridden Asia.

Sprague stopped the vehicle beside a chain fence. David saw a T-shaped building with a low roof and a small steeple.

"The Methodist Church of the Bay," Sprague said. "Nearest thing they have to city hall."

They pushed open a frozen gate, crossed an area where a path might exist under the snow, climbed two steps to a double-door. Sprague banged a cross-shaped knocker.

"You said the pastor is mayor?" David said.

"Honorary mayor. The title doesn't mean much except that he

gets to try to resolve disputes before knives come out." Sprague's gloved hand reached for the knocker again, but the door moved. Unshaven jowls, a bald head and red-rimmed eyes filled the opening. The man, round-shouldered and obese, filled baggy gray sweats. From appearance and smell, he had gotten drunk in the clothes, slept in them, and urinated in them. His feet were buried in fleecy slippers. As the door drifted wider, he pulled a watch cap onto his head.

"Come in for Crissake."

They stepped into a foyer. Sprague made introductions.

The honorary mayor, Silas Merton, didn't offer to shake hands. He just nodded acknowledgement and then shambled ahead of them through a windowless chapel that made David think of a down-at-heels union hall. There were four pews on either side of a linoleum aisle that led to a blond wood altar. Two sets of chairs faced outward from the altar. David couldn't see details; Merton's hips filled the aisle.

Merton spoke with a rumbling cough. "State police asked what I knew about Luther. Said you had an accident?"

"Roberta Gerson was killed yesterday," Sprague responded. "You met her, Pastor."

"The young lady?" Merton halted, turned around. "That's a damn shame. I'm glad I have to explain the Lord's ways to my flock only once a week. So why do the staties want Luther?"

"He's a witness."

"Luther a witness? Heh! So what do you boys want?"

"Dr. Isaac wants to see the church record."

"I should be charging for a peek, like the Shroud of Turin." He led them into a small kitchen. "Coffee's already made. Have a seat."

The pastor set cups without saucers onto a metal table, brought over a coffee pot that was three-quarters full, and disappeared through a curtained doorway. The sound of coughing tracked his movement for a while.

"He seems cooperative," David said.

"Silver crossed his palm. Silas knows a lot of local history, and he tells the townies we're harmless."

"Do they believe it?"

"Nine tenths of them don't believe in evolution. God knows what they think of us."

Merton pushed through the curtain with a cardboard box in his arms. He set the box on the table. Inside the box was a tall, green-bound ledger book. "We don't have all three hundred years' stuff. This is the fourth actual church building. Things get lost. But this record is as whole as you're gonna find."

The ledger's boards were water-stained and flaking. Pages were torn, the edges trimmed by insects. The volume's spine had been reinforced by thick twine wound through several punched holes. With the book open on the table, Merton flipped pages.

"Now, if you're still looking for the Wakelyns, that happened in 1702. You just look down that list and you see it was a bad winter. That year a lot of good Christians found out the truth about the kindness of their maker."

His finger pointed David's attention to the faint sepia runes that provided a bare notation of surname, Christian name, cause of death, dates. Initially the date was preceded by a *d.*, which was self-explanatory, but as the winter had worn on, those notations disappeared as superfluous. All that were being recorded were deaths. One February day, seven names were listed.

"Sad, ain't it," Merton said.

David studied the registry. The deaths dropped to four in March. Three occurred on the same day.

> *Wakelyn, John. Cholera. 9 March.*
> *Wakelyn, Elspeth. Cholera. 9 March.*
> *Wakelyn, Margaret, a child. Cholera. 9 March.*

Nothing indicated whether these were dates of deaths or burials. The ground might have thawed. No more fattening of wolves. He glanced down the column. The next entry was in June; then nothing until August. The crabbed hand keeping the record changed in the summer. David thumbed forward a page, cast backward through births, deaths, marriages, reports of stolen property, minor disputes, offerings of goods from a ship that had arrived. The opening page in the book bore an indictment of the anti-pope leading St. Marys City. David skipped around. A hanging was noted more than forty years later, in 1743.

He knew the period well enough. Life would have been short, many settlers dying within a couple of years of arriving from England. Those who survived would have shared one-room hovels with livestock, if they had any.

David said, "Mr. Merton, it appears the Wakelyns all died on the same day."

"Wouldn't be unusual. Most likely, though, what you've got is evidence the entries were made on the same day."

"It doesn't say where they were buried."

"There's a letter in here somewhere."

David turned pages till he found the photocopy of a letter addressed only to *My Beloved Brother*. It was signed by a W. Kobler. He read down the page to a passage that seemed to answer the question.

> *We helped to bury an unlucky family, Elspeth and John Waklyn and their young daughter. Their festering illness is now well apart, and well hidden, so that it may taint no other in our community. Our sister and I survived the winter by a Greater Mercy. We granted as much of that precious quality as we could to these poor souls.*

"This letter was a lucky find," Sprague said. "I had students go through the archives at the St. Marys City Historical Society. William Kobler's brother remained in the original colony."

Not hiding his dissatisfaction, David focused on the churchman. "No one else got the treatment the Wakelyns received."

"These were prominent people," Merton answered. "It's there, on the next page. John and his wife left an estate valued at ninety-two pounds, thirteen shillings. That was a good lot of money."

David glanced back at the death record. "I didn't know cholera was a festering illness. Are there other references to the Wakelyns in your records? Anything about construction of the crypt?"

Merton shook his head. "No to both. The record's got a few holes."

"Anything stating specifically where the Wakelyns were buried?"

Merton plucked at the book's cover. "There's no records of

that sort. There's plenty of island lore. You ask around, you'll hear it. Folks buried the Wakelyn family at land's end. Don't know how else you'd read Mr. Kobler's letter."

"Land's end."

"That's what old people call it."

"Is there a cemetery?"

"No. You seen what's there."

"Why not bury these people at a churchyard?"

"Well, say folks thought the Wakelyns was devils. That'd be a reason."

"Devils?"

"Maybe they wanted the family sealed up, so they couldn't come back out. The devils raised storms. They made everyone sick. Ewellers blamed the Wakelyn family for just about everything. That's the folk tale. Being bored around here, we like to tell stories." Merton lifted the lid of the coffee pot, looked inside. "You're welcome to look at everything we got. Shall I boil up more coffee?"

The pastor took David into the church basement. The stone foundation, much older than the building above it, enclosed a damp space where a dehumidifier hummed in a corner.

"Plenty of other paper here," Merton said, slapping a stack of cardboard boxes kept a few inches off the floor on wooden pallets. "I won't ask you to keep things in order because there ain't any. The county promised to send an archivist. That was ten years ago. I'll bring down the coffee."

David counted forty-three boxes of various sizes, some as large as moving company cartons. Labels on the sides proved deceptive. "LAND RECORDS" yielded church meeting minutes from the 1940s through the Seventies. "MAIL BOAT" was full of dusty soft-drink bottles. The chore David had set himself was impossible. There were no chairs or tables on which to work. Sprague had remained upstairs.

He gave himself an hour before returning the twelfth or thirteenth box to a stack. He had found nothing remotely useful. He started up the stairs and saw a woman standing in the doorway at the top.

"Silas said a young man was down here," she said.

She was almost as tall as he was, perhaps in her mid-forties, with hair somewhere between blond and gray. She stood with her arms folded, shoulders and hips canted, a heavy tweed coat open across a dark skirt that had collected ice on the hem, suggesting she had walked a long way in her black boots. A thick scarf was folded back on her shoulders. A few drops of water hung in her hair. She had a pleasant, square face animated by light clear eyes almost the color of her hair.

"Silas said you're one of the scientists . . . Dr. Isaac?" Her accent was from somewhere more cosmopolitan than Ewell Island. Stepping aside, she held out a hand that turned out to be cold and firm. "I'm Sydney Wood. You've got some of my new neighbors awfully excited. The police are looking for one of the Michaels boys?"

"As a witness," David said.

"Really? Perhaps someone should have tried to calm the local people. They accepted me so kindly it never occurred to me there could be hostility to your group."

"Is there hostility?"

"You don't know?"

"This is my second day."

"I'm afraid there is. This is a very close-knit community, and most of what passes for information would be gossip anywhere else."

"What sort of gossip?"

"One theme is that you want to prove the islanders committed some awful crime. It would be generations ago, of course, but the same families still live here."

"Do you work with Pastor Merton?" David asked. She didn't look like a Methodist preacher, or what he imagined a Methodist preacher would look like, but neither did Merton.

Sydney Wood laughed. "No, I'm an urban castaway. Assistant professor at the Pittsburgh School of Design. I decided a year ago it was time to do the real thing—spend a couple of years painting instead of teaching." The words sounded as if she had said them before, and he supposed she had. A newcomer would be invited to tell her story many times.

"You're an artist?"

"Mainly portraits, which makes Ewell just about ideal. Where else could I find a character like Silas to paint? Also, living here is cheap, so I can stretch my sabbatical."

"My father is a Sunday painter," David said. The woman was at least ten years his senior, but he wanted to forge a connection with her anyway.

"Is he good?"

"I think so. Since he retired, he's devoted more time to it. He does plein air landscapes."

"Does he show?"

"Sometimes in group exhibitions in Connecticut."

She smiled. "If you're here a while, you're welcome to visit my studio. I've rented the gray house on High Street. They're all gray, I know. It's number 7. I don't have a phone, so just come when you feel like it."

"Thank you," he said.

"It will be a pleasure. Dr. Sprague sent me to look for you in the basement. He wants to get back." They walked to the kitchen, where the ledger had been put away and Sprague stood in his outdoor gear wearing a look of impatience. "I asked Dr. Sprague to sit for me, but he refused," she said.

Sprague moved toward the door.

"Someone already captured his likeness," David said. "Could you see him as a Viking warrior?"

The woman laughed. "I hadn't thought of that, but I suppose I could."

Sprague drove. "Did you find anything?" he asked.

"There was a Boy Scout troop on the island in the Fifties."

"Three members?"

"Five."

"That's helpful. Anything else?"

"No."

"I went through the boxes myself ten days ago. Thought maybe your fresh eye would pick out something. What did you think of Merton?"

"Dickensian. Do you think he's hiding something?"

"I'd bet on it." Sprague snorted. "And Sydney Wood—what do you think of her?"

"She must really have wanted to get away from Pittsburgh."

"I'll tell you something interesting, just in case you're taken with older women."

"What's that?"

"First day I met her, she tried to seduce me." Sprague grinned. "I don't hold that against her."

"Look out!" David shouted.

A pickup truck skidded through the snow ahead of them, spinning in a half circle as Sprague steered past. The other driver's grizzled face twisted as he shouted something they couldn't hear. The man ground his truck's gears and turned onto the lane toward the water.

"Your basic idiot!" Sprague said.

David changed the subject. "Sydney Wood—maybe she's lonely."

Sprague grinned faintly. "That could explain it. I thought it was my good looks."

They reached the camp and found it in chaos.

10

BECKER MET THE ROVER BEARING SPRAGUE AND DAVID. HIS cheeks were flushed, his voice tense. "We've got trouble. Michaels told the police he never entered the excavation. They bought the story. They're interrogating Fane."

"That's ridiculous," Sprague said. He pulled his scarf tight, climbed out of the Rover.

"Fane admitted he was here when Bobby was killed," Becker said. "The sergeant took it from there."

"Took it where? What's the matter with the man?"

"The medical examiner is wondering, too. He tried to talk to the sergeant and got the brush-off."

Charl reached the vehicle. "Noel, these policemen don't know what they're doing. I think we should drive in to Tyler and find a boat."

"Cast Loren to the wolves?" Becker said.

She looked at him. "Get him some help, you asshole."

"We couldn't get a boat in this weather, dear," Sprague said.

The wind had picked up, and snow swirled among the tents. "Let's go see what the problem is."

"They've got Loren in handcuffs. They've taken over the excavation tent."

Sprague headed across the camp.

Becker dropped back a few steps with David. "He'd better go alone. If we all march in, the cops could get nervous."

"Do they really suspect Fane?"

"Hard to tell. The sergeant's acting like an idiot."

Both state policemen had seemed to David to be level-headed that morning. What had happened in three hours?

David thought back. He knew Luther had been underground. He didn't know about Fane. Could the anthropologist have been in the tunnel while David and Becker were airborne? Would he have had time to change his clothes? Michaels hadn't mentioned him. But when David interviewed the islander, Fane had been standing right there, which might have influenced the answers.

Walters joined them, his narrow face grim. David asked if he knew where Fane had been. "It happens I do," Walters said. "If that cop is worried about Loren, he should have a go at me, too. We were playing cards when Michaels began screaming."

"You've told the sergeant?"

"Of course. I made a little headway, I think. The fellow seems mainly confused."

The tent door opened and Sprague and the sergeant came out. The policeman was shaking his head. A few steps behind them, Loren Fane emerged rubbing his wrists. Charl put a hand on his shoulder, and they headed for the dining tent.

The other policeman came out, and the two officers headed for their borrowed car.

"A mistake," Sprague said. "Luther told a plausible story, and we weren't around to counter it."

"*I* was around," Fane said. His attempt at a grin dissolved. "I thought he was going to shoot me."

"Loren doesn't even *look* suspicious," Walters commented. He asked Sprague, "What did the simpleton tell them?"

Sprague looked uncomfortable. "That he wasn't underground,

that he hadn't worked yesterday. Despite what we'd told them, they believed him, and that doesn't make a bit of sense."

At the next low tide, David and Becker measured the tunnel's breach. Sixteen hours later, the weather had cleared enough for a helicopter to bring in three small Asian men, several crates of equipment, and a dozen steel panels pre-cut to fit the underground spaces. The measurements for areas that needed shoring had already been taken. David was impressed by the speed with which the construction team had been assembled. Sprague's bashful sponsor had an impressive command of resources. Sprague prowled the camp impatiently as the newcomers waited for low tide before moving their welding equipment into the tunnels.

David took over the cook's job for an afternoon. Etta Michaels hadn't shown up in more than a day. Six frozen burgers and one omelet did it for lunch. The Asians had brought their own food. They heated trays in a microwave, sat apart to eat, and rebuffed friendly overtures from Walters with pantomimes of not speaking English. The man who appeared to be in charge conferred with Sprague from time to time in broken French.

Charl wandered through, saw David leaning against the stove, and found the picture funnier than he thought it was. "You've got a future," she said, and left, still laughing.

He spotted Becker an hour later and walked out and joined him at the camp perimeter. The larger man's gloved hands cupped a black pistol. "Dr. Sprague is worried about sabotage," Becker said.

"If you want to get coffee, I'll stand watch."

Becker moved an arm stiffly. "You want the gun?"

"I don't need it."

"I'll be back in half an hour."

Becker stalked off.

If he had doubts about the project, they didn't show. In most things in the years David had known him, Paolo Becker was tough-minded. About politics and religion, he was harshly cynical. But when it came to Sprague, he was almost blind.

The old man had earned Becker's loyalty, David thought.

It was Sprague who had gotten Paolo Becker into Columbia's grad program, backing down administrators who were skeptical about the young man's largely European credits.

And it was Sprague who had fought to keep him there, when immigration officials had come around asking questions about the new student's devoutly Communist parents. Had the Brazilian mother and German-Italian father orchestrated a bank holdup in Milan? They hadn't been charged, but there were rumors.

Paolo hadn't done himself any favors when he was questioned. He dismissed politics as a secular religion. He wasn't religious, he said. Therefore he wasn't political. *Mãe* and *vati* were disappointed in him. All that made it into an agent's notes was that Paolo Becker didn't believe in God. Sprague had stepped in and defended his student publicly and loudly. Since the government wasn't sure what it had on the young man, Sprague had won the argument.

Becker would freeze for the professor any time.

David caught a flutter of movement and stared into the woods. A snow devil swirled among the spindly trees, transparent and malevolent and, what counted, harmless.

Forty minutes later, a bright bandana moved among the trees as Walters came out from the camp. "Sprague wants you to suit up. The tunnel's staying dry."

"What about shoring?"

"They spot-welded plates in the west section. It might be a little tighter, but you don't fuss; everyone's in a hurry, you know."

"What about you?"

"Oh, yes, I'm in a hurry, too," the pathologist said. "Haven't had a cadaver since I don't know when."

11

SPRAGUE WAS WAITING FOR HIM. THE CONSTRUCTION CREW had done wonders in nine hours. With the tunnels dry and shored, the men had cleared the rubble that had blocked access to the burial vault. Fane had gone below to install replacement cameras. Whatever happened now, Sprague would have a publishable record.

They want out.

David shivered and tried to ignore the whisper in his mind.

They wanted nothing. *They* were tendon, decalcified bone, maybe scraps of leathery flesh, drained of identity, perhaps drained of the deoxyribonucleic acid strands that had shaped them.

He wiggled forward on his belly, streaming his light ahead. Charl moved just behind him. She had insisted. If Sprague had been able to maneuver in the tight quarters, he would have savored this moment alone. Charl was his proxy.

David elbowed ahead another few inches, playing the light. The vault itself was constructed of stone and creosoted timbers. The close walls and ceiling looked fairly stable. He shifted the light.

Three coffins—

They were unreflecting gray, almost black. Sprague was right about lead sheathing. Fane, who had seen the crypt first after the Asians, had been beside himself with excitement. Lead covering was one thing for big wheels in a large, well-established colony. In London, every subway extension had turned up dozens of lead coffins and ossuaries. But in Ewell the sheathing would have required stripping ballast from a ship, an enormous effort.

But no more than the tunnels. Lots less.

David had built up the moment in his mind. Now the reality was a letdown.

He reached forward and touched the left coffin. Cold and damp. The surface was streaked with mud. If this were a normal excavation, a crew of overworked graduate students would be picking through the mud for whatever tools or other artifacts the burial detail had left behind. Not here. It was a rush job. He shined the light down the length of the center box. It was the smallest, no more than three feet long. A child's.

He told himself he was studying mass populations, cultures, societies—not individuals. Individuals weren't part of the scientific calculus. So he didn't have to think about them, or feel anything for them.

If young Margaret Wakelyn's bones lay here, it didn't matter if she had ever laughed.

If these were Wakelyns. There was no inscription at the foot of any of the boxes. He stretched as far as he could, moving the light along the bonding seams. Whether the vessels had remained air- and watertight was the second question. The first was whether they were sound enough to move.

"You're awfully quiet," said a voice in his ear. Sprague, on the surface.

"If the camera is working," David said, "you can see we have three coffins. All appear to be in good states of preservation."

"They're sound?"

"Good chance of it." He wiggled sideways, opening a space for Charl. "What do you think?"

She squeezed up beside him. Nice—but not quite mud-wrestling. She said, "I'm in awe, Noel, they're beautiful."

"Then let's get them up," Sprague said.

If the roof held, if the bay didn't kill them, the sheer inertia of the objects would be a challenge. David was topside, scraping mud off his boots. He got up and walked over to where Charl and Fane were conferring. Several crates of equipment were open. He saw anchor bolts, tackle, welding tools. "Is this how we get them out?"

"Hope so," said Fane. "The coffins at St. Marys City weighed about fifteen hundred pounds each. We did a lot of the work *in situ*. Testing the air, opening the boxes—can't do that down there."

"We've tried to anticipate," Charl said. "We pour one footing, anchor the tackle in it so our winch can pull laterally. We adapted a Kutcher sled to wedge under the coffins. It will run on steel wheels. We have to drag each box horizontally about twenty-five feet. Then hoist them thirteen feet."

Fane's smile was dubious. "Piece of cake."

"So we bring the coffins up," David said. "It's cold enough we don't need refrigeration for the remains."

"We've got cold boxes for tissue samples," said Charl. "And we plan to airlift the remains out within hours."

Becker and the workmen poured a concrete footing at the bottom of the shaft and anchored the tackle while David watched from above. The Kutcher sled was broken down into three sections, which were reassembled in the tunnel. David watched on a monitor as a small Asian attached a harness to the child's coffin. The hoist cable clanged tight, and as the winch on the surface turned, the box underground grated onto the sled. Becker examined the gap left between the larger coffins. He shined a light on the dull gray containers. David saw a suspicious black streak on the left coffin. "We may have a problem," Becker said.

"What are we looking at?" Sprague said.

"This one has been damaged. Looks like large fissures."

Sprague bent close to a monitor. "Recent damage?"

"No, the end is compressed. I would say it was dropped."

"What about the others?"

"They look all right."

"How long for the first one?"

"An hour?"

The hoist motor whined and the cable snapped taut. The lateral drag resumed.

12

IT TOOK TWO HOURS TO LIFT THE SMALLEST COFFIN. IT WAS hoisted standing on end, feet first. Data were going to be destroyed however they handled the lift, but nobody wanted to chance a detached skull falling the length of the box. Better foot bones, if something had to come loose. David watched on the monitors as Becker worked at the bottom of the shaft. He had wrapped the coffin at six-inch intervals with shipping bands. A two-foot-square section of the Kutcher sled served as a platform, the corners connected by chains to the central cable coming down from the winch. Even after these preparations, David held his breath once the lift began. The box and everything it contained could disintegrate before their eyes.

The coffin reached the surface safely, and Becker and David tilted it onto an industrial weight gurney, activated a pneumatic lift. Becker snipped off the steel bands.

The cold metallic surface seemed to absorb energy: the light from the overhead floods, the last vestiges of warmth in the tent, where the heaters had been off for more than an hour and the temperature was no more than ten degrees Fahrenheit. It absorbed energy and gave nothing back.

Dressed in heavy sweaters and jackets, the team chafed their hands in flimsy plastic gloves. Sprague limped around the gurney, unlocking a cylinder of argon gas, adjusting an overhead camera, exchanging a few words with his wife, who held a second camera.

"Go ahead," he told Fane. The small man had helped in the materials recovery at St. Marys City.

If the coffin had remained airtight, the atmosphere inside was three centuries old. Spectrographic analysis could measure the prevalence of metals and other elements in the Eighteenth Century environment. Bits of fungus and mold might have been preserved. Viral and bacterial contaminants from the period would be present. All useful information, if it could be recovered without contamination from the modern world. Fane used a big, low-speed drill that had a hollow bit connected to an airtight valve. The valve connected to a two-liter sterile tank that at the outset held a vacuum. When an air sample had been drained from the coffin to the tank, Fane closed the valve. He turned off the drill but left the bit in place in the coffin wall.

It was Sprague's turn. He snapped his gas cylinder to the drill, and fed argon into the coffin. The inert gas would help stabilize biological material.

Speaking to himself, Sprague said, "Let's see what else we've got."

He threaded a fiberoptic cable into the drilled hole. On the monitor next to him, an eerie yellow world appeared.

It took David a moment to understand what he saw. It was fabric. The weave was coarse, the magnified threads as thick as twine. There was a weak hint of flaxen color. The camera crept further, exposing a rotted nest that had to be hair. There was a blur that could have been bone. A glimpse of mummified skin.

"You've got good preservation," Walters said.

They stared in silence. The focus shifted a few millimeters and the images blurred as threads curled toward the lens. Then they were looking at bone, but David wouldn't have attempted to identify the object beyond that.

"What is it?" Sprague said.

"Humerus," said Walters without moving closer. "Proximal humerus. You're seeing the top of the upper arm bone."

"Which arm?" said Charl.

"How far into the coffin are we?"

"Two inches."

"So it would be the left arm. Hm."

"What?"

"That's the posterior of the bone," Walters said. "See the depression? That's the groove that carried the radial nerve."

"The back of the bone?"

"It's pretty distinctive."

To David, who had lost the meaning of the discussion, the image looked innocuous.

The focal point shifted. Ribbons? More hair?

"She may be turned face-down," said Walters. "That would explain why we see the back of the bone: it's the right humerus. I think we should open the box."

Sprague nodded to Fane, who pulled a white mask over his mouth and nose. "Unless you need more lead oxide in your diet," Fane told the people around him, "you should mask up."

He used a small circular saw equipped with a vacuum bag. The lead covering came off the top of the coffin in thin slabs, exposing a rough-planed wooden lid that looked almost fresh cut. Sprague circled, inserting a pry lever under the lid every few inches. The hand-cut nails gave way reluctantly.

They took the lid off.

David had no trouble believing that the outer enclosure had been airtight. In the wooden box lay a child's cadaver. Black hair hugged a tiny skull. Bright ribbons shimmered on the dress. The cloth had sunk into the body. Margaret Wakelyn lay mostly face-down, canted partly onto her left side. The exposed flesh was mummified and dark. The bottom of the box was blackened by seepage of body fluids. Coffin liquor. A strong ammonia-like odor rose from the remains.

Coolly, Fane said, "Shit."

Loops of cord bound the corpse's frail wrists and the ankles. A tibia had shed some of its flesh under the conflicting strains of drying tendons and bound ankles. Similar pressure on the shoulder joint had exposed part of the humerus.

"Look at the face," Sprague said.

Charl moved with the camera to where he was pointing, then stopped. Her voice tried for objectivity. "Noel, she was buried alive."

They had all seen this frozen grin before: in photographs of ancient bodies pulled from North European bogs, of concubines buried with their Scythian lords. If nature was cruel, man had adapted to his environment.

I shouldn't feel anything for her, David thought, swallowing bile. The past was a human charnel house. Strangled sacrifices, hammered skulls—

He felt angry at people he had never met. *How could they? To a child.*

"I need space," Walters said. He laid out an electric saw, swabs, forceps, pliers, wipes, containers, multiple pairs of sterile plastic gloves, all on a sterile sheet that a surgeon might use in a minor procedure. Quick recovery of soft tissue samples was essential. Even in the sub-freezing tent, the material would degrade in minutes. Stored in sub-zero canisters, the samples should remain stable for weeks.

Walters clipped tufts of hair and small sections of flesh. Becker held a vial for each specimen, then capped it and stuck on a numbered label while the older man's hand moved to the next area.

"No sign of adipocere," Walters said, referring to the soapy or cheese-like transformation of fatty tissue. "She was probably too young to have caught the more interesting diseases. . . . Franco Rollo has recovered *Treponema pallidum*, the syphilis agent, from a lady who expired in Renaissance Italy. We presume she was a lady. Spigelman found traces of *Mycobacterium tuberculosis* in a fourteen-hundred-year-old skeleton in the Negev. Our little girl here is in a position to tell us much more—"

Walters stopped talking and snatched his hand back as if he'd been bitten. He cursed under his breath. "She wasn't buried alive. She was decapitated. A blade between the fourth and fifth cervical vertebrae. Roughly done."

He turned the body in the coffin, taking his time, glancing now and then at the camera Charl wielded, perhaps imagining himself on PBS, explaining his maneuvers. "You can see here where the neck was sheared," he said. He tapped leathery skin that was raggedly cut. Lifted a skin flap to expose the separated vertebrae. Charl recorded for more than a minute, then looked up and nodded.

"Next, we'll take a peek inside," Walters said. He picked up scissors, snipped open the pretty smock. Traded the scissors for a scalpel and made a long shallow cut across the abdomen.

"We have organ remnants. See the stomach? I hope we've all had our immunizations. It's possible the Wakelyns were ill. Does anybody know how long *Vibrio cholerae* survives in dormancy?"

The question bought him more room to work as he clipped pieces of stomach and gut. He trimmed sections from a dried lump that had been a liver. He began delving into the thorax. "Lungs and heart. You dried out quickly, didn't you, little girl?"

"Bones?" Sprague prompted.

Walters nodded. Slicing dry skin and tendon, he performed a quick surgery that removed the left foot's third metatarsal. Then he tilted the head, forced a blade into the tiny mouth, sliced remnants of jaw muscle and ligament. When the mouth was open, he extracted both canines.

The gruesome procedures had a purpose. If the child's DNA had survived, it would most likely be found in small bones and teeth.

David watched, trying to regain emotional distance. He was too appalled. He had a five-year-old niece he had never met, who lived with his sister in Israel. If this was Margaret Wakelyn, she had been a year younger.

Why did they do this?

How frightened, angry, or self-righteous had they been?

It was snowing again, but Luther Michaels didn't feel the cold.

He had gone outside to hide from the police, and then it had come to him—as many things had come to him recently, as if Etta or someone else smart was telling him softly what he should do—that he had to remain in hiding. The police might come back. They wanted to take him away before his work was done. Huddled against the oil tank behind his trailer, he had grown lumpy when the morning's snow settled on him. His heart rate had sunk to a few beats a minute. His body cooled, and his blood pressure and respiration became undetectable. He didn't notice. He had no conscious thought. But he dreamt.

Etta had brought him breakfast at daybreak. He couldn't eat, but he liked having her talk to him. A little while ago, she had come out again. She had sat beside him, asked him if he was feeling better. She talked to him for a half-hour, and when he couldn't respond she patted his arm.

"You should see yourself," she told him. "You're a snowman."

Was he? Luther dreamt. Was he really?

13

BY THE SECOND NIGHT OF SURVEILLANCE, GERONIMO BIX knew Helen Calder's secrets. He had identified the NIS agent's girlfriend as Judith Mueller, a professor of speech therapy at Georgetown. He had learned Calder cheated on Mueller now and then. A microphone in the apartment fed him chatter and lovemaking sounds. He hacked Calder's home computer, searching for a hint of her informant. He prowled through weeks of emails. In the end, the prosaic business of maintaining visual contact gave him what he needed.

On the second evening, Calder left her apartment for the Italian restaurant across the street, and Bix followed. Twenty minutes later a thin, distinguished-looking man joined her. Bix recognized the man. He was a retired pharmaceutical company scientist, a hired cortex, as Staley liked to say, named Stephan Pogorovich. He had worked for the St. Leger Foundation for a little more than a year, struggling in a tiny laboratory in Baltimore to grow brain tissue from illegally harvested fetal stem cells.

Pogorovich's efforts had been a failure, and there was little chance of the contract being renewed.

The scientist gestured broadly and spoke at length, like a salesman afraid of losing his customer. Helen Calder gave him no encouragement, her face and soft body immobile except for the rhythmic business of eating. Bix wondered how much information Pogorovich believed he had. Every bit of paperwork specified that he was engaged in an altogether legal form of cancer research. The only thing Pogorovich could prove was that his laboratory had diverted funds to an unauthorized—and criminal—use, the stem cells work. Anything else would be his word against the foundation's records and formidable legal talent.

Bix sat three tables away, not close enough to hear the man's words in the busy restaurant, but he could see when Calder abandoned her pretense of indifference. Now both of them leaned forward, like mismatched lovebirds. The conversation was intense.

It was after eleven when Bix took an elevator to Roger Staley's apartment in the Watergate. The rooms were crowded with cherry and rosewood antiques, tangible assertions of money and breeding. Bix gave his report standing in the director's study, while Staley sipped wine.

"What do you think she knows?" Staley asked.

"He could have admitted his own crime," Bix said. "The rest would be guesswork. He would know the foundation violates the law, because of what he was doing for us. But he wouldn't know how, or why . . . or how often."

Was Pogorovich dangerous or only a nuisance?

"You need to review all the firewalls," Staley told Bix, "make certain the coded projects are secure." The code names appeared nowhere in the foundation's offices or unprotected records. More important, no telephone, data communication or travel records would link the foundation to the widely dispersed locations where the main research efforts were under way.

Stephan Pogorovich's project was nothing compared to Lionheart or Crestfallen.

Pogorovich himself was nothing.

As long as nobody could find the projects, the government couldn't undo what Staley and the foundation had set in motion. The key research was funded years in advance. The projects could outlive the foundation.

"I can deal with Pogorovich," Bix offered.

"He isn't our only problem. If Calder looks deeply, she'll find a lot of money we can't account for."

Bix didn't respond.

Staley pondered aloud. "If Calder were unavailable, would her cases become orphans? That's the question. The answer depends on whether we've become an institutional priority at NIS."

Bix was impassive.

"Perhaps there is another solution," Staley said.

He looked at an ancient standing clock. Not yet midnight. He picked up the phone and woke a senior partner at a Washington law firm that handled the foundation's legal affairs. Staley knew that the St. Leger Foundation was viewed as a boring client. It was reputable, which limited the billable hours, and obscure, which limited media notice. But the foundation paid very well for its hours, and the partner took the call.

"A preemptive legal strike against NIS," the lawyer repeated after listening to Staley for some minutes.

"They're threatening a subpoena. I would like to minimize the disruption." Staley had told the partner the foundation was being dragged into a dispute between NIS and an errant research laboratory. The foundation was a bystander, innocent and indignant.

"You're asking whether we could block a subpoena?"

"That's correct."

"The chances are poor, Roger. You've got to understand, federal courts don't slap down the good guys."

"Who says they're good guys?"

"Roger, you or I couldn't *buy* NIS's image. The media love them. So does Congress. And so do the courts." A half-suppressed yawn escaped. "You know the score. Scientists tamper with the natural order, defy the Almighty, rape the little guy. NIS keeps you in check. If you want to avoid disruption, I recommend we accept the subpoena. Give the government what it wants and it will go away."

Staley replied cheerfully, "As usual, Paul, you provide splendid advice. Go back to sleep."

As soon as he hung up, he told Bix, "For openers, we'll silence Stephan."

Bix barely nodded. "And the woman?"

Staley noticed his wine glass was empty. "Too much coincidence would be dangerous."

"Suppose Pogorovich bears responsibility for both deaths?"

"How would you manage it?"

Geronimo Bix told him.

Bix had an enormous file of facts on the informant— personal data, security measures at home and office. It seemed the only thing he had overlooked was the essential character of the man. Believing everyone capable of treachery, Bix hadn't recognized Pogorovich as a specific danger. *Mea culpa*, he thought. *I'm not supposed to be stupid.* He drove back to his office. From a small, very cold refrigerator with a biometric lock, he removed a plastic box that had once held a first aid kit. Now it held six stoppered vials of a size often used for toilet water or crack cocaine. Bix put on latex gloves, transferred two of the vials to a cigarette case.

It was a little after one a.m. when he reached the D.C. Beltway and headed north on I-95.

Pogorovich's laboratory, Canton Oncology Ltd., was in an ancient industrial building a mile and a half from the Baltimore downtown. Surrounding streets were cobbled, sidewalks narrow and empty. Houses were short and cramped. The area was too rough to attract bar-hoppers from the waterfront. In twenty minutes of waiting Bix saw only one police patrol car cruise past on the avenue. Slumped in his car seat, he used an infrared lens to search for security cameras. A building half a block down had surveillance equipment aimed at its front door. He scanned the tops of buildings. He studied lamp fixtures. In the end, he parked a block away, wore his fedora low on his head, and studied the pavement as he walked. There was no reason for anyone to look for an explanation beyond natural causes for Pogorovich's death. But Calder's death would raise the stakes. A federal investigation wouldn't miss much.

He squeezed down an alleyway between buildings. He entered Canton Oncology by key through a rear door and shut down the alarm. He hung up his overcoat, suitcoat and hat, then pulled on a biohazard suit he had brought with him. When he was thoroughly protected, he opened the cigarette case and removed the two vials.

The vials' contents had been stolen from a research laboratory not too different from the lab Pogorovich operated—except that it was legal and its scientists had been trying to combat a lethal bacterial strain, Methicillin-resistant Staphylococcus aureus (MRSA). Because it was resistant to most antibiotics, MRSA killed thousands of people a year in hospitals. The PVL strain, which was especially lethal, didn't require a wound for infection. PVL spread by casual contact with unbroken skin.

Dipping a cotton swab into bacillus, Bix worked his way through Pogorovich's office. Only a touch was needed: on a telephone, a black-glazed mug that said TOP DOC, the refrigerator door, a desktop, a coffee maker, creamer jar, silverware, two lab coats, the bridge of a pair of eyeglasses. He contaminated a culture dish in which something else grew dense and purple. He sprinkled the floor. Investigators would find a scientist had accidentally cultured the agent of his destruction. Terrible that it had gotten loose in the lab. Worse if it infected a few other people.

Bix had shed the beliefs of his grandfather, who had been a devil dancer. There were no spirits in the mountains. No spirit in owls or men. There was no mystery, only simplicity, which he respected.

He would be satisfied to read about Stephan Pogorovich in the newspaper.

He had used up half the second vial when he booted the office computer, composed a polite and meaningless letter to Helen Calder, Senior Investigator, National Institutes of Science. *Happy we could meet, look forward to future discussions. Very truly yours.*

Letterhead into the printer.

A scrawled signature copied loosely from other correspond-
ence.

An envelope printed.

A stamp from the roll in Dr. Pogorovich's desk.

A few bacillus spatters on the letter, two on the outside of the
envelope for verisimilitude.

An accident, a terrible accident.

On his way out, he reversed the process, turning the
protective suit inside out as he removed it, restoring it to its
pouch. He dropped the pouch into a grocery store bag, along
with the resealed vials of pathogen, taped the bag shut.

He handled the contaminated letter very carefully.

A half-mile before the expressway, he found a mailbox.

14

NINE HOURS LATER THEY RAISED THE LARGEST COFFIN. IT WAS obviously damaged. "There is no way this one is airtight," Fane said. "We're not holding a vacuum with the equipment. Shall I peel it?"

"Not yet," Sprague said. "Let's stay with the protocol."

The protocol was a series of steps designed to preserve as much information as possible in an archaeological sample. Fane collected air from the box, then flooded the coffin with argon. When they cut the remaining seals and removed the lid, loose fabric and dust had settled at the top of the coffin. The body, which appeared to that be of a man, was in far worse condition than the child's. Skin and tendons had rotted, leaving brownish lengths of bone.

"Apparently not a live burial," said Walters, for the audio record. "No evidence of ligatures. The body is prone. Bone deterioration looks similar to that of other remains from the period surviving in unsealed containers. Doesn't appear to have been embalmed or we would see white brushite powder from the alum used as a preservative. Little problem with the upper extremities." He picked at bits of fabric and other debris that had shifted during the recovery. "The skull has been damaged."

David looked past Walters's shoulder. Scraps of thin brown hair and scalp clung to the bone.

"The damage is at the back," said Walters. "Both the left parietal and the occipital bones are broken."

"From movement?" said Sprague.

David could see the hole in the skull, three or four inches in diameter.

"It isn't archaeological damage," Walters said. "Decalcified bone fragments in a powdery fashion. There's no sign of that. These bones were broken before demineralization set in."

Sprague spoke. "While he was alive."

"Or soon after death."

"If it occurred while he was alive, we have a second murder victim." Sprague's glee was contained, but barely.

"Let's take our samples," Walters said.

They wrapped the remains in heavy plastic for transport. A helicopter would arrive when the third box had been recovered.

They walked as a group through a screen of sleet to the dining tent, ate in relaxed camaraderie. The project was delivering results. A man and his young child murdered. Journal articles would keep them all busy for a year.

David sat across from Sprague. The older man hadn't scored a spectacular find, but it was respectable. Nothing to apologize for toward the end of a career. Sprague picked at the meaning of the deaths. "That fellow Kobler who wrote to his brother left a few things out, didn't he? 'Dear Family: We rose up and slaughtered our neighbors. God bless.'"

"Is that what you think happened?" David said.

"Isn't it obvious? The family were killed en masse. Perhaps others were murdered as well. Once we've wrapped up this phase, we'll come back with better security and investigate."

"Why couldn't it have been an individual's crime?" David said.

"First, the whole village was complicit in the cover-up. Give me an explanation for that?"

"Don't have one."

"No. The family was relatively well to do. This could have been an economic crime, but it doesn't fit. You murder a family for their silver, you would feed the bodies to the wolves, be done with it. These burials were enormously expensive in labor, especially considering the depleted population. So there must have been a strong motive. The island lore is probably at least partly right."

"What part?"

"That the islanders thought the Wakelyns were devils of some sort. Satanists. Keep in mind, you're dealing with a Seventeenth Century mentality." Sprague leaned back. He had an audience. He was happy. "I think we've got all the pieces of an explanation. Widespread sickness on the island followed by an attack on a family that had survived it. They probably believed the Wakelyns had caused the illness. So they cleaned out the infection. It's possible they were right: perhaps the family were carriers, colonized but impervious. We'll see what microbial DNA can tell us."

"There was disease in all the colonies," David said. "I don't remember that it led to murder."

Sprague gave a sly smile. "Loren and I both think we can find close precedent in Massachusetts." He rubbed his beard, smoothing it for a second. It was a gesture he used when pretending to gather thoughts he had ready. "Think witch hunts, David. A recurrent theme in the persecution of witches was neighbors falling ill. Also, the timing works. The Massachusetts witch hunts hit their stride in 1692 and died out within about a year. The Wakelyns were murdered in 1702. Both events occurred in English colonies, similar cultures, identical belief sets, separated by ten years and five hundred miles."

"You don't believe there was a witch trial down here?"

"Not a trial, David, there's no evidence of that. A frenzy. The mutilation suggests something sudden, intense—survivors wreaking vengeance."

"Is that what your paper is going to say?"

"That depends on what further evidence we find. It's a hypothesis, nothing more. But what Merton says supports it. You know the value of old wives tales. Sometimes they're spot on."

Fane had listened and was nodding. "There's also an economic aspect to some of those cases. Envy and greed played roles. You see someone who's better educated, better off, it's just natural to suspect a pact with the devil. That's Conspiracy Theory Circa 1700."

Sprague nodded absently.

"The real curiosity," Fane said, "is that there weren't more witch hunts in the New World. It was a lively ecclesiastical pursuit in Europe from the Fifteenth Century on. The hysteria was sporadic, but it added up to thousands of people burnt. The Americans scarcely bothered."

"They had Indians to kill," Walters suggested.

"That may be close to the mark," Fane said. "Think of the release people got torturing witches. They lived out the vilest sexual fantasies of degradation. Now you'd have to go to a movie for that."

David said, "What's in the literature?"

"Leaving aside dreary academic stuff," Fane said, "the witch-hunters produced a lot of material. Cotton Mather described his work running the trials in Salem. He became a little repentant, thought maybe people had overreacted. There were textbooks. Bromhall put together one called *Treatise of Spectres* in the sixteen hundreds. Kramer and Sprenger's *Malleus Maleficarum* was printed in the late fourteen hundreds. Lots of practical advice on spotting the hag who sleeps with the devil. The first clue was a person's enemies growing ill."

"It wasn't bad science for its day," Sprague said. "An old woman whose enemies grow ill would bear investigating today."

Becker and David sent up the third coffin. The box showed no damage, and Fane took his time collecting the air sample. David sat with a jacket over his shoulders. If the woman in the coffin, Elspeth Wakelyn, had been mutilated, Sprague would have his evidence of mass murder. As for its cause . . .

Science? Maybe of a sort. Based on sound principles: stomp out the contagion, protect the village. Brutal and superstitious, but rational all the same, and not all that primitive. Modern slaughter wore its own masks of reason; if you wrote its history, a murdered family of three wouldn't rate a footnote.

The lid came off the coffin, and Fane straightened. "What the—"

David looked.

The coffin was a nest of stones and twigs. There was no body of Elspeth Wakelyn.

15

DAVID MOVED UNCOMFORTABLY IN THE CAMP CHAIR WHERE HE had sat to think. The tent was cold. He had a computer on his lap, which he closed carefully and set on a cot.

"We're evacuating in the morning," Charl said. "Noel is sending Walters and the bodies out at dawn."

"That's it, then."

"That's it. The policemen came back. They can't find Luther. They think relatives are hiding him."

"Are they still here? I want to talk to them."

She was standing a few feet from him, red hair tangled. Angry or sad, he couldn't always tell.

"I want you to talk to me first," she said. "You don't agree with Noel's analysis."

"He and Fane need more evidence."

"Do you plan to attack them?"

"Where would you get that idea?"

"Just answer."

"I don't plan to attack anyone. Noel can publish whatever he wants. I'm not going to offer a rebuttal. First, it would be disloyal; this is his project. Second, I don't have an alternative hypothesis. But we don't know what happened. We don't even know that this wasn't an individual's crime, which the community covered up."

"An individual's?"

"Elspeth Wakelyn. Butchering her husband and daughter leaves her a well-to-do widow. She bribes her neighbors to conceal her role by burying three coffins. But why hide them down here? It doesn't hang together. Compared to that, Noel's theory isn't bad. It's premature, in my judgment. But that's between him and peer review."

"Noel's always been ready to defend his findings. He's a strong man."

She was too pragmatic for the role of blindly loyal wife. One of the things David had liked about her was that she had never worn attractive traits—loyalty, compassion, social concerns—out of vanity, like a fashion statement.

"I know he is," David said.

If she had been taller, he wouldn't have felt her breath on his face as he sat and she stood. He wondered if there was a survival advantage in shorter women, because a male could become aware of them under more circumstances. A bit of vulgar doggerel on the disadvantages of tall women popped into his mind. Nose to nose or toes to toes, he and Charl had managed fine.

Driven more by memory than by lust, he grasped her hips and pulled her toward him. She came two willing steps, put her hands on his shoulders, resisted a little. "Good thing you did go away. I love Noel. Respect him, love him, want to stay with him. So I can't hop into the sack with you whenever I want."

"How about every other time?"

"You mean like Wednesdays and Sundays, when Noel's busy at the office. We could have an hour, and then I'd run the kids to soccer."

"I'd coach a team."

She lowered her face, and her hair brushed his face as she stared at him. "Bad idea all around."

"Do you think Ewell's witches will get anyone's attention?"

"Probably not. But Noel's happy."

"He talked about coming back, looking for more victims."

She backed up, stuffing her hands into her jacket. "If he does that, I'll look you up. We can try that island in the Yucatan again." She was joking but only partly. "I don't like this place."

"Nobody seems to," he said.

He found the state police sergeant and his corporal bent over coffee. Both were solid men, comfortable with their authority, unaccustomed to looking like fools. The sergeant, Virgil Vaughn, had a hard, deeply lined face, thick-lensed glasses, two days' growth of pale beard. He and the corporal were sitting with Becker. David joined them.

"The problem we got," Vaughn said, "is people believe Luther Michaels couldn't harm anybody. To a man and woman, they'd rather believe you folks are killing each other."

"We only do that on paper," said Becker.

Vaughn glanced at him curiously.

"In professional journals," Becker elaborated. "The arguments get nasty."

"That's outside my jurisdiction."

David said, "Is Luther still on the island?"

"Nobody admits taking him off. He wouldn't have friends on the mainland. He can hide better here. Wife claims she hadn't seen him since yesterday. If I didn't have to keep peace with these people, I'd arrest her for harboring."

"What about Silas Merton?"

"That old soak could be hiding Luther in the rectory. Silas is local; that's where his loyalties are."

"There's a woman on High Street. Have you talked to Sydney Wood?"

"The artist? Is there a special reason we should?"

"She might have heard something, and she's not local."

Vaughn rubbed his chin. "You're sure she's off-island? Somehow I thought she was Eweller."

"She says she's from Pittsburgh," David said.

Vaughn stirred his coffee.

David asked, "What made you suspect Fane?"

"What?" Vaughn looked up.

"Fane—what made you suspect him?"

"I didn't."

The guy wasn't fooling. "You had him in handcuffs," David said.

Vaughn shook his head. "What are you smoking?"

David leaned back under Vaughn's stare.

Could the man really have no memory?

"I hope I don't have to call you guys as witnesses," the sergeant said. Trace of humor in his eyes, trying to treat it lightly. He stood up, pulled on heavy gloves, strode out of the tent. The corporal hurried to catch up.

Becker said softly, "You been smoking dope again?"

"Not me."

"What would he have done if you'd insisted?"

"I didn't want to find out." David felt coldness creeping up his back.

Sprague came in, trailed by the others. "There you are! We're going to have a little toast. Loren, pop the cork. It's domestic, but we'll pretend not to notice."

Fane produced a bottle that must have come to the island with them. Sprague handed out plastic cups. "Here's to the enlightened folk of Ewell Island!" Sprague lifted his cup.

They sipped the wine, but the mood wasn't there. Ahead would be services to attend for Roberta Gerson, distraught family members, more policemen. The project's success was a matter of perspective.

Becker stood beside David. "You notice how he's not worked up over the empty coffin? He should be running around crying 'Where's Elspeth?'"

"He should."

"So should you."

"I'm off the case."

"I'll be sorry to see you go. It's nice to have somebody around who has resigned from the Sprague cult."

"You could resign."

Becker nodded vaguely. "Truth is, I like the guy." He

wandered over and said a few words to Walters just inside the door. Sprague and Charl talked for a while, then Charl kissed her husband and went out without looking at David. The party had died.

Luther Michaels would never feel cold again.

In the last twenty hours his body temperature had fallen below seventy-five degrees. His heart had stopped twice, and he had closed his eyes in acceptance. Then a jolt, which seemed to come from outside him, sent blood coursing through him again, and dreamy awareness returned.

He wore only carpet slippers and frozen wool socks on his feet. His toes were badly frostbitten. Snow had melted into his jacket and trousers and then frozen so the clothing formed a shiny dark carapace. He was bareheaded, his thin hair strung with ice.

He moved sluggishly among the trees. The head of his firewood axe bumped his unfeeling leg. He had a vague sense that he was late. . . .

Ahead he saw the lights of the archaeologists' camp. This was where he was supposed to be, with these people who were his friends. They had been kind to him and Etta, especially the young woman Luther had had to hurt with the shovel. They paid more money than he needed. They told him he worked good. They praised Etta's crab cakes. A vestige of Luther Michaels's mind knew all that was true.

He crossed the snow toward voices. He would do something good for them. Explain how robbing graves was wrong. How they had to stop.

He saw the woman walking alone between the tents.

He was coming up behind her, and she didn't notice him until his frozen house slipper scraped across crusted snow. She turned but he was lighted from behind and she couldn't see his face.

"Luther?" Charl said.

He couldn't speak, so he nodded.

Then he remembered why he had brought his axe.

Two: The Founders

Founder Effect

The establishment of a new population by a few original founders (in an extreme case, by a single fertilized female) which carry only a small fraction of the total genetic variation of the parental population.

Ernst Mayr, 1963

DNA

DNA (deoxyribonucleic acid) is the giant molecule which is used to encode genetic information for all life on earth.

TalkOrigins.Org

16

COLD SPRING HARBOR WAS LIVING UP TO ITS NAME THIS morning. As she jogged past Vannevar Bush Laboratory, trying to pull ahead of the wind that slashed through her dense coat, Pilar Rodriguez wondered how many of this famed research establishment's staff would kill for the chance that had fallen into her lap. Meeting Roger Staley at the Human Genome Symposium in Turin, Italy had been a fluke at the end of a chain of unlikely events. First a senior colleague had asked her to fill a slot on his symposium team after his protégé's wife miscarried. Then the surprisingly hot weather in Turin had driven conference participants out of the lecture halls at every opportunity and into the surrounding countryside. *Then* she and the Englishman Tom Harris had found the outdoor tables in the hillside village, where by chance Roger Staley had come on his noontime excursion. Recognizing Staley from the conference, Harris had invited the American to join them for lunch. Pilar was condensing the sequence, she realized, as she hurried down the sloping waterfront campus, because chance also had brought her and Tom Harris together in their common interest in speciation. If it hadn't been for that interest, she would never have paid attention to the dour, long-nosed researcher from Oxford who was giving a paper on Galapagos finches. She wouldn't have played hooky with him for a week after the conference ended. She wouldn't have ended up a little pregnant.

More important, she thought, steering her mind back to the subject, she wouldn't have met Staley. And finally, giving chance its due, if dear Tom hadn't gotten an emergency summons back to town from his team's leader, she and Staley wouldn't have found during their private lunch how much their interests coincided. He wasn't a researcher and wasn't affiliated with any of the prominent organizations or corporations sponsoring expeditions in the newly mapped human genetic terrain. But his curiosity was intense, and knowledgeable, and she responded to his focused questions by telling him as much as she could about the process by which new species emerged. It was a broad field of study. The rules were fairly murky. The gray areas were endless. He wanted to understand the nuances.

So she described how species formed new branches, one off the other.

"It happens a number of different ways," she said. "One key variable is whether an organism is isolated"—waiting, wondering if she had lost him already until he smiled encouragement. "Sometimes part of an existing population will become separated from the rest. They might cross a mountain range or a desert, which forms a geographic wall. The environment may be different on the other side of the wall. In that case, the splinter population adapts to different selective pressures. You understand? They may benefit from longer legs, or greater heat tolerance. In time, the changes may become so significant that the two branches no longer can interbreed. That's when we generally say speciation has occurred."

"What if the environments are similar?"

"If the populations are separate, a new species still can emerge just because of genetic drift: random mutation produces changes that aren't shared with the original group."

As Staley nodded, she added, "Where there's geographic separation, it's called allopatric speciation. But species can branch off within a single geographic area, if the new one can fill some environmental niche. That's called sympatric speciation."

Before she could offer an example, Staley said, "That's what your friend was talking about with his Galapagos finches."

"Right. It was really dramatic. Finches with small beaks survived a drought because they could handle small seeds. The birds with larger beaks perished. So only the genetic program for small beaks was passed along to offspring, and there was a change in the species in a single generation."

"That's unusual, isn't it?"

"And how."

He flicked a hand, and a waiter brought a carafe of white wine. "Tell me more."

She did, happy for an audience. She told him about rapid speciation of mice on an Atlantic island. She thought of—but didn't go into—the speciation that had amused her and Tom Harris, in which several lines of male dung beetles from *Onthophagus taurus* were trading smaller penises for larger horns, a reason to be grateful, she and Tom agreed, that men didn't have horns.

In return, she learned a little about an educational organization Staley oversaw. It was active in supporting the social sciences, but the expertise of people in the hard sciences was sometimes needed to put larger questions into perspective. He suggested that an expert in speciation might find a short-term consultancy rewarding.

When she told him she was heavily committed for the rest of the year, he waved dismissively.

"The need isn't imminent, Pilar. The foundation will pay you a modest retainer to be in effect 'on call.' I was thinking of ten thousand dollars for a twelve month period. That's if you never hear from us. If we need help, we would pay your normal consultancy rate." He smiled. "If we can afford you."

For Pilar, a lowly research assistant two years out of graduate school, consultancies at a high level were a mirage on a distant horizon. Her throat tightened, because he expected her to tell him her normal fee. How could you have a norm when you had no data points to average? She thought of an hourly figure that was steep but—

"Our usual arrangement," Staley said, "since we expect people to inconvenience themselves a little for us, is portal to portal pay." He mentioned a rate three times the number Pilar hadn't yet dared propose. "Would that be adequate?"

She tried to appear businesslike as she sipped the wine and decided, after considering the question seriously, that he wasn't making fun of her.

Now she was on the clock, she guessed, since leaving the lab fifteen minutes ago. That meant she had earned half a normal day's pay walking to her car. If she stopped to feed the birds, that would be another fifty dollars.

She threw the satchel containing her clothes into the trunk of her car, placed the aluminum case that held her collection kit gently beside the clothing bag. It hadn't snowed since Sunday, and the roads were clear and the village that lay across the harbor looked crisp and bright.

Dr. Janecke wasn't expecting her back for a week. He had been great—actually, terrific—about letting her take vacation time on short notice. Envy wasn't part of his makeup. He had shared her excitement. He would have jumped at the opportunity himself. The samples she was going to work with were human, from a remote, isolated group, according to Staley. He had refused to tell her more.

As she reached the highway, she speculated on the St. Leger Foundation's angle. They were big on the social sciences, Staley had said. Maybe that should worry her. Social sciences and biology were an explosive mix, lousy for careers. Suppose they were trying to prove a pet theory that ghettos and urban decay were byproducts of specific genetic traits? She needed to steer clear of anybody remotely suggesting racial explanations for social ills. Once you got stuck with that label, the racist geneticist, you were finished in legitimate research. A bright boy named Palmer Cudleigh at the Hopkins, who supposedly could manipulate statistics as well as anybody, had been driven from the field after several papers on IQ.

Pilar told herself to calm down. This wasn't about race or IQ. It was about isolation. And depending on what developed, she might get her name on a paper sponsored by the foundation. Staley had barely hinted at that, but . . .

There was nothing wrong with ambition, as her mother said, if you kept your knees together and your head on straight.

At the airport's small office, a pilot was waiting. He was a solidly built man with burned copper skin, eyes hidden behind reflective sunglasses. Leather jacket, blue jeans—everything but an ace's white silk scarf. He saw the metal case in her hand.

"Dr. Rodriguez? I'm Rudy. The aircraft is ready when you are."

"I'm ready," Pilar said. A sleek blue-black helicopter waited a hundred feet from the building. Whatever else she might decide about the St. Leger Foundation, she liked the fact they were spending money on her. Eight months ago, ten thousand dollars had been wired into her checking account, just as Staley had promised. The retainer had paid off her car loan.

So far so good.

Rudy loaded both her bags. She climbed into a seat just behind the pilot's chair, buckled the belt. It dawned on her that Staley hadn't said exactly where she was going. Not to the foundation's headquarters, he'd made that clear, mentioning a lab they used in West Virginia. She leaned forward as the pilot started the engines and asked, "How long is the flight?"

"About three hours, ma'am. There's a video screen on the back of the seat, if you don't want to nap."

She said thanks and wondered if she should kick herself once or twice for being too embarrassed to ask the city. Not that it mattered. She wasn't a hundred percent sure West Virginia had cities. Maybe it was all strip mines and hollers. Who cared about details? Impetuousness was her middle name, according to her mother. Pilar felt a surge of warmth for the woman who had never admitted disappointment in any of her daughters, whose attitude was always practical: *What do we do about this?* Settling deeper into the seat, Pilar knew the answer. We keep our knees together and cash Mr. Staley's checks.

She had never ridden in a helicopter before, and the bright

cold landscape held her interest for a while. She had seen a model railroad at the Bronx Botanical Gardens, built on a grand scale, its sculptured hills and rivers not quite meant to look real, like what lay below. She tried the video equipment, got lost in something about wild dogs on an island—the heroine was Hispanic—then let her mind drift. The rhythm of the engine was comforting and steady, almost like the reliable murmur of someone who cared about you regardless. When she looked down again, she realized she had been sleeping. The ground was deeply wooded with only a single dark highway that peeked in and out of a haze of winter-browned branches. The aircraft was descending at right angles to the highway. They passed over a hill and on its back she saw a square made up of long, single-story buildings with a paved, open area in its center. That was where the flight ended.

The pilot cut power, removed his earphones, looked around at her.

Straight ahead, Pilar could see a large sign over a doorway. MPC. MILK PROTEINS CORPORATION.

"A dairy?" Pilar said.

Only two cars occupied slots against the north building. There was no sign of activity. No one had come out to greet her. The pilot helped her down to the pavement. Not derelict, the buildings were in good repair. But she had pictured herself arriving at something like the stone and ivy fortresses of Princeton, which would have told her she was at the center of something both important and respectable. But Staley had said a lab, after all, not a university.

The pilot headed for a short flight of concrete steps. A door opened on the landing, and a small, round, dark-skinned man came out. He was dressed in a laboratory coat and baggy black pants, the bottoms of which were stuffed into white socks. His black athletic shoes were huge.

"You must be Rodriguez," he called. "I'm Carter. Seems I'm everything today, including doorman and concierge." His voice was deep, the words drawn out as if he were telling jokes she might enjoy.

He took her bags and led the way inside and down empty

white-painted halls. The place felt empty. Pilar felt unhappier with every step, though she wasn't sure why. Cold Spring's facilities were pretty spartan, at least in the basement where she worked. Carter opened a door. The room had two desks and several chairs, one of them occupied by a man Pilar only glimpsed as Carter moved to the next door. He opened it, and this time the surprise was pleasant.

Here was a well-equipped genetic testing laboratory. She recognized equipment at a glance. The bank of centrifuges was a newer version of the Advanced Biometrics model she and Janecke used on Long Island. There was a 6750 Cryogenic Grinding Mill, an Eppendorf thermal cycler for PCR processing, a Hoeffer minifluorometer.

Carter crossed the lab, opened yet another door, and set down her bags just across the threshold. "Your domain. Lab, sleeping quarters, private bath. We try to treat visiting experts well."

"Thank you," Pilar said. "What will I be working on?"

Carter brought his hands together like an embarrassed host. "We'll know when the job arrives. It's been delayed. Come on out and meet Minh. Would you like coffee?"

"All right."

An Asian man with thinning hair was slouched at a computer. Carter introduced them. Pilar Rodriguez, Louis Minh.

"Any word?" he asked Minh.

Minh typed again, sat back and waited as nothing occurred on the screen. "They've forgotten us."

"Where are the samples coming from?" Pilar asked.

"Some island. Everything with these people is a big secret." Minh turned in his chair, noticed the pilot standing in the doorway, pretended to ignore him.

"You talk a lot," the pilot said.

Minh waved a hand dismissively.

Pilar had the pilot in her peripheral vision. He had been distant and professional to her, almost invisible as he carried out his job, for which she'd been grateful. She got tired of being chatted up by horny strangers. Busboys thought they could talk to a Latina. Every jerk thought he had a chance. The clipped tone Rudy used on Minh surprised her. He was still in the doorway, medium height, solid, a square unrevealing face. Not Puerto Rican. Possibly American Indian. The pilot went to the coffee urn, filled a metallic container, left them. Minh watched him go.

"Do you work for Mr. Staley?" Pilar asked.

Carter responded. "Sort of. We do contract lab work for a number of small pharmaceutical companies. Staley advises us and sends us business. You're here for St. Leger Pharmacal, right?"

St. Leger Pharmacal. A pharmaceutical company. So it was commercial.

"You may as well get your equipment set up and make yourself comfortable," Carter said. "I'll show you the cafeteria, if you're hungry."

"I am," she said.

He walked with a pronounced wobble, like some big-shoed carnival doll. Pilar decided that Carter was a perfect example of the effects of a minor genetic variance, presumably harmless, though a roly-poly figure with circus-clown feet would have made his life hell as a kid. And of course she couldn't be certain that the genetic quirk was harmless. A mutation that expressed itself in one visibly unkind way might cause a host of other problems.

"You have a lot of space here," Pilar said.

He was flicking wall switches as he went, spilling light down uninhabited passages.

"We've got ten times more space than we need," he replied. "You may have noticed there aren't a lot of towns nearby. We got the property cheap. If we keep growing, we'll keep upgrading. The hard part is getting techies to work out here. Right now it's just me, Minh and another fellow, and now you."

"What is St. Leger Pharmacal doing?"

"Mr. Staley didn't tell you?"

"He was vague."

"That's our Roger. A secret's better in his pocket than in somebody else's, that's how Roger thinks."

Carter pushed through double doors into a linoleum-floored room about twelve feet square. There were three orange-topped round tables, ten or so bucket chairs, several lighted vending machines.

"Everything from pot roast to candy, canned apple drink, corn chips," Carter said. "We go first class. There are no pretzels because I stole them all and hid them. Here's the microwave and condiments. This is another reason we have trouble getting people to work here. If you want a beer, or God forbid, some company, the nearest town is thirty-four miles around the other side of the mountains. I don't go there. They don't like people of color too much. Minh doesn't go either."

She peered through a couple of vending windows, looked around the drab room. "I thought you said you had a cafeteria."

"Misspoke. I guess I meant 'canteen.' You aren't planning to be here long?"

"I don't think so."

"After a week, some of this food starts to taste good. Especially after a power loss knocks out refrigeration." He patted a sandwich machine.

"Are the bathrooms out-houses?"

"Oops, that was going to be my next surprise. You want anything here? Just push the buttons, we don't make you pay."

Pilar selected a couple of chocolate bars and followed Carter through the labyrinth back toward the lab. One saving grace of the long twisted route was that she wouldn't find herself trying the pot roast soon.

She said, "Has Mr. Staley shared his secret with you?"

Carter slowed and glanced back. "Nope. Sorry."

"Do you know what we're waiting for?"

"Tissue samples. Isn't that what you've been told?"

"Genetic material from an isolated population, according to Mr. Staley. Minh mentioned an island."

"That's interesting," Carter said vaguely. He had stopped. "Basically you don't know why you're here—except you're doing a DNA sequence. Suppose it's a ruse and you're really being sold into white slavery? Or you're here to service Minh and me as we struggle to overcome a life-threatening disease, no time for R and R? Don't be offended, I'm queer as a duck, and Minh's addicted to satellite porn. I don't know. Staley didn't tell me the purpose of your job. I'm just supposed to set things up, make you comfortable, let you work. But an isolated population, huh? That's interesting."

They resumed walking. She asked, "Why's it interesting?"

He stopped again. "Did he make a point of the isolation thing?"

"Pretty much."

"You know the term 'Founder Effect'?"

"Of course."

"Well, you know what a pharmaceutical company would be looking for. Profitable therapies. St. Leger Pharmacal isn't a factor in the industry. But maybe Roger thinks he's on to something hot. You're young. You haven't worked for big pharma, have you?"

"No. I've been at Cold Spring."

"Good research place, I hear. But where the rubber meets the road, it's all about money. Now, isolated population. What happens to DNA in isolated populations? Mutations gain strength. Grandma the genetic founder has a hare lip; after a few generations ten percent of her clan have inherited hare lips. Maybe Staley hopes there's a medical angle in these people. An illness, maybe."

Pilar caught on. "An illness needing a treatment."

Carter stared at the ceiling. "Possible."

When they reached the lab, Minh was absent. Pilar began putting away her clothing. She had packed enough for only a few days. She opened her collection kit, wondered if she would need any of it. Carter tapped on the door and came in.

"Everyone's looking for rare disease therapies," he said. "The big players spend billions. If I'm lucky, a few hundred thousand will drop off the table into MPC's hands. I don't know what Roger has in mind, but you know what I would do?"

"What would you do?"

Carter didn't like to go at anything straight. "Some genetic diseases deliver benefits, don't they?" he said. "A Jewish woman I know carries the Tay-Sachs gene. Awful thing, right? Very very bad if she marries another carrier and they have children. But the gene also makes a carrier less vulnerable to tuberculosis, which is why it wasn't flushed out in the *shtetl*. Children who get two copies are doomed. A parent with one is TB-resistant."

"I know that," Pilar said.

"Of course you do. Suppose instead of trying to eliminate the Tay-Sachs allele from the genome, you decided to harvest its beneficial side to fight the new drug-resistant TB. I'd like to own stock in the company that pulled that one off. You know, I hope Staley isn't onto something like this. It's such a good idea I'd like to try it myself."

"You'd need a research budget," Pilar said.

"What's fifty or a hundred million to a dreamer?" Carter said cheerfully.

She opened the lab cupboards and checked supplies. Pipets, centrifuge tubes, gel chambers, PCR plates, reagents. Much of the material was still in boxes. Just to be on the safe side—because she didn't know what might be wrong in the tissue she was supposed to sequence—she went out and pestered Carter for a set of goggles, a solid-front gown and other gear suitable to Level 2 Biosafety. Carter's talk of Tay-Sachs didn't bother her, she didn't plan to get pregnant again soon if ever, but she'd had an uncle who contracted tuberculosis in a veterans hospital.

17

THE FRAGMENT OF IDENTITY LEFT IN LUTHER MICHAELS thought about pretty Dr. Gerson—he hadn't wanted to hurt her—as his frozen hands swung the axe. Dr. Gerson had been his friend. But there had been no choice then, and there was none now. His arms felt the force of the impact against Charlene Sprague's head. A fan of blood sprayed the snow. She turned to stumble away, and again he lifted the axe. He had to get the devil's head off now. That was the way it had been done forever.

A voice called words he couldn't comprehend.

He began the downswing of the axe—*first things first, one thing at a time, as Etta would say*—and from twenty feet away Sergeant Virgil Vaughn fired four shots into Luther's chest.

What was left of the islander died instantly.

They got Charl into the tent, onto the long table. Her mouth opened, leaked meaningless sounds. Sprague squeezed her hand, his face colorless. Walters pressed his fingers to her neck. He thumbed an eyelid. Drawn by the shots, Fane arrived. Walters told him, "Get some saline bags. And alcohol. They're in the supply tent."

"How bad?" Sprague's voice was thin.

"The bleeding isn't arterial," Walters said. He fingered the ragged flesh. His gaze rose and stopped at David. "Dr. Isaac, there's a first aid kit with bandages in the excavation tent. Can you fetch it? We'll stop the bleeding, get the blood pressure up. She needs a hospital. When's the helicopter due?"

"Five hours," Sprague said. "I'll get them here tonight."

"We've got massive tissue damage. Possibly a skull fracture. There'll be swelling—"

"I can't lose her," Sprague said.

Fane returned, and Walters started an IV.

The helicopter arrived before dawn. Sprague loaded the blanket-wrapped woman on board, climbed in beside her. Right behind them, metal tissues case in hand, Walters climbed aboard, and the helicopter lifted off.

David watched until its lights were distant specks.

He was too numb to feel, and he thought that that was a good thing.

Becker nudged his arm. "Come see this."

Luther lay where he had fallen. A green tarp weighted with pieces of wood had been spread over him. The younger policeman looked the other way as Becker kicked away wood and lifted a corner. Frost had spread across the dead man's face, blurring the already vague contours. Becker pulled the canvas back further, exposing the length of the corpse.

"Bare fingers, slippers on the feet, no boots, no hat, no overcoat. The ice on the sweater and the shirt isn't just on the surface; it permeates the material."

He dropped the tarp.

"Look around. Most of the blood is Charl's. For a man with that many holes in him, Luther didn't bleed much. He had to be hypothermic," Becker said. "It's too bad Walters didn't get a chance to examine him. I had a look ten minutes after the shooting. Luther's skin was already icy to the touch, almost hard.

He had been outdoors a long time. It explains why the axe blow didn't kill her. It's a wonder he could lift the thing. A wonder he could move."

Becker stood back. "I offered to shove a thermometer up his rectum. Just from curiosity. Sergeant Vaughn wouldn't let me. He doesn't want anything more he can't explain."

18

HELEN CALDER ARRIVED EARLY AT NIS HEADQUARTERS ALONG the Dulles Access Road, parked in Building C's underground garage, took an elevator up six floors. Knowing her section chief never arrived before eight-thirty, she went straight to her office and telephoned Timothy Berman. Her honey, Timbo. She had never met Berman, the NIS's new head of electronic surveillance, but six weeks of telephone contact had created a superficial intimacy. Even if Timbo didn't share her sense of mission, he was a techno-geek adept at his craft. Talking to him, she pretended to be slim and pretty, her voice a mix of sweetness and pepper, Miss Mall Slut.

NIS had been eavesdropping on the St. Leger Foundation for nine hours. Her last meeting with Stephan Pogorovich had produced enough raw innuendo for her section chief to sign the order. Life had gotten much easier for federal investigators since the executive branch had gained the authority to issue extra-judicial surveillance warrants.

"We've intercepted eighty-four calls in and out of St. Leger," Tim Berman reported. "I'll download the recordings to your desk. Nothing rang a bell with my team. No key-word hits. But we don't do analysis, honey, we just splice wires, *si?*"

"What about cell phones?"

"No intercepts so far."

"Data lines?"

"Several pipes seem to be in regular use. I could get in and crack their internal e-mail, but the warrant doesn't cover that. It will take a while to break the encryption, if we can do it at all. If they're violating other laws, illegal ciphers may not bother them."

"They're violating laws big-time," Helen said.

"You and me, we'll catch 'em. Are you still dating that Redskins stud? Or do I have a chance?"

Mall Slut liked jocks. "Sorry, Timmy. One man is enough for me."

By the time she came back with a mug of canteen coffee, Berman had sent the download. Wanting privacy, she plugged in the earpiece and began skipping through the digitized recordings of intercepted calls. Before she was half through, a file icon pinged, informing her that another forty-five documents had arrived. There was no way a single investigator could keep up with the flow.

She skimmed for something recognizable. A reference to secret cloning experiments would have been good, but the software would already have flagged anything like that. She searched for the sound of Roger Staley's voice. She heard his name twice, as a secretary told a caller she had reached Mr. Staley's office. In neither case was Mr. Staley available. Both calls, according to Tim Berman's equipment, had come in a few minutes after seven this morning. That might be interesting. Foundation executives started their days at ten, ate long lunches with their lobbyists and went home at four. St. Leger had been up and running at seven a.m. and—her glance dropped again to the file count, which had swelled by another thirty-one calls— was going full tilt at eight-fifteen.

The calls she jumped through seemed innocuous. At least two-thirds were from a floor full of energetic young social science researchers, who were pulling together statistics on urban ills that might be susceptible to St. Leger-style medication. The others, from the fragments she bothered listening to, were from secretaries scoring lunches for second-tier executives, or ordering office supplies, or stealing a minute's sex talk with men they probably knew. If there were any secrets in that sea of apparent blandness, they would have to wait for later.

It struck her as odd that there hadn't been any calls to or from an outside law firm. A man threatened with a subpoena would want advice from counsel.

She called Berman and asked how the data deciphering was proceeding. Her best chance was tracking the money. Berman was her only hope on that front.

"*Ees* very *deefeecult* to work when the senora keeps asking her gardener in for coffee."

That meant no luck. As a point of principle, she wished Berman wouldn't use a stereotypical Latino accent, but she didn't know how to tell him this. She didn't want to end their cuddly friendship.

She brought her voice down an octave from the silly slut register. *This* was the mama who knew how to deliver. "I *really* need it, Tim, do you follow me?"

If that voice didn't have him grabbing his pants, nothing would.

"Okay, I'm getting back to work," he said.

Berman called back. "I've got bad news, sugar. Staley used his cell phone twenty minutes ago. We tracked the call, but he's got state-of-the-art encryption. He might as well be talking Ket."

When she didn't ask what Ket was, Berman volunteered, "They speak Ket in parts of Siberia. NSA might be able to unravel the encryption."

"Where did the call go?"

He read off a number. "That's a company called MPC out in West Virginia."

She consulted her database. MPC had the lowest level federal bioresearch license.

"Can you get records for his other calls?" she asked Berman.

"Officially?"

"Informally."

There was a moment's silence. "Sure, I can do that."

"*Thaaank* you," Helen purred.

"I'll also work on decryption," Berman promised.

Her in-box pinged and she began working through a data dump of Staley's cell phone records. He didn't make many calls. He'd gotten a few incoming in recent days from a satellite phone. She could track the phone, or have Berman do it; more hours invested. Three mornings ago Staley had called a landline at the Cold Spring Harbor Laboratory in New York. Helen paused. That might mean something. She scrolled on. Most of Staley's traffic was with other numbers registered to the foundation. No telling who carried the phones. She glanced back at the 516 number. Cold Spring Harbor Lab. You couldn't get more distinguished than that in the genetics field. For decades the laboratory had been directed by James Watson, co-discoverer of DNA's double helix. Helen punched the number Staley had called.

"Dr. Rodriguez's office."

"May I speak to him, please?"

"I'm sorry, Dr. Rodriguez is away. May someone else help you?"

"No, this is personal," Helen said. "When will he be back?"

"Dr. Rodriguez is a she, and I'm not at liberty to say. May I take a message?"

"Do you have a number where she can be reached?"

"Personnel might, or Dr. Janecke, her supervisor. Do you want me to connect you?"

Helen put on her best starchy-aunt tone with Rodriguez's supervisor, who sounded too harried to argue. He said that Rodriguez had a week's leave to do work for the St. Leger Foundation.

"What sort of work?" Helen said.

"Something on insular population genetics."

Helen phoned her section chief as she walked toward his office, told him she needed a minute's audience, and ignored his secretary as she opened the door to the office. Helen walked in and sat down heavily.

"Staley has somebody at Cold Spring Harbor," she said. That was overstating it by a mile, but she could always back down later. Having a bulldog like Helen building cases had been good for the career of the chief, Philip Marburg. They both knew it. So she pushed. "I want to tap Staley's home phone; we should have done it before. And I think we should listen to Cold Spring's traffic for a few days."

Marburg groaned. She understood his uneasiness without caring about it. James Watson, Coldspring's director, had testified before Congress more than twenty times, wearing the Nobel laureate's mantel like a superhero's cape.

Marburg gestured feebly. "If Watson caught on he was being bugged, he would denounce NIS from the rooftops and people would listen. We know they're not running a eugenics program. So let's forget that idea. Don't tell me about Davenport and Grant."

"I won't." But she wouldn't forget them. Eugenics, a dubious scientific theory of racial purity, had been respectable in the United States in the early Twentieth Century, and people like Charles B. Davenport, a Cold Spring director, had made it so. Davenport had set up Cold Spring's Eugenics Records Office, had written tracts against racial mixing, and had called for forced sterilization of the mentally "unfit." Madison Grant, keeper of the eugenics records, had denounced the "soiling" of the white European race by immigrants. Their ideas had gained traction in universities, Congress, and the courts. Her fear wasn't misplaced, Helen knew. A modern eugenics movement would have first-class scientific credentials.

"What about Staley's home phone?"

"Sure, sure," Marburg said, "go get him. Who cares if Staley screams?"

Tim Berman was businesslike. "There's been more traffic on Staley's phone. Whoever he's talking to is in a cell near you."

"Can you identify the number?"

"It's listed to the foundation. He's got one of his people baby-sitting your office."

She felt an adrenalin rush. "No shit?"

"You know you're on the right track."

"I've known that from the start."

"You're a confident little minx."

She giggled like a confident little minx and broke the connection. She unlocked the left bottom drawer of her desk, removed a compact nine-millimeter Sig Sauer, and slipped the weapon into her handbag. Then she asked her section's secretary to get her on an early afternoon flight to New York.

Geronimo Bix had parked his black Mercedes in the driveway of a farm a mile behind NIS headquarters. The tilt of a rusty FOR SALE sign and the absence of curtains in the farmhouse windows had satisfied him nobody was living here. He walked into the field, like a prospective buyer sizing up the land. A buyer would notice that the ground hadn't been tilled in years. So Bix noticed that and kicked speculatively at the clumps of dead grass and chicory that had taken over. If he could crack an access code at NIS, this would be a suitable way in and way out of the government buildings. The ground was hard. So far, there was no snow to take footprints or tire tracks. A physical entry would be high risk. . . .

If he could just penetrate the NIS computer firewalls, he could plant a virus that would disrupt the agency for a month. Maybe long enough for them to forget about Pogorovich and Agent Calder.

His phone pulsed, and Staley said, "I need you here."

19

HELEN CALDER HAD TO CHECK HER HANDGUN BEFORE boarding the commuter plane to New York. At La Guardia, she signed for the weapon's return, rolled her carry-on down to an auto rental counter, and picked up the keys to a large sedan. All the while she looked for faces that might have been with her from Washington. She was confident that nobody had followed her from NIS headquarters to Dulles Airport. But the knowledge that someone had been babysitting the NIS offices—if Tim Berman's information and conclusion were accurate—made her alert.

She drove out the Long Island Expressway, picked up 25A north, and entered Cold Spring Harbor as freezing rain began to blow in from Oyster Bay. The pretty little town looked like money even in the rain.

It took her fifteen minutes to convince the management of Cold Spring Harbor Lab that she meant business. An assistant director, after weighing the government money that was in the pipeline, decided that of course an NIS representative could visit Rodriguez's work station.

A bearded young man took her across the campus to a low brick building where Rodriguez worked in a basement full of centrifuges and DNA analyzers. He said, "Her supervisor, Dr. Janecke, is in the city."

"What does Rodriguez do?" Helen asked.

"*Arabidopsis.*"

"What's that?"

"*Arabidopsis thaliana*, it's a plant in the mustard family. We did the genome several years ago." He sounded slightly proud, slightly embarrassed. "It's got an extremely dense gene structure. About half the plant's DNA is occupied by genes, compared to five percent in humans. So we got a lot of result for the effort."

"I see."

"It was the first plant to be completely mapped." When she didn't respond, he went on: "We sequenced about one hundred million DNA pairs. Now we're trying to identify the function of each of *Arabidopsis*'s twenty thousand or so genes. You know, what causes the plant to go dormant in cold weather? Knowing that could be a boon to winter farming. And we're playing around with alternative splicing of mRNA. That amplifies the number of proteins a gene orders up. You understand?"

"Not exactly."

"Like if you add a letter to a multi-digit number code. The possibilities go up by factors of twenty-six."

Helen nodded. Looking around the cramped lab, she knew there was no baby farm here. No human parts warehouse. The campus was too open for anything illegal. Besides which, Cold Spring had enough money flowing from NIH, NIS and other legitimate sources that it didn't need under-the-table gifts from St. Leger.

If not here, then where? At which of the thousands of licensed bio labs? Never mind an unlicensed operation.

"What does Rodriguez do?" she repeated.

"Pilar's working on the gene functions. We randomly insert material that tells us which part of the tissue a particular gene operates in, during what stage of the cell's life. So we can deduce its function."

"A function such as telling the plant to go dormant?"

"Exactly."

There wasn't much in the immediate work area that gave her a sense of Rodriguez. A photograph of two teenaged girls, hugging each other and laughing, was stuck to the top of a carrel. On a back corner of the work bench, a plastic frame held a picture of a young woman with teasing eyes sitting beside a middle-aged, darker-skinned woman who smiled as if it hurt. Thinking of her own working-class mother, Helen suspected she was seeing the generation that went to college as a birthright and the one that washed other people's floors. She didn't like family memories. She looked away.

She ran a finger through a small stack of publications, found that somebody had turned back pages of an article reporting on rapid speciation of European mice. She read a paragraph:

> On the island of Madeira, where the founder population of common European mice arrived by ship, six separate mouse species have evolved in less than five hundred years. Multiple chromosomal fusions underlay the process, according to Janice Britton-Davidian, who conducted the research. Where the ancestor mice had forty chromosomes, the species that have evolved on Madeira have between twenty-two and thirty chromosomes. . . .

Helen got the point. The chromosomal compression had been incredibly rapid. If you played with genes in a lab, change could come even faster. That would be the next step for these bastards. Arctic grown tomatoes, laboratory grown humans.

She wondered if the bearded young man fully understood the history of the place he worked. Understood all the human damage that had been done in the name of racial improvement. It was the eugenics movement that had armed the likes of Justice Oliver Wendell Holmes Jr., who had approved the State of Virginia's forced sterilization of a woman in 1927 with the glib comment, "Three generations of imbeciles are enough."

If he knew, he probably didn't believe history could repeat.

While the bearded young man watched uncomfortably, Helen tore apart Pilar Rodriguez's work area.

Staley called, and you immediately took vacation. Where to?

20

DAVID ISAAC SPENT THE LATE MORNING WITH BECKER AND Fane, packing instruments. There had been no word on Charl. She had looked like death when Sprague lifted her into the helicopter. Unconscious, pale—slipping.

David had felt powerless to help. Now he was both depressed and jumpy. All his adult life he had sought answers in science and nowhere else. If he couldn't understand something, it meant he hadn't collected enough data points, nothing more. There were no hidden corners in the natural world that light couldn't reach. No separate reality. One had to settle for what there was. But he felt the malevolence of Ewell Island as if it were a personal presence. The whisper in his mind had changed. It was no longer, *They want out.* It was, *They're out.* He asked himself exactly what he believed the words meant.

He walked to the edge of the camp, stood still as snow tapped his shoulders. The police sergeant was somewhere around, waiting for a shooting team to finish up. David and the others had given statements. The corporal had gone to Tyler to meet the police boat that would take Luther's body to the mainland.

He let the snow come down and wondered if this was how it happened. You stood out in the cold on Ewell Island for a while listening to the giggling in your head and then went and got an axe.

He had dreamt of Charl. Breasts cool, sand under them hot. She had never been far from his subconscious. His father said his inability to let go of her was evidence a man could be intelligent without being the least bit realistic.

Fane came across the ground.

"You want to take a little trip with me?" Fane asked.

"Where?"

"Talk to Etta Michaels. Give our condolences. Ask where Luther was hiding out."

"Sergeant Vaughn's people will interview her."

"Nobody says we can't. And I want to hear, I really want to hear. I thought he was harmless."

"Why would she tell us anything?"

"Maybe she won't. Maybe she'll brag about spitting in our coffee. Either way, I want to talk to her."

"Okay," David said.

As they backed the Rover out, Becker approached. David lowered his window.

"The helicopter arrives at four," Becker said. "We're going to leave immediately."

"We won't miss it. We're going to have a chat with Etta Michaels."

Becker pulled off his gloves and blew on his hands. "I know David is nuts, but you, Loren? Suppose Etta has another axe? Or you run into Luther's thirteen cousins who've all got axes."

"Do you want to ride shotgun?"

"I'd rather wait for the helicopter."

Fane held out a hand. "How about lending me your gun?"

"Forget it. But after they cut you up, I'll shoot them, if I'm still here."

They drove out along the gray spit of land. No one came to the door of the Michaels trailer. Fane went around back, and

David followed. A hundred years of junk had piled up in the rear yard, spreading toward thin trees further back. In the shadow of an oil tank, David saw a patch of flattened snow, from which tracks shuffled toward those trees. How long had Luther waited here?

"Let's try the neighbors," David said.

They knocked at the next house without getting a response, though television noise was audible.

"Fuck 'em," Fane said.

"They wouldn't tell us anything anyway."

"They don't know anything. I'd like to see the autopsy results on Luther. People survive in cold water. They shut down. Kind of hibernation. I've never heard of anyone swinging an axe in that condition. Becker's right. Luther should have been dead."

"We can't be sure of his core temperature."

"Who are you kidding? He was *iced* on the outside. So he could settle down and hibernate until he decided to go kill someone."

"The obvious answer is that he wasn't that far shut down."

Fane looked past David. "We got company."

A car was coming, muffler rasping. It stopped near the Rover, and a woman got out. David recognized Sydney Wood, the artist. She wore ear muffs, with her gray-blond hair loose. There wasn't much color in her face, a little darkness under the eyes.

"I didn't know if any of your group was still here," she said. "Pastor Merton says Luther went crazy. How badly did he hurt Mrs. Sprague?"

"We haven't heard." David introduced Fane to the woman. "An artist from Pittsburgh," he said.

Sydney Wood's smile came and went. "It's terrible," she said.

"Maybe living here does that," Fane said.

She had pulled an insulated box out of the back seat. "I've brought food. It's the only thing I can think of for Etta. I don't know if care packages are customary here. Did you try her door?"

"She's not answering. Maybe if we leave she will."

"I'll try."

David took a couple of steps around the front of the Rover,

but he was in no hurry. Once again he wanted to prolong a conversation with the woman. She had continued to watch him as if expecting something more. He asked: "Have you finished your portrait of Silas?"

"It's difficult. He drinks and tries to get my skirt up." She grinned. "He passes out in late afternoon, but by then the best light is gone."

They were almost back to the camp when Fane said, "I wouldn't mind getting her skirt up."

"No," David agreed. She had the same effect on him. It had nothing to do with the kind of longing he felt for Charl, just a matter of *let's get that skirt up*. That basic.

"I must have done without too long. She's not that young."

"No," David agreed. And he didn't care.

"Probably experienced, though. There's nothing wrong with experience."

Becker met them. "No word," he told David. "What about you?"

"Waste of time. Have you packed Sprague's stuff?"

"Yes."

"Show me."

Becker showed him the crate with Sprague's personal belongings. David pulled out the professor's laptop, switched it on.

"What are you doing?"

"Just curious."

There should be something—emails or memos—that identified the project's sponsor. Maybe explained why they were here. Who had found the site. The computer booted.

A password demand came up.

"Any ideas?" David said.

"Try 'you're fucked.'"

"In Urdu?"

"For starters."

David shut down the machine.

Mid-afternoon came without a helicopter.

21

PILAR RODRIGUEZ CAME AWAKE AS THE PHONE RANG AND Louis Minh said, "The stuff's here. Staley wants you to get right on it."

Pilar switched on the lights. Her watch told her it was before six. Evening, not morning. She had been dozing. "Okay, I'll be out in ten minutes," she told Minh. She hurried through the bathroom. A two-minute shower brought her fully awake.

In her lab, a very tall, white-haired man in a dark suit was leaning over the Hoeffer minifluorometer. His back was to her. Although he must have heard the door open, he gave no sign. She opened her mouth to tell him to get the hell away from her equipment. Something stopped her.

She cleared her throat.

He turned his whole body, straightening slowly, and inspected her from head to foot. Her jeans and polo shirt, which were typical lab attire, were noted in a way that suddenly put her back among soiled undergraduates. He extended a bony hand. "I'm

Gus St. Leger. You're doing very important work, Dr. Rodriguez."

"I haven't begun." She wondered if this St. Leger was *the* St. Leger. He looked old enough to have founded Harvard. His face was cadaverous, with hollow temples, age spots on deeply lined cheeks. The eyes were so pale she thought of bleach. His suit was heavy and old-fashioned.

"Start small and build quickly, that's my motto," St. Leger said. "One of them. Diversify, diversify is another." He had the low, sonorous voice a general would use for speeches he wanted people to remember.

"Minh said some samples have arrived for me to process."

"Eager to get at it, that's a good character trait. You won't mind if I hover, will you? I promise not to get too much in the way."

"Well . . ."

"Believe it or not, I know my way around a modern laboratory." He turned the last word into five syllables. "My hired man, that's Roger Staley, tries to keep me away from the sharp end of the business. Have you met Roger? Pedantic lad. I picture him as a little boy who cried often to his mother. My mother didn't believe in that sort of coddling. Accomplished woman, but she had no interest in being 'mama' to a crybaby."

Pilar had heard that men never got over their mothers. She had even dated a couple who pretty much proved the point. But St. Leger seemed to be going for a longevity record with his issues. He had to be in his late seventies, or older.

"I'll just watch," he promised. "Minh has the specimens. Let's go bother him."

She could see Minh through the glass door, conferring with a man who looked like a middle-aged bicycle messenger: slim, a little stooped, with a bright bandana on his head. She wondered if white guys called them do-rags. The men were talking across a brushed aluminum box that she guessed held frozen tissue.

Minh and the other man looked around when she opened the door. The newcomer said, "I'm John Walters. Are you going to run the sequencing?" He had English or Australian in his voice.

Pilar nodded. She shook his hand and introduced herself.

St. Leger loomed a half foot over the tallest of them. He asked, "What kind of time are we talking?"

"Twenty hours, approximately," she said.

Walters handed Pilar the aluminum case. He said, "I'll brief you while you're preparing to extract the DNA, if that's all right."

"That's fine."

"We've got multiple specimens from two human bodies, an adult male and a female child. The man was in his thirties, the child approximately four years old. The remains are a bit over three hundred years old."

Pilar knew that most of the time she looked reasonably sexy. But she had a suspicion she looked stupid when she was surprised. Most people did. Staley hadn't told her the material would be old.

"Were the bodies well preserved?"

"The child's was."

"You collected the samples?"

Walters offered a hint of a smile. "There's no chance of contamination, if that's your concern. I'm a forensic pathologist."

Goody for you, Pilar thought. Contamination was indeed part of her concern, but only part. Old tissue and bone samples often contained none of the sequences of nucleic acid that made up DNA. Oxygen and water destroyed genetic material. She might do the sequencing and find that nothing had survived. Or the DNA she amplified might turn out to be of some basic organism that had lived on the human host. Short strands of primitive bacterial DNA survived the centuries better than the long strands of more complex organisms.

She wondered if St. Leger understood there was no guarantee of success.

She let Walters open the metal case, which released cold air. Inside were more than two dozen labeled containers.

"Where were the bodies?" she asked.

"Place called Ewell Island."

She looked at him, the question still there.

"Bottom of the Chesapeake estuary," Walters said. "Parents probably were from Cornwall—that's in Southwest England."

I know where Cornwall is, she thought in annoyance. *Not exactly . . .*

"I'm surprised there's anything left of the bodies," Pilar said.

"The coffins were sheathed in lead. The practice was common in England at the time. Pretty rare here. This family got top treatment."

"I'll bet they didn't do that for native Americans."

"No, you had to be important."

She wondered if he meant the early colonists didn't consider the native Americans important, or he didn't, and then wondered how this very white middle-aged dude felt about Puerto Ricans from Brooklyn. She didn't care if he was a racist; it was only one test she used to separate particular idiots from the herd. She could take it either way. She got along with a lot of bigots. Even had dated a couple of Anglos who thought they were being open-minded going to bed with her.

"The girl is better preserved," Walters was saying. "There's a '1' on her containers. A '2' on the man's."

"Were they related?"

"Father and daughter, we think. Probably named Wakelyn."

She pulled on plastic gloves, used a clamp to unscrew the first extremely cold canister. The contents were wafer-thin slices of bone. She transferred the material to the Cryogenic Grinding Mill, which would reduce the bone wafers to dust from which any surviving DNA could be extracted. She and Minh had spent two hours decontaminating all the lab's equipment—needlessly, she suspected. Several of the machines were barely out of their bubble-wrap and apparently had never been used.

The first task was recovering whatever DNA might remain in the specimens. The next job was purification, followed by amplification. The most she could hope for were short, broken strands. The computer would do the hard work of building a sequence from recognizable markers—if there were enough clues to work with.

The basic biological map of the girl and the man would be the same as her own. That was the *basic* map. There would be many small differences, markers distinctive to the Wakelyn girl's English stock, others identifying Pilar's Spanish-Taino heritage. Geography would account for most of the differences, not time.

Human genetic change was rapid, particularly in the mitochondrial DNA that passed mother to daughter, but "rapid" was a relative term. Almost nothing happened to a complex species in three centuries. Unless you were a Galapagos finch, or a European mouse.

Which brought Pilar back to wondering what Staley and St. Leger Pharmacal were seeking.

If these islanders had originated in Cornwall, or descended from recent immigrants, they might have some distinctive traits. Nothing as dramatic as Tay-Sachs, she was pretty sure. But other things, maybe. She remembered reading about a clan named Kerr on the Scottish border, who had shown such a tendency to inherited left-handedness that the name had entered the language, kerry-fisted meaning left-handed. So you never knew.

She wondered if the islanders remained insular today. Quirks from three centuries ago could have been magnified over time. As she ground the bone slices, she toyed with the protocol for a study of not just the long-dead family but also current islanders. The Left-Handed Hare-Lipped Alleles. St. Leger Pharmacal wouldn't get a billion-dollar patent, but Pilar might get her name in *Cell* magazine, if she could put herself in charge of the study, find funding, little impossible details like those.

She found herself curling her tongue like a straw and remembered one of the stunts a biology instructor had pulled. The instructor couldn't curl his tongue sideways, but he predicted with confidence that each student who could do the trick would find that one or both parents also could do so. "And if neither can," the instructor had said, "then you'd better suspect that either you were adopted, or your father should be wearing antlers, because your mama was entertaining another gentleman." This talent, which he regarded as useless, lay directly in the genes. If one parent had it, the odds were fifty-fifty that each child would have it.

Pilar's mother, it developed, curled her tongue very nicely. So did Pilar's kid sister, which proved to her that while genetics were predictive, statistics were not. The fifty-fifty chance had come up heads for both of them.

The cryogenic grinder had done its job while she daydreamed. She removed the stainless steel cylinder, transferred the powdered bone into a clear 50 milliliter tube, and added 15 milliliters of disodium salt EDTA, which would chelate the calcium from the powder. Two years ago, the chelation step would have taken overnight. Now it required four hours.

She repeated the process with the other samples. There were twelve in all. By the time they were rotating in their chemical baths, she noticed that she was alone in the lab.

She discovered that her abhorrence of canteen food hadn't kept her from becoming hungry. Stripping off the plastic gloves, she wondered whether she would eat pot roast or a week-old hotdog. At the moment, she could eat both.

Walters was in the canteen, drinking very black tea. "Your soup must be on," he said.

"Slow cooking," she said.

"Have you done this before?"

"Not for a couple of years."

"Since graduate school?"

She felt embarrassed that he found her inexperience so obvious. "We had fragments of Neanderthal bones," she said.

"Not Svante Pääbo's project?"

So the bicycle messenger wasn't just a pathologist, or was a well-read one. "My adviser was trying to amplify more base pairs than Pääbo had done. We weren't very successful," Pilar said. She looked in the foggy windows of the vending machine, decided to roll the dice with the pot roast. After microwaving the cardboard package longer than necessary, she got a can of soda and sat down across from Walters. "The amino acid racemization was too high in our samples."

"The bones hadn't stayed dry?"

"Right. There wasn't much material to work with, but I still enjoyed the experience. We got a few dozen pairs that did nothing to upset earlier research." She pushed a plastic fork into something that resembled cooked meat, possibly Neanderthal. "What more can you tell me about our specimens?"

"I don't know much. We dug them out of a hell of a deep crypt. We're pretty sure both the man and the child were murdered. The bodies were mutilated."

"I hope they don't think I can help with an investigation of that?"

"No. I talked with St. Leger on the flight down here. I think he just wants a DNA profile."

"Have you worked for him long?"

Walters shook his head. "Never heard of them till yesterday. What about you?"

"I was hired for just this job."

Walters lifted his tea mug an inch. "This place is pretty out of the way."

"Pretty?"

"Probably a hundred labs around D.C. could sequence DNA."

Pilar shifted. "I've thought about that."

"Conclusion?"

"The man who seems to be in charge here, Carter, thinks they may be after therapeutic products. You'd want to keep a lid on the research, wouldn't you? Especially early on, when anyone could grab the idea."

"There was disease on the island in the Wakelyns' day, probably cholera," Walters said. "Where are the therapeutic possibilities in that?" He meant there were already vaccines. "Where else do you work, Pilar?"

"Cold Spring Harbor Laboratory." She felt proud as she said it.

He nodded. "Impressive. What are you doing there?"

This was the bad part. "Working on mustard plant genes," she said.

When she returned to the lab, it was nearly nine p.m. Lights had been switched off in the anteroom, but not in her lab. Pilar transferred the chelated material to the centrifuge, set the speed for 2,500 rpm. Twenty minutes later, she added extraction buffer and turned up the heat.

By the time she was ready for the serious stuff, the radio station she had been listening to had played its last hillbilly love ballad and faded into static. It was after one in the morning.

If she had recovered any human DNA, now was the time to turn it into something useful. The process she launched was called a polymerase chain reaction. It would uncouple the double strands of any surviving DNA and reattach them to segments of polymerase enzyme, creating in effect two molecules where there had been one. The process would repeat again and again for the next several hours, creating sequenceable DNA samples from the smallest chemical fragment.

So she hoped.

A lot could have gone wrong with the Wakelyns' tissue. Water could have destroyed the fragile data altogether. A few weeks of exposure to oxygen could have done almost as much damage. DNA chains consisted of almost endless variations of nucleotide bases, chemicals classified by four letters: GCAT. The letters stood for guanine, cytosine, adenine and thymine. Oxygen could have wrecked pyrimidine bases, which contained the cytosine, thymine and RNA uracil. The purines, which contained adenine and guanine, would have fared better, but you couldn't make much sense of a GCAT sequence when half the pairs were missing. When there was a biological host to pass it on, DNA survived forever, changing a little with each replication. But out in the world on its own, it was no more durable than a digital code without an electron. She remembered the wild enthusiasm in the 1990s when a team believed they had extracted DNA from 20-million-year-old plant leaves. In reality, the relentless process of depurination had leached out all the ancient DNA molecules. What the scientists had amplified were bacterial contaminants.

A lot could go wrong even in sterile labs. Paleozoic insects caught in amber—an airless, waterless medium—had promised to yield genetic patterns that hadn't been seen on earth for a quarter-billion years. But all that information had been long gone, and amplifications yielded mixes of animal and fungal sequences. Old dinosaur bones that had excited scientists and movie makers yielded up nothing more exotic than strands of DNA from the men and women who had worked with the bones.

Goodbye, Jurassic Park.

She had been as careful as she could be in handling the material. She had changed gloves with every sample. She had scrubbed down the lab table with ethanol, had sterilized the grinding mill.

Now she had to wait.

She figured her chances were good. Bones and soft tissue could have retained significant amounts of their nucleic acids for three hundred years. Bodies pulled from a Florida sinkhole had yielded genetic secrets seven thousand years old. In the absence of water and air, broken strands of DNA could survive much longer—long enough to provide a glimpse of the evolutionary dead ends that had shared the earth with early man. Svante Pääbo had amplified several hundred base pairs of 50,000-year-old Neanderthal DNA.

Compared to that, this was easy.

Her mind wandered to what she was being paid.

Too easy.

22

HELEN CALDER TOOK AN EVENING FLIGHT BACK TO Washington. When a steward who wanted to play air marshal told her to turn off her cell phone, she showed him her badge and went ahead and completed her call to Tim Berman. It was six-twenty, and he was still on the job.

"We picked up a lot of traffic between the foundation and a group of scientists," Berman told her.

"What kind of scientists?"

"Archeologists. There was radio and telephone communication. Some of it was open. We called on NSA to decrypt the rest. The people had an accident. Woman was injured, a man was shot by the state police."

"Where?"

"An island called Ewell."

"Does it matter to us?"

"I called the state policeman who was in charge. He said that pretty weird things were going on. But there was nothing about biological research."

Staring at the night sky, wondering—just for a moment—if she was missing something, Helen said, "So not our bailiwick. What else?"

"Let's stick to the archaeologists."

She suppressed her impatience.

"Okay, archaeologists," she said. "What about them?"

"What was the name of the woman you were looking for in New York?"

Berman knew very well. He had something and was playing with her. "Give it up, Timbo," she said flirtatiously.

"It was Rodriguez, wasn't it? One of our intercepts from the archaeologists mentioned cadaver specimens. Five minutes later, Staley alerted the MPC lab to have Rodriguez stand by."

He sounded hugely pleased with himself, but Helen felt deflated. MPC was nothing. She had been on the wrong track. Whatever Rodriguez was doing for Staley, it wasn't eugenics research.

"Do you want to hear the recording?"

"No." Then she thought, *What else was she going to do?* "Yes, please."

She heard the voices of two men. Roger Staley, ordering a man he called Carter to have Rodriguez ready to work specimens that were being flown from the island. Archaeological specimens. Her heart sank. Berman let the recording run.

Staley's voice: "*St. Leger will bring the samples himself.*"

Carter, unhappy: "*He plays with the equipment.*"

Staley again: "*He owns the equipment, so let him.*"

Who was St. Leger?

Berman broke into her thoughts.

"A helicopter flew from the foundation's headquarters to the island to pick up the injured woman. There's been a jump or two out to West Virginia. If I were hiding something, that would be a good place."

Helen didn't answer.

"And why hire someone from New York?"

She reached a decision, with regret because it meant the death of Miss Mall Slut.

"You do good work, dear," she told Berman. "Can you meet

me at Reagan Airport? I'm the short fat woman with the pretty voice."

Tim Berman knew what Helen Calder looked like. The first time she had called him, he had checked her personnel file within minutes, knowing that a face and body to go with the voice were too much to hope for. *Weight: 165. Height: 5' 3".* Oh yeah, oh mama. And a face to scare children. But he kept up their flirtatious telephone relationship. He was tall, with sandy hair and boyish features, and he considered it his moral duty to flirt with unattractive women.

And he could close his eyes once in a while and imagine a sexy, sexy lady behind the sweet voice. Then it was like phone sex without a phone bill. There was nobody real in his life right now. Women were afraid of his good looks.

He got to the gate as the shuttle plane was taxiing into its slot, and Helen Calder was one of the first passengers off. When he waved and introduced himself, she managed to hang onto her outward dignity by being brusque as they shook hands. "Is Staley at the headquarters?"

"We think so."

She looked at her watch. Seven twenty-eight p.m.

"Where's the surveillance van?"

"On the street, a hundred yards from their building."

"Any activity this evening?"

"A helicopter came in. Satellite traced it to MPC. No cars in or out since about seven."

"I want to see what's going on," Helen said.

His car was outside, and to Helen's total lack of surprise the car was as flashy as the man. "Were there other references to a St. Leger?" she asked.

"None."

"We'll do a data search on the name."

"Of course. I just assumed—"

"That we knew who St. Leger is? Sorry, honey—" and her tone mocked their old intimacy "—we don't know shit."

□□□

Stephan Pogorovich scratched absently at his cheek as he listened to the telephone ring. The NIS switchboard was closed for the night, and he had used the electronic directory to select Calder's number. Typical, he thought. Between five-oh-one and nine the next morning, the world could go to hell and nobody at the National Institutes of Science would be the wiser.

He glanced around his laboratory.

He couldn't be certain there had been an intruder last night. All day he had second-guessed himself. He could be mistaken.

But he *knew*. He knew just how security-minded was the organization that had funded his off-the-books research. If he'd had a visitor, it was someone who had entered without breaking locks or setting off the alarm. It might mean Staley had learned of his talks with Calder.

In which case, he had reason to be uneasy.

He wished he could reach Calder.

He scratched his cheek. His lab assistant Jenny had gone home sick. One more pressure on him. His face was breaking out. Nervous hives?

His cheek burned like fire.

23

SIX-THIRTY A.M.

Pilar Rodriguez stared at the screen, trying to make sense of the DNA profile of the island girl.

The analyzer had done the heavy lifting. It had filled the capillary array with LPA gel, loaded the samples and run the program that identified the genetic material by the seemingly endless variations of the GCAT bases. Then the program had compared the girl's genes against the human genome reference database. And the little girl—Pilar had begun thinking of her as Chiquita—this little Chiquita was unusual.

Seriously weird.

She had the D variation in the microcephalin gene (MCPH1), which regulated brain size. No big deal. The allele, or genetic variety, was common in Europe and parts of Asia, rare in Africa. There was evidence that the variation was a fairly recent evolutionary development. Pilar switched to the database. Okay, it might go back 37,000 years—that was recent, sort of. She'd come across this one in school, working with the Neanderthal DNA. There had been a study raising the possibility that the allele might have been a product of interbreeding between humans just emerging from Africa and Europe's Neanderthal population*. Pääbo had debunked the idea. No matter. Whatever the source, Chiquita had the D variation.

Pilar frowned. She realized she was avoiding thinking about the things that mattered. These things . . .

She seldom used foul language. She bit her lip, hard. Hissed, "*Shit!*"

She had been so careful.

She had handled the specimens correctly. She hoped St. Leger believed her. Looking at the screen, she said "Shit!" twice more. Once you got used to foul language, it was a comfort. Like two or three deep breaths.

She went back to the human genome database and began searching for answers.

It was six-forty-five in the morning.

Eight-fifteen a.m.

Augustus St. Leger listened, allowing the young woman to see just a hint of sternness on his face. He stood slightly hunched, arms folded, following her finger as she pointed to the discrepancies in the analysis. "I'm not certain I understand," he said.

"First off, we didn't get any human DNA from the adult male. There are bits of DNA that match a common mold in two of those samples. No human chains have survived."

"How disappointing."

"If the remains were exposed to water or air for several hundred years, it's not surprising." Pilar glanced sideways and found she couldn't read St. Leger's expression. Serious, businesslike—but the washed-out eyes could be concealing boiling

* "Evidence that the adaptive allele of the brain size gene microcephalin introgressed into Homo sapiens from an archaic Homo lineage." Patrick D. Evans, Nitzan Mekel-Bobrov, Eric J. Vallender, Richard R. Hudson, Bruce T. Lahn. *Proceedings of the National Academy of Sciences*. November 28, 2006.

rage, or professional disappointment, or nothing. She found her inability to read him a little scary.

"This set of analyses is from the fourteen samples we had from the girl," Pilar said. "There are some obvious contaminants, bacterial—not important; the program separates them out. But we've got a couple of other differences that I can't explain." She swept a hand across the screen. "These are *wrong*."

He asked his question calmly. "In what way, my dear?"

She'd asked herself the same question. It wasn't as if a single tissue sample had been contaminated. The girl's sequences were consistent. Almost as if the genes had been spliced, new material inserted. But nobody had been conducting genetic experiments three hundred years ago.

"This program we're running, you understand what it does?" she said.

"Tell me."

"It analyzes the sequences and compares them to the database developed by the Human Genome Initiative. The project has accurate sequences on about thirteen thousand human genes. The program compared the girl's genes to the reference genes. That's where we have a problem. The girl has variations that aren't in the database."

"Is that unusual?"

"Definitely. Not impossible. New alleles show up all the time. The database keeps expanding. We all have small variations, and some not so small. But for one subject to have several that are new . . ."

"Is there any significance in the changes?"

"I can't tell. If this person had been sick, it's possible we're seeing the genetic cause of an illness. But if the illness had been seen before, it should be in the database."

"Any other possibilities?"

"It's possible there's a contaminant, but I don't think so. The program should identify anything viral or bacterial."

"What else?"

Someone manipulated the genetic structure? That was possible only if the tissue samples were from someone who had been alive very recently, who was a product of genetic experimentation. She wasn't going to say that, so she said nothing.

"Well, I must ask you one question," St. Leger said softly. "Are you certain, Dr. Rodriguez, that you didn't sneeze into the machinery?"

She looked around and saw that he was smiling. "No, I didn't sneeze," she said.

"How likely is contamination?"

"It happens." The answer was almost honest. He hadn't asked if contamination had caused *these* results. Chances of that were zero.

"Suppose you took your own samples from the cadavers. Would that help?"

No, she thought. But she said, "I can do that."

Because she wondered now just what had made Chiquita so strange. And what the strangeness meant. For a heady moment, she saw her name not just in *Cell* magazine but on the cover.

A messed-up genotype, that was what she had. Really messed up.

And she hadn't told St. Leger the worst of it.

As he left the lab, Gus St. Leger was halfway to believing he was the most important man in the world. He was an unlikely candidate for the role, so old he couldn't help smelling of piss, survivor of half-a-lifetime of bad habits, one potentially fatal illness, three treacherously stupid wives.

None of which undermined the importance of what he was on the trail of.

None of which undercut *his* importance.

The chosen are seldom worthy. He supposed he wasn't any more unworthy than most.

24

WHEN HE WAS FORTY-THREE YEARS OLD, GUS ST. LEGER HAD discovered a consensus among the people he knew that he had outlived his usefulness. There was some dispute among two of his three ex-wives whether he had been born useless or had had to cultivate the art. He had no friends, though an expansive circle of cronies sailed with him on his catamaran and rode the train with him to the races at Saratoga. Besides placing complicated bets designed to lose, he had no real interest in horse racing. Nor in much else. A hired crew handled his boat. A white-shoe law firm handled his inheritance. He had given up women—temporarily, he supposed—after the last one left his New York mansion in a rage. Gus had chuckled—taking a larger, historical view—at the news of her beloved president's assassination.

In fact, he had no real interest except drinking. He did that as he thought a gentleman should, with good manners for as much of the time as he could remember.

The Upstate New York racing season, which began in late July and ended in late August, provided him an opportunity to be intoxicated from breakfast until the last lawn party ended in the cool morning hours. By eleven a.m., he was noticeable on the upstairs porch of a grand Victorian hotel, sockless in penny loafers, almost elegant in deep tan shorts, a rumpled collarless shirt, seersucker jacket, squinting under a straw fedora. It was the getup a spoiled twenty-year-old might have affected. Gus felt he was twenty at heart, misunderstood and underappreciated. A woman who sat at a rattan table near him in mid-August thought that with his shaggy hair and dissolute good looks, he could have passed for an older Peter O'Toole. She was close enough to notice that he smelled bad and had dirty ankles.

He saw no reason to bathe. Money accumulated in New York faster than he could wager it, and his constitution resisted his attempts to kill himself with rum, gin and vodka. He had no reason to do anything except puff on a long cigar between sips of his Bloody Mary and lament the fact that the day ahead held sixteen or eighteen hours of unwelcome consciousness.

At forty-three, he was friendless and loveless, and the money depressed him. A better man might have shot himself.

As much as he bored himself, he loathed his ancestors. His maternal grandfather had amassed the kind of fortune that usually flowed from a great industrial breakthrough. Jonah Cable had done it by investing North European money and keeping part of the profits. Cable's daughter Phoebe, Gus's mother, had become the first female cardiologist certified to practice in New York State. At age thirty-two, she married Roland St. Leger, who two years later retired from his own surgical practice and began writing verse that won praise from Ezra Pound. By then Augustus was eight months old and had uttered several clearly enunciated words to form a sentence. His mother, who had expected a brilliant offspring, distanced herself from the little boy whom she found insufficiently clever. When Jonah Cable died in 1928, Roland St. Leger made his final practical decision of consequence, selecting the Broad Street law firm that became conservator of the family's wealth. The firm got the Cable-St. Leger estate through the Depression with a mix of high-grade bonds and gold held in Europe. The next generation at the firm, convinced that wealth could be protected only by increasing its bulk, compounded its clients' fortunes through the war years and the economic booms that followed.

By the time he was thirty years old, Gus desperately hoped that the lawyers, trust officers and bankers would wreck what they had made. Both parents were dead—too early in the case of his beautiful but remote mother. St. Leger was between wives but intensely interested in a young British actress, and he had found an avocation that suited him temperamentally and intellectually. Pub crawling in South London, which occupied the hours between his encounters with the actress, brought him into contact with people who skated on the edge of self-destruction. He found their cowardice—their unwillingness to go over that edge—a telling weakness. He outdrank and out-caroused the wildest of them. Those pursuits left him no time for money managers trying to reach him from New York.

In his mid-forties, he spent an entire summer at Saratoga, and there he met Arnold Benoit, a statistician who enjoyed both horses and whiskey. Benoit's mathematical work was at best marginally effective against the pari-mutuel betting system. His grand preoccupation was society. He confided to St. Leger that behavior which seemed an impenetrable mystery when one considered human beings singly and in small numbers became predictable—if still not understandable—when the numbers were large. St. Leger was ready for a wallow in pseudoscience. He was also charmed by the little hustler's insistence on being called *Ben-wah*. He considered playing with the pronunciation of his own name, which his father had unaccountably anglicized.

"There have been four wars in my lifetime, including the present idiocy," Benoit commented as the United States sent its first advisers to Vietnam. Benoit and St. Leger were perched in an owner's box at Saratoga, on an afternoon hot enough to melt the collars of the well-dressed people around them. Gus St. Leger was amusing himself by wearing garters, black socks and yellow linen shorts to complement a sleeveless undershirt and a boater. Arnold Benoit wore a dark suit that was shiny at the knees. He spoke to St. Leger's half-averted ear. "The wars seldom provide a net benefit—that is, after their cost—to any group and certainly don't serve the interest of the masses of volunteers and conscripts who will be slaughtered. Yet wars come periodically, like cycles of insects. What is at work, my friend, is a *collective* human dynamic. It stretches across societies of every sort. A scientist asking the right questions could bring about a profound reevaluation of social behavior. Now, St. Leger, in the seventh race you notice we have a small field, eight nags running, and three are quite heavily favored. I propose to bet each of the five others to win. The wager will cost me ten dollars and will pay, you see, a minimum of twenty-four dollars if successful. Only three horses can beat me. Thus there is statistically a thirty-seven and one-half percent risk of my losing, a sixty-two and a half percent chance of my winning, and a one hundred forty percent gain if I win. The risk-reward ratio therefore is 2.23 to 1 in my favor. So I am being well-paid to bet against other people's expectations."

"You're not being well paid if the favorite is a better runner," St. Leger replied. "Which he is."

"Perhaps."

"The form book—"

"I can generate any history in your form book by random numbers. What you see as a record of superior performance, I know contains a large element of chance. When the odds reflect a popular belief that the record is predictive, I bet on randomness."

Benoit happened to win the bet, which did not impress St. Leger. But they talked into the evening, and Benoit confided his lifelong dream of establishing a very small statistical research center.

"The thing could be run on a half-million a year," he said, "and the rewards of understanding social trends could be worth many times that."

St. Leger refrained from pointing out that if Benoit's statistical theories were any good, he should be able to pick up a half-million at the track. He knew that his new friend's ambitions had nothing to do with money. Arnold Benoit dreamed of finding and then pulling the strings of a world of compliant puppets. Stimulus and response, predictable, reinforced behavior. St.

Leger doubted that anything would come of the little man's research. He knew that Benoit's statistical center soon would cost him more than a half-million a year. Bloat was inevitable. It was also part of the entertainment value of the project. The managers on Broad Street would twist in anguish over every year's budget. Gus would check in now and then when Benoit might have concocted some absurdity, and meanwhile he could offend the sober people he encountered by announcing himself as a philanthropist. He developed a small comic performance that consisted of confusing that word with philanderer. Few of the society people who had to tolerate him found the farce objectionable. They were philanthropists, too.

Three years into the life of the Benoit Statistical Institute, its director forecast a resurgence of religious fundamentalism across the globe that would cause stresses to civil society. Seven years into the decade, St. Leger admitted that the little shaman might have some worthwhile analytical techniques. Islamists had sacked an embassy. Appalachian preachers were fondling rattlesnakes. In spite of himself, St. Leger had developed an interest. Benoit, who had taught him to be wary of the random correlation, was suitably modest about his forecast. The events could be coincidence. Correlation didn't prove causation. "We may be investing meaning in a series of random blips, Gus," Benoit said. "Have we discussed cancer clusters?"

"Many times."

"Most of them are meaningless. Fools observe a pattern and demand meaning. They can't stand coincidence. But random distribution produces many apparently non-random results. Have we discussed the much-predicted new ice age?"

Benoit's interests were eclectic. Sometimes St. Leger couldn't tell whether the little man had changed a subject.

Benoit taught St. Leger to doubt the significance of any outcome that veered dramatically from the norm. "A big run at the craps table is statistically certain, if enough people play enough games. The run doesn't mean the winner is skilled. The same applies to great investors. Luck says there have to be a few who shine brightest. These runs of success are all rare birds at the far end of the distribution curve. Rare and inevitable."

"And great sopranos—is their success random?"

Benoit waved a hand dismissively.

Watching the statistician's glittery eyes, St. Leger suspected his friend was insane. But he was clever—as St. Leger had known he would be—at suggesting ways to increase the institute's budget. In a few years St. Leger's outlay had risen fivefold and Benoit had recruited two additional scholars. One of the new hires had written a book on the decline of urban population centers. The other had published papers in journals suggesting that among students of human behavior, psychological man would give way to biological man. Money was needed for research in both areas. The budget rose another tenfold.

By his sixty-eighth birthday, Gus was spending seven days a week at the institute's offices in rural Virginia. They might be producing gibberish, but he had never cared. That year a doctor told him he had a small cancer growing in his colon. Before his surgery, Gus directed his lawyers to establish the St. Leger Foundation to succeed Benoit's institute. The change seemed only proper. The work he was financing stretched well beyond the original studies. Benoit had died the previous summer. Gus fully expected to join his crazy friend in purgatory—an outcome that was unlikely but possible, so he didn't dismiss it. The foundation, on which he lavished the bulk of his estate, would be the St. Leger family's monument.

The irony of not dying during his dissolute years of indifference—but succumbing when he was caught up in splendid mischief—seemed inevitable. Two days after the section of cancerous bowel was removed, Gus left the hospital on his feet. He was burning with purpose.

That fall he hired Roger Staley as executive director of the foundation. Staley, who had come from a family of New England Quakers, was too prim for the old man's taste. But he was intelligent, conversant in a number of sciences, hard-working and efficient. Fiefdoms had sprung up under Benoit. While appearing to stamp them out, Staley consolidated them all in his own office, then turned his attention to information security. There was no reason, he told St. Leger, that information should flow like gossip among the departments. A sociologist in Virginia gained nothing by knowing that the foundation sponsored a project on African paleontology. Chinese walls were erected around the foundation's areas of interest. St. Leger chuckled in private. He understood exactly what the Machiavellian prick Staley was up to. Information that no longer traveled haphazardly among disciplines flowed only to Staley. This suited Gus very well. He had wondered if the foundation would continue after he was gone. Staley's accumulation of power answered the question. The St. Leger Foundation would be in capable hands.

They disagreed on little, even when Staley felt secure enough to drop most pretense of deferring to the old man. The future of humanity lay in biotechnology. St. Leger permitted Staley to dabble in his areas of interest, genetic augmentation and cloning. Neither pursuit addressed what St. Leger saw as the main conundrum of the human species—its ability to produce an Aristotle in the Fourth Century B.C. and a hundred generations later, whole nations of superstitious jackasses. A eugenicist promoting racial doctrines had given him a possible answer. Mankind had evolved along several lines, all but one of which had died out. Suppose—suggested the eugenicist—the die-out of man's cousin the Neanderthal hadn't been complete? Suppose *Neanderthalensis* had interbred with early *Homo sapiens sapiens*? Suppose this hybrid line developed in parallel with the *sapien* line? A bifurcated species could explain so much. It could explain the struggle between reason and zealotry. It could explain periodic group madness. Part of humanity just wasn't up to snuff. But which part? The eugenics quack had let slip the fact the Neanderthal's cranial volume was larger than modern man's. Which species had polluted the other?

Suppose *Homo sapiens* wasn't wiser. Suppose it prevailed because it was a faster breeder.

Or a fiercer predator.

Man was definitely that. Ferocious, carnivorous—even cannibalistic.

Traits of *Homo sapiens sapiens* or *Homo neanderthalensis*?

Gus liked the theory either way. He made a note to himself: "Be vigilant of small things. Human and Neanderthal DNA are

99.5 percent identical. The half-percent may be a gulf separating Earth from moon."

The standard version of human history said modern man had spilled out of Africa fifty or sixty thousand years ago and dominated the planet in short order. Whether he had slaughtered his cohabitants or merely passed them by could keep anthropologists squabbling for decades. No one could deny that the Neanderthal had died out . . . unless his genetic material had been preserved in a hybridized species. St. Leger found a quote from Thomas Hardy that he scribbled in his journal: "Flesh perishes. I live on. . . . "

But the genetic evidence pointed to no mongrelizing. So the conundrum wasn't explained. And St. Leger was frustrated, until gene science gave him a new theory.

And a means to find the evidence.

He would look for anomalies. An anomaly was a fact that didn't fit its surroundings.

Most of the data that came to the foundation was meaningless. St. Leger looked for the anomaly that wasn't.

He expanded the foundation's support of anthropology and archaeology. He became an amateur student of myths. In the evenings he read *The Golden Bough* and speculated on the persecutions he found in the old religions. Persecution could be a marker. The primitive rises against its better.

When Staley showed him a memorandum from one of the foundation's bird dogs about a possible burial site on Ewell Island, St. Leger said go ahead, fund an excavation. Almost a year ago, Staley had put a young woman on retainer who had worked with Neanderthal DNA. It had taken Staley months to track down someone with the qualifications the old man demanded. Expertise in speciation, familiarity with *Homo neanderthalensis*. None of it made sense to Staley, who suspected St. Leger was slipping into senility. Gus understood and didn't mind. He had just turned eighty-nine. He thought he was entitled to little flights of fancy.

25

"KICK FANE AWAKE," BECKER SAID. "WE'RE ABOUT TO LAND."

The helicopter had departed from the island well after midnight. The pilot had said the destination was near Washington, but David saw no sign of the city or its familiar landmarks. A minute ago they had crossed a sparsely lit highway. Now there was a low office tower rising ahead, black steel and glass. They dropped toward a lighted square on the roof.

David nudged Fane. "Wake up."

There were thumps from the undercarriage, sounds of wheels being locked down, then the door behind the control console opened and a man in a dark suit leaned in. "I'm Roger Staley," he said. "Let's get downstairs."

Snow had come up the Potomac River from the ocean and was blowing like dry sand across the roof. They skirted men in lab coats who wheeled medical gurneys to the helicopter's cargo bay. The remains of the Wakelyns had been kept cold. In a warm environment, fungal growth would enshroud the girl's cadaver almost before one's eyes. As Staley led them onto an elevator, David forced the fear out of his voice as he asked, "Is there news on Mrs. Sprague?"

"She's doing nicely."

"*Nicely?*"

"Noel is with her now at GW—George Washington Hospital. It's an excellent facility. He'll join us in a few hours." Staley had a thin voice, a finely boned face that was nonetheless masculine. "I don't want to wait till then to congratulate you on your success. We're all tremendously excited."

"Who's 'we'?" Becker said.

"All of us at the St. Leger Foundation. We sponsored Noel's project. I've kept the kitchen open in case you're hungry. I'm eager to hear your report on Ewell. But I suppose you're exhausted? Your rooms are this way. If you're up to it, we've got a gym and a pool."

"Nice place," Becker said.

"And a laundry service. Leave anything you want done in the hall."

David was indifferent to the fact his windowless suite had the anonymity of an airport hotel room. He slept for six hours, showered, and found his clothes hanging washed and pressed outside the room.

Fane tapped on the door and came in. "This is a secure place. I left my room to look around. A guard comes out a door and asks if he can show me to the dining room. When I say no, he tells me I can't wander without an ID badge."

"Why are you whispering?"

"Good point. If there's electronic surveillance, we'll never spot it. I tried in my room."

"Why would they have surveillance in our rooms?"

"Why is a guard babysitting this floor? Is there a telephone in your room?"

"No, but my cell phone works." David had already called his father. "Do you want to borrow it?"

"No, I have one."

"Then what are you worried about?"

They met nobody from security in the hall but found Becker coming back from a swim, accompanied by Roger Staley. Staley was grinning. "Those specimens you recovered are fabulous! We ran the young female through an MRI. Extraordinary preservation. You handled things well."

"You have an MRI here?" David said.

"Oh, yes. It's important to Dr. Sprague to preserve as much data as possible. Just as an aside, we're going to sequence the Wakelyns' DNA. I gather you've some familiarity with that field, Dr. Isaac?"

"Some."

"A young woman is on loan to us from Cold Spring Harbor Laboratory. We'll get you introduced to her and then have breakfast."

He took them down a couple of hallways and onto an elevator that needed a pass card. Two levels up, they got off and wound their way to a laboratory with a cold room. The temperature was a degree or two above freezing.

A dark-haired woman, bent over the cadaver of the girl, didn't look up as they entered. She wore a lab coat made bulky by the sweaters under it, double latex gloves, a plastic mask. Scissors and a scalpel lay on the metal table. Sealed jars held hair and tissue she had collected. Using long forceps to probe organ remnants, she ignored them for several minutes, moving quickly, dropping syringes into small metal barrels, sticking labels onto jars. After a while, she looked around.

"I'm doing a clean job, guys. Would you back away?" Her tone was pleasant.

"Dr. Walters already took samples," Becker said.

"And here I am, taking them again. Who are you?"

Staley spoke up. "These men recovered the remains on Ewell. When you're ready, Dr. Rodriguez, I'll introduce you."

She was ready a minute later.

She shook hands perfunctorily, nodded at names David knew she wasn't bothering to remember.

Staley said, "Would you like to join us for breakfast, Dr. Rodriguez?"

"I have to clean up here."

"Take your time. The dining room is on the fourth floor."

As the others left, David hung back, returning to the exam table. There had been little apparent deterioration of the child's body.

He said, "Do you need help packing your specimens?"

She squinted, ready to tell him to get lost. His face was youngish, too young for the flecks of gray in his short hair. It was a long, thin face, open and likeable. She thought he didn't pay much attention to his looks, wouldn't bother raising a two-day beard, though he might look good in one. Finding that a little dull, she looked for something else before giving up and settling for *nice* and *dull*. Sometimes that's all there was. The bigger guy with the Prussian look had given her a little rush.

"Sure, you can help," she said. "Canisters go into this case. I'll zip up Chiquita."

"Chiquita?"

"She needs a name."

"It was Margaret Wakelyn."

"Walters told me."

"What happened to the samples Walters collected?"

"Nothing. I just decided to do it again. Come on, hurry up. I'm freezing. And I'm hungry. I've been eating out of vending machines since yesterday."

"What about the dining room?"

"That's here. The sequencing lab is in West Virginia." She saw his doubtful look. "The equipment is first rate. So's the software—the whole Wisconsin package. You could run a university lab on it."

They used Rodriguez's key card to take an elevator down two levels. The dining room was mahogany paneled, with thick carpet showing parquet at the edges and brocaded armchairs scattered along a twelve-foot-long table. David heard Noel Sprague's voice before he saw him.

"There was no skull fracture," Sprague was saying. "I've never seen anyone recover so fast. The blessings of youth." He looked around as David and Rodriguez came in. "The doctors plan to cut her loose this afternoon."

Sprague occupied the seat at the head of the table as if it were his by right. Roger Staley sat to his left.

"Help yourselves," Staley told the new arrivals. He gestured toward a long side table with covered buffet trays.

The food was delicious. David ate hungrily.

"The cat's rather out of the bag regarding our support of your project," Staley said, addressing mostly Sprague. "We'd like to keep the location of the crypt confidential for a while. There may be more work to do there."

"More burial sites?" David asked.

"It's an exciting possibility."

Fane looked up from his plate. "The whole island was onto us. I'd say the secret is out."

"What's the foundation's interest in the excavation?" David asked.

"Pure science," Staley responded. "We support humanistic research on whatever front we can."

"I hadn't come across the St. Leger Foundation in archaeology."

"We frequently remain in the background, David. But these excavations were special, I'm sure you'll agree. As sociologists we like to know why people act. What belief drives them? If not belief, then what circumstance? We wonder about day-to-day actions, of course, but when behavior is extreme, the question is potentially even more rewarding. Human sacrifice points to a particularly intense state of the collective mind."

David traded glances with Becker, who was keeping a straight face. Normally a phrase like "collective mind"—describing something that didn't in fact exist—would have brought a snort of derision from Becker.

"Dr. Rodriguez," Staley said, "bring these gentlemen up to speed on the DNA work."

She wore a deer-in-the-headlights look for a moment. Then she said, "We're in the preliminary stages. . . ."

"But it's still of interest. The families are believed to have come from Cornwall. Dr. Rodriguez will help us confirm that. Or perhaps we'll have a surprise?" Staley smiled encouragement. "I'm reminded that identifying small genetic variations has solved old mysteries, for example the origin of European Gypsies. A distinctive blood factor traced the tribes conclusively to India."

"Language had already done that," Fane said softly.

"Yes, yes. But the biological evidence might have pointed elsewhere. Then the theories based on linguistic similarities would have had to be re-thought. Evidence that negates a theory is important, too."

David watched the smiling man. Staley should have left it alone. He could have just said that DNA analysis was routine with archaeological specimens. Apparently he didn't know that, so he thought they needed an explanation. That implied that it wasn't routine in this case, that there was a purpose, and that he didn't want to disclose it.

David aimed his question at Rodriguez. "Are you looking for anything in particular?"

She hesitated. "Adding to the database is useful in itself."

Staley stepped in. "We won't know until we see the results."

Rodriguez nodded.

Nobody asked why she was taking new tissue samples.

David followed Sprague out of the dining room. "You don't need me anymore," David said. "I'm going to hitch a ride to the airport. I'll stop and see Charl on the way."

Sprague extended a hand, which David shook.

"She'll be happy to see you. Please stay in touch."

"I will." A lie. They both knew it.

Sprague pretended to gather stray thoughts. "Your assumption is way off, in any case."

"Which assumption?"

"That the project doesn't need you. There is plenty more for you to do if you want to. We're short-handed. In a few days, we're going back to Ewell. Turn the place upside down if we have to, find out what really happened. You could help with that."

His old mentor grinned through his beard. It was a display of fondness, if only of the master for an apprentice. But it was also a declaration that he wasn't worried about anything. He hadn't been afraid to invite his wife's old lover back for the project. He wasn't worried about her affection. He was in command there as well as in the field.

David shook his head. "I don't think so, Noel."

26

A MAN WHO SAID HE WORKED SECURITY FOR THE FOUNDATION drove David as far as the last stop on the D.C. Metro's Orange Line. They were in Oakton, Virginia. "You'll get downtown quicker on the Metro than if I take you," the driver said.

"Thanks," David said, collecting his bag. He took an escalator, crossed a pedestrian bridge over the highway, found a train waiting at the platform.

It was a clear, bright day, bitterly cold, snow on the ground catching shadows as a few high clouds slipped along. The train car he boarded held a dozen or so passengers, several the right age for college students, a few who might have been government workers, all settled in, a couple reading, most listening to music, all of them passive, switched off.

David sat down, away from the others, as the last passengers came aboard and low chimes sounded before the doors closed. He glanced down at the highway, where automobiles raced along parallel to the train, and thought about what Staley had said about behavior. Whatever their destinations, the men and women around him were as caught up in rituals of belief as the old Ewell Islanders. The beliefs were different, the rituals contemporary. Off to university, off to an internship, off to a prosperous and perhaps influential life. There wouldn't be a simple driver for any of that. Belief and circumstance, Staley had said. Studying it, you would find contradictions and omissions in every idea, conflicting pressures in every circumstance.

You might learn what had happened on Ewell. You might learn what the islanders had believed. But *cause* was more elusive. The cause might lie hidden in a dozen things the island people *didn't* believe. Any lesson drawn would be an off-the-rack cliché: Don't let fear, resentment, superstition—or whatever else you disapproved of—get out of hand.

David wondered what theory Staley would gravitate toward. Not that it mattered. . . .

He got off the Metro at Foggy Bottom outside George Washington University Hospital. The Neurology Center was overheated, and he paused a few steps inside the doors to loosen his coat. He looked back to make sure he wasn't blocking the flow of visitors. A man had stopped on the sidewalk, a man of medium height in a fawn topcoat, who stared at the entrance. On the train David had marked the man as a bureaucrat, a studious reader of his square-folded newspaper without musical accompaniment. Sun glare on the Neurology Center doors prevented his seeing inside. He turned as if he were lost and walked on.

David got directions at the security desk and found an elevator.

Charl was sitting in a bedside chair, clicking through an email program on a laptop. A red knit hat covered most of the bandages on the left side of her head. Her color was good. He waited a minute before moving because his eyes were stinging. He felt a heart-stopping rush of disbelief that he was seeing her. He knocked lightly and stepped through the doorway.

"David!" Her smile was warm. She pushed away the computer table. "Is Noel with you? He's supposed to pick me up."

"He said he would be by later." David squeezed her hand, bent and kissed the right side of her face. "You look great. How do you feel?"

"Wobbly. If I move my head fast, I want to throw up. They said I'm really lucky." She patted the bed, and he sat. She said, "Noel told me everyone's off the island and safe. Thank God. Luther must have been insane."

"He was in odd physical condition."

"What do you mean?"

He told her.

She worked on it, couldn't get anywhere.

"The cold could have affected his mind," David said. "But it's pretty clear he killed Gerson."

"Insane," she repeated.

"As good a theory as any. I spent the morning at the St. Leger headquarters."

"So, your mystery is solved."

"Not exactly."

She noticed his bag. "And you're leaving."

"Six o'clock flight."

She stuck her hands under the blanket on her lap. Her face was pale. "I wish you were staying."

He wanted to stay and talk, stretch it out. Beg her to fly to New York with him, then drive up and spend the night in a snug, breakable bed at his father's house in Westport.

"There's something else," he said. "A man followed me to the hospital."

"Followed you. Are you sure?"

"Not a hundred percent."

"Well then."

"Fifty-two percent?"

"Don't make me laugh. It'll hurt. Why do you think he followed you?"

He described the man from the train.

She said, "How do you know he wasn't just coming to the hospital like you?"

"I don't."

"And who would follow you?"

"He could be a private detective. Maybe Noel thinks we're having an affair."

She touched the fringe of the bandage, wincing. "I told you . . ."

"Sorry."

"You'd have an an affair with a married woman."

Honesty was never a good idea with women, but he said, "In a heartbeat."

The neighborhood around the hospital was full of students, red-faced, hustling along. He walked a couple of blocks and noticed that the man who had come out of the hospital after him was a half-block behind. David strolled at random along the narrow sidewalks. The man was a block behind. Fawn topcoat, dark trousers, no hat. Hunched to expose less of himself to the frigid air.

David came back around the campus and walked into the Foggy Bottom Metro entrance. An escalator carried him down into the underground complex. At the bottom, David turned left instead of heading for the ticket machines. The man in the fawn topcoat was halfway down the moving stairway, several steps behind a woman holding a child's hand, a dozen steps below a group of Asians who had gotten on after him.

David walked to the UP escalator and bounded up the rising steps.

He had gone a block when a woman detached herself from a group of pedestrians and opened a wallet so that he could see a holographic ID card and a badge. The name on the card was HELEN CALDER.

"We would like to talk to you," she said.

Coming up behind, the man who had been following grabbed his arm and spun him around.

"That was cute." He had a square face with a short upper lip, reddish blond hair standing in cold spikes, light blue eyes. He was puffing.

"That's all right, Agent Kushner," the woman said. She turned to David. "May I see your identification?"

"No, I don't think you can."

"We're with the federal government."

"And I'm on a public sidewalk, minding my own business."

Calder's tone stayed pleasant. "You identified yourself at the hospital as David Isaac. You visited a patient named Sprague. Apparently you've both been working on Ewell Island. And you're both affiliated with the St. Leger Foundation." She smiled warmly. "Is that about right?"

Kushner had let go of David's arm. He stood close, coat unbuttoned, gun butt deliberately exposed, even so not very intimidating.

"There's a place a block from here where we can have coffee," Calder said.

"Another time," David replied.

He stepped away, and Kushner moved in to block him. "The lady asked you nicely."

David stared past him, at the busy sidewalk. "And I said I didn't want a date."

Kushner reached again for his arm, and David swung his bag into the man's face. Kushner stumbled back, blood running from both nostrils, spattering the fawn topcoat. He groped for his gun. "You're under arrest, asshole!"

Helen Calder stepped between them. She put a hand on Kushner's shoulder. His eyes were streaming.

"Let's put that on hold," she said. "It would be better, Dr. Isaac, if we talked. There's a restaurant down the street. Agent Kushner will get himself cleaned up while we drink hot toddies."

Her voice was cuddly, almost sexy, as her face held its lumpy smile. "It's in your interest as much as ours," she said. "We can decide about arresting you later."

27

ROGER STALEY WALKED FROM MONITOR TO MONITOR IN THE security office. There was little of this building and its surroundings that wasn't scanned twenty-four hours a day by Geronimo Bix's cameras. An outdoor scene had captured his attention.

"When did this happen?"

"Hour ago," Bix said. "There's been a van parked up the road eavesdropping on us. This one arrived an hour ago."

The van, so white and anonymous it cried out government, had pulled into the driveway approaching the foundation's entrance. It was as if they were inviting someone to send out a guard to tell them they were trespassing. And then what?

"Arrogant," said Staley.

"I sent Rudy to fuck with them a little," Bix said. Rudy Little Horse was Bix's second cousin, man of many skills including helicopter pilot. Bix tapped a key and a time-stamped recording showed a large SUV with blackened windows—presumably driven by Rudy—as it drove up and parked beside the white van. Staley watched. He half expected to see a window of the van buzz down and a badge appear. But nothing happened. Arrogant indeed. The SUV pulled around and stopped close to the rear of the van.

Rudy stayed in the SUV. Nobody got out of the van. Thirty seconds passed. A minute.

"I told him to come back," Bix said. "Big radiation leak out there. They're monitoring us."

"We don't seem to have solved our problem with NIS," Staley observed.

"NIS picked up that archaeologist outside the hospital. I have someone on him."

Gus St. Leger, slouched in an easy chair out of sight of the monitors, spoke up. "You should have killed him."

Staley wished he could ignore the deep voice. Since his arrival, St. Leger had taken charge and issued orders, often contradictory, to every staff member he came across. So far, the staff showed no doubt about the lines of authority. Edicts that mattered were referred discreetly to Staley, who told St. Leger that everything was being taken care of. Only Geronimo Bix had escaped the flood of directives. St. Leger seemed reluctant to distract the small man.

"Isaac is harmless," Staley said.

"He's ignorant. That's not the same thing."

The old man was joking. He knew they couldn't kill every person NIS might interview. St. Leger met Staley's glance with the loose grin he had worn in his drinking days.

"You don't understand, do you?" St. Leger said. "The Puerto Rican girl is holding out on us. Betcha girls have always done that to Roger, don't you agree, Heronimo?"

Bix ignored the Spanish pronunciation of his name. St. Leger viewed Indians as not much different from Mexicans—not truly human the way a lanky European with no color in his skin was human.

Not ready to mock Staley, Bix didn't respond.

St. Leger's voice rose. "You've got good projects underway, Roger. But Ewell may be the most important."

"How is Rodriguez holding out on us?"

"She knows the child's DNA isn't tainted." The old man met Staley's glance with placidness that was a barrier. "We're looking in the right place, Roger. Small, isolated population. Exactly the place for an abnormality to flourish. Rodriguez will tell us if we're right."

"It's probably a fluke," Staley said.

"Permit me to be excited, please. I'm close enough to the grave that I have no illusions about myself to preserve. You youngsters have much more at stake." St. Leger balanced a foot on the seat of a nearby chair. "Suppose you're a member of a mongrelized race, Roger, how would you feel about that? Would you want to purify it? What if it turned out that Heronimo here is the purer representative of humanity? Pretty nasty shock for a gentleman like you."

Staley didn't answer.

"Cat got your tongue? Good! If there's something truly interesting, we may want to keep it to ourselves."

"Sprague plans to publish."

"I know. He plans to publish some tabloid sensationalism about a murder of witches. If that's all, we may let him. Or we may not." His expression changed as he looked over his shoulder at Geronimo Bix. St. Leger was ever so glad that Staley had hired Bix.

28

THE RESTAURANT WAS ON THE GROUND FLOOR OF A BOUTIQUE hotel that was crowded with lithe young people who moved like dancers. Perhaps they were; the Kennedy Center was a few blocks away. Helen Calder pushed back her coat off a bright green sweater and ordered Irish coffee for both of them. "I'm going to loosen you up at taxpayer expense," she purred.

Despite himself, David liked her. "Your technique is better than Kushner's."

She smiled in reply. "We've talked to official people who were on Ewell Island—a state policeman and a medical examiner. I gather you were new to the excavation. The machinery of government is running slowly today, so I can't recite your c.v. We'll have it by this afternoon. Are you the same David Isaac the State Department had to extract from Mexico two years ago?"

"You've got the basics," he said.

She fell silent as steaming tall cups arrived. When the server had left, Calder said, "I would like you to answer some questions about the St. Leger Foundation."

David pushed his cup away.

The line between being a good citizen and being an informer had blurred in recent years. Federal agents were apt to pop up with questions about anyone. He had seen it at Columbia with Becker. He had seen it closer to home. When his sister had moved to Tel Aviv to marry an Israeli, the questions had been about his own family. Questions and whispers. To which nation was the Isaac family loyal?

To none, he had thought. But he had never dared say it. His father was loyal to healing. His sister to her belief in the Jewish people. And he, he was loyal to other things: science, reason, whatever truths those two disciplines could wrest from the world. Even then, loyalty was the wrong word. He had seen what damage reason, wielded by fools, could do.

This woman with the lumpy face wanted something important enough to overlook Kushner's bloody nose.

So where did that put his loyalty? Charl, Becker and Noel all had different claims on it.

"I don't know much," he said.

"I understand. Have you met Roger Staley?"

"Only today."

"Have you met other scientists—outside your group?"

"A geneticist has been brought in."

"I'm not much of a scientist myself," she said, "flunked my chem labs in high school. Maybe you could tell me a little about your project. Just in layman's language."

"We excavated a burial site and recovered some human remains from the early Eighteenth Century." He told her about the deeply buried coffins, the exhumations of the remains of the man and the girl. He didn't mention Luther's attacks. If she had talked to the state police, she might know all about that.

"It sounds interesting."

"If you're an archaeologist, it is."

"Why is a geneticist involved?"

"It's routine. Another way of tracking populations, diseases, minor traits."

She showed a glimmer of interest, but it was faint. She asked, "Has Staley mentioned the foundation's other work?"

"In broad terms. Sociology of some sort."

"Have you met a man named Bix?"

"No."

"Or heard the name Stephan Pogorovich?"

"No."

"Are you aware it's illegal to clone human beings?"

He couldn't suppress a laugh. "Where did that come from?"

The woman's smile was perfunctory. She stayed silent.

Cloning? What did she imagine? The Wakelyns?

For a breathless moment, he wondered. Was it feasible? It would be insane, but the only question that might occur to certain people was: Could it be done?

"Do you think they're planning to clone the Wakelyns?" David asked.

Finishing her drink, Calder set down the cup. "No, I don't believe they're doing that," she said. "Thank you for your help, Dr. Isaac."

"That's all?"

"It wasn't so bad, was it?" She made gathering-up motions with her coat. "I hope you enjoyed your coffee."

He hadn't touched it. "Can you tell me why we had to talk?"

She handed him a card. "In case you think of anything."

He had plenty of time to take the Metro out to Reagan Airport and catch a shuttle to New York. Instead he walked aimlessly for a couple of blocks. Past narrow townhouses, within sight of the Kennedy Center, back toward the hospital. Kushner and Calder had given up on him, as far as he could tell. If he was being followed, he couldn't spot anyone doing it.

He circled back toward the campus, trying to decide where he was headed. There were two choices: the airport or GW Hospital.

A bag was on the hospital bed. Charl, standing beside an obligatory wheelchair, was admiring a long black coat her husband had brought for her to replace her bloodstained field jacket.

Noel looked around. "David! Still on your way home?"

David sat down heavily. "Tell me what you know about the St. Leger Foundation. What you *really* know."

29

SPRAGUE SEEMED TO DRAW BACK AS HE LISTENED TO DAVID describe the run-in with the government agents. He said, "Are you certain they were with NIS?"

"Her badge looked authentic. The guy was armed."

Charl spoke. "Assume they were real, Noel. Why would the National Institutes of Science investigate the foundation?"

"I can't imagine. It's absurd. Staley's bunch have a little bit of a reputation as do-gooders, which I overlook. A distinguished board. No scandals."

"How did St. Leger wind up backing your project?" David said.

"Actually, Roger approached me. Someone had stumbled across the site, and he was interested. There was the local lore of burials. I made a preliminary survey six months ago. The shaft was largely unobstructed. An excavation looked feasible, and the foundation was willing to back me. I don't know how any of this could offend NIS."

"What's the purpose of the project?"

"That's obvious, isn't it?"

"Tell me."

"The Wakelyns were murdered by their neighbors. All we need do is find a single document mentioning witchcraft—"

"That's your purpose. It may not be Staley's. The foundation put a lot of money into your project. Suppose they had another motive?"

"Such as?"

"Calder mentioned cloning. She asked if I knew it was illegal to clone humans. Then she denied suspecting the foundation was doing it with the Wakelyns."

Charl leaned against the bed. "What would be the point of cloning a person from three hundred years ago?"

"It seems far out," David allowed.

"'Off the wall' would be closer," Sprague said.

Charl's glance silenced him. "David, what names did the woman ask you about? Bix and—?"

"Bix, no spelling, no first name, and Stephan—with an f or a ph—it sounded like Pogorovich."

Charl reached across the bed, dug her laptop out of the bag. "Let's start with Pogorovich. Are you sure that's how it was pronounced?" She sat with one hip on the bed, typed in a search. "There's a page for something called Canton Oncology Ltd. in Baltimore. Stephan Pogorovich is director. It looks as though they do cancer research. . . ." She read silently. "Contracts from hospitals. You think it's him? It says Pogorovich won a MacArthur award eleven years ago. How could he be important to NIS?"

"I don't know," David said. "How many Stephan Pogoroviches did you find?"

"Looks like just this one. He's in medicine, so he's probably the one."

"Try him with St. Leger."

She did. Nothing showed. "I'll try Staley." She got the same result. "Wonder how you spell Bix." She went through several spellings and didn't get much until she tried the phonetic B-i-x , which produced several million hits. The first twenty or so seemed to be about a jazz musician. "Bix Beiderbeck," she said uncertainly. She typed BIX+ST. LEGER and got a mix of jazz and genealogical sites.

David pushed off from the wall. "There's still Canton Oncology."

Trying to recover, Sprague said dryly, "I don't think NIS has it in for cancer research. But I'll ask Roger to clarify matters."

David and Charl exchanged glances.

"Yeah," David said, "why not. Did you come by car? I'll hitch a ride back."

"You think I'm still hiring?" Sprague said.

"Are you?"

Sprague chuckled. "Only people who promise to agree with me."

Sprague had a driver—not the man who had taken David to the Metro but a dark young woman, who negotiated the Beltway traffic and had them back at the St. Leger Foundation headquarters in an hour. She parked in an underground garage, keyed the elevator and took them up to the executive level. Loren Fane was standing outside an office suite, arms folded, pale with rage.

"What's going on?" Sprague asked.

"These bastards won't let me leave! They're got us locked down."

David almost said he'd been out, but had he been on his own?

"You don't believe me, try it yourself," Fane said. "The elevators are restricted to the upper floors, and the stairway doors are locked."

Sprague made a calming motion. He disappeared into the suite of offices and emerged less than five minutes later. "Loren is correct. It's for our own safety, I'm afraid. Roger will meet us in a few minutes and explain."

30

PILAR GOT BACK TO MPC IN LATE AFTERNOON. MINH greeted her like a man desperate for company and helped carry her cases into the lab. The helicopter lifted off while they were still climbing the steps. That suited her fine. The fewer eyes the better.

"Is Walters here?" she asked.

"Carter took him down the mountain for R and R."

She dumped her coat, accepted a large mug of coffee from Minh, tuned the radio to hillbilly heartache, and got to work. As she repeated the steps from yesterday, she wished she could run the problem past someone like Janecke at Cold Spring. Or one of her old professors, Henry Wald, except he was too formidable to approach. She wasn't afraid of Rick Janecke. She respected his objectivity, and in a purely professional way she liked him.

She knew one thing he would say: Don't jump to conclusions.

Pedestrian, but true.

There were probably more explanations for Chiquita than she had considered.

The child's skeletal structure had looked normal. Pilar knew she really wasn't qualified to judge that. Anthropologists waged war over the meaning of a small cranial variation that Pilar wouldn't notice if she saw it. But the remains hadn't *looked* like those of a freak destined for an early, painful death.

Yet the first sequencing of her genes pointed in that direction.

Pilar glanced around the silent lab. Minh was beyond the glass door, bent at a work station. She checked her pocket phone. No trace of a signal. No phone on the wall or the desk. She peeked out at Minh. No phone that she could see out there either.

She stepped out and saw that Minh's diligence was being spent on video solitaire.

"Louis, is there a phone in the place?"

"Carter's office."

"That's the only one?"

He looked up warily. "Carter told me when I was hired that the clients like keeping work proprietary. He meant they're anal."

"That's proprietary. Where's his office?"

Minh led her into the hall. Two doors down, Carter's office was unlocked. She entered, switched on a double-bar of overhead lights. A telephone set was half buried under paper on a shelf. She lifted the receiver and heard a faint dial tone. When she glanced at the doorway, feeling like a spy or a sneak thief, Minh had withdrawn.

She dialed Rick Janecke's direct line from memory.

When he picked up, she spoke quickly. "Rick, it's Pilar. I wonder if you—" She was going to say "—could spare me a moment," but he cut her off.

"Rodriguez, where are you, and what are you up to?"

He sounded unfriendly, which she hadn't expected.

Pilar said, "I'm in West Virginia, doing the work I told you about."

"There was—" his tone softened to a high-pitched whisper "—there was an agent from NIS looking for you yesterday. What the hell are you doing?"

"What did he say?"

"*She* scared the shit out of the assistant director. Were you dabbling in illicit cloning? He said not here. The old man went nuclear. You shouldn't count on having your job. I'm sorry."

She felt shocked, and upset. "Me, too."

"What are you doing? Wait, I don't want to know. What are you calling me for?"

She hesitated. "Advice."

"Call the NIS agent, that's my advice. I've got her card."

She let him read a name and phone number. Then: "Rick, tell me one thing: how many variations can you have in a genotype before you decide you're looking at something different?"

He didn't hang up. His silence lasted a few seconds. "What do you mean?"

"Suppose I showed you a mouse with major alleles—genes where they aren't supposed to be, substitutions that aren't recognized by the sequencing programs."

The line was silent.

"What are you talking about? You told me you would be working with a person from an isolated population."

"I am."

"How many differences?"

"Four big ones. I let my let my client think the sample was contaminated. He doesn't know better. Tonight I'm running the sequences again with fresh material. If it comes out the same, what do I tell him?"

"Was this—person—alive?"

"Till the age of four."

"Well, there you have it. The alleles were lethal."

"She was murdered, Rick." She stared out the doorway of Carter's office. Nobody was in the hall.

Janecke cleared his throat. "You've thrown this at me sort of sudden. Most genetic mistakes are fatal—or so awful you'd wish they were fatal. Major ones abort spontaneously."

"I know."

"I know you know. Which makes me wonder why you're asking. How big are these mistakes?"

"Big enough that I figure I screwed up." She was lying. She wondered if he could tell.

"Which genes," he asked, "which chromosomes?"

"I'll tell you everything after I've run them again."

Janecke spoke as if he hadn't heard her, reciting what they both knew. "An evolved species works pretty well. Tweak the coding, you're more likely to get two heads than an improvement. If you're talking several significant mutations, the subject should be a mess. What's this isolated population you're looking at?"

"I don't think I can tell you."

"Well, then, fuck off." Once more, however, he didn't hang up. He asked, "What are they like?"

"Islanders."

"Good start." She could almost hear him thinking. "Your donor is dead. What are her relatives like—two heads, four arms?"

"We don't know. She died three hundred years ago."

"Is the island still populated?"

"Don't try to figure out where it is, Rick. It's populated; I don't know much about it."

"If this child was killed on an island three hundred years ago, you need to ask was she part of the local population or an outsider? If she was part of the population, you've got to wonder if some of her differences were inherited. If so other people might have them. You get ugly stuff on islands. You see, Rodriguez, I'm assuming you didn't mess up. How long have you worked for me?"

"Twenty-three months."

"So even if your professors didn't teach you, I've taught you how to do the basics."

"And I'm grateful, Rick. Let me ask you one more thing. Have you ever heard of the St. Leger Foundation, or St. Leger Pharmacal?"

"The foundation, vaguely. When you said they had a job for you, I knew I'd heard the name before. What about them?"

"I had to sneak into a guy's office to make this phone call. They're big on security." Turning her back on the doorway, she added, "And they fly me around in a black helicopter."

She heard a suppressed laugh. "That cinches it. You're working for spooks."

"I don't think so. It's a private fiefdom."

"Doesn't mean they don't do contract work. You should hope I'm right. Then the NIS lady was just doing a background check."

She could tell he didn't believe it.

She hung up the receiver, glanced into the hall before flicking off the light and leaving Carter's office.

She should have been more candid with Janecke. He might have concluded that she'd botched the sequencing, or that she was crazy. Or he might have accepted her findings and run around with his hair on fire. She didn't want that. Even at Cold Spring, hair on fire would draw attention. And she *sure* didn't want attention. Not yet. Not when any of a hundred people with big reputations could elbow her aside on this project.

It probably wouldn't come to that. Chiquita would be just another of nature's freaks, soon to be indexed and forgotten.

But this freak was more interesting than anything she had found in mustard plants.

31

ROGER STALEY WAS MAKING A SHOW OF BEING RELAXED. Perched on the side of his desk, Staley knew he looked convincing. You would trust your checkbook to this guy. Or let him train your children at a private school that favored cold baths and enemas. It wasn't hard to deceive people who wanted to identify with you.

"I'm afraid this is my responsibility," he told Sprague. All the Ewell team were present except Sprague's wife. "I should have warned you all that certain groups are attempting to undermine our research."

"What groups?" David Isaac was slumped in a leather chair, farthest from the desk. The tone of the question wasn't belligerent, but it annoyed Staley anyway.

"We've been supporting research toward cancer vaccines," Staley responded. "Some results are promising." He let it hang. It was like a seduction. A little bit at a time. "A Swiss consortium isn't happy. We at St. Leger, as you know, are a nonprofit. Any patents that come from this work we support will be open source. That could close off many profitable avenues for the Swiss."

He didn't look directly at Isaac but wondered how the story was being received. Swiss villains were made to order for a Jew. "The security lockdown was temporary, an overreaction on a junior person's part." It had been St. Leger's call, pending a decision on how to handle the NIS interest. When Staley heard, he had almost screamed at the old man that they couldn't lock people up.

"Where does NIS enter the picture?" Isaac asked.

"We filed a complaint with NIS some months ago, asking that they investigate the Swiss group. They may be following up on that. Did the agent who met you mention a man named Pogorovich?"

"Yes," said Isaac.

Staley knew she had. Bix's person had sat several tables away from Calder and Isaac, eavesdropping with a directional pickup.

"There you are," Staley said. "Stephan Pogorovich has done cancer research for us. The Swiss have tried to steal his data. When money is involved, unfortunately, people become quite ruthless."

Noel Sprague nodded acceptance of the story, as if he knew all about greedy pharmaceutical companies.

"NIS may have picked up recent chatter about the Swiss consortium's activities," Staley said. "If we stay with tightened security, I'll make sure it doesn't interfere with you." He dug around in his desk, passed out laminated cards to each man. He offered a ten-watt smile. "This gives you the run of the building—including the exits. Noel, how is Mrs. Sprague feeling?"

Becker came up beside David. "Follow me. You'll like this."

They took an elevator to the upper floor where the Ewell bodies were stored. They entered the cold room, and Becker pulled back a plastic sheet from the remains of Margaret Wakelyn. Rodriguez had been thorough. The abdominal and thoracic cavities gaped. Becker brought a strong light to shine on the head.

"Is this your line of work now?" David asked.

"Something has been bothering me. Look at the teeth, remarkable for a four-year-old from that period. There are no signs of decay. A relatively well-to-do family would have had sugars in its diet. Papa's teeth are good, too."

David looked at the girl's leathery skin. A bluish cast of fungal growth was barely visible in patches around the shoulders and the lower abdomen.

"What does Rodriguez say?"

"Left this afternoon. Abrasive creature. Ignored my charm. Let me show you the father's teeth."

Becker led the way to the deeper cold storage, opened the metal door and switched on the lights. At the back of the room, John Wakelyn's skeletal remains lay in a bag on a trolley.

"Even Loren doesn't believe they monitor the refrigerators," Becker whispered. "Otherwise, he's pretty far off the deep end. What about you? What do you think is going on?"

"I don't know. Sprague was quick to believe in big pharma spies."

"He has a vested interest," Becker said. He sounded unhappy at admitting disloyalty. "Also, Staley didn't explain why he's fast-tracking the DNA work. I talked with Rodriguez. She didn't tell me anything. But she isn't that hard to read. Something went wrong when she sequenced the material Walters brought out. So she's starting from scratch, getting flown back and forth on one of the foundation's 'copters. Does that sound like routine DNA analysis?"

"No."

"They're looking for something in a hurry. I have an idea or two. What's the most likely disease to have hit Ewell? Cholera. Suppose Staley wants a genetic reason the Wakelyn family didn't die of cholera? They could have just been lucky. . . ."

"The island mythology made them special."

Nodding, Becker said, "Try this. If you can look for a therapy, you can look for its opposite. Suppose the Wakelyns did make their neighbors ill."

"Carriers."

"Disease-resistant carriers. If you could replicate the trait, it would make a dandy biological weapon."

"For whom?"

"Our side, their side. Anyone with enemies."

In Becker-speak, that meant every government. "Do you have any happy ideas?" David asked.

"Not at the moment."

They emerged from the cold locker talking about teeth. John Wakelyn had had spectacular teeth.

32

JOHN WALTERS LEANED OVER PILAR'S SHOULDER READING the computer screen. Two hours after midnight. The place dead. Walters had come back from his expedition with Carter smelling of beer and sweat. He was fighting yawns.

"This isn't my field," he said. "What is it?"

"Chromosome 3, a key marker," Pilar said. "Its banding is virtually identical in chimpanzees, orangutans, gorillas, and humans. Nothing unusual in our specimen. It's this other one—number 4. When I first saw this, I thought someone was playing a trick on me. This is a big chromosome. More than two hundred million base pairs, a thousand genes, a hundred and some disease genes. Everything from Alzheimer's to Huntington's to Parkinson's to macular dystrophy to fertile eunuch syndrome has its origin here." She had spent hours at the genome initiative database. "*This* gene, APBB2, is linked to late-onset Alzheimer's. That's in its normal state. Chiquita's version has about fifty percent more base pairs than normal—

around six hundred thousand. There's major duplication within the gene."

"Would that prevent it from encoding its normal protein?"

"It would do something."

"This is what you found on the first sequencing, isn't it?"

"Yes."

"And?"

"I've been thinking. One possibility is she came from a degenerate family. You know, badly inbred. She might not have been viable beyond a certain age. There might have been physical deformity we can't detect. She might have had a predisposition to a certain disease, or resistance to it." She floated that, got no response.

"You can't tell from this analysis, can you?"

"No."

As a pathologist, Walters would know how the gene hunt worked. The presence of a particular sequence of nucleic acids at a certain position might not matter. What counted might be how they acted in combination with other genes. Or how they were expressed. Medical research meant working backward— observing a condition and then chasing down a cause. Sickle cell anemia, for instance, traced to a tiny mutation that substituted GTG for GAG at one position. But if your starting point was the unfamiliar gene, you wouldn't know where it led.

"It could be nothing," Walters said.

"That much change isn't nothing. There are other things wrong with her. Three new alleles on Chromosome 4, plus a whopper on 8."

"Look at the bright side," Walters told her. "Finding the answers could take you years. You'll be gainfully employed, and you might run your own lab."

She relaxed. "That part sounds okay. Did you and Carter have a good time?"

"Can you picture Carter line dancing? In a honky-tonk saloon?"

"No, I can't."

"Be grateful for that. I'm going to bed."

Pilar wished she could do the same. She remained in the lab.

St. Leger had complicated the job by emailing her an unidentified genome program. He'd written:

SEE HOW THE CHILD MATCHES UP WITH THIS.

She had loaded the program, sent a message back:

WHAT IS IT?

A response came:

EUROPEAN SUBSET. DON'T WANT TO BIAS YOU SO I'LL SAY NO MORE.

So she stayed later, running Chiquita against the European subset. She ran it, studied the results, thought St. Leger was playing games with her. Chiquita's DNA matched the human genome database ninety-nine point nine-nine-nine-nine percent. However important her variations might be biologically, they were statistically insignificant. The matchup with St. Leger's program was a lot less. About ninety-nine point six—but she couldn't be sure because St. Leger's program was incomplete. Parts of the "European subset" were missing. But enough pairs had been in the program that Pilar wondered what group it belonged to. For sure, not any Europeans she had run into.

She fell into her bed at 3 a.m. Slept badly.

At 7 a.m., both St. Leger and Staley were visible on the laptop screen as Pilar reported the results of the second sequencing. She went through the new alleles gene by gene.

CHROMOSOME 4, GNRHR . . .
CHROMOSOME 4, APBB2 . . .
CHROMOSOME 4, AIS4. . .
CHROMOSOME 8, SNTG1. . .

She gave the same explanation she had given Walters about the impossibility of finding instant answers to the variations' significance. "It could take years to isolate the effects," she said. "If we knew the girl had a certain physical defect, we could work backward. If we knew some pathology ran in the family, or in that group of colonists, we would have a place to start. As it is, we don't know if she inherited these traits or just got a bad break when her genes were put together."

"What about the current Ewell population?" Staley said.

Pilar felt a stir of excitement. She'd been thinking about them.

"If her alleles existed in other colonists, they might still be present," Pilar said. "It would depend on how damaging they are."

St. Leger said, "So there could be a public health problem on Ewell."

"There could be."

"A simple genetic test of the present residents would tell us about the alleles, wouldn't it?"

"Yes."

"Well, then. We should do that, shouldn't we? There's nothing like seeing for oneself. That's one of my mottoes. I'll have Rudy pick you up—you and Minh. We'll see what these Ewell folk are made of."

"I'm not licensed for public health work," Pilar said.

"Don't worry, Minh is qualified. You'll observe, analyze the results when we get them. Now—that program I sent you . . ." There was something eager in his expression. "Did you get any matches?"

"There were similarities, but not much closer than you'd get comparing our DNA to a chimp's," Pilar said. She wanted him to understand it was *he* who had wasted the time, not her. "None of the new alleles showed up in your program."

"So . . ."

"So whatever that subset is, she's not part of it."

"Are you certain she's no match?"

His disappointment was obvious. And puzzling.

"It's about all I'm certain of," Pilar said. "Where does this subset come from?"

St. Leger seemed to recover. "Oh, it's nothing important, my dear. My little exercise in whimsy. Well, we press on then. I'll see you later today."

His hearty tone was false.

The call ended, and Staley turned to St. Leger. "What 'program' did you send her?"

"Svante Pääbo's latest Neanderthal sequences."

"How did we get them?"

"I imagine someone stole them." Crossing his legs, St. Leger stared at the ceiling.

"Did you really think we would find Neanderthal DNA on Ewell Island?"

"I considered it possible." The old man put his elbows back on the desk, stared down at the cascade of his necktie. "The Neanderthal hypothesis has its weaknesses, but I like it. They shared southern Europe with us for thousands of years. They had speech. They may have had red hair. I find it hard to believe that none of them sampled the neighboring hominid's nookie."

"Which wouldn't matter," Staley pointed out, "if they couldn't interbreed with humans."

"Well, that's as may be. What do we make of the Ewell flock? Odd birds indeed. They're not much to look at from what you've shown me. The modern ones, anyway. They've had three hundred years of humping their sisters. I'm supposed to say 'consanguinity,' aren't I?"

"Say whatever you like. There are some spectacular misfits among them."

"Yes, and that still intrigues me," St. Leger said. The old man's grin was never pleasant. The teeth were amber and crooked. His breath stank worse than his trousers. "The Wakelyn girl must have been a vile little monster. Loaded with defects from Chromosome 4. Better off dead. Hm. Do you know much about the SNTG1 gene from Chromosome 8, Roger?"

Staley shook his head.

"I've seen it mentioned," St. Leger said. "I don't recall the context."

"You're sending Rodriguez and Minh to Ewell."

"I may go, too," the old man said. "You run along, Roger. I need to do some reading."

He found it almost immediately online. A University of Chicago researcher who had studied SNTG1 found heavy natural selection of the gene across all humanity's races. The researcher didn't pretend to know why. The gene, along with MCPH1, helped regulate brain size. A tiny mutation was disastrous. If a couple of sequences were deleted from the gene's short arm, there was a chance of spinal curvature at birth.

Margaret Wakelyn's variety had no deletion. Instead there was a long insertion of coding, borrowed from elsewhere on her family's genetic map, spliced—by an accident of parentage—into an area where it didn't belong. What did all that extra coding do? Was it gibberish?

By rights the Wakelyn girl could have been ejected from the womb at eight weeks, never to have drawn a breath. But she had drawn four years' worth.

And then had her head cut off.

33

STEPHAN POGOROVICH'S LAB ASSISTANT TOOK HERSELF TO
Bayview Medical Center when the tiny pimples that had begun
on her lips the previous afternoon had spread across her chin,
down her neck, and onto her chest. At nine thirty-three a.m.,
two hours after she was admitted, much of her torso was
covered with what the emergency room doctors had tentatively
identified as a virulent strain of Methicillin-resistant Staphylococcus aureus. By the time the woman died of multiple organ
failure a few minutes after noon, a nurse in the infectious
disease unit wasn't feeling well.

The head resident hesitated for twenty minutes. Meth-resistant
staph was endemic in hospitals. It was hard to combat because
several strains could withstand most antibiotics. It was aggressive,
traveling through the body to attack at multiple locations. The
hospital's infectious disease specialist did not like the look of the
dead patient's infection. It had moved faster than he had seen
before. It had killed faster. The head resident consoled himself

with the thought, *She didn't get it here*, as he phoned the Centers for Disease Control. It was CDC's second call that day from Baltimore. The first call had come two hours earlier from Stephan Pogorovich. By three in the afternoon, both the hospital and Pogorovich's laboratory were under quarantine. Several hospital employees were receiving massive doses of vancomycin. The MRSA variant was nasty, but the outbreak was limited and the health responders believed they had it under control.

They believed that for almost an hour.

Helen Calder heard about the incident while she rode in Kushner's pool car, a hand over her eyes, weary and demoralized. Apart from Pogorovich's allegations, which a defense attorney would eviscerate standing on one leg, she had nothing to prove that Staley had violated any law.

When her phone went off, she was tempted to ignore it. She answered and Tim Berman said, "We've been monitoring your boy in Baltimore."

"Pogorovich?"

"He phoned CDC saying he thought he had an outbreak of MRSA in his lab." Berman pronounced it "Mersa." "Pogorovich is sick and his lab assistant may be, too."

"MRSA," Helen repeated.

"Resistant staph. CDC is quarantining things up there."

She tried to shake off her lethargy. Pogorovich hadn't mentioned working with pathogens. She looked out the windshield. They were a hundred yards from the NIS front gate, and Kushner was slowing with his turn signal clicking.

"Drive on past," Helen told Kushner.

"It's apparently pretty aggressive," Berman's voice persisted.

"What else?"

"That's all we've got so far."

"Let me know if that changes."

She disconnected from Tim Berman and ordered Kushner to head for Baltimore.

A CDC officer in a moon suit met Helen Calder on the cordoned street where Pogorovich had his lab. The officer was tall and angular, with small, narrow-set eyes. "I'm Voight. I can't authorize you to enter the building," she said.

It was nearly dusk. The site was swarming with people in biohazard gear. Even the local police who were directing traffic away from the neighborhood were suited up. Helen found it amusing without being certain she should. There was a tendency of local responders to play an incident to the hilt. Here they had white protective suits, decontamination chambers and—a block or so away—a post where the mayor and police commissioner could tell the media how they were handling the emergency. The mayor of Baltimore, she had heard, would raise an alarm at the sight of talcum powder in a barber shop.

"Was this guy working with bacteria for your people?" Voight asked.

Helen felt her jaw clench. "Of course not. Where would you get such an idea?"

"He was babbling your name."

"He's my confidential informant."

"Maybe he didn't inform you of everything. The MRSA in this building isn't your typical hospital infection. We're having seventy percent fatalities. It survives on sterile surfaces, transmits by contact, penetrates skin, attacks the heart and other organs. A third of the cases involve necrotizing fasciitis—the flesh-eating disease. We're not having great success with clindamycin or vancomycin."

"How many cases?"

"Right now, thirty-some confirmed."

"Is it contained?"

"No. The guy's assistant contaminated her family. Her husband went to work last night at a truck stop on Broening Highway. He's a grill cook. Just a few hundred contacts. Bayview Medical's a mess. They didn't take precautions soon enough."

As they talked, Voight moved away from the brick building on which the name Canton Oncology was blurrily visible through sheets of plastic. She asked Helen, "What was this idiot doing?"

"He said stem cell research," Helen said.

"That's all?"

"Using material from aborted fetuses is illegal."

Voight glanced back at the building. "His lab doesn't have even elementary precautions for working with an aggressive pathogen. I don't think he knew it was there. The organism could have ridden in on fetal material. Or maybe someone brought it from a hospital. We haven't tracked everyone's movements. I hope this thing hasn't taken hold at a family planning clinic."

"Where is my informant?"

"We took him to Bayview. He was on life support an hour ago."

"I need to speak with him."

"Good luck. I'll give you my cell number. Let me know if you get a new angle on this."

Helen walked back to the car, gave Kushner orders. They weren't far from the waterfront. The windows of warehouses reflected swollen, dirty clouds that didn't seem to move. A few office buildings painted the sky with a sickly orange haze. The city felt immobile, like something dying.

As he drove, Kushner complained, "We could have gotten something out of that Isaac guy."

Besides a bloody nose? She almost said it, but Kushner was right. She shouldn't have let Isaac go.

She stared out the side window at row houses slipping past, blocks of them, identical in their fake stone fronts, drawn shades, narrow steps, houses twelve feet wide containing lives that were cramped into narrow sitting rooms and attic bedrooms, like her mother's house. Helen looked away from the houses. Their car crossed an intersection that had neon tavern signs on two of the four corners. A laundromat, a small grocery. Set a pathogen loose in these neighborhoods where everyone lived close and it could infect half the population in forty-eight hours. Then again, it might stay put, because many of these people wouldn't leave the neighborhood for weeks on end. They might not even go to the hospital, as rashes turned to abscesses and they slipped into painful sleep in front of the television.

At Bayview Medical Center, she sat in the car with the heater blowing and sent Kushner to run the gantlet of cops and CDC agents. She checked phone messages, touched base with Tim

Berman. Her section chief's line didn't answer. Kushner came back, talking before he had the door closed. "You're not going to get anything out of Pogorovich. They pulled the plug."

"That fast."

"What do you do with a guy who hasn't got a heart, kidneys, liver, lungs." He made washing motions with his gloved hands. "You shouldn't have sent me in there. Everyone is dressed like bubbleboy."

"If you're infected, please get out of the car."

"I've got a family. I don't like this. Where do we go next? You got a leper colony to visit?"

Helen shook her head. "We go downtown, before CDC gets all the hotel rooms."

34

EWELL ISLAND.

Pilar Rodriguez had never seen a more grim and desolate-looking place, if you didn't count parts of Brooklyn, New York. As she saw the stooped, weathered houses—which would have embarrassed her cousins in the La Perla slum—she laughed quietly until St. Leger turned his gaunt face questioningly at her. She looked away. You had to have been a poor Latina to enjoy the absurdity of it.

So this is how white people live.

And the Ewell Islanders couldn't claim to be recent immigrants, poised on the first rung of economic ascent that Anglo culture promised.

She wondered where her ancestors had been three centuries ago. There must have been at least one bloodthirsty conquistador among them, raping Indians, inserting the aggressive genes that drove little Pilar to complete not just her degree but post-doctoral work that had led her to Cold Spring. *Post-doc ergo,* she thought, no longer amused.

The pilot Rudy brought them down fifty yards up from the harbor where Pilar had glimpsed a dozen small boats, with no sign of anyone working them. Passing over the village, she hadn't seen a single car moving or anyone walking. What she supposed were roads were pristine snowy strips. Smoke trickled from a few chimneys.

Pilar climbed down from the aircraft and sank calf-deep in the snow. St. Leger opened a cargo hold, withdrew a metal box about a foot square. The box could accommodate a hundred blood samples. The pilot came around and pulled a larger steel box from the bay and motioned to Minh to collect other equipment. St. Leger stopped beside Pilar. "The man we're going to see is Silas Merton, local preacher. I had to fabricate a small story for him. Explaining our real concerns would have been too complicated."

What he said was probably true, she thought, but the mission itself was a lie. If St. Leger cared about the Ewell population's health, this investigation would have taken months to set up and would have had official support. St. Leger wanted something now, right now.

Silas Merton didn't match her image of a preacher, not that she had a flattering mental picture of the clergy. She had been denied communion for more than a year after her abortion. This man was fat, dressed in a tattered jacket, dirty gray sweat pants, and a stretchy cap from which spikes of thin hair escaped. He shook hands with St. Leger and watched the equipment being set up. They were in the main church hall, where the light was gray in the corners and the air was cold.

Merton said, "People got a bad taste from the last batch of visitors."

St. Leger didn't overplay his surprise. "You had previous visitors?"

"Archaeologists. Grave-robbers. We lost a good neighbor who'd never injured a soul."

"However did that happen?"

Merton looked away. No answer.

St. Leger had opened his outer coat, beneath which he wore lab whites. Pilar grimaced. He would play TV doctor, hustling joy-in-a-pill. St. Leger used his general's voice. "As my office explained, Pastor, we're investigating a variant of post-polio sequelae. A nasty business. You said you remember receiving polio shots as a child?"

"Yes, sir."

"Post-polio sequelae occurs in people who had the polio virus. They recover but decades later suffer neurological deterioration. The damage can be terrible. Unfortunately, we're finding a similar problem among people who received a vaccine that was widely dispensed in the early Fifties. The vaccine used a weakened virus instead of a dead one. Terrible thing: recipients are coming down with polio symptoms in middle age."

Merton nodded. Pilar felt the blood drain from her face. *A little fabrication?*

"Health records," St. Leger went on, "show that your neighbors got the original vaccine, so we're deeply concerned."

Nodding again, Merton said, "So you want to do a little blood test."

"That's right. The test will tell us if anyone is pre-symptomatic."

Merton looked at him slyly. "And there's a hundred dollars for volunteers?"

St. Leger clapped the pastor's shoulder. "Pastor, nobody likes needles. People might not want to roll up their sleeves even for money. We need you to help your neighbors understand our project."

Pilar thought of heading for the door. St. Leger's deception was too reminiscent of criminal things the government had done a half-century ago, brutally turning patients into test subjects. And St. Leger's methods would be seen as *her* methods.

She felt sick. Pretending she hadn't known wouldn't save her career. She should have bailed at MPC and hiked to the nearest town if she had to. She couldn't hike off this island.

She fought down her panic.

"Who's the cute one?" Merton asked.

His brow was low, his eyes slightly popped, teeth bad—she could tell that by the staleness of his breath, which enveloped her five feet away. He had the appearance of premature aging that

188 JOHN C. BOLAND

she associated with Appalachia, narrow-boned bodies not meant for long survival. That Merton's bones were cloaked in fat didn't change the type.

She remembered Henry Wald, her professor at NYU, telling a seminar that from a biological perspective, a human being was disposable after child rearing. You've done your duty by your genes, he said. Wald had been at least seventy years old. He joked that his ongoing existence was an imposition on the future, that we weren't designed to live this long. Pilar had thought Wald harsh, even in jest. *We aren't disposable*, she had thought. Looking at Merton, she had the thought again—and knew she was arguing against nature.

Pilar approached the man, extending a hand, which disappeared into the grasp of his large fingerless glove. She realized she was casting her lot with St. Leger. She didn't like it, but she was. She said, "Pastor Merton, I'm Pilar Rodriguez. I'm pleased to meet you."

"Same here, honey."

Who was she to reject a compliment even from a gray whale. She said, "May I ask if you were born on Ewell?"

"Sure you may ask." He kept her hand. "I'm umpteenth generation Eweller. End of the Merton line. Never had a woman put up with me long enough to marry. Never sired no children who'd acknowledge me."

Pilar got her hand back.

St. Leger walked back from conferring with Rudy. "What I was thinking, Pastor, was let's see how many of your neighbors want to come in for a screening. Doing it here makes more sense than all of us going door to door. Agreed?"

"A lot of people don't have phones. I'll send a boy out, make what calls I can. It's okay if I mention the hundred dollars?"

"Absolutely."

"That's per family?"

"Per person," St. Leger said, "in cash. And the foundation has authorized me to make a donation to the parish for your help."

Merton grinned. "We accept donations," he said.

The first islander arrived at the church an hour later. She was a young raw-faced woman who wore a frayed yellow sweater over a housedress. She folded the five twenty-dollar bills into a pocket, looking around with a mix of shyness and dread, then let herself be led to a metal folding chair where she sat as Minh drew blood from the inside of her elbow. As others trickled in over the next hour, Pilar glanced now and then at St. Leger. There was no sign the old man understood the significance of what she was seeing.

The islanders looked pallid and weak. Faces dull. Speech clumsy. Movements sluggish. They showed little interest in the scientists, didn't talk much to each other. If you could judge intelligence from appearances, the average IQ was in the low eighties. Pilar ran through her skimpy knowledge of medicine, looking for an explanation beyond debilitating genes. Environmental poisoning by some metal such as lead or mercury, perhaps even a metalloid such as arsenic, was one possibility. She decided to have the blood samples screened for toxic materials. If there was an environmental explanation, these people deserved to know. If the cause was genetic, knowing wouldn't help.

She would bet it was genetic. Something of the Wakelyn mess had survived and ruined these people.

She settled at the back of the hall. A feeble current of warm air blew from somewhere. It didn't warm her. It just made her more aware that she was cold. She opened her laptop. No wifi here. She shut the machine, leaned back, and watched St. Leger's test subjects. She wished she had opened up to Janecke. Wished she could talk to him now. Or Wald. Funny how she kept thinking about him. A die-hard evolutionist, still scribbling journal articles. She'd found a recent one describing the transformation of a European mouse on the island of Madeira, where in a few hundred years it had evolved from one species to six, giving up as much as half its chromosomes along the way. A lot of evolution in a small period of time.

She wondered what Wald would make of these people. Natural selection was supposed to improve a species. Well . . . not exactly. Natural selection *changed* a species according to its environment. Not quite the same as improving.

Merton was sitting in a corner, rubbing the ear that had been pressed to a telephone. Pilar walked over to him. She said, "Your neighbors must respect you. You're getting a lot of them to come in."

"They might feel different if they knew the bounty I'm getting." He eyed her. The look wasn't unfriendly. "You folks remind me of someone."

"Really?"

"You're like the archaeologists we had. Their camp is still down there, watched over by some Koreans or Chinese or something. You haven't asked what they were doing."

"You said robbing graves."

"That doesn't interest you?"

"It does. But it's not my field."

"What *is* your field?"

She sat next to him. "Epidemiology, right now, but I started out in cellular biology." She assumed neither term would mean much to him. He nodded vaguely. She said, "We're not into grave robbing. How do we remind you of them?"

"Bunch of smarty-pants digging up our past." His lopsided grin softened the words. "I fed those people quite a yarn about early islanders who were devils."

"As a religious man, do you believe in devils?"

"Tell you the truth, I'm not all that religious. But I believe there's people who can do harm. Devils is one way to describe them."

"*Ojo malo.* My mother talks about the evil eye."

"And you tell her it's nonsense."

"I don't tell my mother that *anything* she says is nonsense."

Merton grinned. "I bet you did once or twice."

"When I was very young," Pilar said. She heard something and turned. A small group of people had gathered inside, waiting their turn. A woman Pilar hadn't noticed before, stout and middle-aged, was arguing with the others. Her voice was loud.

"You know what happened to my Luther! Why are we lettin' more strangers on the island!"

Merton got to his feet and started toward her. Pilar followed.

"Now, Etta!" Merton called.

She wheeled on him. "You bastard! They shoot my Luther, and you kiss their asses!"

"These people want to help us, Etta. They had nothing to do with Luther."

Rudy was coming up behind the woman, and Pilar didn't like his expression. She moved to block him. His eyes were no darker than his skin, not at all impenetrable. That made it worse. She saw something deep down in them that stopped her.

"Etta?"

The voice came from the doorway. A woman stood there, just out of the snowfall, wearing a heavy tweed cape, dark trousers, hide boots. She looked both mature and youthful at the same time, which made it impossible to guess her age. Her skin was smooth. Eyes pale and liquid. She was nervous, but her voice was soft.

"Etta?"

Etta looked at her.

"Etta, why don't you come with me, dear? We'll have some tea." She glanced at Pilar, who was close. "I'm sorry. Etta's been upset."

"That's why I didn't call her," Merton said.

St. Leger had closed the distance. He was frowning, mouth open—surprised and disbelieving as he stared at the woman in the doorway. He spoke to Merton. "Pastor, please introduce us."

Merton nodded. "Sure, sure. Miz Wood, this is Dr. St. Leger, who's doing research involving polio. This is Miz Sydney Wood, our artist-in-residence."

"I'm pleased to meet you," said St. Leger. His gaze moved across the woman's face. His eyes were glassy with excitement. "Would you like to be tested? Post-polio syndrome might be present here." He made it sound infectious.

"It wouldn't affect me," she said. "I'm familiar with the illness, but I was never vaccinated."

"Your parents took quite a chance."

"No. Disease doesn't like our family. It was a pleasure meeting you. I'll take Etta home and we'll have tea and honey."

Beside her, the island woman was docile. Pilar watched in amazement.

Where had all the anger gone?

35

"HOW LONG HAS SYDNEY WOOD LIVED ON EWELL?" ST. LEGER asked Merton.

Merton rubbed his cheek. "It seems about a year."

"She's an artist?"

"Paints anyone who'll sit still. Me included. Would you folks care to break for lunch? I don't have much, but we can make do."

"Thank you, Pastor, but we've brought food. I hope you'll join us."

The pilot went out to the helicopter and returned with two stainless steel boxes that contained hot food. They set up chairs at the table where Minh had been working.

Pilar ate quickly, seated across from Merton.

"Have you been to the archaeological site," she asked him.

"Couple times. There's a stone well ten or fifteen feet deep. The coffins were at the bottom." He raised a sparse eyebrow. "You could build a lot of tales around that. If we had more ambition here, I suppose we'd have a tourist attraction."

"How many people were buried there?"

"Three coffins," he said, and his voice trailed off. "One of the sheriff's people says there were only two bodies. Don't know if that makes the story better. I could tell folks we had three and one got loose."

A few islanders came in over the next hour. Minh bound their arms, drew vials of blood. Rudy handed out twenty-dollar bills. A couple of the islanders asked questions, one stout bearded man pretended to faint, but mostly they showed no curiosity. They struggled into their heavy coats, pulled down woolen caps, and left quietly. St. Leger sat with his long limbs bent, head tilted back, his mind seemingly far away.

Pilar asked Merton for directions to the ladies room. He pointed her deeper into the building, which was a warren of small rooms. The toilet almost made her gag. She used it anyway, washed in a sink that could have bathed Jesus's feet. Then she got out her phone. The signal was weak. She stared at the screen. Who was she going to call? Janecke? Tell him she was up to her neck in trouble? If she had been fired at Cold Spring, Janecke might not care what trouble she was in.

She wished she had talked more to the archaeologists. Gotten more on Margaret Wakelyn. She didn't have a number for any of them. They might be as overpaid—as bought off—as she was. She thought about the big guy, Becker, who had tried his Prussian charm on her. Proud of his studliness, she thought and smiled. She sort of liked that.

She opened the bathroom door.

Two loud *booms* froze her in place.

A moment later, two sharp *cracks*.

Gunshots. Inside. Close.

36

HELEN CALDER WAS WALKING TOWARD THE ELEVATOR OF the downtown Hyatt when her phone went off and Tim Berman's calm voice said, "If you're at the office, I'm too late."

"What are you talking about?"

"Where are you?" His calm sounded fragile.

"I'm in Baltimore, honey, shacked up with a married man. What's 'too late'?"

"I came back to the office. Bad move. There are a couple of sick people on the sixth floor of Building C. Our security guys think we may have been the target of a bio attack. How does the MRSA in Baltimore present?"

She felt ice on her back.

She said, "Rash, fever, sores—" She wet her lips. She had stopped walking. "Kidney, liver, pancreatic failure, sometimes flesh necrosis . . ."

"Don't come back."

"Where are you?"

"Building B. We don't have any sign of contagion here, but security has locked down the whole complex."

Somebody pushed past Helen with an annoyed grunt. She didn't notice. She stared at the pattern in the carpet. It was incomprehensible. Ugly beyond reason. She stared. If there was a chance she was infected, she had to put herself into quarantine. Herself and Kushner. But they had been out of the office since the previous afternoon. So how could they be infected by anything at headquarters? The heat she felt in her face wasn't from a pathogen. It was from an almost uncontrolled anger.

Staley, she thought.

"Agent Calder?"

"Yes, Tim."

"I've got to get off the line. Security wonders who I'm talking to."

"Okay," she said, but he was gone.

She stood immobile. Her feet had been on a mission. What was it? The phone in her hand buzzed.

Her section chief, Phil Marburg, spoke fast. "We've got two people up here with rashes. I'm one of them." He was trying to sound hearty to avoid sounding afraid. "This thing seems pretty contagious. Did you enter Pogorovich's lab?"

"No, sir."

"That's good. While I'm out of commission, you're in charge of the department."

"Yes, sir."

"Report directly to Dr. Starns." Starns was director of the National Institutes of Science.

Helen heard a sharp intake of breath. In the background were loud voices. A woman began screaming. Marburg said, "Got to go."

She saw Kushner moving away from the registration desk. In the garage, he had pulled a small overnight bag from the trunk of his car. Kushner, at least, would use his own tooth brush tonight. She intercepted him. "You'd better call home and tell your wife you're okay. Headquarters is under quarantine. It sounds like MRSA."

Kushner's ruddy face lost color. "How—?"

She moved toward the elevators, forcing him to hurry.

He said, "Have you talked to the chief?"

"Phil is infected. Several people on the floor are sick."

As they got off the elevator, she checked her watch. "Don't unpack. We may be leaving. I'll know in half an hour." She entered her room, didn't bother disturbing the drapes or the air-conditioning. She pulled a chair away from its small desk, kicked off her shoes, stretched her feet onto the bed as she started working through the numbers programmed into her phone. The first call was to the CDC officer, Voight.

"Give me an opinion. You said this wasn't typical hospital staph."

Voight sounded like she welcomed the interruption. "That's a misnomer. There's no such thing as typical staph anymore. We've identified more than a hundred varieties. It reproduces every twenty minutes, and each time there's a chance of mutation. That's tens of billions of individual organisms reproducing seventy-two times a day. The attrition is high or this stuff would cover the earth." Her voice was puffy, the sound of a person walking briskly. "The planet would look like one big petri dish, Calder. Think about that."

"I'm thinking about something else. How unusual is this variety?"

"It puts out PVL—that's Panton-Valentine leukocidin, a toxin that kills white blood cells. That's why it gets ahead of the body so fast."

"Could it have been bred in a lab?"

"You mean deliberately? What a thought. Sure it could've. Do you have information?"

"I'll get back to you," Calder said.

The next question was whether NIS was in such an uproar that the legal department had shut down. She tried a couple of the litigators she had dealt with, first on their office lines then on their cells. A woman she knew answered with aircraft noise in the background.

"Where are you?" Helen demanded.

"Outdoors in Addison's SUV."

"On a runway?"

"Just about. We couldn't get back into the office after court.

We're getting some civilians dumped out of suites at the Dulles Marriott. The department is going to set up shop there. The top guy will be at the Willard. Actually, we're the only law department people who aren't in quarantine. You know what's going on?"

"Some of it. How many people are sick?"

"Five, six—I don't know." The woman's voice dropped. "Maybe more because Marburg's assistant went home a couple hours ago. We're pulling up at the hotel—"

"Tell them it's MRSA," Helen said. "Just like Baltimore."

"How do you know?"

"That's the next thing. I want us to get a no-knock warrant to take down the headquarters of a thing called the St. Leger Foundation. I'll direct the raid, but we'll want FBI and Fairfax support. The place may be hardened. A hundred agents, airborne capability."

"What the hell are you talking about?"

"There's a helicopter pad on the roof. We'll want to seize control of that before anything else."

"Slow down. If the FBI is involved, they're not going to let you lead a raid. And we're going to need a lot more information to get a warrant, never mind recruit the Bureau. If we do this under the Patriot Act, we'll need Homeland Security to sign off. The will require a formal submission through the director—"

Helen cut her off. "We've got what we need, honey. My confidential informant at Canton Oncology died of MRSA complications this afternoon. The symptoms at HQ are identical. My CDC contact says this MRSA strain could have been manufactured in a lab. The only link between Canton Oncology and NIS is my investigation of the St. Leger Foundation. Get working on the warrant. It should cover biological and medical research material, physical and electronic documents relating to genetic research, bank records related to funding of genetic research, anything involving pathogens. I'll email you a draft affidavit in the next half-hour. You've got my cell number."

She hung up. The warrant terms were broad enough that she could reach an arm down Staley's throat if she wanted to. She opened her computer, took down an affidavit template and began filling in details. Stephan Pogorovich was the common factor. She described his suppositions and conjectures as if they were proven fact. *"Illegal cloning, in violation of the Omnibus Medical Research Advancement Act . . ."*

After she emailed the affidavit to the NIS attorney, she phoned Kushner, told him they would be staying until she heard back from Legal.

"I've been watching TV," he said. "It's on CNN and Fox."

"What are they saying?"

"Research lab had an accident. I'm having lunch sent up. Do you want some?"

"No." Anything she ate wouldn't stay down.

She clicked off the phone and turned on the television. A local station was showing the old warehouse neighborhood from a helicopter. Streets were choked with official vehicles. She didn't mind a little alarm, if it overcame the qualms of judges and the FBI. The scene switched to Bayview Medical, where a reporter was interviewing a CDC officer outside a taped barrier. The CDC man was wearing civilian clothing, not biohazard gear. He projected confidence. "We've had a few patients, but no more are coming in. Your viewers should understand this is a common hospital infection. Our responders have it contained. There's no cause for panic."

"Ask him if it's a new strain," Helen whispered as if they could hear her.

"That's good news, then," the reporter said. She paused as she listened to her earpiece, then thrust her microphone out. "There's a report that a government office in Washington is under quarantine. Are the events related?"

The CDC man turned patronizing. "You and I both know it's premature to speculate."

Helen switched off. She had threatened Staley. Threatened the St. Leger Foundation. That was the starting point. And they had responded. Knowing that somebody thought she was worth killing made her feel light-hearted, almost girlish, and not the least bit intimidated.

37

Pilar leaned into the hallway, listening.

She moved silently. Two or three gloomy rooms, then a closet-sized space that had a daybed and a footstool and smelled musty. How many rooms had she passed through to reach the bathroom? She stopped and listened.

Loud voices.

She didn't think she wanted to go toward them.

There was a door to her right. She pressed a hand against the wood, felt coldness seeping through that told her it led outside. She could get away from whoever had fired the shots. But that meant abandoning her coat, gloves and stocking cap, which she'd left with her equipment.

A deeper boom rattled the building. Dust sifted from the ceiling. She didn't think it had been a gunshot.

She crossed a small bare floor and looked out in the main hall.

The church's double front doors were wide open. A man sat against the wall near the doors, legs outstretched, head bent.

From his beard and green parka, she thought he was the man who had pretended to faint a while ago. The front of his parka was shiny with blood.

Another figure was on the floor, closer. She realized it was Minh and abandoned caution, running to him, stopping only as she saw the ruin of his chest.

There was no one else in the hall.

She followed the sound of voices. She reached the doorway, and a wave of heat struck her face. The helicopter they had arrived in was burning, flames and oily black smoke twisting into the thick air. Rudy stood near the fire, a handgun sweeping the surrounding area, which was empty. Silas Merton, his face twisted with rage, stared at the pilot.

St. Leger noticed her.

"Could you take a look at Minh?" St. Leger suggested. "Perhaps first aid?"

"He's dead."

"A shame," he said.

"What happened?"

"One of our patients came back with a shotgun. He would have killed all of us if Rudy hadn't been alert. Someone else poured gasoline on our aircraft." He turned away from her. "Why don't you go inside, Dr. Rodriguez. Freezing won't do you any good."

"How are we going to leave?"

"We don't need to, not immediately."

Rudy was coming back, the handgun out of sight, a satellite phone to his ear. Pilar followed Merton, who entered the church and knelt beside the man in the bloody parka. Beside them lay a single-barrel shotgun. Merton's lips moved soundlessly.

There was nothing she could do.

Pulling on her coat and hat, she paused beside Louis Minh. There were three red splotches on his chest, where the heavy shot from the long gun had penetrated. The business of dying had drained his face of experience. Bent beside him, she watched from under the table as St. Leger and his pilot conferred near the open doors.

Rudy lifted the shotgun and pumped out two cartridges that he caught in midair. He reloaded the gun and handed it to St. Leger.

Pilar slipped around the corner, retraced her steps deeper into the building, finally running until she reached the tiny room with the door that felt cold. She stopped and held her breath. There was no sound of pursuit. No reason for them to come after her. Except that the blood-collection scheme had blown up in their faces and two men were dead.

She could find a safe place in the village, phone the police, and wait for help. In the furor over the shootings, maybe nobody would pay much attention to her role. Fat chance of that. Her mother was going to see her daughter in handcuffs and die of shame. Pilar opened to door onto a small, snow-covered porch that lay in deep afternoon shadow. The fire was out of sight behind the church, but greasy black soot was floating over the building and falling onto the snow. She took two steps off the porch, slipped on hidden ice and fell jarringly. She got up, breathing hard. There were houses ahead. Boats to her left. She waded ahead through ankle-deep snow, reached an area where the footing was better, and began running.

She saw no sign of anyone.

Rudy pulled the preacher up by the shirt front, told St. Leger, "He set us up."

"Don't be naïve. Destiny, my savage friend, set us up. Your people believe in destiny, don't they?"

Rudy didn't know who the old man meant by "his people" or what most of them believed in. His Apache parents had believed in selling trinkets to tourists along Highway 73. His sister had believed in selling six-dollar blow jobs to Air Force men near Glendale. Rudy Little Horse believed in computer games. He let the part about being a savage pass.

Rudy nodded at the man he had killed. "Why did he come back?"

St. Leger treated the question as rhetorical—or presumptuous, as it wasn't his job to provide insights to the Indian—and didn't answer. He had studied the archaeologists' reports. One similarity stood out in the attacks on the Sprague woman and Louis Minh. Neither assassin had seemed to care about self-preservation. After killing Minh, the man with the shotgun hadn't even turned to flee before Rudy cut him down.

St. Leger gestured, and the pilot lowered Merton. St. Leger

crouched stiffly beside the preacher. "Brother Merton, was your neighbor a violent man?"

"Neither of them was."

"Neither?"

"Luther either."

St. Leger looked away from the preacher and studied the face of the dead islander. Low brow, narrow-set eyes, misshapen teeth. The poor fellow would have been at the top of his game slinging a towel at a car wash.

What would Benoit have thought of this?

The woman who called herself Sydney Wood stood beside the curtained window of her front door, which gave an unobstructed view of the burning helicopter. This shouldn't be happening. It was out of control. . . .

She knew some things without seeing them. Inside the church there had been death. She didn't know who had died—only that the low babble of islanders' minds had been reduced by one small, meaningless presence. She could tell that her friend Silas was still alive, and she was glad.

She turned her attention to her visitor. Slumped on a worn sofa, Etta Michaels wasn't quite asleep, but she was subdued and no longer a bother.

Poor Etta. Like a dog that had lost its mate, she should be put down, humanely. The woman who called herself Sydney Wood spoke softly. "Close your eyes, Etta. Close your eyes and go to sleep. It's all right. You can stop worrying. Just rest."

Things were out of control, and they were going to get worse. She had sensed the intruding presence. Terribly old. It had come home, like a wayward beast. . . .

"Etta, you can stop breathing."

She could feel the beast's power in the air, humming like a current. She didn't fear it. She was strong, and she was wise. She had known its like before.

It had no compassion. But neither had the woman who called herself Sydney Wood.

She glanced down at the islander woman. Etta had stopped breathing.

38

PILAR RAN TOWARD THE HARBOR.

She went down an unplowed path between garages and a fenced warehouse yard. Battered workboats were wintering at concrete piers where a couple of tracks had been shoveled through mounded snow. Several buildings across from the water, with steel drums and fishing gear stacked in front, seemed to promise more immediate shelter. She climbed the steps to the nearest, which had a hand-drawn window sign saying HINES OYSTERS. She could see a light inside and an angular section of pressed metal ceiling. She kicked a path to the door and went in. A man in a plaid shirt and corduroys sat on the floor just inside, knees at his chest, fists pressing his temples. He didn't look up when cold air whipped his hair. Pilar stopped.

"Mister," she said.

His shoulders moved but he didn't raise his head.

There were parts of the room she couldn't see: behind islands of waist-high barrels, past a counter that supported a napkin holder and bottles. A mix of chairs—aluminum and vinyl and old ladderbacks—leaned against tables. It looked like a seafood restaurant that might draw a tourist or two in summer.

Attracted by motion, she glanced back. The man was hugging his knees, rocking.

She used her hip to shut the door.

Better the devil you don't know.

"Mister."

He stopped moving.

"I need help," Pilar said.

He rocked sideways, twisted toward her, and she saw a bloodshot brown eye peeking past his arm.

"Are you hurt?" Pilar said.

The eye closed. The shoulders rose as he drew a breath. She moved closer and saw more of his face. Broken capillaries colored the cheeks. A ragged mustache overhung bleeding lips. The lips didn't look chapped, exactly.

. . . Red spittle trailed from a corner of his mouth. His teeth were locked so tight his jaw trembled. The tiniest voice crept out. "He's in my head. . . ."

He buried his face. She saw the jaw flexing. He was chewing his lips.

"Who's in your head?"

"Does God ever scream when he talks to you? He never talked to me before. Now he tells me burn it, burn it, burn it. Everything. Myself, the village. Maybe he's really the devil. He's a fooler, ain't he?" The nearer hand crept from his temple, clawed absently down his cheek leaving red tracks. The hand disappeared, and Pilar heard sucking as he cleaned the fingers.

She scanned the room for a weapon. There were pans stacked behind the counter, a greasy dark cube sprouting knife handles . . . The man rolled onto his side and she jumped, but he was pulling his knees to his chin, eyes squeezed tight. Not a threat.

She backtracked to the door, turned the lock under the doorknob. She found a wall switch that darkened the ceiling light. She moved around the dim room, guided by a little daylight. In a drawer behind the counter she discovered a flashlight with a strong beam, stuffed it in her pocket. Grappling in the same pocket, she searched for her phone. If there was a signal, she would call the police. . . .

Until they arrived, she would huddle here at Hines Oysters.

She rummaged in her other pockets. The phone was gone. She must have lost it when she fell. She walked to the back of the shop, pulled aside a plastic window covering. Frost whitened the glass. She scraped clear a small patch near the bottom of the sash, stooped and peeked out. She couldn't quite see the way she had come. A small building was behind this one, blocking part of the view. Then there was a fenced lot. She could see a little past the building, toward the church. Even if she retraced her steps, she probably wouldn't find the phone.

She focused on the room. There was a payphone on a wall, half-hidden by an apron. She went over, lifted the receiver and heard silence. The store's cash box was on the counter. She pilfered two quarters, dropped them in the coin slot, rattled the hook. *Nada.*

She searched the shop, opening drawers, aiming the flashlight at shelves, anywhere someone might tuck a cell phone. She checked a bathroom and a storeroom. Then she went back to the man, handled him gently as she patted his clothes. Thinking. At best, the island's population was degenerate, Etta Michaels, the man in the parka, this man. . . . Insanity could run through them like a family curse.

She didn't find a phone on the man. He was withdrawing into silence.

Pilar returned to the rear window. Pressing her forehead to the frost, she could see a sliver of the area where she had fallen. The afternoon light was blue and fading, providing so little clarity that she almost missed the motionless shape. Not a tree. Not a snowman. It was obscured by a utility pole, immobile.

She took a second look at every shadow. There was a second human shape beside a tree. She couldn't tell for sure which direction either person was looking. She had the uncanny sense they were looking at *her.*

Stationary, like sentinels.

Slowly, she pulled herself below the window level. With the sun heading down, the air temperature was dropping. They should be dancing in circles to keep warm.

She was making assumptions on flimsy evidence. She didn't *know* that they were watchers. All she had seen were two bundled shapes standing in the cold, *as if* they might be watching. They might have been drawn by the helicopter fire. They might have heard gunshots. They might have phoned each other.

Or God might be inside their heads.

Even with a breeze disturbing her tracks, she had left a trail anyone could follow. She shivered.

The man on the floor had not moved since adopting the fetal-retreat posture. She approached him cautiously. His breath trembled. As she knelt, his head turned, but his eyes remained shut.

"It's not quite so loud now," he said.

"I've got to go," Pilar said. "I'll send help."

"I fear the voice wasn't God."

"Probably not."

And she wondered about that. A delusional person should be pretty sure who he was hearing.

She stepped away from him, stood near the door. Stayed still, listening. There was a small whistle of wind in the eaves. Nothing else. Her target, she decided, would be the nearest boat. If there was a working radio, she would figure it out. She unlocked the door, twisted the knob and eased through the half-open doorway.

She heard the scrape of a boot on ice.

Thick arms wrapped around her. Wet breath scented with chewing gum splashed her cheek.

She threw herself against the railing, twisting, digging an elbow backward. There was a squeal, and her attacker let go. Pilar saw a small pink face of indeterminate sex. She swung a gloved fist into the pink nose. The attacker pitched backward.

Pilar leapt the porch railing, evading a man who had run to the bottom of the steps. The pier and the boats were out unless she wanted to be trapped there. Or to try swimming in ice water. If she could get out of this dead end, she might find a house for refuge. She ran past the neighboring warehouse, hearing heavy feet behind her. She hurled herself into a narrow cut between buildings. Then stopped. Twenty feet ahead, snow had drifted almost six feet high. It blocked the way. She spun, but her pursuer was already there, closing off retreat. He had a cherry-red face, blue watch cap, quilted jacket, bare hands. He was at least six feet tall. She wished she had gotten a knife from the oyster shop.

She turned and tried to scale the drift. Even with a running start, she came to a stop after ten feet, caught thigh-deep in powdery snow. She tried to push forward. And fell. Her arms plunged up to her shoulders. Her face hit the numbing coldness.

She heard *whump-whump* and glimpsed the man descending on her.

Hands clutched her shoulders, pushed her down.

She ordered her legs to kick. They barely moved.

A hand pressed the back of her head. She couldn't move, she couldn't hear. Against her eyelids, red bolts lanced through a thickening blackness.

His weight crushed her. Hundreds of pounds.

She tried to scream and snow filled her mouth.

39

RUDY CAME BACK FROM SEARCHING THE CHURCH FOR Rodriguez. He told St. Leger, "She's gone, or in hiding."

"So much for your tracking skills, Mr. Little Horse." St. Leger casually inspected the shotgun. "I want to talk to the other woman. Miss Wood." He raised an eyebrow at the pilot. "Ask Pastor Merton where we can find her."

Eighty-nine years had stuffed Gus St. Leger's memory with faces, some detested from the start, a few admired, several loved for a while, one loved forever. Most of the images were blurry. St. Leger closed his eyes. The image of one person remained clear. It had taken a while for that face to occur to him, because it was so illogical.

He compared the memory to the face of the woman who had stood in front of him two hours ago. The resemblance wasn't perfect, but it was strong. And inexplicable. He crossed the room, following Rudy, and stood beside Merton. The pastor's face had been beaten bloody.

"He says she's at the top of the street," the pilot said.

"Thank you, Pastor. Tell me what you know about her."

Snuffling blood, Merton said, "Just what I told you."

"Tell me again."

"She's an artist on sabbatical. A painter. Been here about a year."

There was a singsong tone in Merton's voice. St. Leger frowned. "What else?"

Merton looked up blankly. "I don't know anything else."

St. Leger almost believed him.

Evening was coming. Rudy studied the scrambled snow around the church. It showed jumbled footprints of forty-eight islanders who had come to be tested, plus the tracks of the people with St. Leger, and—moving away together—the trail left by the crazy woman and Sydney Wood.

"The pastor told the truth," Rudy said. "Two women went this way."

He led the way up the gentle grade toward the outermost line of houses. A number of buildings were clearly vacant, with buckled porches and boarded windows. One stood wide open, windows and doors gone.

St. Leger followed, thinking. He knew the term "devolution" was meaningless, a contradiction in terms. If an organism changed, whatever the nature of the change, it would be adapting to its environment, wouldn't it? Evolving to fit a niche? Adaptation didn't make value judgments such as "improved." It only adjusted a species to circumstances. Dumbed it down if necessary?

What was he seeing here?

If we look back far enough, he thought, *would we find Wakelyn-type anomalies in primitive man?*

St. Leger closed the distance with Rudy.

He scanned the houses that stood at the edge of a thinly wooded area. Individual trees were blurred by the approaching dusk. The houses must have belonged to the island's Brahmins, when it had any. They were two stories, with millwork on porches; signs of shutters on the wide siding; a decorative inset on what remained of a chimney.

"Does it bother you that people didn't come out to watch the fire," St. Leger asked.

"Not much bothers me," the pilot said. "But as a point of information, I noticed."

St. Leger chuckled. *You're not such a savage*, he thought. *At least not a "primitive" savage.*

St. Leger had already seen the furrow that shuffling feet had cut through the snow toward a porch.

"You want me to go in and quiet the woman down?" Rudy asked.

"No. Wait here."

St. Leger strode onto the porch. He turned the shotgun, swung it underhand, smashing the stock under the doorknob.

The door opened.

He stepped into the dimness, and sensed her waiting.

He was slack-jawed and weaponless five minutes later when he came out and beckoned Rudy.

"Go keep Merton quiet," he told the Indian. "I'm going to be a while."

St. Leger walked back into the house. He hadn't told anyone whom the woman resembled. He hadn't let himself know—really know.

The resemblance had to be a coincidence.

His mother had died eighty years ago.

Rudy Little Horse stopped walking halfway down the hill, literally in his tracks.

He looked back at the houses. He lacked a sense of mystery, but he thought the woods behind them looked evil. Snow swirled lightly, and in the fading light it was easy to mistake the motion of air for substance, especially at the edge of houses where something could be moving mostly out of sight.

The church was no more than fifty yards ahead. He couldn't bring himself to think of it as a refuge. He didn't need a refuge. He was stuck with crazy white people outdoors or in. But he could look forward to getting out of the cold, now that the wind was picking up.

He heard a voice on the wind.

Specks of snow, hard as grains of sand, stung his eyes.

He blinked, and tears froze on his cheeks. He hadn't meant to stop walking.

The voice on the wind was speaking so softly he had to hold his breath to listen.

It was whispering about blood.

He told his feet to move. When he got to the church, he would see if the preacher had a bottle of whiskey.

Something fluttered across the snow.

He glimpsed it from a corner of his eye. Fifty feet to the left, a scuttling shadow, dark and shaggy. Bigger than a wolf, smaller than a bear. The long-armed shamble of an ape.

He laughed soundlessly. These people *were* apes. Now they were running around acting the part.

Something hit him from behind, knocking him into the snow. As he rolled onto his side, he glimpsed the figure scampering away. He pulled his gun and fired.

The next attack came from his blind side. He felt a jolt, not too bad. Numbness in his shoulder. Numbness in the arm. Nothing painful. Another blow came, not nearly as surprising as the first, on the side of his neck. He tried to turn, but his body wouldn't respond. He had to drop his gun, which somehow didn't matter, to reach across his body and feel the knife handle protruding from his neck. *Stuck me like a bull.* A shadow swept past. It hung in the darkness, then moved in deliberately. The face that took shape in front of him wasn't apelike. The dull, sallow features looked slightly familiar—perhaps one of the men who had come to trade blood for money . . . except that Rudy Little Horse could see very little.

Amateurs fooled me.

There was a stunning blow to the back of his neck. He felt himself spinning forward, falling, rolling ear over ear, while a separate, distant part of him remained kneeling in the snow.

40

HELEN CALDER HAD NEVER MET THE DIRECTOR OF THE National Institutes of Science face to face. This was as close as she expected to come. She was seeing Carsten Starns over an Internet link from his command post at the Willard InterContinental Hotel near the White House. He was long-faced, with round cheeks and a lick of cornsilk hair dangling across his forehead. He had been governor of Oklahoma twice, a retired obstetrician who declared every newborn was God's handiwork and therefore perfect. His political platform had called for banning genetic engineering and imposing capital punishment on abortionists. Those positions had made Carsten Starns a shoo-in for the President's choice to run NIS.

"Agent Calder, I'm happy to put a face to the legend." Starns spoke graciously—gallantly, he thought, given that Calder's face could blind a toad. "I knew Phil Marburg personally, and I'm damned angry about his loss. Now. What can you tell us about the St. Leger Foundation?"

Helen described the foundation's secret accounts—actually she had identified only one—and her investigation of Pogorovich's allegations. Illegal cloning, that was the one that would get Starns's back up.

He listened until she was finished. "You don't have evidence that this lethal virus was planted?"

Helen stopped herself from correcting him that MRSA was bacterial not viral.

"We have circumstantial evidence, sir," she said. "It's theoretically possible that Dr. Pogorovich was working with MRSA and inadvertently transmitted it to our headquarters. But I don't believe that, and neither does CDC. Pogorovich didn't have the most basic precautions at his lab for dealing with pathogens. CDC hasn't found any documentation that he was aware of MRSA in his lab. Finally, there's that letter. Its only function was to carry MRSA into my office. Our people have read the text. It said nothing. He had no reason to send it."

Starns spoke to someone out of camera range. "That is the opinion here as well. The letter's contamination level was too high to be accidental. If you could stay with us, I'm going to have Judge Ramsey patched in. Tell her what you've told me."

Helen made her presentation to the judge from the U.S. District Court for Northern Virginia, who immediately authorized a broad warrant for a search of the St. Leger Foundation headquarters.

Helen tried not to let rage blind her. But she kept imagining her lover Judy opening an innocent piece of mail at home. Anger curdled in her belly.

While she waited for Kushner to get himself together, she watched CNN. The reporter at the scene in Baltimore had withdrawn a mile from Bayview Medical, and the mayor was no longer in front of cameras. The reporter was tripping on his own doubletalk. But the news was clear.

The infection wasn't contained.

It was loose.

□□□

Evening.

David uploaded his notes on the Ewell excavation to Charl's computer. She could do with them whatever she and Noel decided. He had left out all opinion, limiting himself to what he had observed directly about the crypt and its contents. He glanced into the other office. They were working in a two-room suite provided by Staley, who seemed to want the archaeologists out from under foot while he dealt with something else—*the treacherous Swiss*, David thought with contempt.

He watched Charl, moving back and forth in the next office, coffee in hand. Her physical recovery was extraordinary. Her bandage was off. Across her temple a long faint scar was receding into healthy new flesh. The deep bruising around the wound had all but vanished.

He stood in the doorway. She looked about twenty-five years old. His heart stuttered at each sight of her, as if he had come round a corner and been pleasantly shocked. A sort of *Aha! Look at that!* moment. It made it hard to concentrate on business.

"I wish I had the girl's DNA report," David said.

Charl looked up from a table littered with CT scans. "What would you do with it?"

"Make a guess at what Staley's up to."

"What would it tell you?"

"Not much, but I'm guessing now with even less."

"So you'd have more data to confuse yourself with."

"That's how I do it. Bury myself in facts and take a shot in the dark." He hadn't told her about Becker's wild guess. It had seemed nutty. Not impossible, just a little paranoid. But then he had remembered that disease carriers had been used against enemies in the past—plague victims hurled over the walls of besieged cities, infected livestock set loose by Hittite schemers.

"I know Staley is a liar," David said. "The question is what kind."

"Supercilious?"

"A little."

"Graceful?"

"As a dancer."

"Habitual?"

"We don't have enough data."

"That old problem."

Loren Fane came in, didn't speak to either of them. There was a small TV screen on the wall. He turned it on, stood back.

They looked.

A chaotic scene. People jostling against a police barricade. It could have been a rock concert, except people outside the barricade wore biohazard suits. Before David could make sense of it, the picture was replaced by an airborne shot of a multilane highway blocked by stalled cars.

"It's been going on for more than an hour," Fane said. "Parts of Baltimore are quarantined. The second shot is on Dulles Access Road."

"What's it about?" David said. He watched a crawler at the bottom of the screen, read "MRSA" and something about panic.

"The Dulles scene is at NIS headquarters," Fane said. "They've had an outbreak of methicillin-resistant staph, MRSA for short."

"The hospital illness," Charl said.

"Yeah, well," said Fane. "One of the Baltimore locations is a lab run by a Mr. Pogorovich. Remember the name? The NIS person asked about him. So what's all this got to do with our friendly, lying hosts? I tell myself not to jump to conclusions. Then I think, 'Oh, why not?' You can put NIS, Pogorovich, MRSA and St. Leger Foundation together in a single sentence. But what should the sentence say?"

David shook his head.

Charl asked Fane, "Do you think you know?"

"I was counting on you. Your husband has the connections here."

She turned back to the screen. There was a subdued report that David missed.

Charl came over to him. "You should have left when you could. They say the airports are closed."

"Where's Noel?"

"With Paolo. They're taking more pictures."

"I think we should pack our gear."

"Where would we go?"

The crowds in Baltimore looked like a mob, frightened and ready to break loose. "Maybe nowhere. But let's get ready." He turned to Fane. "Have you heard St. Leger mentioned on the broadcasts?"

"No. But I was wandering around downstairs, chatting up the guards. This place has a lot of guards. One of them points outside. There's a van inside the grounds. No markings."

"TV?"

"She didn't think so."

Not the evil Swiss.

"I'm going to try to reach the NIS agent," David said. "Let's get Noel and Paolo and meet back here in fifteen minutes. Then we decide what to do."

The difficult part would be getting Noel Sprague to leave. He wouldn't want to turn his back on his benefactor, run away on hunch and rumor, drop the project midstream. The research could be resumed later, but Sprague wouldn't see it that way.

If Sprague he didn't go, Charl wouldn't.

And if she didn't go . . .

David didn't bother to finish the thought. He knew he would be here too.

He tried phoning Calder as he took an elevator to the cold room level. All he heard was a persistent bleat. Fane would love it. Either the nearest towers were down, or the signal was being suppressed. He found Sprague and Paolo examining images of the dead girl. He told them enough about the MRSA outbreak to get them downstairs for a pow-wow.

When they reached the office suite, Fane was gone.

"Where's Loren," Sprague asked his wife.

"He got upset when his phone wouldn't work. He went to pack."

Sprague gave a sigh designed to sound patient. "I don't understand what any of this has to do with Roger or the foundation."

"Or NIS?" said Becker. "For starters, the explanation Staley gave us is crap."

"It doesn't imply a connection—"

"Why the rush job on Ewell? Why the rush to sequence the Wakelyn genes?"

Sprague showed his disappointment in a patronizing smile at Becker. "Well, Paolo, tell us. What's that have to do with pathogens or NIS?"

"If you're playing with pathogens, why not have more than one? People were sick on Ewell. Maybe Staley wants to replicate a three-hundred-year-old illness. A viral or bacterial strain that old—we would have lost our immunity against it. If they recovered a few DNA strands, amplified them, spliced in more aggressive genes . . ."

Silently, David, who knew how Becker thought, supplied the rest. You could give your army immunity and unleash an old, stepped-up bacterial strain on an enemy. Or immunize your entire population, if you cared that much about them.

Sprague rubbed his beard. "I know you're sincere, Paolo, but what you're saying is paranoid. Our government wouldn't be involved in anything like that. And Roger certainly wouldn't be."

David felt his spirits fall. They could debate with Sprague for an hour. The man would resist, rebut, mock. When you came down to it, they had no evidence.

He caught Charl's glance. She was worried.

There was a young woman's face on the television. "It spreads fast," she said. "We're advising people to remain at home. That's the safest place. To facilitate that, mass transit has been suspended."

Questioner: "Are you admitting patients?"

"At the moment, we aren't. We're recommending that people who feel ill isolate themselves. Fluids are important, and bed rest."

David felt the hair on his neck rise.

Triage had begun.

Sprague turned from half-watching the interview. "We may be better off right here, don't you think?"

He looked directly at Becker, met a grim, angry stare.

Sprague said, "But, of course, if one of us wants to go . . ."

His glance traveled to David. It was an empty flourish. They both knew he was staying.

41

IN HIS OFFICE, WITH THE DOORS LOCKED AND THE MONITOR audio turned off, Geronimo Bix worked the slide of a compact .45-caliber pistol, chambering a round. He set the safety and dropped the pistol into his suitcoat pocket. A nine-shot .32 was strapped in a holster at his back. He didn't know what had gone wrong. The lab that had developed the MRSA was legitimate, financed by a prestigious teaching hospital. The pathogens it cultivated for research would have been grown from hospital specimens. Such strains were potent, and mortality from them had been climbing for years. But nothing in a hospital had ever moved like this. Pogorovich should have died quietly three or four days after Bix's visit—Calder a few days later. If they had strong constitutions it was possible neither would have died. Their months of recovery would have served his purpose almost as well as their deaths.

So what had happened?

Forty minutes ago, watching the chaos filmed by news

helicopters circling the headquarters of the National Institutes of Science, Bix had considered the possibility he was seeing a propaganda stunt. But if it had been that, things would have been under control by now. That would have been the whole point, the government mastering a crisis. This chaos was real.

He glanced at the security screens. They were being actively monitored by two young staff people one floor below. But he looked anyway, saw nothing had changed, the van was still there, trying to eavesdrop on his every trip to the can. There would be more of them before long. Once it started, trouble came in a rush. You didn't want to step in front of it. But you might deflect it a little. He turned back to his desk, where a laptop was transferring his savings from a suburban Washington bank to an HSBC office in Panama. He bore more than a passing resemblance to Panama's former dictator, who also was short and pock-marked, heavy-lipped and thick-chested. He never expected to visit Panama, so he didn't bother to worry if the likeness would be a liability.

He rode an elevator down to the second garage, took a black Mercedes and drove up the ramp out of the garage, along the driveway where the surveillance van squatted. There was nothing to be done about the fact they would note the departure. The question was whether he would be followed. As he rounded the congested Beltway twenty minutes later, he was satisfied that nobody had stuck behind him. His spirit soared above the traffic in the winter dusk, above the countryside, over the ghetto streets, over law offices, banks, political bunkers, cozy restaurants filled with chittering. He liked to imagine himself an eagle without succumbing to the fatuity of mistaking metaphor for reality. An eagle, after all, never carried C-4.

A small African woman who worked for the lab's executive director had stolen the MRSA, selling it to an intermediary she didn't know who sometimes worked for Bix. The likelihood of that transaction ever leading to the St. Leger Foundation was remote. But Bix would talk to her to make sure.

He circled the College Park neighborhood from a mile out. Watched the mirrors. Repeated the loop two blocks closer, and worked his way toward the center, the circle tighter each time. He saw no sign of surveillance of himself or his destination.

He drove into a retail square with two-story buildings enclosing a dozen rows of parking. The building he cared about was on the west side, with two outside stairways leading to a brick-arched gallery on the second floor. A dental clinic on the ground floor was having evening hours. A man emerged from the lighted foyer carrying a toddler, crossing the recently plowed parking square. Bix drove past them and slid the Mercedes into a space on the square's east side. He crossed the lot, went up the stairs. The upstairs tenants were mainly professional offices, closed for the night. He stood for a while looking down from the gallery. There was a small commotion across the way. Two teenagers were play-wrestling on the sidewalk outside a karate studio. Flapping scarves, flailing arms, exploding breath, hooting screams.

He scanned the lot. That was it. Nothing else.

He walked down to East-Med Labs and opened the door to the reception room. Miriam N'yang, professionally dressed in a blue suit and gray topcoat, sat in a visitor chair. Her red-lipped mouth was smiling. Bix stopped breathing. He wondered if contamination could have reached him in these few seconds. N'yang's black skin glistened below her close-cropped hair.

Bix pressed a handkerchief to his face, closed the door. If the bacteria was loose here, a handkerchief wouldn't help. But he had to know.

He moved around her, got a different view of the dead woman, and felt a little better. She hadn't died of bacillus. N'yang had been shot twice, once high in the head, once through the right eye. He hadn't been mistaken that she was smiling. Many people smiled at death. It terrified them, but it also promised release.

Bix stood and listened.

He didn't need to go into the suite's back rooms to know that East-Med's chief, if present, would also be dead. For a moment, Bix wondered if Staley had sent someone ahead of him to sanitize the clinic. But Staley didn't know about East-Med. And Bix did the foundation's cleaning up.

He wondered if N'yang had understood she was selling a highly mutated strain of MRSA. He doubted it. People who ordered things like that to be bred wouldn't be people you stole from. So she hadn't known. But someone had seen the news today and recognized the telltales of their property. He wished he could ask N'yang and her boss who the client had been. He knew the manufacturing hadn't occurred here. The site didn't have the security or containment facilities. He was following that thought when the door to the back of the suite opened.

The man who stood there was unusually handsome. He was well over six feet tall, with dark blond hair, gray eyes that reflected light, and a face that would look youthful and strong when the man was in his sixties or seventies. He wore a black topcoat. He didn't seem surprised at Bix's presence. He possessed supreme self-assurance. The silenced pistol in his left hand came up fast.

Bix fired first.

He squeezed the trigger five times in little more than a second. The explosions of the .45 left him deaf. He crouched with the muzzle aimed at the empty doorway, waiting for any flicker of light or movement. He counted to ten. He couldn't afford longer than that. The gunshots would have been heard in adjoining suites, if anyone was there, and in the dental office directly below. The man with the beautiful face had stopped moving the instant two of Bix's slugs crashed through his heart. Bix rummaged through the dead man's jacket, found car keys and a billfold, which he thrust into his pocket. His silent counting of seconds had reached fifty. He skipped over the body, explored the back rooms and confirmed that the lab's executive director was indeed dead in a lavatory. He didn't enter the big sealed-off rooms where East-Med's scientists worked in sterile conditions. The rooms were brightly lighted. Bix moved along a window until he could see down an aisle. Two men and a woman lay shoulder-to-shoulder on the floor. The blood around them trembled as a breeze from a ventilation grill disturbed the wet surface.

He thought about leaving the scene as it was. East-Med had no link to the foundation. But that kind of thinking was why things got worse. He had brought plastic explosive automatically, the way a smoker brings a match. It was in the left pocket of his outer coat, wrapped in a flimsy supermarket bag. He uncovered the block, connected a timer. The lab's computer stood under a desk beside the sterile room. He set the timer at thirty seconds.

The sound of gunshots had brought a white-jacketed woman from the dental office. She looked everywhere but up. Twelve feet of the upper front of the building blew off when Bix was halfway down the outside stairway, and then the woman was screaming—though he couldn't hear her—as fragments of brick, glass and wood hammered cars and distant building fronts. A section of roof tumbled in the sky like a flaming raft and came down on parked automobiles a hundred feet away. Heat boiled from the building. Bix circled to his car as if he were deaf and blind to the chaos around him. None of the dozens of people who spilled from offices and shops ever thought about the Mercedes that crawled away between buildings.

He was several blocks south, cruising the university neighborhood with the driver's window half open, when he heard the first siren.

He stopped at a fast food restaurant full of college kids, remained in his car and examined the contents of the dead man's wallet. The leather pockets contained several thousand dollars in cash but no credit cards, ID or personal papers. Bix didn't know much about pathogen research, but he knew you wouldn't play with amplified MRSA in a sterile room at East-Med. You did it fifty miles from anywhere in a microbial suite with negative air pressure wrapped in a cocoon of airlocks. If containment wasn't two hundred percent, things still got loose. The Russians had learned that with anthrax. Now somebody was learning a different lesson. Bix didn't spend a lot of time wondering who.

A vibrant sense of self-preservation told him his best course was to drive to the nearest airport and disappear. Instead he headed toward the D.C. Beltway and Virginia.

Another anonymous van had moved onto the foundation's property. They were getting ready for something. Bix passed the entrance and parked underground. He took an elevator up and found a small man with a patchy beard and sharp features waiting on the sixth floor. In a winter jacket, with a rucksack on each shoulder, the man looked overheated and frightened. Bolting. It was in his eyes. He would run straight into the NIS agents. Straight *to* them. They would ask questions. He wouldn't have many answers. At most he could provide logistical color. Was the staff busy? Was there much of a security force? What had he seen on the sixth floor?

Bix started to pass the man. Then he made a decision. It was a decision against letting NIS have more information.

He turned only halfway, knowing eye contact could panic the man. He asked, "Are you leaving us this evening?"

The man nodded.

Bix took a step to continue down the hall. "I don't think many cabs are running, but we have a car service that's reliable. If you'd like, I'll make a call."

"Thank you," the man said.

"No problem. You'll need a new pass, too. We're locked down tight. Come to my office, I'll get you a pass."

"Thank you," Loren Fane repeated, and followed.

42

BIX ENTERED STALEY'S OFFICE AT QUARTER TO EIGHT.

Staley raised a silencing hand.

A brusque woman's voice came from the speakerphone on Staley's desk. "I'm sorry, sir, Mr. Essen isn't available this evening." Essen was the senior partner at the law firm the foundation used. "He asked me to tell you he wouldn't be able to speak to you before tomorrow afternoon."

Staley cut her off. He looked shocked. "They scared off our lawyers," he said.

Bix wondered if Staley had really expected the rules to stay the same. He brought Staley up to date on East-Med, described the man he had killed. "No identification. He probably had a car, but I didn't stay to look. He was there on the same mission I was. Sanitizing."

"For whom?" Staley didn't sound as if he expected an answer.

"Somebody we don't know about. There's worse." Bix told him. Fifteen minutes earlier, three large armored trucks had converged on the St. Leger building, forming a half-ring that blocked the exits from the underground garage and flooded the lobby with light. Bix handed his PDA to Staley, who flicked through the images fed from security cameras. So far the vehicles hadn't deployed their passengers.

Staley got to his feet. "How long do you think we have?"

"Maybe fifteen minutes. We can hold them to the ground floor for a lot longer if we lock the elevators and the stairways."

"No. We'll let them come."

Bix wondered if Staley really believed he could litigate his way clear.

"You know what we have to do," Staley said.

"I know." Basic memory erasure. Nothing could be left for government techs to reconstruct. St. Leger had made it clear: Once compromised, the foundation would have to die to preserve the secrecy of its projects. Research funded years in advance would be the old man's claim to immortality.

Staley understood only part of it. He had managed the foundation affairs so long he thought they were his own.

Bix stepped behind Staley's chair, bending to access the computer on the side desk, and as he did so he lifted from a holster in the small of his back the .32 pistol. He reached across his body and pointed it at the spot where Staley's skull met the spine. The director was pulling on his suitcoat, planning his reception of NIS agents, weighing how far he would go to protect the old man's legacy, how far to protect himself, when the gun went off. Staley gave a snort. His right hand squeezed the air. He fell onto the desk, pin-striped hips jerking as if the body were receiving electric shocks. Bix fired twice more and the jerking stopped.

St. Leger had been explicit on one point. The foundation's secrets mattered more than transient lives.

Having erased one dangerous memory, Bix turned to the computers. Making them safe was a more complicated task but less important. He removed the hard drives, returned to the security office, extracted the memory disks from the drives and ran them through a shredder.

From his safe he removed two packages of C-4, several

boxes of ammunition, and the remaining vials of MRSA. He packed the ammunition, half the C-4, and the bacteria into a hard-shell attaché case. If he placed the rest of the explosive correctly against the first floor columns, he could bring down the building. He felt no temptation to do so. There were innocent people in the building, clerks, secretaries, junior researchers, several members of his own staff. None was a threat to St. Leger. Bix set the charge behind his safe, where much of the released energy would be driven through the building's outer wall. The PDA showed armor-clad figures exiting one of the trucks. Not much time now. He locked his office door as he left.

In the second basement, he entered a concrete tunnel that ran several hundred feet straight away from the building. When he was half the way through the tunnel, he touched a button on his PDA.

The brain and memory of the St. Leger Foundation disappeared in a ball of fire.

A door opened from the tunnel onto a hillside in a wooded area where snow hid tangles of raspberry vines and fallen trees. Bix followed a slope down a quarter mile, to a bulldozed no-man's-land at a townhouse development. The houses were empty and dark. Bix walked out to the highway and in ten minutes was entering the lobby of a chain motel.

There was a bar to the lobby's right, which was full but strangely quiet. A muted television showed a distinguished face trying to appear confident as texts swum along the bottom of the screen. The captions said a quarantine had been imposed on the District of Columbia at 7.55 p.m. First responders had set up triage at the back of the U.S. Capitol. It was believed there were few injuries. No fatalities had been reported. . . .

"Yeah, right," someone said.

As he moved into the room, Bix saw that a second screen at the other end carried a different station. There was no reporter on camera. A river of winking taillights had been dammed by official vehicles strung across upper Connecticut Avenue, blocking a flood of people trying to leave the district. North of the barrier the road was empty, except for a police motorcycle tracing slow circles. Nobody was trying to get *into* Washington.

Someone spoke up. "Radio says people are sick in Congress. Plus Baltimore and Herndon."

"My wife's sister lives in Baltimore. Things are looking up."

Nobody laughed.

Bix watched as the images and captions changed, realized he wasn't registering some of it. In his life, he had killed three people before this week, if he didn't count those done when he was a soldier. One killing had been personal, a matter of honor. Two had been in the line of business, years before he had joined the foundation. He accepted that death was sometimes necessary, when one set of interests conflicted with another. He accepted that there was a stoicism in his heart that enabled him to act without regret. But he did not kill indiscriminately. If things had worked as planned, a handful of people might have died because of the MRSA release—at least two of them direct adversaries of Mr. St. Leger, the others collateral damage, people who were close to his targets. What was happening now was different.

This was mass murder. Something nations did.

He thought about the tall blond man at East-Med. And suddenly he understood. What *he* had inadvertently started by releasing the MRSA, someone else was pushing forward. Someone was spreading it.

A murmur passed through the room, a collective release of breath. Conversation rose. Bartenders poured shots. The crawling letters on the screen reported that Reagan, Dulles and BWI airports were closed. Incoming flights were being diverted to Richmond and Philadelphia. Flights that had originated in the Baltimore-Washington-Virginia area were being held in quarantine across the country.

Bix left the bar. Outside, in a plowed parking area, he found an older SUV, broke the steering column lock, started the engine. He might have only a few minutes before a customer emerged from the bar and reported his vehicle stolen, but tonight it wouldn't matter. Tonight cops had other priorities, and a stolen car wouldn't make the air. He picked up the Ox Road heading south. He dialed his phone with one hand, and when a deep voice answered he told St. Leger he would see him by morning.

43

THERE WAS LITTLE LIGHT IN THE ARMORED COMMAND vehicle, which faced the ground floor of the headquarters of the St. Leger Foundation. Calder's face, quilted and sallow, sagged from hours of fatigue. She had lost track of Kushner in the confusion of the staging area and suspected he had slipped away to be with his family.

"Do you think there's any real chance of contamination?" Tim Berman asked. He sat behind her, half his attention on the links to the monitoring van. The quarantine at his NIS section had been lifted two hours ago. Calder thought: *Poor sweetie is afraid of contracting something that will spoil his looks.* She glanced at his reflection in the dark glass, tried to imagine the handsome face running with sores.

"Nobody goes into the building without biohazard gear," she said. She had dropped her voice, so only Tim could hear. "When we reach the labs, don't fuck anything that's dead. Observe that rule and you should be okay."

Berman shivered. In the past hour, Calder's banter had taken an ugly turn. Since learning that Marburg and four other members of the NIS investigations unit were dead, she had barely been in control of herself. She had suited up in black nylon protective gear, which made her look like a frog in a turtle shell. Somehow she had come out on top in the jurisdictional wrangling. Except on tactical matters, Calder was in charge.

The building had been silent for more than an hour except for small bits of internal babble that Berman's team had intercepted. Things were going wrong in there. Infrared showed the ground floor empty, the upper floors sparsely occupied. Someone inside the building had quashed all communication with the outside.

Calder watched the digital clock. Most of the people with her were on loan from the FBI. Slow to get organized. Too much time was passing.

She spoke into her radio on the tactical commander's band. "If your people are ready, let's serve the warrant." She kept the impatience out of her voice. A second later, she heard an affirmative.

She climbed out the back of the APC, using the vehicle to shield her body. The building a hundred feet away was brightly lit on most floors. An FBI helicopter hung on station above the top floor, its floodlights sweeping the rooftop landing pad. An agent inside the APC handed out folded biohazard suits. Helen shook hers out, struggled into it, and secured the tabs on the plastic helmet. She saw the tactical commander start across the snow and hurried to join him. Neither of them expected gunfire from inside. The infrared sweeps showed nobody positioned to resist. Two snipers stood behind each vehicle, mounted scopes searching windows.

Calder was twenty feet from the building.

First came a gout of flame from midway up the structure. Glass, twisted metal and burning paper shot from the side of the building like small rockets. The explosion shook the ground and deafened her.

Several agents threw themselves flat and opened fire on the lobby. The building took several seconds of punishment before the commander ordered the men to stop shooting.

Calder realized she was on her knees and struggled upright.

The hole in the building was only about three windows wide. It hadn't been meant to bring the structure down.

She strode past the entry team, closed the distance to the building. Most of the door glass had been shot out. She kicked loose a fragment and ducked into the lobby. There was no one else here, dead or alive. The tactical command officer caught up with her. "The whole building could be rigged to go," he said.

"I guess we'll see," Calder said. "But I think they took care of what they wanted to."

"I'm not risking people."

"Then send them home. If anyone does stay, have them secure the elevators. Detain anyone who comes out."

"Listen, Agent Calder—"

"Shut up. I probably just lost the information I came for. Now I'm going upstairs. Do you want to come along?"

Calder led the way directly to the fifth floor, squeezing past buckled walls, climbing over shredded debris, ducking scorched ceilings. It was impossible to guess what had been in the offices that stood exposed to the outdoors. The water distributed by the sprinklers over the walls and ruins was turning to ice. Calder searched the floor and found two unconscious people, apparently low-level employees. She called downstairs for paramedics. Her interview with Staley had been on the sixth floor. She headed for the stairway.

David saw them come out of the stairwell forty minutes later, two bulky figures in white biohazard gear, both moving heavily, both carrying automatic weapons on their shoulders—not expecting ambush, apparently. When they closed in, he recognized Calder. She might or might not recognize him with plaster dust in his hair. He raised his hands.

"There are three other people here," David said. "No weapons."

"Put your hands down, Dr. Isaac," Calder said. "You're going to wish you'd helped me earlier."

Three: Survival Traits

The potentialities for rapid evolution of the human species haven't been depleted, since the environment continues to change and genetic variance remains plentiful. Mankind assuredly continues to evolve, both culturally and biologically.

Theodosius Dobzhansky, 1963

Suppose the great genetic drift—this mindless tide with no predetermined shore—picks its survivors from the artless and the stupid?

Henry E. Wald

44

FOR TWO HOURS, DAVID SAT HUNCHED AGAINST A MARBLE wall in the lobby, hands cuffed behind him, separated from the other archaeologists, as the government team searched the building. Calder had lost interest in him. Several doors down, she had turned up a young man in a navy blazer who worked for building security. He promised to help.

David had no idea what the search was finding on the upper floors until Calder came back.

"How dangerous is that mummy?" she asked.

"Mummy?"

"The dissected cadaver. How dangerous?"

"It's host to the usual bacteria and fungoids. I'd wear gloves."

She turned and went away.

Winter air blew into the lobby. He tried to get comfortable. He couldn't see Becker or the Spragues. He had an unobstructed view of the front doorway, through which the government's agents came and went. He pulled his knees up, ignoring the cold.

When Calder returned, she wasn't wearing the biohazard suit. Her tone was mild. "Do you know the whereabouts of a man named Bix?"

"No."

"The security officer informs us Bix is chief of security. We can't locate him. Can you think where he would be?"

"No."

She jerked her head at a uniformed man, who stepped over and pulled David to his feet.

"What about Roger Staley?"

"He was here earlier."

"Uncuff him. And the others. Come upstairs with me, Dr. Isaac. How about your colleague Dr. Fane—do you know where he is?"

"He was talking about clearing out," David said. The agent cut the plastic restraints on his wrists. David said, "We were all thinking about it. You're not in a bubble suit. You didn't find MRSA here."

"We've got an idea where it originated," she said. "A lab in College Park blew up this evening. Sort of like this place." She walked quickly. Elevators were back in service. Entering a waiting car, she seemed to be talking to herself as much as to David. "The lab was on our inquiry list because a foreign national managed it. We thought they did contract work for hospitals."

As the elevator doors closed, David saw Charl in the lobby, supporting her husband. Noel was white-faced and trembling.

"I'm going give you a chance to help yourself," Calder said. "Tell me what you know, every bit of it."

"We had nothing to do with staph—"

"I assume as much. What *were* you doing?"

He told her again about the excavation, but in more detail, about the murdered family, about the evidence of illness.

Her eyebrows lifted slightly. "What was the foundation's interest?"

"Social science, according to Staley."

"Any reason to doubt that?"

"A little," David said. "They were rushing a DNA workup on the young female."

"'They' being Dr. Rodriguez, yes? Was she doing the sequencing here or in West Virginia?"

"The latter."

Calder halted, as if she had bumped into a wall. "Goddamn. I knew about that place and let it slip." She raised someone on her radio, stepped away from him as she spoke for half a minute. She came back, waved him down the hall and into an office. "Here's the kind of people you're dealing with." She stepped aside and David saw Staley's distorted, dead face. "He took three shots in the head. *Not* from us. In addition, the computers have been stripped. I wanted you to see this in case you're holding back anything."

"I'm not."

"Anything else unusual about the DNA work?"

"You tell me. What was NIS's interest?"

"We had an informant who said they were working on human cloning. How old did you say the remains were? Three hundred years. Why would you want to clone someone from that far back?"

"I don't think you would. Except . . . if you had a natural carrier, and you could copy that trait . . ."

He watched her small eyes. She said, "You mean a biological weapon. It may fit. The MRSA didn't evolve in a hospital sink."

"You'd better secure the girl's remains."

"We've taken care of that. There's something else I want you to see."

They rode an elevator to the cold room floor. She took him into the room, pointed to a gurney that supported a black body bag. He knew it contained the bones of John Wakelyn.

"We found this. Take a closer look."

He walked over, looked into the unzipped bag and saw the frost-covered features of Loren Fane. He felt sick.

"Just so you know who the good guys are," she said.

He turned away.

"You and your friends can make yourselves comfortable downstairs," she said. "Stay out of the way. Don't try to leave. I don't think you'll want to. You've got food and water for the time being. So far nobody's sick. Count your blessings. Half the people in my department are dead."

She dropped him off in a third-floor conference room, where David saw a man with a stethoscope bending over Sprague, who was stretched out on a leather couch.

"Chest pains," Becker said.

David moved to Sprague's side. "How are you, Noel?"

"Just fine. Charl takes alarm at every excuse."

The other man was folding the stethoscope. He addressed Sprague. "The pain seems atypical. I don't think you've had a heart attack. If it comes on again, have someone find me. I'm Dr. Taylor."

David followed the man toward the door. "You came along on the raid?"

Taylor nodded. He was thin and bald. "We weren't counting on a friendly reception. This is an easy gig compared to being on call outside."

"How bad is that?"

Taylor considered before answering. "D.C. is sealed off. NIS has lost a dozen people. We're hearing seventy percent mortality from the MRSA, but nobody really knows. It could be close to a hundred percent."

"Only a damn fool would think we had anything to do with this," Sprague called.

Taylor ignored him. "The fact it presents within a few hours is good news. If this thing had two days to incubate before anyone showed symptoms, and the contagion rate was the same, I heard CDC people talking a few million dead."

"From staph?" David said in disbelief.

"CDC and Homeland Security think it's a terrorist attack." Taylor picked up his medical bag. "I'm glad I don't have a family."

An hour later, Calder looked into the room, saw Sprague sleeping, and motioned for David to join her in the hall.

"We hit the lab in West Virginia," she said. "The man in charge says he expected Rodriguez and a technician to return this evening. They haven't. They're on Ewell Island with the founder of this organization."

"The founder?"

"Gus St. Leger himself. Why would they be on Ewell, Dr. Isaac?"

"I don't know."

"Then guess."

"Something to do with the Wakelyns."

"I'd say that's a given. My people found the child's genetic workup and are uploading it to me here. Rodriguez left behind some notes, which are being scanned. If you get an inspiration, come tell me."

45

ST. LEGER STOOD IN SYDNEY WOOD'S DIMLY LIT STUDIO. Underfoot were patterned rugs, torn in places, the designs reduced to shadows, wood floorboards speckled with paint, spattered tarps under the room's two H-frame easels. Canvases framed and unframed were tilted face-to the walls. Others hung by wire from molding along the ceiling. There was also death in the room. The old woman who had screamed at Merton lay curled on a deep, ancient sofa, head back, face slack. St. Leger didn't find that as strange as he thought he should.

He approached an easel, admired the portrait.

"Who the hell are you?" he asked.

He saw her clearly enough. She had features he would call handsome rather than pretty, a look of comfortableness about her. But tension, too. Her hair was what he guessed they called ash blond, or maybe it was a mix of blond and gray. He didn't know. It was the kind of thing one of his wives would have talked about while he ignored her. He doubted he would ignore this woman. There was a formidable intelligence in her eyes, as much as you tell anything that way. She watched him patiently. She was giving him time. He tried to tell himself the resemblance he saw was a mistake. A portrait of his mother hung in his New York townhouse. He imagined he would have remembered her perfectly without the painting or album photos. Phoebe Cable's face had been rounder than this woman's, her hair russet. What had jarred him more than a similarity of features was the sense that he had met this sort of gaze before—so intelligent, so without sympathy. His mother had looked at him like this. Without love.

"Who are you?" he repeated.

"Not who you think," she said. "I'm an artist. Would you like to see my work?"

She beckoned, and he returned to the nearer easel. The large square canvas showed signs of recent work—a wiped-out background, a loosely painted face full of sallow grays and rheumy blues, ragged creases, shattered veins. . . . St. Leger had the fanciful thought that the painter had scraped the flesh off her subject, searching for something deeper, then had stuck the flesh back on, none too carefully.

She said, "You recognize Silas?"

"Of course."

"I have to anesthetize him with whiskey, so that we can get a bit done. When the anesthesia wears off, we use the couch."

St. Leger nodded. "Without a corpse on it," he managed to say.

"It might not matter."

He looked past the portrait of Merton. The room held hundreds of canvases. Hundreds of completed paintings. He tugged himself free of her influence long enough to think, *Generations of work.* Few of the portraits flattered, but they had the clarity of truth. He wandered along the wall. It couldn't all be her work. Here was a profile of an old woman. The paint was discolored, the varnish crazed. The subject's clothing was drab, old-fashioned. She could have sat for her portrait hundreds of years ago. He stopped at the second easel. It held a picture of a young girl. Black curls flew every direction. A wild, open-mouthed laughter. Eyes as bright as lightning. St. Leger had never been a connoisseur of art, but he understood he was seeing an admission of the deepest possible love. He examined the canvas. The colors lay deep under glazes that had darkened over many years. He looked from the painting to Sydney Wood. "Who is she?"

"My daughter."

"She's beautiful."

"I had to do it from memory. And from imagination. How old would you say she is?"

"I'm not good on children's ages. Seven?"

"Seven is close enough. She never reached that age, so I had to imagine what she would have looked like."

"Beautiful," St. Leger admitted. "But you say she died? That's a tragedy."

"I thought so." The woman smiled. "Her name was Margaret Wakelyn."

He tore his glance from the woman and stared at the very old painting of a young girl who had died. How long ago?

He wanted to close his eyes, but the woman was near him. A gentle but strong hand brushed his caverned cheek. It was the comforting touch of a mother toward a child. Or of a person toward an animal that couldn't be brought along.

"My name is Elspeth," she said. She was near but her voice sounded distant. "Do you understand? Margaret Wakelyn was my daughter."

"That's impossible," St. Leger said.

46

THE GIBBERING PULLED SILAS MERTON TO THE CHURCH DOOR. He didn't want to know what was out there, but he had two souls to protect, besides his own. For sure one of the two was worth more than the skin of a drunken, disbelieving preacher. So he went to the double doors, opened them and looked into the darkness.

He whispered, "Christ Jesus." Not praying.

The shapes flitting across the snow looked like ragged apes. They were armed with clumps of wood, knives and axes. He recognized several of them as neighbors.

Silas backed into the church.

He tottered into the chapel. The body of the bearded islander was sprawled where it had fallen, covered with a not very clean sheet Silas had thrown down. The little Chinaman under the table had had to do with a ragged towel. For some reason Silas hadn't thought to call the state police. Things had been moving too fast, and help was a long way away. Whatever was happening would play itself out tonight. People he thought he recognized would go shambling through the snow like monkeys swinging axes. For the first time, he considered it likely that poor Luther had done everything they said he had.

He went into the room where the young woman was bundled under covers. She was awake again.

"How are you feeling?" he asked.

"Grateful," Pilar said. "Thank you for rescuing me."

"Tom Mears's never acted like that before. Neither's his wife." Feeling self-conscious, Silas sat on the edge of the bed. He'd piled blankets on her after heating them in the oven. He hadn't had the courage to strip off her clothes and dunk her in warm water. The devil he didn't believe in was doing enough mischief tonight without him looking at her body. If he hadn't interrupted Tom and Hildy Mears, they would have smothered her in the snow. They'd come close to turning on *him*.

"Why did you come after me?"

"Saw Tom following you. He didn't look right. *Nothin's* right, honey. What's going on with old Crispin? Tom wasn't looking out for him either." The oyster shop owner was in another room, alternately ranting and unconscious. Silas had brought him back after the woman, both in a fireman's carry. He'd thought his heart was going to explode.

"Mr. Hines said God was in his head."

"It would be the first time. He's a heathen that only comes to church on Christmas. Now I'll probably see him on Easter. Whoop-tee-doo! We gotta get a boat that'll take you and Crispin over to the shore. If we get to Crisfield, there's a town nearby called Salisbury that's got a hospital."

"I don't need a hospital."

"Crispin does, and you should get off the island." He leaned forward and patted her folded hands. "Something's got into a lot of people's heads. I think they hacked up that pilot. There's a body out in the snow."

"What about St. Leger?"

"Don't know. Wouldn't hurt my feelings if they got him. You rest, ma'am. I'm gonna see about a boat. You think you can help me get Crispin down to the dock?"

"I can help."

"Good. I hurt myself getting you two up here. I'll need a hand."

He checked on Crispin, who was snoring, and settled down at his desk and called Johnny Shaffer, who ran the mail boat. In an emergency, Johnny would take out his boat in any weather. Silas listened to the third ring.

He didn't think he had seen Johnny swinging an axe. When he'd come to give blood, he hadn't looked any worse than usual. Silas heard a guarded "Hello?"

"Johnny, we gotta get Crispin to the hospital. He's having seizures."

The silence lasted a few seconds. "Wife and me've been sitting with the lights off. Someone was shooting a bit ago. You know what's going on?"

"Crispin said God was talking to him."

"I saw Tom Mears an hour ago, holding his head like a cracked egg. Celia told me not to go help him. She's telling me now I'm not gonna come help you."

"Would you just meet us at the boat if I get Crispin down there?"

"Come morning I might."

"Crispin will be pretty dead by then," Silas said, hoping the irony would budge Johnny. But the mail boat captain had hung up.

47

HALFWAY THROUGH THE DNA SEQUENCE, DAVID DIDN'T believe his eyes. He looked up from the computer, asked Calder, "Are you sure this is right?"

"It's the sequence they ran. What about it?"

The program had isolated the deviations in Margaret Wakelyn's DNA. They were numerous, and several were massive. If he had seen the analysis in isolation, he would have assumed a stillbirth. Knowing the girl had survived until she was four, he didn't know what to think.

"This isn't—"

He stopped himself. He was wary of what he had almost said. Ethicists would have a field day with the subject. If a fetus's genetic code was so messed up that it couldn't survive in the womb, was it a mistake to say the DNA wasn't human? In a sense it was true. The magic code hadn't produced a living human being. It wasn't anything else, either, absent a successful life form. *This* code had produced a successful life form—at least one that had survived a number of years—but did that mean it was a human life form?

Not exactly.

Which was where the academic ethicists would jump all over him. *Define human!* they would cry. Is a Down child human? Answer the wrong way and you would be in big trouble.

So all right, David thought, Margaret Wakelyn was human. However you defined it. But profoundly different. No wonder Rodriguez had taken new samples.

Then he got to Chromosome 8 and the SNTG1 gene and revised everything he had told himself. "Different" didn't cover the Wakelyn girl.

David pointed out the gene deviations for Calder.

"I don't know what Staley was after," he said, "but I could make a guess why St. Leger went to Ewell. He wants to know if they are others like Margaret there. And if there are, he wants to know *what* they are."

"But we don't know why he cares."

"No, we don't know why he cares."

Calder thanked him and headed downstairs. The building was filling up. Carsten Starns along with a mismatched entourage of military and civilians had driven down into Virginia after abandoning the Willard Hotel. Starns had told Calder he felt like he was ensconced in the devil's sitting room. But he was adjusting. Now Starns's main concern seemed to be making sure the soldiers kept out anyone who arrived after him. A refuge ceased being a refuge when the doors were wide open.

He listened to Calder's report and asked, "How does this tie in with our affliction?"

"St. Leger is on Ewell," Calder said. "With Staley dead, he's our best shot at answers. We can pick him up in a couple of hours."

"Of course, of course." Starns suspected he sounded vague. Reports from CDC and Homeland Security were reaching him, when he wasn't bypassed, and they scared him to the depths of his soul, where a Christian had no business being scared. For a while he had been virtually paralyzed as the truth sank in. MRSA had appeared in New York, Boston, Los Angeles, Denver,

248 JOHN C. BOLAND

Toronto. All air hubs, he thought. We didn't get on it fast enough. Then CDC's epidemiology experts told him these weren't secondary contagions. The morbidity made it clear the pathogen was being released deliberately in large cities.

Starns was almost glad that the big decisions were out of his hands. The President had ordered thousands of law enforcement people into the field to contain the outbreaks, which meant containing populations that might want to move. In an hour every airport in the country would be closed.

Calder prodded him. "Ewell is a small place."

Starns focused on her. "Do you think the island is infected?"

"No, but our guys will wear protection. And if St. Leger is responsible for the staph, we'll be the agency rounding him up."

Starns buried the urge to laugh. So she thought turf wars still mattered, did she? Wasn't thinking that if a single infected person happened to be walking around in this building, she and he both were dead. Fat lady would have sung. Not the fat lady in front of him, but the one who showed up for funerals at the Nazarene Church in Boise City, Oklahoma to sing "Lamb of God, for Sinners Slain" and "In Me Thy Spirit Dwell! In Me Thy Bowels Move!", arm flesh wobbling as she reached for the high notes.

He felt his jaw clamp. For all he knew, *Calder* was infected. Or some of the Homeland Security people, or military folk. They'd all started the day in D.C. This would be a safer place with them gone. He wished he could get rid of all of them, except his own guard. Humming "Lamb of God," he told Calder to go ahead.

Calder found a dozen marines bivouacked in a small auditorium. Their commander was a weekend fight-club habitué named Dott, whose cheeks and brow ridge were padded with scar tissue. His misshapen nose made hers look pretty. Calder liked his appearance. If she had to have a man around, this was the kind to have.

They would have St. Leger by daybreak.

"Wake up, boys," she said.

48

THE BOAT PILAR BOARDED HAD AN ENCLOSED CABIN ABOUT fifteen feet long with benches under dirty windows on either side. She touched the kitchen knife in her pocket for reassurance. The boat's captain had appeared out of nowhere when they were halfway to the waterfront, carrying Crispin Hines in a bedsheet tied to a closet pole. Pilar's knees were shaking. When she saw a shadow come toward them, her heart almost stopped. Johnny Shaffer stepped out of the darkness and took Pilar's end of the litter. "My boat's down to the left," he said.

Shaffer made up a bed on the inside deck for Hines, who was unconscious. Pilar knelt beside the islander. His breathing was frail. She wasn't trained in medicine, but she thought he was dying. There was little she could do to prevent it.

"Crispin wouldn't be much of a loss," the captain said. "He sniffs oven cleaner when the TV goes out."

He took the boat out a quarter mile, then headed east along the island. Pilar could see nothing through the windows except an intermittent wash of spray as the boat rolled. A stove gave off oily fumes and too much heat. After fifteen minutes fighting nausea, she lurched onto the open rear deck where the cold air saved her from fainting. Waves slapped over the boat's sides. Ice slithered across the deck. Pilar clung to a stanchion through a series of twisting rolls, then went back into the cabin.

Shaffer's head turned. "What's the matter with Crispin?"

"We don't know," she said.

"Bet he's been hearing voices." The captain glimpsed her expression. "Easy guess. I suspect everyone's hearing them, except the pastor here, who's too drunk to notice. What about you, ma'am? Do you drink?"

"No."

"So do you hear the whispering? After a few days it gets to you."

Merton said, "You hear whispering, Johnny?"

"Now and then." He looked back at the black window in front of him. Pilar saw his eyes watching them.

She glanced at Merton, who shook his head. No, they wouldn't ask Shaffer any more about the whispers.

They didn't have to. He volunteered: "Sometimes it's so soft I have to listen hard. Then I catch on. He wants me to kill Celia— that's my wife. Kill the strangers. I guess that would include you, ma'am."

The bottom dropped out of Pilar's stomach.

"Sometimes, an idea comes along, you don't know where it came from, think it's your own. Maybe it is. Can't really tell if it's a good idea or a bad one. Like how I could turn the boat so the seas are following, see if we could get swamped."

"You don't want to do that, Johnny," said Merton.

"No, no I don't." Shaffer had already turned the boat a little without making a show of it. A wave took them broadside, and the boat heeled until the opposite windows were awash. Crispin rolled off his blanket onto the linoleum. Pilar got him back onto the blanket and half-wedged him under a bench.

The boat righted itself, sluggishly.

Merton called out, "Let's see about heading back, Johnny!"

The captain looked over his shoulder. His face wasn't made for grinning. "I said I'd take us across. Now you want to go back? What about poor Crispin?"

The boat's engines rumbled. Shaffer kept talking, but it was to himself as he pounded the wheel with a fist.

"Poor Crispin, poor Crispin!"

Pilar saw the sick look on Merton's face.

"Get 'em off my boat! That's what I should do. . . ."

The boat rocked, and Shaffer staggered, clutching the wheel.

Merton shut his eyes as water flowed under the door from the back deck. He murmured, "We can go back, Johnny. Radio for help for Crispin."

"Radio, hm?" Shaffer leaned forward and yanked a flat black box with an attached microphone from its brackets. "Problem is, Pastor, the radio ain't worth shit." With both hands, he hammered the box on the wheel. Shattered plastic from the radio flew at his face. "Maybe that'll help." He flung the box away, gave the wheel a jerk. The deck tilted as a wave slammed across the stern.

Pilar climbed to her feet. She stumbled past Hines to the front of the cabin. A fire extinguisher was clamped under the controls, two feet to Shaffer's left. She knelt and released the catch. She guessed the cylinder weighed ten pounds. Shaffer was shouting something to Merton, turned away from her, as she swung the cylinder at the back of his head. His peripheral vision caught the movement, and he spun three-quarters around, enough for her to take in the raw eyes and the bloody trail from his nose, before the metal slammed his ear.

Shaffer pitched onto the wheel, dragging it to the right. As the deck heaved, Pilar grabbed his shoulders and pulled him loose.

The wheel was turning on its own, the bow lurching. She tried to see outside but got only her own reflection—and then sudden movement behind her, a figure vague and dark like a man risen from the sea, and she turned and saw the face, red-eyed, teeth gritted.

"Take it easy, honey," Merton said.

He stepped past her and took the wheel.

She did what she could for Johnny Shaffer and Crispin Hines

as Merton nosed the boat into the weather. She was afraid she had fractured Shaffer's skull. Even as she prayed he wouldn't die, she dug through bins under the seats until she found a coil of narrow rope that she used to tie his hands.

"What's wrong with these people," she asked Merton.

"You're the doctor."

"I'm no doctor. Please tell me you're not hearing voices."

"Like Johnny said, I'm a drunk. But I hear it, not much, but it's there. Don't you?"

"*No.*"

"It started after those archaeologists arrived," Merton said.

Could the excavation have released a pathogen? A spreading virus might cause a kind of encephalitis that brought on insanity. But she couldn't make that fit. The archaeologists had all been as close to Chiquita as she had. None of them had shown symptoms. And *she* wasn't hearing voices, was she?

Was she?

Maybe just a whisper?

The cabin tipped down. A thunderous crash jarred the boat.

"Are we okay?"

"We will be in a minute," Merton responded.

As they entered protected water, the boat steadied. Pilar went out on the deck with a hand lantern and called out directions to Merton as he approached a pier. It wasn't the pier they had left from. There was heaped snow along its length that hadn't been disturbed. She wrapped a line over a piling and held tight, and Merton cut the engine. The boat crunched against the pier. What followed wasn't really silence. She could hear wind blowing and waves chopping against the hull.

Merton came out and tied another line.

Pilar looked around. There were no lights. "Do you know where we are?"

"Half mile from the muni docks. Not sure whose place. Hope it ain't the Angelos'. They're mean without hearing devils. I don't want to go back to town. If it's calmer come morning, we can set out again. Just keep Crispin and Johnny comfortable is all we can do."

Merton went on: "This has been building, I think. If you're

God and you want someone to hear you, you probably gotta search around. Maybe Luther liked what he heard right away. Maybe others've been fightin' it, like Crispin."

She heard it then, *WHACK WHACK WHACK*, and cringed, but the sound wasn't inside her head.

It came from behind and above, faint a second ago but rising. A strong light flicked across house tops a hundred yards away, rushing toward the village, rotors hammering the air.

Help?

Merton said, "Someone better go see. I'll do it."

He was barely upright. He couldn't make it through the snow.

"No," Pilar said, "I'll go."

"You still got your knife?"

She patted her pocket and climbed up onto the pier, kicked her way through snow along the edge. When she reached the end, she flashed the lantern and Merton waved and went into the boat's cabin. He switched off the last cabin light. He preferred to wait in the dark. She couldn't blame him.

She felt abandoned. Her mother had never sent her alone into dark urban streets, where anything could lurk. It occurred to Pilar now—belatedly—that she had never learned a useful survival skill.

She used she lantern beam sparingly, not wanting to draw attention to herself. Far off to the right, the bottom of a cloud brightened for a few seconds. Lightning? Or a reflection from the helicopter's searchlight?

She crept between houses that she couldn't see. It was impossible to tell whether the houses were abandoned or their occupants were waiting in the dark, feeling the edge of their knives and listening to

kill kill kill kill kill kill kill kill kill kill kill kill

and she tightened her mouth, forced herself to listen to her breath

puff puff puff kill kill kill

and then she reached an open stretch that seemed to lead north.

The warmth from the boat cabin was draining from her. She heard a distant *whup whup whup* of rotors.

Another area of cloud turned silver for a moment. The light dipped, drew a wide circle and flashed on the side of a house. It was less than a mile away, maybe half that. She was afraid of St. Leger, but if the foundation had sent the helicopter it still represented a way off the island.

She ran.

She covered a hundred yards, heart thudding, and as she stopped, sucking cold air, something flickered between her and the lights. After the jarring run, she had trouble seeing anything but jumping red suns.

She switched off the lantern and held her breath.

The helicopter had settled onto an open space. She could see floodlit snow drawn up like a dazzling aura by the whirling blades. Sound reached her dimly. Voices, radios. The aircraft's doors were opening, men in biohazard gear dropping onto the ground.

The movement between her and the helicopter wasn't an illusion. A dozen jerking silhouettes shambled toward the landing site. They swung shadowy objects that suddenly flashed as they caught the light. Axes, knives, a long gun. The men from the helicopter saw the danger. She heard a shouted order, then a gunshot.

Then a ripping burst of fire. Other shapes stumbled into view from behind the helicopter. Screaming carried across the snow.

Pilar dropped to her knees and searched for cover.

49

DAVID ENTERED THE COMMAND CENTER THAT HAD BEEN established on the fourth floor of the St. Leger building. Calder was already present, along with a dozen military people. Outer coats and protective vests were piled haphazardly in places not occupied by coffee cups and computers. The soldier who had roused David from bed backed out the doorway.

A man with a blond cowlick who wore a rumpled navy suit seemed to be in charge. He sketched a wave. "Thank you for coming, Dr. Isaac. I'm Director Starns. Perhaps you can help us."

David couldn't read the man's expression. Or Calder's. A wall clock said it was three-forty in the morning.

"I'll try," David said.

"Good, young man. Tell me what you think is going on on Ewell Island. Ninety minutes ago we sent a helicopter to secure Rodriguez and St. Leger. They landed, set out to find these people. Here's the last transmission." That was a cue for a subordinate to adjust one of the machines. Crisp voices filled the room.

"... *clear.*"

"*Yates on point.*"

"*Aim the light here—*"

"*Yates?*"

Five seconds.

"*Yates?*"

"*Yates ... ?*"

There were explosions of static, which David suspected were gunfire, and shrill, stabbing cries. Words lost. Screaming. More gunfire.

"We had to listen to that for almost two minutes," Starns said. His voice trembled. He flicked a hand and the sounds were cut off. "You were there. What's happening on that island?"

The voices had been confident. Then chaotic.

"An ambush," David guessed.

"Who on that island could ambush a marine unit?"

"Nobody that I saw." But the island had been wrong from the day he landed on it. Saying so wouldn't explain anything.

"I heard what happened to your people. It sounds like somebody's nuts down there. What do you think, Agent Calder?"

"I haven't been there," she said meekly.

A man with short gray hair and a battered face had lingered in the background. Now he stepped forward. "This isn't helping my people. They need extraction."

"They'll get it, Major Dott." Starns waved a big plowman's hand at David and Calder. "You can take these two with you. You'll get to see the problem first-hand, Agent Calder."

Dott turned to them. "Get yourself ready in ten minutes so I don't have to send someone after you. We muster on the roof."

"How many of your people are on the island?" David asked.

"Six. We'll have a satellite map in the air. You can show me where we'll meet resistance. What's the terrain like?"

"Low and flat."

"The chopper landed at the edge of the village. You know where the village is, what it's like?"

"It's at the north end of the island, maybe a hundred houses."

"They were going after St. Leger. Could he have an armed group?"

"I don't know."

"How big is the population?"

"Two or three hundred."

"Armed?"

"Not well."

Dott gave David a dour look. "Your ass is going to be on the line, too. I hope you haven't forgotten anything."

50

PILAR PRESSED HERSELF FLAT AND MOTIONLESS ON THE SNOW. To move, and be seen, was to die.

The screams had stopped, and the gunfire had stopped, but the images of what she had seen remained.

Forehead resting on her arm, she fought the urge to close her eyes and accept the cold. Her body shivered violently, trying to sustain itself. The organism wanted to keep going even as the conscious mind thought perhaps enough was enough. She raised her head a few inches. The light was still there, but she saw no movement. There had been no movement the last half-dozen times she had checked. How much time had passed? A half-hour, an hour? Long enough that her body was stiff and lifting her head was an effort.

She didn't know how many people had been on the helicopter, but she was morally certain what the silence meant. The islanders sliding out of the night with knives had overwhelmed the men with guns.

She got to her knees. It was all she could do for the moment. The higher vantage let her assure herself no one was near. She studied each shadowed mound for signs of life. She lifted the lantern but didn't switch it on as she forced herself to her feet.

She had her bearings, more or less. The helicopter had set down in an open area at the south edge of the village. There were two possibilities of shelter. One lay behind her, on the boat. The other was maybe a couple hundred yards ahead, if she could find the church. There would be a phone at the church. . . .

She avoided the lights—and the bodies. If anyone was alive, she couldn't help. She could barely move herself ahead.

She did it by counting steps, promising herself to quit after fifty steps and then reneging and starting again.

Four hundred seventy steps later, she knew she was being followed.

There had been a crunch several minutes ago, back somewhere in the dark. It had been loud enough to be audible over the wind sloughing in off the bay. She remembered a place a hundred feet back where she had stumbled on boards buried in the snow. They had clacked a little, and she had been horrified. Whoever was behind her had stepped on them and not cared.

She didn't look back. There was so little ambient light that she couldn't see more than a few feet in any direction. She put each foot down carefully. If she fell, she suspected she wouldn't get up.

She guided herself mainly by picking out rooflines against the slightly paler sky. Twice she flashed the lantern quickly against a building. The church was still ahead, not too far she hoped. After each use of the lantern, she moved away as fast as she dared in case anyone had marked her position.

Now she stopped and listened.

There was breathing. Not far behind her.

Her numb fingers dug for the kitchen knife. She crouched. Feet crunched toward her, slowly at first and then running like something smelling prey. She aimed the lantern and flicked the switch.

She had a momentary glimpse of a face, wide-eyed, bloody-eyed, crazed, not a half-dozen feet from her, and she thrust out the knife, felt the impact, heard the choked scream. The attacker staggered back. Pilar switched the light off. Footfalls crunched away.

She was shaking uncontrollably. She wept, and tears froze on her cheeks.

She almost had her breath back when she heard it.

Crunch, crunch, crunch.

Coming back.

Coming fast.

51

DAVID ISAAC WATCHED THE GROUND AS THEY SWEPT OVER the south end of the island, aiming floodlights down on the excavation camp where all but a single tent had been dismantled, and then hovering over the cluster of small houses at land's end. The ground and the bay were a continuous, inhospitable moonscape.

"You dug up bodies, huh," Dott said. Before David could answer, Dott spoke to someone else. "Anything on infrared?"

"Weak signatures in a few of the houses," a voice reported.

"All right, swing north. Follow the shoreline. Tell me if you see signs of a hostile unit."

Half a minute later:

"More signatures, forty-some. Nothing like a unit. They're scattered. Most of them aren't moving. Maybe asleep. Some are inside houses, some outside. The ones outside are weak, they're cooling."

David spoke. "If that reading is from the village, there should be a couple hundred."

"You hear that?" Dott said.

"I'm telling you what I got, sir," came the reply.

Dott spoke to the second helicopter, which hung somewhere off in the blackness. "What are you picking up?"

"I think we've got our missing bird, sir. Two o'clock, hundred meters. I'm lighting it up."

They lost altitude, and David could see it ahead, the grounded helicopter swept by the approaching floodlights.

"There's bodies, sir. I count thirteen."

"Heat?"

"Not significant. I'd say they're dead."

Dott spoke into the microphone to the second 'copter, the one Helen Calder was aboard. "Stay aloft and cover us. We're going in."

David couldn't hear the response.

"Swing around once more," Dott ordered. The first chopper's floodlights slipped across rooflines, lingered on walls, swung back to the grounded helicopter. David heard the reports. No sign of hostiles. A couple of heat images. Nothing close, nothing moving.

They landed and eight men set up a perimeter while Dott and a medic examined the scattered bodies. Fewer than half the dead were soldiers. Dott put a toe to a dead islander.

"Come take a look," Dott called to David. "You ever met St. Leger? The people with him? Is this them? There's a woman."

She was middle-aged, stringy-haired.

"It's not Rodriguez," David said.

"Look around. Could any of these guys be St. Leger?"

"They all look like local people."

"Why would they attack my men? Look at this shit. Shotgun, knives, axes. Anything at hand."

"Luther used a shovel."

"What?"

"Doesn't matter."

A gangly soldier came up. "We haven't accounted for Lieutenant Yates. Got tracks going north. Military boots. There's some buildings that way."

"Show us."

The man led the way away outside the perimeter. "See these

prints? He was running. There's others mixed in—maybe the lieutenant was chasing them."

"How many sets we got?"

"Least five, sir."

"Let's see where they lead." Dott communicated with the airborne helicopter, asked for light between the buildings that lay ahead. They were ramshackle cottages. Larger structures that could be commercial flung their shadows around. Walking two places behind Dott, David felt they had entered a maze, four of them going single file, the medic last. Twenty yards and the grounded helicopters were out of sight. The tracks veered. Half a minute's huffing progress and the searchlight, moving haphazardly, swept the side of a house twenty feet ahead, and the sight jumped out at them, a dead man sitting against a wall in a lake of frozen blood.

"Shit," said the medic. "It's Yates." He went over and knelt beside the man, an empty gesture, and stood up quickly. He spotted something, took a few steps and retrieved a weapon. He pulled off the clip. "Empty, sir."

Dott ignored the medic, listening to something on his tactical channel. "Don't put a light on it till I say so," he ordered. He told the others, "There's a double heat signature two hundred feet north, eleven o'clock. Corporal, you're on point. Use your night vision. Don't fire until you're told. Let's move!"

They followed the tracks between buildings, and the soldier reported, "Got 'em in sight. Thirty feet. One's got a knife."

"Get those goggles off," Dott shouted. "Light it up!"

The helicopter's searchlights swept over them, pinned two struggling figures. Their arms were intertwined like dancers. The bigger shape on the right was swinging down a knife. The one on the left buckled. David glimpsed dark hair, a bloody slash on the forehead.

"That's Rodriguez!" he said.

Dott snapped, "Take the knife!"

There was a crack from a rifle and the attacker was flung back as David ran to Rodriguez. Her eyes were unfocused. She shivered violently. He couldn't tell how much of the spattered blood was hers.

She mumbled, "There are people on a boat . . . Merton . . . they need help."

Dott bent over her. "Did St. Leger attack my men?"

Her eyes rolled back. She was unconscious.

The medic didn't think the bleeding was serious but pronounced her hypothermic. While he gave her a shot of epinephrine, David pointed Dott's attention to the church, which stood at the edge of the light's range. "You're going to need a base, aren't you?"

Soldiers came and went from the building. Dott had ordered all three helicopters to come in close to the church. He set up a patrolling guard. There was no sign of St. Leger. No sign of islanders. David stood outside, watching the dark houses. No lights, no smoke. He told Dott, "You should have gotten more heat signatures. Two hundred maybe." He stood and stared at the houses.

Helen Calder closed her satellite phone. The conversation with Starns back at St. Leger's building left her mentally numb. MRSA outbreaks had been reported in more than a dozen cities. Buenos Aires. Sao Paulo. Vancouver. Tokyo. It went beyond terrorism. The entire human race seemed to be the target.

She cornered the medic. "Where is Rodriguez?"

"She's awake." He had raised her body temperature in hot water. She was curled in a narrow bed, an IV line taped to her arm. There were thin bandage strips on her forehead.

Helen stood over her. "What happened here?"

"We've got to get off the island. There's a sickness."

Helen's stomach sank. "Sickness."

"Mental sickness, viral, I don't know. But people are out of their minds. If you're here a while, you start to think you're hearing voices. A dirty little whisper. I'm not sure it's an illusion."

"You hear a voice and you think it's real?"

Rodriguez sank back. "What I think doesn't matter. We can get the answers later. But we need to evacuate the island. All of us. The local people are crazy. One of them killed Louis

Minh. They killed St. Leger's pilot. The boat captain was insane. . . ."

"Why are you and St. Leger here?"

"There was a girl . . . an island girl . . ."

"I know about her. We collected your records. What's her significance?"

"You saw the sequencing report?"

"She was defective."

"No, there's more to it than that. St. Leger thinks there is. I'm not sure. But that doesn't matter. We *have* to get off this island. I can hear the whispering. If you stay here, you'll hear it, too. So will all these soldiers. If only one of them is weak-minded and has a gun, he'll use it on us."

"You don't know what's happening elsewhere, do you?"

"What do you mean?"

"Shooting us might be a favor," Helen said.

52

ANGUISH TORE THROUGH ST. LEGER. HE ROLLED ONTO HIS side. His throat convulsed, and he choked out sobs. With her glancing touch, Elspeth Wakelyn had shown him everything. Had forced her knowledge on him. Had forced him into Margaret Wakelyn's mind as the child died. He tried to smother the grief he felt. It had been imposed on him as crudely as if he were a goose with a feeding tube crammed down its throat. She was making him feel what she had felt. The endless grief, the self-pity . . . the loathing for the creatures that had deprived her of her long life's first loves.

He fought back. He didn't *care* about a child who had died three hundred years ago. Millions of children had died since Margaret Wakelyn's head was severed. Their deaths were decreed by nature. If he had learned one thing from Benoit, it was that human life was ruled by the same relentless laws of chance that drove the rest of existence. A thousand zygotes times a thousand risk factors: a deformed child was a statistical certainty. A billion children times a thousand varieties of death: Why weep over what randomness made inevitable? He squeezed his eyes shut. He didn't want to know.

She huddled in the dark. Ragged men and women searched the village. Frail voices rose. Feeble minds raged, no more than animals, they should all have died this winter. . . .

She had no sense of either parent. Her father had been within her mind's reach a little while ago, shivering in terror. Then awareness of him was gone—so completely gone that she thought this must be what death was, the void where he had been.

In a gap between storage bins and barrels, amid animal smells and dampness, in the numbing cold, she moved stiffly as she heard the shed door scrape open. She could picture the searcher, a man with a pocked face, clawlike hands wrapped in rags, his glance sweeping the dim space. She could hear his teeth rattling as he lifted the scratchy bag that had hidden her. He screamed, "Here! Here! I've found her!"

Others crashed through the doorway, doubled over in pain she sent them. The first man lifted something sharp.

The blade of a shovel.

"They killed my husband, and they killed my daughter," a far-off voice told St. Leger. "Do you know, I've never been certain I've captured Margaret's likeness. Wouldn't that be sad. If I've painted her a hundred times and gotten it wrong."

He sat up. The woman was standing beside the portrait of Silas Merton. She seemed to have forgotten him.

He wanted to disbelieve what she had shown him. But that was impossible.

"How did you escape?" St. Leger asked.

"I was unconscious. They didn't hit me hard enough. By the time they realized I wasn't dead, I had crawled away. A woman who wasn't quite so afraid hid me."

"And you've been here, all this time?"

"No. I come back only at intervals."

He tried to stand, but his legs were weak. "To wreak your vengeance?"

"Why would you think that?"

His voice seemed too loud. "The average intelligence of the

people here is a little better than a dog's. You've done something to them."

"No. You know what nature does to inbred populations. They're degenerating on their own, without my intervention. I try to be a realist. The people who killed my daughter were pathetic, frightened things. They have been dead for centuries. Their descendants owe me nothing."

She was beside him. He must have lost minutes, or hours. His mind was battered, his thoughts almost incoherent. The vision of his left eye was blurred. He suspected he had suffered a small stroke. He tried to clear his mind of the images she had forced on him—the random gleanings of how many lifetimes?—garish nightmares, a madwoman dancing in a burning village, cutting her wrists with a rusted blade, an infant hung upside down at a crossroads, forests of white bones—the images weren't all dreadful, but their weight had been more than he could bear. He had never been hypnotized, and he had never been raped. What the woman had done to him had felt like both. His mind had been hers to play with. She had stuck all sorts of objects into that orifice. He knew he couldn't bear such an assault again.

He found himself stepping sideways, slowly, along a wall of paintings. He saw a handsome bearded man in a black coat, standing before a window opening on rivers and deer. Without willing it, he moved left. Another portrait: the woman was attractive, almost beautiful, with dark red hair—

He stopped. She had wanted him to see this. It wasn't a self-portrait.

He recognized the sitter. He would always recognize the woman he had loved.

He stared at the portrait of his mother and wept.

"Phoebe is one of my great-granddaughters," Elspeth Wakelyn said.

He heard the word "is." He had missed her so. All his life he had missed the woman who kept him at a distance. She had never loved him.

St. Leger turned his head. "She didn't die?"

The response was silent but clear: *No*.

"She left me."

She had to. She wasn't aging. People noticed.

She left me! he cried without speaking.

Now the tears that squeezed from his eyes were acidic with rage.

She left me, because I didn't matter.

He had a thought, an unwelcome one. If this woman, and his mother both had had a gift . . . He asked, "How long am I going to live?"

You could live a few more years.

He felt relief, but didn't understand. "Why not longer?"

You had only one gifted parent. Something in her mind was hard and cold. *We're very careful about reproduction. We've learned the hard way.*

She spoke audibly. "You can do something useful for me, Augustus. You can tell the men who've come to the island to leave. Some of them are already dead. If they stay, they'll all die. I can't protect them."

Protect them? This vileness, this ancient *thing* speaking of protecting them?

"I'm too weak," she said.

"You—weak?" He tried to see her clearly.

"I've always been weak. I couldn't save my husband or my daughter."

A wave of grief. He rejected it.

"You seem to have a pretty good hold on me," he said.

She smiled, almost kindly. "Now I'm letting you go."

He found himself walking in the dark, the air still and heavy with the stench of burned plastic, the blackened ruins of the helicopter collapsed ahead like bones in a sacrificial fire. He had paused by the corpse of the shapeless woman on the couch. Elspeth Wakelyn had given him an unspoken thought. *She deserved peace.*

"You killed her."

I gave her release.

Like a veterinarian would release a dog from its pain, with a needle.

He was near the church when a soldier stepped from behind the building and aimed a rifle at him.

"Put that away," St. Leger said.

53

"HE'S RANTING," CALDER SAID.

David stood beside Major Dott and looked through a narrow, off-plumb doorway, into the tiny room where St. Leger warmed himself beside a stove. It was Merton's office, bookshelves lined with pornographic statues, along with books that might have been scripture. Below the shelves, a tall, spindly old man seemed convulsed, knees jumping, a wild animation in his face as it reflected changing emotions. He was frightened, he was deliriously happy, he was vengeful, he was reflective, he cried into his hands. After five minutes of interrogating him, Calder had decided she was dealing with a madman.

"He says if we don't kill this woman, she'll destroy us," Calder said. "The rest is gibberish."

"What is the rest?"

"That the woman is three hundred years old. Or older."

David looked away from the old man. He almost knew the answer, but he said, "Who is she?"

"An artist named Wood."

No surprise.

Calder went on. "He says she's really named Elspeth Wakelyn. Calls her a six sigma mutation. I've never heard the term."

David said, "A six sigma event is six standard deviations from the norm. A woman who's lived three hundred years would qualify. But I've met Sydney Wood. She's not three hundred years old."

"You don't have to tell me that," Calder said. "The man's crazy. But we've got him and we've got Rodriguez. We're going to pull out."

"Let me talk to St. Leger," David said. "With Rodriguez."

"Why should I?"

"You've nothing to lose. You saw the DNA sequence of Margaret Wakelyn. You've seen what's going on with the islanders. You want an explanation."

Helen Calder shrugged. "You're not going to get much rational out of St. Leger. Or Rodriguez. She's hearing voices."

"So was I," David said, "from the day I arrived. I just didn't realize what it was."

Rodriguez looked ten years older than she had two days before. Someone had gotten her several layers of oversized clothes to wear from Merton's closet. Under the plaid shirts and frayed sweaters, she appeared frail but determined as Dott opened the door for her to Merton's office. David followed her in. Dott and Calder remained in the doorway.

St. Leger was chuckling to himself, rocking back and forth, fingers laced, eyes slitted. He saw Rodriguez and beamed happily. "Oh, my dear! I'm so glad you're all right!"

She nodded stiffly.

"You've no idea how wrong I've been," he said. "I looked at the evidence you showed me and ignored it. I stayed fixed on my pet theory. You showed me major mutations in the Wakelyn girl. I couldn't escape the idea we are a mongrelized species—some of us, anyway, those who can think. I loved the idea. Man the brutal hunter, raised up by interbreeding with the bigger-brained Neanderthal. It would have been amusing, wouldn't it?"

"There's no genetic evidence of interbreeding," Rodriguez said.

"I know that. But I asked myself how much of the human race has had its genetic heritage mapped. So in theory the possibility remained. Some of the aborigines in southern Africa were genetically isolated until a few hundred years ago. Think of that—a hundred, perhaps two hundred thousand years of biological isolation. Who would have expected that? Why couldn't human-Neanderthal hybrids have survived somewhere a mere fifty thousand years? A black swan event, my dear. You can never rule out the improbable.

"I don't blame myself for an *idée fixe*. My fault was ignoring all the evidence you came up with. The Wakelyn girl carried several mutations. All that extra coding in the SNTG1 gene. Why was it there? I assumed it didn't matter. Or that it was harmful. That the kid was a half-wit like these islanders." He snorted in derision. "But that many mutations in a viable organism suggested they had been under selection for generations. They couldn't all have occurred in one generation."

David said, "Where is this going?"

"Where do you think?" St. Leger waved a hand. "I got my bifurcated species, just not the way I imagined. A new species of hominid has been evolving right under our noses. It's as different from us as we are from the apes."

Dott said, "Old man, you're out of your mind."

"That's a separate matter." St. Leger leaned back, resting his head against the wall. "You can't model improbable events. I learned that truth from someone you never met. If you roll the dice often enough, nothing is sufficiently *un*likely to be ruled out. Elspeth Wakelyn showed me. She opened a door inside my head and poured it all in. The experience almost killed me. She did something to a local woman. . . ."

"What did she do?" David asked.

"Got inside her head and switched her off. Stopped her breathing, stopped her heart; I'm not sure." St. Leger's eyes rolled side to side. "She says she's weak. A matter of perspective,

I guess. She let me see something she didn't mean to. There are others like her that aren't weak."

"I don't have time for this," Dott said.

St. Leger ignored him and said to Calder, "The infection out there is worse, isn't it? What do you think its purpose is?"

Her voice was barely audible. "Tell me."

"It is to eliminate us. We're a competing species." His eyebrows rose. "It's wise social engineering. They live a very long time, and they're clever. Before we leave this island, you need to destroy Elspeth Wakelyn. You need to hunt down all of her kind and kill them. Every one of them. Every last one. I can help. I know something about them."

Dott turned his back. "Keep him under wraps. We're going to head out."

"Wait," Calder said. "I don't want you to kill this woman, of course. But we should take her into custody."

"You're buying his crap?"

"I don't buy anybody's crap, major. I just want her in custody." She brushed by him, gestured to David and Rodriguez. "You two, come with me. He's talking a major evolutionary change. Could it happen?"

Rodriguez looked stunned, struggling to focus. "I need to think about it."

"We don't have time."

"Then all you'll get is a guess. If I was looking at mouse DNA and saw that many deviations, I'd say that if the animal was alive and healthy, it was well on its way to speciation. That's not a conclusion you jump to with a human being. The idea is just too far out."

Calder turned to David. "What about you? You didn't like the sequence."

"No, but I'm not an expert in the field," David said.

"I'll go with my first instinct," Calder said. "The old man has a screw loose. But we'll round up this woman anyway." She strode off in disgust.

David watched her go and said to Rodriguez, "What do you really think?"

She jerked her head toward a hall, and they wound up in Merton's kitchen.

"I looked up everything I could find about the SNTG1 gene," Rodriguez said. "There's a fellow at the University of Chicago, Jonathan Pritchard, who thinks the gene is under strong selection across all human races. If it does influence the brain, it's an important change. All that duplication could make the girl something special."

"Would it make her live hundreds of years?"

"I haven't seen it connected to longevity. But look at her other alleles. There are plenty that could do *something*." Rodriguez opened cupboard doors, looking for food. There was none. Merton's larder had been stripped by the soldiers. "There's a woman named Cynthia Kenyon at the University of California. She's worked with two genes, daf-2 and daf-16, and extended the life of small round worms by about fifty percent. Other people followed up and found they could alter daf-2 and make mice live longer. Daf-2 codes a protein sort of like insulin in human beings. Some people think that if you lower carbohydrate intake, you produce fewer insulin receptors and live longer."

"Okay."

"But the human gene that codes insulin, IGF-1, was normal in Margaret Wakelyn."

"So?"

He watched her as she gave up on the cupboards. "A team at Albert Einstein College of Medicine studied human longevity in the Nineties. They found that a certain variation in the CETP gene was several times more likely to be found in people a hundred years old than in the general population. If I remember right, the gene affects both good and bad cholesterol. Chiquita didn't have that variation, either."

"That's not very helpful," he pointed out.

"Look, I'm not an expert in the human genome. I was sequencing a damned mustard plant at Cold Spring. But there are literally billions of possible human gene combinations. Who knows what any combination might do. Only about two percent of our DNA seems to do anything—that is, provides coding for proteins that make us what we are. Yet twice that much appears to have evolved under pressure of natural selection, suggesting it *has* a function we don't know about. The so-called junk DNA contains hundreds of ultraconserved elements—sequences evolution has protected—that stretch pretty much across all vertebrate genomes. There's some speculation that they regulate development from embryo to adult. But we don't know any of this. It's all hypothesis."

"So hypothetically?"

"So hypothetically, a tiny variation—a single nucleotide polymorphism—could have changed this family, possibly a long time ago. A protein works more aggressively—or less aggressively —and the organism lives longer."

"Hundreds of years longer?"

She shrugged. "Scary thought, isn't it? If I was at Cold Spring, I wouldn't buy into any of it. Here, it's easier to believe." She looked at him sharply. "We've really got to get off this island."

"Are you still hearing voices?"

"I don't listen. And I'm not suggestible."

"And you don't have an IQ of eighty. When I was here before, the whispering was faint. I thought it was my own bad mood. What do you think it is?"

"Elspeth Wakelyn?" Her mouth moved crookedly. "No. It isn't a woman. One man told me it was God. But God wanted him to burn things."

"In a few days, it's gotten more powerful."

"Which is why we have to leave," she said.

Before dawn two of Dott's men swept the area around the church. Except for several corpses, they reported nothing. Dott came out, cradling a machine gun. From here he could see the house where St. Leger said the woman lived. It didn't look like much of a challenge, so he turned the job over to his sergeant. "Go arrest the woman. Take St. Leger along so you get the right one."

The sergeant disappeared into the church. Dott played, just for a moment, with the idea of burning down the village as they left. Something here needed cleansing.

He had abandoned the idea when the sergeant returned, looking embarrassed. The sergeant reported that the man he had left guarding St. Leger had been knocked unconscious. The old man was gone.

54

BIX HAD STOLEN THE CABIN CRUISER FROM A MARINA IN southern Virginia. He reached the island in the bloated gray pre-dawn, surprised that he had lived through the night. All the way down to the Atlantic, the radio had played nothing but spirited patriotic marches. He took it as a bad sign.

He docked where St. Leger had ordered, at the foot of an oyster cannery's pier. Then he stuffed his pipe with rancid herbs, opened several windows and climbed to the fly bridge. Even to himself, the boat smelled of death.

St. Leger came aboard at daybreak, shouting, "Mr. Bix! Make ready!" His breath froze.

From the deck, Gus St. Leger could see most of the town's harbor. There was no sign he had been pursued, but his sense of urgency was acute. Bix was supposed to have brought the remaining MRSA vials. If Major Dott didn't end up killing Elspeth Wakelyn, *he* would do the job—even if it meant sacrificing himself. That would be unsatisfactory, leaving how many generations of her offspring unaccounted for?

Not to mention possible sisters?

He called for Bix again. The engines were silent. The boat felt abandoned. He entered the saloon, found it empty. There must be a half-dozen cabins. He ignored them and hurried to the bridge. "Bix?"

There was a second bridge, for fish-spotting, just above him. He climbed the steps. Geronimo Bix was sitting in the captain's chair, facing the stairway. His bronze skin was a lavafield of sores. Black eyes swam in bloody craters.

St. Leger's breath caught.

"It doesn't like the cold." Bix must have been in agony, but his voice was flat. "The cold has slowed it down, I think."

St. Leger backed away. "Did you bring the vials?"

"They're in the box. It's over there on the seat. It may be contaminated. Up to you."

St. Leger stole a glance at the small plastic box.

"I'm so very sorry, Mr. Bix," St. Leger said, wishing he had a gun, in case the man tried to get off the chair.

"It must have happened at N'yang's lab." Bix raised and examined a hand that was a red-streaked candelabra.

St. Leger stared in wonder. "It's eating you alive."

"I also brought plastique. I can't bear much more of this."

"I understand." St. Leger glanced at the MRSA vials. They would be swarming with microbes. Every surface in the boat would be lethal. He was wearing gloves, which he could peel off as soon as he escaped. But if the pathogen was airborne . . . He tried to calculate how many liters of air he had breathed, how many million microbes might exist in each liter. He shook his head numbly. If he was exposed, he was exposed. He needed to spend another few moments with the man who had served him. "This thing that's loose isn't your fault, Mr. Bix. The people who made it would have used it later. If anything, you made them move before they were completely ready." He didn't know why he tried to reassure this dying man. If he could absolve Bix of guilt, perhaps he absolved himself.

"Do you want the vials?" Bix hissed.

"I think not."

"Then it's time to see how this bug likes fire."

St. Leger fled.

The explosion, when he was ten yards from the boat, lit the waterfront and knocked him from his feet. He got to his knees, face scorching as a dirty orange balloon of fire lifted skyward. He brushed a burning ember from his leg.

He probably hadn't been infected. If he had been, he would know soon enough. He started walking. He needed a new strategy for dealing with Elspeth Wakelyn and her progeny. He was near the church when two soldiers grabbed him and manhandled him inside.

Dott's men had taken no chances with their target, firing a concussion grenade through a window of the gray house, and finding when they entered a dead woman on a couch and an unconscious woman on the floor. The medic drew a syringe of ten milliliters of Haloperidol, injected it into the unconscious woman followed by five milliliters of Diazepam. He said to nobody in particular, "She'll be out for several hours." He studied the glistening needle and wondered, without having thought about it previously, how many times he would have to jab his own neck with the needle to open an artery. Not that he wanted to do that. They unfolded a litter and carried Elspeth Wakelyn down to the church.

Dott walked through the building, shouting, "We leave in five minutes!"

Rodriguez followed behind him. "What about Pastor Merton?"

"He's going to have to make out on his own."

"I promised I'd get help."

"You tried. I can't take islanders back to Virginia. You know why."

"You could drop them on the mainland. They could get an ambulance."

Dott's tone softened. "Miss, you don't know what's going on outside. Hospitals won't take anyone. Your friend's got a better chance here." He didn't know if it was true. He thought it might be.

He looked at the people around him. All you needed was one infection. He might get back to Virginia and find somebody had brought it in. Any of them could have. That crazy bastard St. Leger, who had run away only to come back. Or Rodriguez. He might be bringing it in himself. He had talked to Starns twice in the last hour. The guy was panicking. Matter of time before they fired on any incoming aircraft. *Matter of time till I shoot anyone who comes near me.*

Rodriguez had gone over to the litter where the three-hundred-year-old woman lay. Yeah, as if things weren't crazy enough.

He had options. He could set up a perimeter at the church, hunker down, wait it out. Ignore orders for the first time in eighteen years.

"Load the choppers," he ordered.

A security ring protected the aircraft as the civilians boarded, then the men fell back in groups of three and climbed aboard and the birds lifted off. Dott looked down. There was nothing, no sign of attack, no sign of anyone. Just a boat burning itself out a half-mile away. . . .

St. Leger spoke quietly. "You have an opportunity, Agent Calder."

When she ignored him, he continued. "What I'm saying is easy to prove or disprove. We have a full sequence of Margaret Wakelyn's DNA. If you run this woman's DNA, you can know for certain whether she's the girl's mother. That knowledge, in your hands, would be worth more than the discovery of penicillin. Run the sequence quietly, Agent Calder. If I'm wrong, you've lost nothing. If I'm right—you'll have the key to something other people only dream about."

"What key?"

"The key to longevity."

She met his gaze.

"I would be careful who I shared it with," he said.

"There are two things wrong with that," Calder replied. "First, I think you're nuts; I don't believe you. But even if I did, I couldn't sell it to Starns."

St. Leger settled back. "Sell him on something else then. You're down here looking for answers to MRSA. I had nothing to do with the illness. Wakelyn, I'm pretty sure, had nothing to do with it. But let's suppose—let's allow Mr. Starns to suppose— she has a natural immunity to drug-resistant staph. Wouldn't he want to know why?"

He watched her considering. He had forgotten who had found the connection between the mutated CCR5-Delta 32 gene and resistance to bubonic plague. But he remembered the excitement when the same deletion was found to provide resistance to a version of the human immunodeficiency virus, HIV-1.

There were *dozens* of medical precedents to justify running Elspeth Wakelyn's DNA. He wondered if Calder was thinking about them.

In the back of the helicopter sat a tall, handsome man.

He watched, and he listened, and he let the feelings of the people around him flow past, as meaningless as dust. He didn't bother noticing the emotions, the endless fear, anger, envy and regret that dominated the human mind.

None of his fellow passengers noticed him, because he had encouraged them not to. Boarding the aircraft, a man had stepped around him, still not seeing, never registering a thought that there was a person to avoid. As long as nothing caused them to focus, he was safe. Even then, he could confuse a few of the weaker-minded ones, set them against the others. He'd had no trouble doing that on the island.

He had little to fear from them.

The unconscious woman the soldiers had whisked aboard in the first helicopter was another story. He feared her a little. He hated her deeply. Even sedated, she was aware of him. She held him at bay contemptuously. He could focus on a feeble-minded soldier, have him bring up his gun, shatter the woman's half-sleeping brain. He could do that. But it wasn't what he wanted. He imagined her chained to a bed, where he could have her whenever he wanted. Fuck her every hour for a hundred years. See what brilliant things popped out of the union. Every day for a thousand years, filling the earth with *his* dazzling light.

55

THE HELICOPTERS LANDED AT TEN-MINUTE INTERVALS ON THE roof of the St. Leger Foundation headquarters, discharging passengers, unloading their cargos of dead, then dropping to protected areas inside the security perimeter on the grounds. David's craft came in last, behind the command ship carrying Dott and Rodriguez. The seventeen people returning alive from Ewell Island were met by armed men in hazmat suits. The atmosphere at the building had changed dramatically in the five and a half hours since they had flown out. The headquarters had become a bunker. Armored vehicles near the entrances aimed their spotlights and weapons outward, warning off any refugees seeking shelter from the biological storm.

David and most of the others returning from Ewell were shuttled into a dormitory-style room for twelve hours of isolation. Even if a symptomless carrier had come back on the helicopters, people around him would begin dropping within twelve hours. In which case, David knew, the reaction from the soldiers and FBI agents outside the containment area would be pragmatic. Fragments of news leaked through, revealing a spreading panic. Troops had fired on people trying to flee quarantined cities. Movement meant spreading the contagion.

David spent most of his twelve hours of confinement sleeping. Charl flitted through restless dreams, sun-darkened, moving like liquid copper on sandy sheets.

Awake he heard a continuous, soundless scream.

The woman.

What were they doing to her?

The quarantine subjects had been separated into two groups. Calder, St. Leger and Rodriguez had gone with the stretcher bearing Wakelyn. That left David sharing a dormitory with Dott and his team, who batted around war stories about the men who had come back in body bags. David listened and thought about Rodriguez's remark. These men liked things simple: orders, objectives. None of them said anything about having heard voices. David didn't ask.

When Taylor cut him loose, Charl was waiting.

"They said you would be okay, but they were guarding the door with machine guns," she said.

"They weren't sure. How is Noel?"

"He's fine." Something in her tone. "He's frightened. So am I. What happened on the island?"

He told her as they went upstairs. The archaeologists had reclaimed their old space. Noel was deciphering records that had been found on other archaeological projects the foundation had backed. The great die-off in the Jamestown Colony in 1607 had caught the organization's attention, as had the colony's early rebellions. The foundation had investigated upheavals, looking for something deeper.

Noel's color was back, but he was shrunken and uncertain. He realized he had been the foundation's pawn.

David moved over to the television. The screen was filled with an image of a wind-whipped American flag. There was no sound. No news crawler. He realized he had been looking for news of Connecticut. His attempts to call his father hadn't gone through.

If the Westport hospital had asked for volunteers, David knew, Bernie Isaac would have headed in.

Sprague's exclamation—not a word but an incoherent explosion—pulled him around. Charl looked at her husband in shock. She had started to describe St. Leger's claims about Elspeth Wakelyn when he cut her off.

"I don't believe any of it!" Sprague thundered.

He got out of his chair, throwing down papers. "It's all a lie!"

David watched. His old teacher was seeing everything he had done in life becoming obsolete. He wouldn't be alone. Not much that anyone had done would matter.

Becker was waiting in the hall. He told David, "Rodriguez has an office. She's begun sequencing the woman's DNA. Do you believe St. Leger?"

"No."

By silent consent, they headed higher in the building. The stairway lights flickered, went out, came back weaker a few seconds later. "Even money that was the power grid collapsing," Becker said. "I'm surprised it stayed up this long. No grid means water pumping stations are out. Next come fires. You figure firemen showed up for work today? Or grocery people, or police? It's going to happen here, too. When Starns's team can't hold it together, this place will get ugly."

They came off the stairs into the sallow light of a hallway. Rodriguez was in a hastily arranged lab next to the refrigerated room, the space crowded with a sequencer, centrifuge and other equipment. Carsten Starns leaned over Rodriguez's shoulder, studying a monitor. Both the NIS director and Rodriguez looked haggard.

"What have you learned about Sydney Wood?" David asked.

"Nothing useful," said Starns. "Whether we have a naturally immune carrier time will tell. We flew equipment in from West Virginia so that Dr. Rodriguez can run a complete genetic profile. If that's normal, we'll have to test the subject's immunity."

David listened, feeling cold. Immunity to what? He suspected he knew. Starns would try out the MRSA on her.

"I was working this morning in a bubble suit while you were locked up," Rodriguez said. She shifted her attention to Starns. "This will take another twelve hours, sir."

"Call me when we have something."

Becker spoke up. "Will the building have power in twelve hours?"

"We can run on generators for seventy-two hours," Starns said. "This building was designed for self-sufficiency. Solar imbedded in the window glass can provide heat almost indefinitely. We have food for a hundred, slightly more than our current complement, for a week. More if we reduce calories. We're in a good place." Starns focused on David. "Do you believe in The Remnant, Dr. Isaac? Of course you don't, you're not a Christian. It's a religious concept. We know The Remnant will be saved."

Starns was halfway out the door when he paused. "None of you have heard the good news, have you? Our affliction is near its end. Whoever engineered this monster made it too ferocious to maintain a chain of living hosts. If we enforce the quarantine for another four or five days, CDC epidemiologists believe the beast will consume its last victim. Not enough people believe it, but ultimately God is kind to us."

David said, "At least to The Remnant."

Starns gave him a sad look and headed down the hall.

"You're an idiot for antagonizing him," Rodriguez said.

"Probably. You haven't told him everything. What happens if she's Chiquita's mother?"

Rodriguez looked troubled.

"Who leads the vivisection team?"

Anger flashed across her face. "There won't be any vivisection. They won't do anything like that."

"Starns is talking about testing her immunity to MRSA."

She hesitated. The sequencer blinked silently behind her. She pushed the monitor around so the two men could see it, typed a short code into the keypad in front of her. A color diagram flashed onto the screen, displaying bars of genetic coding.

"This is Chiquita's mitochondrial DNA, which she inherited directly from her mother," Rodriguez said. She clicked and another sequence appeared beside the first. "This is the mitochondrial DNA of the woman upstairs. I'll lay the second pattern over the first. Watch."

The patterns slid together, overlapped and merged perfectly.

"You said you hadn't completed—"

"I know what I said. Fortunately, Starns doesn't know how long this job takes. The *fact* is right in front of me. Whether that woman is Sydney Wood or Elspeth Wakelyn or Rosalind Franklin, she is the mother of the child." She leaned back, eyed the two men. "So what do you make of it?"

"How sure are you?" Becker asked.

"Sure. Mitochondrial DNA doesn't change much generation to generation. With Chiquita and this woman, the mt-DNA is identical. Now—logically—that leaves three possibilities. Chiquita could be the woman's mother *or* daughter or twin. So I looked for and found a marker that Chiquita inherited from her father, one the woman doesn't have. That establishes parentage. The woman is Chiquita's mother."

"Maybe you fucked up," Becker said.

"I didn't. What about you guys?"

"What about us?"

"Did you really dig that girl out of a three-hundred-year-old grave? Or is this some kind of stupid hoax? We haven't run tests to confirm the age of the girl's remains. So I can't be sure. Maybe the kid died five years ago, in which case who cares who her mother is?"

"We were both present when the coffin was opened," David said. "The burial was twelve feet underground. There was a water trap. It wasn't a hoax."

She turned to Becker. "That's your story, too?"

"No hoax."

She stared at the perfectly matched DNA ladders on the monitor.

"Will you tell Starns?" said David.

"I don't think so."

"You could get your name in the history books. First to vivisect—"

"Quit it, all right? If this woman is Elspeth Wakelyn, she didn't just pop out of an egg, *sui generis*. Her parents would have possessed most of her traits, probably all of them, and their parents, and so on. If she's several hundred years old, there are others like her . . . and must have been for centuries."

"Unnoticed?" said Becker.

"Persecuted. That's St. Leger's theory. He intends to put it into practice." Rodriguez turned off the screen. "How long does the Bible say the first descendants of Adam lived? I remember Noah, because he had a round number. Noah was supposed to have been six hundred years old at the time of the flood. A lot of them supposedly made it past a hundred."

"If you believe their record keeping," Becker said.

"I don't, of course. But it's interesting that the idea of an enormous lifespan goes back a long way. Did the pre-Christian writers just make it up?"

"They made up other things."

"Okay, but where did they get the *idea* of people living hundreds of years?"

Becker snorted. "Where did the Greeks get the idea of gods in the shape of mortals?" His tone was derisory. Rodriguez's dry smile stopped him from saying more.

She filled the silence. "People who lived hundreds of years would be *seen* as gods, wouldn't they? I can tell you something else that fits. If I remember right, the Greek gods toyed with us mercilessly."

"Do you think Wakelyn's kind have toyed with us?"

"Something was doing it on Ewell."

"There's another question," David said. "Would longevity be a survival advantage? Would a gene that conferred it survive?"

"An animal that lives longer gains experience, accumulates knowledge," said Rodriguez. "That's an advantage. But it's a good question. Sexual maturity comes later. Genes don't get shuffled as often. Mutations come slower. Long generations could breed stagnation."

"Where is Starns holding the woman?"

"What are you planning?"

"I haven't got that far. Where is she?"

"There's a place on the top floor—a cross between a holding cell and a clinic."

Every foundation needs one, David thought.

"If you're going," Rodriguez said, "I'm coming with."

Carsten Starns returned to his office.

St. Leger had warned him not to trust the little Hispanic gal, but that was really the least of his concern. He wasn't a fool. He'd had Carter and John Walters debriefed. He understood where the trail of bread crumbs led. Rodriguez could pretend not to know, but she knew, and so did he.

He had been outfoxed by nature. He had fought cloning. He had made war against tampering with the human genome that the Creator had designed and made perfect.

But he'd been fooled.

All the while, nature was changing the design.

Carsten Starns was a believer, but he wasn't an ignorant man. The basics of human evolution were undeniable. The human species, *Homo sapiens sapiens*, had existed for two hundred thousand years. This, Starns believed, marked the point at which God had invested His creation with the immortal soul. Different racial traits had shown up over the last forty thousand years. These were normal responses to the environment as man spread from Africa; northern latitudes required lighter skin for Vitamin D absorption. Some specific genetic traits—such as the lactase gene, which enabled adults to digest dairy products—spread through the European population in just the last six or seven thousand years: another adaptation to the environment, as man developed animal husbandry. Perhaps that was God's greatest gift: that his creation could adapt, and grow.

But at some point, Starns thought, the game had changed. *Homo sapiens sapiens* had gained a competitor. Could *it* possess an immortal soul? Starns hoped not. Because if it did, then God had breached his Covenant with man, and chosen a successor.

Starns could never accept that. God had rejected the angels for man. He had set man above the beasts. He had made a promise of eternal life. Now, if St. Leger was right, divine grace was a lie.

56

ELSPETH WAKELYN APPEARED TO BE ASLEEP. SHE LAY ON A tubular-framed bed, partly covered by a hospital gown. Her wrists and ankles were strapped down. The medic who had been on the mission to Ewell stood behind the bed, garbed in biohazard gear. There was a window between that isolation room and the hall. Calder and St. Leger stood outside the window, looking in.

Calder spared a glance for Rodriguez and the two men. "You don't belong here."

"Is your prisoner violent?" David asked.

"She's sedated."

"Then why is she restrained?"

Calder turned her back, chewing her lip as she stared at the woman behind the glass.

"It's an extra precaution," St. Leger said. "Prudent, since we don't know what we're dealing with. Have you completed the sequencing, Dr. Rodriguez?"

"Not yet. The software is acting up."

"We'll have what we need to prove her lineage." St. Leger folded his arms. "We could run the sequences after euthanizing her."

Rodriguez drew in her breath.

"No?" St. Leger asked.

"We'll do nothing of the sort without evidence."

"The evidence might leave you unable to act." St. Leger leaned so his nose almost touched the glass. "You saw what she's capable of on the island. That's one ability she didn't explain to me—getting inside my skull. You would think a mutation would confer a single advantage. Perhaps longevity, perhaps a psychic talent. Yet she has both. Explanation?"

"Maturity," Rodriguez said.

"What?"

"When you were a two-year-old, you couldn't multiply numbers; your brain hadn't grown enough. If she's had hundreds of years to build neurological paths, it could explain a psychic ability. That's just a guess. But I don't think she was the one influencing people on Ewell. I heard a voice in my mind. It wasn't a woman's."

"Of course it was her, who else?"

"When she was in your mind, did she tell you to burn, murder? Did she make you do anything you didn't want to do?"

St. Leger stared through the window. She had made him forget himself. She had made him listen—or permitted him to listen; the opportunity had been its own compulsion.

"Then who?" St. Leger said.

David followed St. Leger's stare. Even unconscious, the woman behind the glass held his attention. Under the pale hospital garment, her body had an earthy sensuality that he couldn't ignore. Was this, too, something that developed if one lived for centuries? For a moment, he let himself wonder what it would be like, getting the hospital gown up around her waist, lifting her knee, rolling with her in the ancient rhythm of oceans and blood. The rhythm was older than identity, older than human awareness, as basic as the first self-replicating chemical, a thing buried in the cells demanding continuation. If he lifted up her gown and bent her knee aside, he would share in everything that had gone before, and in whatever lay ahead.

Blood hammered in his ears. He blinked hard and turned away from the window.

Calder stood motionless, lips loose, face flushed.

Rodriguez backed away from the window, glassy-eyed, her face sweaty. She looked embarrassed. "Jesus Christ," she whispered.

Was it good for you, too? he thought.

"What *was* that?" Rodriguez whispered.

"Maybe she's dreaming."

"About all of us?"

He heard, faintly in an ear that had no physical existence, the cry that had tormented him as he lay half-awake. Rodriguez was hearing it, too. David watched as Calder shivered violently—an orgasm?—and seemed to struggle, like a sleeper reluctant to wake.

Becker was nowhere to be seen.

St. Leger grabbed David's arm. "You see? You have no idea how dangerous that thing is. She'll eat your mind."

St. Leger's jaw froze, his eyes popped. His hand loosened from David's arm.

David looked past him. In the glassed-in room, the medic was slumped in a chair, head tilted, chest rising rhythmically. The prisoner had her face turned toward the window. Her eyes were open.

She was watching them.

57

HELEN CALDER, STILL SLUGGISH, BEGAN TO DRAW HER PISTOL.
David caught her wrist, twisted the gun away.

He said, "Who are you planning to shoot?"

"Give me that!"

As he dropped the weapon in his pocket, Calder's face emptied and her shoulders sagged. David turned on St. Leger. The old man was studying his clawlike hands with a look of wonder.

David looked through the glass. The woman on the bed returned his stare.

He pushed open the door and stepped into the isolation room.

Her voice was husky. "Can you help me sit up?"

He undid the restraints. Feeling the warmth of her hand, noticing the smooth perfection of her skin, he thought: *It's at the cellular level, whatever it is that makes her what she is.* But it had to be that. She wasn't just getting by. She was healthy and—despite the effects of the drugs she'd been given—she was strong. He felt her awareness at the edge of his mind, not intrusive, a polite hesitation at the threshold, and he knew he had sensed the same presence when they had met the first time, when he was in the church basement. He hadn't recognized it then for what it was. He had thought only that he wanted to know her better, which was another way of thinking he wanted to let her in.

Now he said, "Who are you?"

Names flooded his mind. *Elspeth Wakelyn, Sydney Wood,* and before either of those, a dozen names from Cornish villages where a woman dared not remain too long if she didn't grow old.

"Help undo my ankles," she said.

He unbuckled the straps. "What did you do to Calder and St. Leger?"

Distracted them.

Her voice was clear in his mind.

"And the islanders?"

Shaking her head, she spoke softly. "I'm not strong enough for that."

He felt the thrill of her fear. She swung her legs off the bed. Close to her, he could smell her sweat, feel the sensuality of her presence. He knew he was being *urged* at some level that didn't approach control.

Rodriguez was bent over the medic, stripping off his biohazard gear. There was a separate conversation going on between her and Wakelyn. Rodriguez began unbuttoning the man's uniform shirt. Elspeth Wakelyn dropped the hospital gown and waited for pieces of the uniform.

"Help me get out of here."

"Not until you tell me who you are."

You already know.

"More."

There isn't time!

He felt the fear crawling through her. For an instant he saw the object of her dread—brilliant sun-filled eyes, flowing blond hair, long flat muscles, a glorious, idealized Wagnerian image of heroic manhood, *a Greek god*—and then the beautiful mouth opened and he saw a snaggle of shark's teeth as the fingertips curled into talons and the bright godlike eyes burned holes in his mind—

David squeezed his eyes shut.

Wakelyn said, *He believes he's a god. They all do.*

The image faded.

She said, *He came from the island with us.*

David swung around, imagining breath on his neck.

You won't see him unless he wants you to.

"Who won't I see?"

He couldn't tell how much time passed. Part of what she told him came in words. Part was an avalanche of images. Part was wordless, pictureless *understanding.*

Elspeth and John Wakelyn. Both had the longevity trait.

The trait had been in the isolated Cornish villages a long time. Fewer than a dozen strange people were scattered among the coastal enclaves. They knew nothing about themselves except that they were different. And at risk. The ones who had exposed their differences had been crushed under mounds of stone or burned alive. Elspeth's mother believed the long-liveds were descended from fallen angels. It would have explained so much. They were strong and healthy. They aged very slowly.

They all traced themselves to a woman known as Little Sophie, who was still alive when Elspeth was a child. Sophie claimed she couldn't remember when she had been born, or where, but as a young woman she had been a camp-follower of Charlemagne's army. That would have been at the end of the Eighth Century. Sophie's mother had lived a long time as well. They viewed themselves as witches.

If one of the long-liveds made it past late puberty, she developed a small ability to influence normal people. The *Push,* Little Sophie said. The talent didn't go much beyond a power of suggestion, like whispering into a sleeper's ear. When Elspeth had been in one place too long—she was in her thirties and looked eighteen—she moved to a distant village. Her new neighbors had no memory of her. She supplied one. She was fourteen years old. She had lived among them all her life. They knew her and loved her. It was easy. Elspeth knew that all human memories were at least partly false anyway.

One member of the scattered long-liveds was far more powerful than others. Both his parents had had the trait, which was unusual. This young man, this perpetually young man, had the strongest *Push* Elspeth had ever known. His name was James Seeker.

As Seeker's talent developed, he discovered that he could make any mischief he wanted. That would be a dangerous thing in any young man. It was worse in Seeker, who had no conscience. He could rape a woman, a man, or a child—and command the victim to forget. He could pass through a market like a shadow, urinating on food, starting brawls, lighting an old man's hair on fire. By the time Elspeth was in her forties, Seeker had shed all self-restraint. He ranged across the countryside, an invisible terror. People were maimed in their beds. Twelve-year-old virgins gave birth. On the Feast of the Assumption, an old woman, disemboweled, swung from her cottage roof. Seeker had begun doing something else, as well. He conjured apparitions. Ghosts screamed from chimneys. Demons swirled in the clouds. Only the weakest-minded people were vulnerable to the most extreme illusions, but their ravings stoked the fear of others. Someone was calling up demons. Who? The witch hunt began. Anyone could come under suspicion. You didn't want to stand out. Eccentric habits, unusual intuition, good health—anything could be a lethal marker. The only person above suspicion was Seeker. The villagers worshipped him as a saint.

Elspeth and her mother lived in terror. All Seeker had to do was whisper a name to have anyone burned alive. His mind was strong, sensitive to every nuance, every eddy around it. He was greedy for sensation. He was difficult to deceive.

Elspeth and her mother laid a trap. The women chattered to themselves about luring a child into the countryside, among the ancient burial mounds where followers of the old ways had slaughtered enemies. They would slaughter the child. Propitiate the old gods. Elspeth Wakelyn brought the knives. She filled her mind with images of young flesh. James Seeker came, demanding to share the thrill. He stepped from among the cairns. There was no child. The Lerryn River carried away what was left of the tall, beautiful man.

Elspeth was ninety-three years old when she and John Wakelyn came to the New World. Her husband had the mutation, weakly expressed, and was beginning to grow old in his eighties. Their daughter received a copy of the longevity gene from each parent. It was fully expressed.

Margaret Wakelyn would have grown into a wonderful woman. She would have lived for centuries.

"Who are you afraid of?" David asked.

Not James Seeker.

She picked up his thought. *No, not James. But there have been others like him.*

It's only in the last hundred years we've begun to understand genetics. If I have a child and it gets one copy of the key gene, there's a chance the longevity trait will show up. It depends on other conditions whether the autologous gene will be expressed. If the father is like me the child will get two copies of the gene. If she's female, she will live a very long time. But in a male . . . Do you understand? Mutations are most strongly expressed in the Y chromosome. In males.

When we recognized the danger of long-liveds interbreeding, it was too late. There are several hundred offspring like James. They consider themselves to be the purebreds. You've no idea what they're like.

David said, "I have an idea."

No.

(dead, hollow, burning cities, reefs of human bones, man and man's works swept away)

That is your future. There will be none of you left but slaves. And playthings. They love to have playthings.

But her fear wasn't abstract. It was personal. David said, "Who are you afraid of?"

Wakelyn had finished dressing. She spoke aloud. "The Ewell people murdered my daughter and my husband, just as I told you. When I escaped the island, I was pregnant. With a son. He came back with you on the helicopter."

"You're afraid of your son?"

"I haven't seen him since he was nineteen. He was already

worse than James Seeker. In the last few months, I've sensed him—coming for me."

David said, "Why?"

"By Philip's standards, I'm an evil person. I never again had a child by a man with the longevity gene. Instead I've polluted the new race, tainted it with the old human strain. What would *you* think of a woman who procreated with mountain apes?"

"What can Philip do?"

"Alone—he can do to you what he did to the people on Ewell. Control weak individual minds, chip away at dozens of them with a mantra or chant. If he forms a circuit with several others of his kind, he can destroy every mind in this building. Except mine. He has to get at me physically. But he could have one of you do that for him."

David looked out through the glass. St. Leger and Calder stood motionless, not frozen but like people who had lost their trains of thought.

"You could have killed them."

"It wasn't necessary. Augustus has a special reason for hating me. The woman—she's afraid of so many things. . . . Will you help me?"

He felt no pressure. She was subtler than he imagined, or she was leaving the decision to him. Yet he could sense that she had left part of the truth unsaid, perhaps the major part.

"Why do the purebreds want to destroy us?" David asked.

"Because you're not human. Not fully human." There was no trace of humor in her smile. "The old order gives way to the new. Doesn't it?"

He understood what she hadn't said. She had no need to be *for* the old order or *against* it. In time, nature would eliminate *Homo sapiens sapiens*. The emergence of the new gene had started the clock. The end could come quickly, if Philip Wakelyn had his way, or slowly. Perhaps not all that slowly.

How many more Elspeths were there? He couldn't begin to guess. If the trait had been present in a woman more than twelve hundred years ago, the question was one of fertility . . . and exponential growth. Fertility had to be very low, to balance the low mortality rate. Otherwise the variants already would number in the trillions.

The touch of the woman's mind—the gentle bump of an aged and almost alien consciousness against his—had resolved all his doubts about the significance of the variation. It might take years to unravel the complexity of the woman's genome. She spoke as if longevity came from a single gene. Which one?

"Do you know where Philip is?" David asked.

"He's near. He's good at hiding himself."

She hadn't told him the full truth, and he probed for it. "He doesn't really want to kill you, does he?"

She came nearer. He felt the blinding sexual attraction. "Why do you say that?"

"He had opportunities on the island. He could have gotten the locals to do it. Or the soldiers."

"He could have."

There was something in the woman's patient tone that made David hesitate. Then he understood. "Your parents both had the longevity trait."

The woman didn't answer.

"So you are homozygous. Purebred. Just like James Seeker and your son."

"Not 'just like'."

"No, you lack the Y chromosome. But if you had been born male, you would have been like them. The gene would have been fully expressed."

She didn't answer.

David said, "But if you had children by a purebred male . . ."

"If the children were male, they would be like my son. You're right. Killing me isn't his first objective."

"What is?"

"He wants to use me as breeding stock. With the right partner I could produce hundreds of his kind."

And who would be the right partner?

She answered: *My son.*

A voice from the doorway said, "The world has enough monsters."

Carsten Starns entered the room. Beside him crowded three men and a woman, dressed in civilian clothes but armed. FBI, or NIS, or Homeland Security. People who would do what they were told.

He caught Elspeth's desperate thought:

There are too many—

She couldn't protect herself. As she hadn't protected her husband and daughter.

The man next to Starns aimed his weapon squarely at Wakelyn's chest and fired.

58

DAVID AND RODRIGUEZ STOOD TOGETHER, AGAINST THE WALL, under a soldier's watch. The room was full of armed men, a few women, half of them military. St. Leger lowered the gun he had taken from David. His expression was astonished. "Do you really think humanity should lie back and say go ahead, wipe me out, evolution decrees it?"

"I don't know what evolution is going to do," David said.

"You were going to help her!"

"I was going to prevent a murder."

St. Leger spoke between set teeth. "You can't afford to be so squeamish. Fortunately, Director Starns isn't."

Elspeth Wakelyn lay on the hospital bed, unconscious from the taser shock and sedation, blindfolded, strapped down. After St. Leger warned of what he called her hypnotic power, the guards were put on ten minute rotations. The old man strode around the bed, looking down, like a crane inspecting something curious in murky water.

"If this woman carried a lethal virus," he said, "you would isolate her—at the very least. If there was a risk of her escaping, and the consequences of it were dreadful enough, you might even support euthanasia. This is how we have to look at her. Not as a virus carrier. But as a deadly virus itself. If she lives, she's a death sentence to the human race." His sharp shoulders rose and fell in a shrug. "We're done talking."

"It's too late," David said.

"We'll see."

Rodriguez spoke. "You're going to stop the evolutionary clock?"

"Actually, I'm going to turn it back," St. Leger said. "Destroy this new master race. Why not? We fight every day against the evolutionary advances of microbes. You think we should let nature take its course because this bug walks on two legs?"

"It's too late," David repeated.

St. Leger didn't seem to hear. "She's no better than us. This isn't some new improved version of the ape. It's just *different*. An ape with six heads would be different. We don't have to bow and worship it when we can kill it."

"It's *too late*."

"Starns sees it my way. So will the public, if you think the public matters. Once we tie her to the epidemic, the old witch hunts will be nothing compared to what we do to the Wakelyns."

St. Leger started to turn away, and David said, "She didn't tell you everything, did she?"

"She showed me more than I wanted to see. The bitch showed me—" Rubbing his temple, he turned reddened eyes on the unconscious woman. He pushed a thought at her: *We'll farm your fucking DNA. What's left of you will be a few scattered cells floating in alcohol. Does that prospect appeal to you as much as it appeals to me?* There was no response. But St. Leger heard the murmurings of her sleeping mind. Incoherent, too scattered to understand. Casting a surreptitious glance at the people around him, he saw no hint that any of them shared his awareness. Most of them were too primitive to be receivers. She could control them, if she struggled up several levels toward consciousness, but she would never fill their minds with her pain.

Blessed are the stupid.

St. Leger watched the soldiers. *There* was the state of humanity. Morons who moved when they were told to move, ambulatory guns that someone else aimed. Calder and Starns were in the doorway, heads together, hatching plans, imagining they were in control. They were the hominids who, if Wakelyn's gift could be harvested, would count their useless days in centuries. Starns might view Wakelyn as a stain on Creation, but he wouldn't turn down a few hundred extra years, would he? And St. Leger wondered: *What about me? Is that what I want?* Schoolchildren singing hymns to *Au-gus-tus-Sane-Lay-ger, G-i-i-iver of Life.* He should be around for that, to make sure it was as grotesque as he imagined, except he couldn't bear the thought. He had no appetite for a longer life. He didn't want to live forever. Or for that matter, any longer.

You won't.

The words stole into his mind.

He looked down. She was unconscious, but on some level she had become aware of him.

No? He directed the thought, got no response.

It occurred to him he might have been hallucinating. He had no scientific verification of any of Wakelyn's black magic. Anything he had experienced could have been the product of an aged, delusional mind. He might indeed have suffered a stroke. The blurred vision of his left eye fit that. Perhaps his cognitive power was blurred as well. Everything he saw and heard could be products of his dementia. He considered the problem. It had an amusing aspect. What could be more solipsistic than supposing the external world was a mere expression of one's madness?

"We're taking her downstairs," Calder said. She stood a few feet from him, brows arched—hadn't she seen a madman talking to himself before?—hands on her hips, mouth confident, something Starns had given her: the first hint that she could be invaluable in the new world: it would need a lot of policemen. The gift of longevity would be parceled out carefully, only to the deserving.

"The General wants her terminated," Calder said. "She's too dangerous. We have evidence she designed the plague bacillus herself."

The General? And, *You do?*

St. Leger followed Calder's gaze. The man who stood beside Starns wasn't in uniform. St. Leger couldn't make out exactly what he was wearing. He might be tall and fair-haired. St. Leger tried to focus, but his attention slipped away.

"I didn't know we had a general in the building," St. Leger said.

"He came directly from the President."

"Really."

"With orders to terminate the variant."

"Splendid idea. Why take her downstairs to do that? It could done right here. Right now." He watched Calder, who looked as mindless as any Eweller. He said, "Go ahead, then," trying to block the thought, *So you've come to rescue her?* He brushed past Calder, groping his pocket for the gun—

The pain blinded him.

It was an explosion, a hundred times worse than the nails Wakelyn had driven into his skull.

You could have been like me, said a dreadful whisper in his mind. *If you'd had a better father.*

Another explosion.

Your mother despised you. Half your mind was dead. You were an animal to her.

St. Leger screamed.

You disgusted her.

N-o-o-o!

But why else would she have left him? Not only to hide herself . . .

She must have despised him.

A jolt took him to his knees.

It's too bad you won't live to see what your mother produces when I breed with her. We'll chain her to a bed, beside this one.

The image stabbed his mind. He wept.

He stared blindly. The room was shadowy. He knew another gasket had blown inside his skull. Felt like a major one. There was so much that Wakelyn had tried to tell him. That he hadn't wanted to absorb.

He didn't know if he was dying. If this was death, it was about time—and yet so unfair. With a different father, he could have been with *her* forever.

A rocking explosion. This one from outside.

St. Leger didn't hear that sound. It came as Helen Calder fired a pistol into the back of his head.

59

DAVID SAW THE GOLDEN MAN STEP OUT OF THE SHADOWS, tall and commanding. He could have passed for a god if there was a small-time Nordic race that needed one. The face was too sharp-featured and feral to be called handsome, but it glowed with conviction. The green eyes had the jewel-like clarity that might come from a brilliant mind looking out on a world it knew it could shape. What was missing was any trace of the shared experience of being human: the experience of pain and fear and guilt.

Something invisible moved toward David, a wall of emotion, of loathing and indignation, as if the sight of a frail, soft soul—David's soul—was a moral affront, to be wiped away. It struck like a hammer blow and flung him into darkness.

Rodriguez was on her knees, fingers on his wrist. Her face was the first thing he saw. "Thought you were dead," she said.

"He tried," David said thickly. He ducked his head between his knees. His mind was sluggish. With each heartbeat, nausea swept him. His face was sweaty. Hands shaking. A soldier lay beside the hospital bed, unconscious or dead. Another man—the medic—was doubled up, retching. The bed was empty.

Becker was kneeling beside Rodriguez. "What happened?"

"Her son came. Philip Wakelyn. She tried to protect us from him. Where did you go?"

"I got off this floor after the old man went limp." Becker rested a hand on David's shoulder. "Did she have control of you?"

"Not exactly," he said.

"Who shot St. Leger?"

"Calder pulled the trigger," Rodriguez said. "She wasn't acting on her own."

David straightened and said, "There was a general—"

Rodriguez shook her head. "No, that was Philip Wakelyn." As she explained to Becker, David listened and realized that he had partly succumbed to the purebred's influence. Part of his mind wanted to accept Philip's made-up version of reality.

"Where are they taking her?" Becker said.

"Out of here, if Philip can manage it. If he breeds with her—" David pulled himself to his feet. "If he breeds with her, there will be more like him. We've got to get her back, Paolo. She's not our enemy."

"You believe her?"

"Enough."

"How do you know you're not under her control?"

"None of us can be sure. We have to act anyway."

Becker spoke softly. "St. Leger was right, David. Wakelyn's genotype puts us all in the crapper."

"No. We'll change, but we would do that anyway. We've been doing it for thousands of years. If Elspeth's genes don't confer an advantage, they'll be flushed out of the human genome. Maybe longevity is a plus, maybe not. We'll find out gradually, and our children's children will be around for the answer." David knew he was sugar-coating the truth. He felt no need to preserve a species whose time had passed, even if it was his own species. No need to preserve, but a need to protect its final generations from Philip Wakelyn.

Elspeth's way was better. Her children were no longer purebred. They were half-and-halves. Mixed species. *Hybrids.*

The hybridization of humanity would take centuries. Everyone he loved would be dead long before its end, with no claim on the future. He wondered: Once the process was complete, would there be tribes, would there be Jews, even secular, non-believers —or would the new generations say goodbye to all that? The old, troubling questions of humanity wouldn't vanish. There would be people who thought about those questions, but what would they call themselves? He didn't know, but he suspected he was clinging to an anachronism.

"Philip Wakelyn plans a clean sweep," David said. "Did you see Major Dott among the soldiers?"

They both said no.

"We've got to find Dott. If Philip and his mother are still in the building, we need Dott to hold them."

"Why wouldn't Philip have left with her?" Rodriguez asked.

"He needs to set something moving. He'll want to turn this building into another Ewell Island, with no survivors."

He walked over to St. Leger's body, searched pockets and found a gun.

For whatever good it would do.

60

THE BUILDING FELT DEAD, AS IF PHILIP HAD PASSED FLOOR TO floor, shutting off minds, stilling hearts. David started down the south stairway. Becker and Rodriguez followed.

"I hear her," David said. The mental cry was faint. He didn't think it was directed at him in particular. She was pleading for help from any mind she could reach.

Which made him wonder: what minds did she *think* she could reach?

The light was dim in the stairway. The building had grown darker since Philip's appearance. Emergency lights had sunk to faint orange. *Was he hallucinating?* The mutant could not have tapped the building's energy source. No organic brain, regardless of how powerful, could drain a mechanical system. The generators might be failing, or might have been sabotaged. Or his perceptions could be distorted.

The feeble orange glow made the air seem *thick*.

"If it comes to it, we can't let him have her," David said.

He left the alternatives unstated.

"You're right." Becker sounded eager. "We can't."

They heard shots. Two sharp cracks and then dozens of reports, the echoes high-pitched like shrieks bouncing up the stairwell.

Rodriguez looked at David without seeming to recognize him. In the last few seconds the stairwell had gotten darker. In a way he couldn't identify, it was changing.

Ghosts from chimneys, demons from clouds.

The stairwell wasn't changing. His perception of it was.

A blunt-nosed man in uniform emerged from the command center on the second floor and stared straight through Philip Wakelyn. He sketched a salute to Carsten Starns and jerked a questioning look at the two men who carried Elspeth Wakelyn strapped to a litter.

"Where are you taking her?" Dott asked.

Starns answered. "The general wants her transferred. I concur."

"The general?"

Philip clapped his mouth, smothering a giggle.

The man was going to say, *What general?*

"What general?" Dott said.

"The general standing beside me," Starns replied stiffly.

"There's nobody standing beside you."

Philip whispered: *A traitor!*

Dott scowled. Next to Starns, the air rippled. Dott squinted. He could almost see something. Like heat in a desert.

This man's mind was hard, Philip found. You could chip a tooth on it. He especially enjoyed breaking people like the major, because they sensed what was happening to them. Then they struggled as feebly as a baby when you held its head under water. He didn't have time for that now.

He told Helen Calder: *Use your pistol.* Calder had barely struggled. She could be convinced of anything.

He whispered: *Execute the traitor.*

She did.

The two shots knocked Dott backward onto the floor.

Philip played a game with the mind of the first marine who charged out of the command center. Instead of letting him square things with Calder, who stood with her pistol extended, Philip turned the young man around to unload an ammunition clip into the chests of the officers right behind him. They died. Philip watched benignly. He could feel the minds of the dead for a few seconds—if there was no structural damage to the brain, sometimes longer as neurons discharged, synapses collapsed, the subconscious vanished. It went nowhere, as far as he could tell.

It was a concept he had trouble accepting. He felt as though he had always existed. He knew he hadn't, but he could remember no time when he hadn't. He smiled at the fallacy.

He lifted his mother from the litter.

You have work to do, he whispered to the remaining marines. *Use your guns. There are other traitors. Hunt them down.*

He was sorry he couldn't stay to watch.

The gunfire had stopped. But the stairway was definitely darker. It seemed narrower and steeper and *damp.* David retreated up several steps. "We'd better try a different way."

They emerged into a fifth floor hallway. He froze, and the door bumped his shoulder. He closed his eyes, forgot to breathe. When he opened his eyes the image was still there. Thick white stalactites hung from the ceiling, feeding brackish water into streams at his feet where four half-submerged bodies strained in their final contortions, gasping, eyes bulging. The faces were coated with years of lime, but he still recognized his friends who had perished in Mexico. Rodriguez and Becker were rooted. David wondered if they were seeing substantially the same thing or were being shown their own versions of hell.

"It isn't real," said Rodriguez.

Becker's gun pointed into the oozing darkness. "Are you sure?"

"It's Philip. *It isn't real.*"

"She's right," David said.

But it could become real—their reality, subjective, insubstantial, delusional. If one of the purebreds was this strong, what castle of horrors could a family of them build? How would a person trapped in it find his way out?

A lime-slicked face turned upward, pleading. David looked away.

As he took a few steps, he could detect the illusion's weakness. The black, enclosing walls were translucent, like a smoked window through which he could see into small offices. Several men in white shirts and dark trousers sat at a round table loaded with electronics gear. Their faces hung slack. David heard an insinuating whisper and wondered if it reached them.

Isn't it time you did something?

One man's face pinched with sudden rage. He was staring straight out of the office at them.

"Come on," David said.

The configuration of the building showed through the illusion like shadowy bones under flesh. All he had to do was ignore appearances. As a scientist, he relied on the evidence of the senses, interpreted by his mind. Now he relied on the knowledge that his senses were being deceived. He grabbed Rodriguez's arm and walked straight through a stalactite. It was no worse than negotiating a carnival fun house, better in the sense that no papier-mâché faces leapt at them from the walls.

"This is building toward something," David said. "He doesn't need a magic show to get his mother out of here."

They followed the corridor until David thought they were near the office the archaeologists had used. He was desperately afraid for Charl. He pushed through a hanging garden of tormented bodies, unfocusing his eyes because he did not want to share the inside of Philip Wakelyn's mind. The more one shared it, the more it would take over.

The office was empty. He backed out.

"They're not here," he said. He wondered if the murderous rampage had already begun. Had caught Charl and her husband.

"We can search for them," Becker said. "Or we can try to intercept Philip."

"Can you tell where you are?"

"Yes, mostly."

"What about you?" he asked Rodriguez.

"I'm seeing past it."

The next door opened onto the north stairwell. David led the way down, moving quickly to the second floor and into a wide kitchen. Becker cringed away from some imaginary threat, almost fired on the apparition, then lowered his weapon and shuddered. He was pale and sweating. "I found a way out of here earlier," he said.

"Where?"

"Take the service elevator. There's a loading dock in the second basement. Across the garage, a door gets you into a tunnel. You come out in woods. If this goes wrong, whoever's left might want to try it."

"Then what?"

"Look for shelter."

Something swam across David's vision, a crawling blackness that tried to sweep him into its world.

He wondered how far afield Philip could broadcast his horrors—whether Philip and his cousins had been stoking the chaos in infected cities.

"Shelter might not be worth much," David said.

He felt a flicker of awareness. "She's awake. On stairs . . ."

"Where?"

"I can't tell. He'll need transport. You two try the stairs. I'll try the garage."

"What do you plan to do if you find him?" Becker said. "You can't sneak up on him. Do you know how to shoot?"

"No."

"So you haven't got a clue, have you?"

David admitted, "No."

61

THE DREAM IMAGES FADED AS THE ELEVATOR DESCENDED. AS HE neared the garage, David cast a thought outward—*Where are you?*

There was no answer. He wondered if he had really sensed her or if this was another of her son's deceptions.

Becker and Rodriguez had taken the stairway. Their priorities were set: Find Dott or other soldiers. Intercept Philip. All else failing, head for the men and women on the armored vehicles that cordoned the property.

Hope whoever they encountered was sane.

How do you plan against a creature than can read your mind? David had a faint hope. If Elspeth was conscious, she might distract her son.

Might.

The deepest garage looked empty, except for a bright orange utility vehicle. Across the floor he could see the closed door that might provide them an escape, if he could find Charl and they could reach it.

Fifteen feet behind David, the elevator murmured. He threw himself behind a concrete pillar as the doors opened. Two soldiers emerged, swinging their weapons in tight arcs, trotting across the floor. The taller man spotted David.

"Come out! Hands up!"

"I'm not armed." Leaving the gun in his pocket, David stepped around the pillar. Two young men who had been on the Ewell team closed on him. A short, dark-haired boy lowered his weapon. "You're one of the scientists. Do you know what's going on?"

"We brought the island's trouble back with us," David said. "Can you reach Major Dott?"

"The major's dead. So's half our unit. Guys are killing each other. What'd we bring back?"

"A form of mental contagion."

"Like a virus?"

"That's right. How many of your men are acting normal?"

"Five, six. Corporal Stratton has his head on straight, but he took two in the belly. No one can find the medic."

"There's a man calling himself a general—have you seen him?"

"Yeah, he's trying to bring some order. Him and Director Starns."

"Is there a woman with them?"

"Couple. One's sick. The other one's helping us find traitors."

"Traitors."

"Like the ones that killed Major Dott. The general showed us. We got a real fifth column at work."

David tried to keep the dismay out of his voice. "Can you take me to the general?"

"I don't know. . . ."

"There are things he needs to know about the contagion."

The second man chuckled. "I don't think there's much the general doesn't know." He lifted his radio. "Stratton? You still with us? . . . Raynes, who's covering? Anyone?" He scowled. Then he pulled his face away from the radio and looked up. Both men had heard it.

Brrrt-brrrt-brrrt.

Three bursts, muffled by tons of concrete.

"Maybe they caught some of the bastards," the taller guy said. "We better get back to base."

David started to turn away when lightning exploded behind his eyes. The pain drilled through his optical nerves, fired nails through his cortex. He was on his knees, palms on the concrete. Choking vomit. He had been shot, or slammed with a rifle. . . .

Another blinding jolt.

He clenched his eyelids. Dazzling light burned through them, boiled away the gray matter, incinerated the brainstem. Turned bone to dust. Left nothing.

Bits of him came back. He remembered to breathe. Air was acid in his lungs. He cracked his eyelids.

He lifted his head and saw the two soldiers ten feet away. The smaller man was twisting like a worm pinned to a board. The other lay face down, unmoving.

The storm had come and gone and he was alive. He guessed at its source. Neither Elspeth nor her son had that kind of power alone.

David forced himself to his feet.

He headed for the garage's up ramp. It switched back and forth, with sharp turns at the middle and the top. He heard engines when he was two-thirds of the way up. Then he rounded the last corner and emerged fifty feet from the front of the building. Dozens of cars were parked along here, some civilian, some official. The doors to the outside were open. At the threshold, Helen Calder climbed into a large SUV that spilled exhaust across a half-dozen inert bodies. A man in uniform was pushing Elspeth Wakelyn into the SUV's back seat. Her son, coming from behind the vehicle, sensed David.

A wave of pitiless loathing—

Another traitor, Phillip told the soldier. *Kill him.*

The soldier stepped into the open and fired as David hurled himself behind ranks of cars. The sound of the shots drowned out every other external sound. As the soldier came deeper into the garage, David ran behind vehicles for the exit and plunged into the darkness.

Snow fell heavily. Floodlights were barely visible at the distant perimeter, casting vehicles as silhouettes. Closer, tires whirred on ice. Letting the sound draw him, David felt the denseness of the air, the presence of electricity before a storm, atoms packed so tight that movement was like plunging into a smothering foam wall.

The SUV was a hundred feet ahead, halfway to the perimeter, engine idling, exhaust trickling, and as he neared, the back door opened and a lumpy figure rolled out onto the ground, blood spraying from the throat. He reached the body, recognized Calder. He hadn't heard a shot.

The SUV whined for traction, fishtailing across the open area. The guard posts lay ahead. In front of the vehicle, something large and white rose from the snow, swirling upward. A snow devil, David thought. But there was no wind. At first it was a flailing white curtain, transparent and insubstantial. Then it took on shape. And the shape became solid. *Ghosts from the chimneys, demons in the clouds*, David remembered. Mammoth jaws appeared, and expanded. Claws scythed down toward the military cordon. A guard saw the apparition and screamed and was swept away. The SUV plowed ahead, crushing bodies.

The thing descended on the vehicle. Silently, a section of torn roof whirled into the night.

A man levitated out. A man who could have been a god.

He twisted in the garish light, rising, thrashed by snowy claws. He began coming apart. There were four inaudible convulsions. Legs fell to the snow. Arms tore from their sleeves like stricken birds and fluttered into the darkness. The head twisted, came free, and spun away like a small bright moon. The torso hung in empty air. Fifty feet past the perimeter, the SUV slowed to a stop.

Men with weapons ran after it, then became lethargic. David reached the vehicle before them. The roof was intact. Philip Wakelyn occupied the driver's seat, head back, blowing crimson froth at the ceiling. Lines of red had soaked through his coat. The red marked the junctures where arms and legs joined the torso. In his mind, Philip had been dismembered.

Soldiers drifted up but lost interest.

David pulled open the passenger door, took Elspeth's arm. "You did that?"

No.

He felt the comfort of her mind.

The feeling was warm, almost maternal, and for a giddy moment he wanted to laugh because she had everything reversed, she wasn't entitled to be maternal. In a sense she was younger than he. She wasn't humanity's parent but its child. Not quite the old species' first born, but its future.

A soldier went rigid, then relaxed.

David heard the silent scream.

Kill her.

She's your death sentence.

Kill her.

The voice fell silent.

The froth on Philip Wakelyn's mouth was still. His breathing had stopped.

Becker was beside him, aiming his pistol at the woman's head.

"He's right," Becker said. "We can end this."

"No." David blocked him. "It won't end anything."

"It will buy us time."

"We're too late. It's been going on too long."

Becker's grip on the weapon tightened. Elspeth Wakelyn watched him, then turned her back. She told David, "This way."

On the road outside, a dozen or more vehicles sat, engines running, lights dimmed, windows opaque, modest vehicles, unmemorable, like the woman who got out of the nearest car. She could have been his next-door neighbor, Sunday school teacher, office clerk. She looked thirty years old. Attractive without beauty, fiercely healthy. Somewhere in his mind he felt a gentle probing, assessing—and a whisper of information, that this young woman had changed little since Lincoln spoke.

"My daughters came for me," Wakelyn said.

David wondered: *How many?*

She didn't answer. Instead she gripped his wrist. *Remember this.*

Sunlight blazed in his mind. Not lightning. Sunlight.

Becker came out of the darkness. The cars were gone, moving slowly into the chaotic night. Elspeth Wakelyn was gone with them.

Becker said, "What did she do to you?"

David tried to make sense of the images that had filled his brain. He knew he would try many times, until he imposed order and sense that Elspeth Wakelyn might not have intended. He would do the best he could. This was what happened to religious revelations. Someone had to work them over into comprehensible form. He had no intention of becoming Wakelyn's prophet. He had never embraced the traditions of his father, and he could never accept the role of Saul to this new species. But he wondered if any of humanity apart from himself knew what lay before them.

Assuming she told the truth.

62

THERE WAS NO SIGN OF ALARM AROUND THEM. SOLDIERS WERE wandering away, indifferent to the corpse in the SUV. One young woman in battle gear moved off, kicking clumps of snow until she disappeared in the darkness. David wondered whether the damage to their minds was permanent. He wondered if the dead man had done it or Elspeth and her daughters.

"I tried to shoot her," Becker said. "Couldn't move."

"You were lucky." David took a last glance inside the SUV. If the dead man *was* her son, if she had told even that much of the truth, Elspeth wasn't sentimental. She had arranged his slaughter. David shivered. What else could you do to a monstrous offspring? That would be Starns's thinking about anyone with the mutant gene. A lot of other people's, too. Perhaps his own.

When they reached the building, he thought he had an answer. The soldiers who had survived here were as mentally crippled as those outside. Philip hadn't done that; he had gotten free of the building. This had been Elspeth Wakelyn's parting message. Joined with others of her kind, she could inflict horrible damage. Better leave them alone.

He doubted the message would be understood—or heeded.

Carsten Starns sat on the floor in the laboratory. Behind him the room was dark. David found the specimens and the gel trays Rodriguez had prepared, tossed them into the lab's autoclave, set the unit for sterilization. At the monitor, he deleted all the files containing both Margaret and Elspeth's DNA profiles. There would be no chain of evidence linking the living woman to her long-dead daughter.

After watching him for a while, the director of NIS said, "Who are you?"

David didn't answer.

Looking up at him with childish intensity, Starns said, "Who am *I*?"

Nobody who matters.

"You've chosen sides," Becker said.

David wasn't sure. "We can't conceal the truth for long, but Starns won't have a monopoly on the information. That might make a difference."

"Look around you. If a few of them can do this much damage, it may not matter who knows."

"Not to the outcome. But to how we get there." David imagined Starns leading a campaign of eradication, a crusade to save the human race from the interloper, defending biblical lies while the truth was still obscure, as some of it would always be. The crusade would be futile, but it would destroy any chance for coexistence among man and his successor—if coexistence was possible. David thought it was. Elspeth had no use for the purebred male. A common enemy could unite them, for a while.

He started for the door, and a voice behind him said, "You aren't going to leave me?"

Elbows on his knees, Starns waited for an answer.

"Only for a few minutes," David said.

"I *order* you not to leave me!"

That much of the personality was intact. "I'll send somebody," David promised.

□□□

Dr. Taylor was working floor to floor, gathering a flock of men and women who wore childlike expressions. He stopped, and the daisy chain stopped. Each person stood with a hand on the shoulder of the person ahead. Some of them giggled. Most just stared.

Taylor looked back at them anxiously. "What the hell is this? They have a mental age of six. I haven't heard of the disease presenting this way. Why aren't you and I affected?"

"I don't know," David said.

"We're going to have to feed all these people."

"We'll help."

"Assuming they don't die. If this is a new form of the disease—" Taylor considered the eight people had in tow "—it's coming just as I was getting optimistic." He patted a young soldier in his charge. "Come on, fellas. Keep a hand on your buddy's shoulder. Downstairs we go."

"Have you seen Professor Sprague?"

Taylor shook his head.

"What about Rodriguez?" said Becker.

"No, sorry."

David watched them go.

Becker said, "Rodriguez and I split up at the first floor. I'm going to find her."

He did, in the lobby, looking after uniformed men who wandered aimlessly in and out the shattered windows. Two men in dark suits lay in pools of blood. Rodriguez followed Becker's glance and told him, "They were executing traitors when the storm hit. I was going to be next."

"Are you okay?"

"Brutal headache. But I know my name. These guys don't."

She ran to restrain a man who was standing under a guillotine-like shard of glass, trying to pull it loose.

The horrific scenery had vanished. But the halls were crowded with puzzled-looking men and women, and bodies.

David came off the stairs and Charl was running at him. "You're all right! We were hunting for you upstairs."

"Where's Noel?"

"He's trying to find someone who isn't sleep-walking. What about Paolo?"

"He's okay. So's Taylor. We've got a lot of people to take care of."

"You saw what happened? It was like we were underground—"

"Elspeth Wakelyn had a son. We were in his nightmare." They returned to the stairs, started up, and David told her what he knew and what he had done.

Charl stopped. "You destroyed the evidence? What if Philip's kind launch another attack?"

"They're going to be busy hiding—from us, and from Elspeth and her daughters."

"You believe that because she told you."

"No, she told me other things."

"Like what?"

"Later." Without Wakelyn's help, he had made another guess. He studied Charlene Sprague's face. The wound she had suffered four days ago was invisible. Her smooth skin could have been an undergraduate student's. Her vitality had always amazed him, and drawn him. Now he suspected he knew why. He wondered just how deeply variant genes had made inroads into the human population. How many generations had they been at work?

A bridge still existed. The break between species wasn't complete.

They could still interbreed.

"You really should have children," David said.

She stood still. "Where did that come from?"

"Just an idea."

"You'd better forget it. I'm staying with Noel."

"And I wish you both long, happy lives." She would probably have that. Not the longevity of Wakelyn but if his guess was right a pretty good stretch. He thought of her thirty years from now, still beautiful.

"Come on," she said, and grabbed his wrist.

For a moment, he felt Elspeth's fierce grip. Her command: *Remember this.*

She had showed him.

At first, the images were connected to the world he knew. Cities and towns and farms, skyscrapers and hovels, more or less recognizable. Then they changed. Pestilence and wars cut them down. They grew again. It was the story of the human race, forever grasping, forever unperfected. Scores of years passed. Then hundreds. Then much more.

A barren place. It had never supported life under its black sky, but a woman stood there. She bore a small resemblance to Elspeth Wakelyn, though her dark skin carried the signature of a dozen races. She operated a towering machine, brow creased as she worked at a task he couldn't imagine, her face bathed in the luminescence of a blue sphere half-hidden by the horizon, its continents familiar, its seas blazing in sunlight.

He knew the things Wakelyn wanted him to know:

The woman was more than eight feet tall.

The ancient myths of giants had been a premonition.

She had lived for more than a thousand years.

The myth of Lazarus had been fulfilled.

She had never been ill.

The torments of Job were a distant human memory.

Unless an accident cut short her time, she would live another four or five millennia, her knowledge and her species' knowledge rising in an ever steeper exponential curve until the last question had been asked—and answered—and he glimpsed both the question and its answer.

The final sentient species had halted the wasteful biological lottery of evolution. Man and woman chose what they would become.

There had been no god in the natural universe, but Wakelyn's children had become gods.

This time the jump forward was far, far longer. . . .

Another barren place, another distant sky. Rising from a dry sea was a blue sun under which no member of *Homo sapiens sapiens* had ever walked but under which the new species thrived. Behind the blue star, trillions of miles distant, swelled a giant orange sun, his sun, bloated and aged. This was what lay ahead, however many millions of years. Someone carrying Wakelyn's genetic gift would be alive, to witness the death of the sun.

The young woman squeezed his hand. "Are you daydreaming? Come on."

David knew there were things he wouldn't tell anyone, just yet.

Epilogue

GUEST COLUMN BY HENRY E. WALD, DIRECTOR EMERITUS, Department of Cellular Biology, New York University, published in *The New York Times Magazine* (online edition, August 8).

I used to tell my students, "Nature is the ultimate terrorist." The line was pithy and provocative. I explained, "Nature wipes out every sentient being within a hundred years or so. It will do the same to you, to your favorite boyfriend, to your sweetest child."

It's a wasteful beast, starting over again and again. Like a mad scientist, nature creates experiments, then tosses the results into the rubbish bin. More than 95 percent of all the species that have ever inhabited the planet are now extinct. All the early hominids—every last one that did not evolve into modern man—became a dead end. There is no reason to expect nature's wastefulness to change.

It is early to do more than speculate about the eventual significance of the discovery of the Ewell Variant. But if I were still in the classroom, with an audience that could only fidget but not escape, I would offer a few thoughts. Human evolution has been incredibly rapid. Four million years ago our distant ancestor the australopith diverged from the apes and began to walk upright. Let's call that, in evolutionary time, twenty-four hours ago. Five hundred thousand years ago—after many subspecies had risen and died out—early *Homo sapiens* and the Neanderthal split from our common ancestor, *Homo heidelbergensis,* and went their separate ways. On the biological clock, that was three hours ago. Scarcely two hundred thousand years ago, full *Homo sapiens sapiens* emerged in Africa and populated the earth. On evolution's clock: a mere 72 minutes ago. We're vain enough to believe that that was it—modern man is evolution's end game. Leaving aside that view's chauvinism, it ignores the observable fact that mutations occur constantly. Most of the changes are fatal to the recipient, but it's clear that this aspect of biology hasn't stopped functioning. Evolution isn't over.

Observing the rapidity of *Homo sapiens sapiens'* ascent, we should have been expecting something new to come along.

The process by which individuals and species are replaced may seem cruel. What is more pathetic than an aware being saying, "I won't be here tomorrow—I won't *be.*" A few paragraphs ago, I used the term "wastefulness." I concede—at age seventy-eight—that I have a vested complaint against nature's throw-away scheme. A man has just enough time to accumulate a morsel of wisdom before being wiped out. In part because of that, societies repeat mistakes century after century. I would like to say that this represents bad planning by our genes, but I'm afraid that such "Wald-centricity" is misguided. Biologically, wisdom counts for nothing—it's the new experiments that propel evolution. Even in human affairs, wisdom is a bit overrated—often hard to distinguish from the clogged arteries of orthodoxy. If each hominid had lived longer, we might still be huddled in the African bush, listening to a wise old man tell us the dangers of fire. Short generations mean that a fresh young mind comes along and knocks wisdom for a cocked hat. The species that adapt best live very short individual lives. How long does a single bacterium have to contemplate its uniqueness? It's here and gone. Yet it belongs to a family of genetic winners, whose rapid mutation can handle pretty much anything a sentient species' science throws at it.

Long-lived generations contribute nothing to the DNA's development. They yield stagnation. As species compete for places in the ecosystem, stagnation can mean death.

Does that mean we should welcome the Ewell Variant?

Personally, I like my friends and neighbors without the odd attributes of the Eweller. But nature didn't consult me.

Nature may have set humankind on this path long ago. There remains debate over the extent to which evolution is random. Natural selection, scientists agree, is not random—it rewards advantage, the enlarged cortex, the fleeter foot. The question is whether mutation itself is completely random. Here we risk straying into the folly of "intelligent design," so I want to be especially careful about my next point. The scientifically respectable argument goes this way: that the designer is not a supernatural intelligence but our genetic heritage itself. Once you have eyes, the next step is eyelashes. Until you make that improvement, nature will keep trying. It will throw off horny lashes, nictitating membranes, anything you can imagine to protect the useful organ. Inversely, without the development of eyes, you will never get eyelashes.

This brings us to a key question of evolutionary theory. Do certain mutations repeat? If they do, that reduces the role of natural selection—the survival advantage, for instance, of speech over tooth and claw. If they do repeat, then species' genetic makeup does a lot of the selection by repeatedly throwing up a particular variant. Even then, of course, its eventual success depends on its conferring an advantage on the organism. So we are back to natural selection.

Some games, the moment they're set in motion, determine the outcome. One player has an advantage that no luck or craft among the opponents can overcome. An example is the number game "Run to 20." The game is fatal to my opponent every time. He can't win even if he knows the pattern, once I've made the first move. My grand-niece drives her brother crazy with that, beating him every time.

We don't know the pattern of the game nature has set in motion with the Ewell Variant. The Variant may succeed or it may prove to be a dead end. But longer term we can know the outcome of nature's game. It is ruthless and unsentimental.

If I were in the classroom today, I would give students the bad news this way: "The replacement of our species by a newer model is a foregone conclusion. The only questions are *what* and *when*." It's just possible we've seen the *what: Homo sapiens ewellensis.* The *when* may be sooner than we think.

Nature, March 23

EXCERPT FROM COMMENTS BY DR. HENRY E. WALD, FORMER director of celluar biological research at New York University, at the Smithsonian Symposium on the Politics of Biodiversity, Washington, D.C., February 13-15:

Last spring's NIS report suggests that a quarter-percent of the live births in the District of Columbia are at least part Eweller, that is, they contain at least one copy of what we believe to be the key mutated gene. Whether this is from successful interbreeding over an extended period of time—or a product of a mutation that existing *Homo sapiens sapiens* is programmed to throw off again and again—is a topic of lively debate. With rare and repellent exception, mothers coddle these infants as they would a "normal" offspring.

How long does the separation of one species from another take? The fossil record suggests hundreds or thousands of generations. When would you have recognized it—that your child is different from you?

And which cousin is the dead end? It's hard to think of Man as a dead end. A Neanderthal forty thousand years ago would have had a similar problem imagining that his big-brained, muscular family would soon be extinct. The remnants of *Homo erectus* living on Java fifty thousand years ago probably considered—if they thought about the matter at all—themselves to be well-established survivors, when in fact their species had already died out on most of the earth.

If Ewellers truly are splitting from us, the process has just begun—a few thousand years are nothing in evolutionary time. It's too early to say for sure if Ewellers will be recognized as a separate species. If they are, let us bid them a hearty "Welcome!"

EXCERPT FROM COMMENTS BY CARSTEN STARNS, FORMER director of National Institutes of Science, at the Smithsonian Symposium on the Politics of Biodiversity, Washington, D.C., February 13-15:

I saw how easily they killed. How easily they controlled. If these mutants bear humanity no ill will, why do they remain in hiding? I believe they recognize—as we should—that it's a question of which species will survive.

FROM THE PAPERS OF HENRY WALD (UNDATED):

Who says it's an advance? Movement isn't always movement forward. Change isn't always for the better—it's just written up that way by the winners. Did civilization benefit when barbarians swept into Rome? Europe was set back a thousand years. Technology withered. By the time Columbus sailed, sea-going ships were half the size the Romans had used for trade. The knowledge of how to build bigger ones had been lost. That's history, not evolution, but the processes are similarly blind. We believe that evolution rewards a survival advantage, but what constitutes "advantage"? A variant with big teeth and a tiny brain might thrive for a thousand generations. But its small brain can't foresee an ice age. So the species perishes. Is a big brain a decisive advantage? How about in a random event, a volcanic eruption? All those big-domed, erudite monkeys go down with their island. Their evolutionary "improvements" aren't right for the circumstance. Instead, a few peanut-brained animals with wings fly away and survive to breed. So a billion years of natural selection gets wiped out. A newcomer could exterminate *Homo sapiens sapiens* and a bit later join the long list of anthropoid extinctions. Too bad for us. To bad for the newcomers. Evolution wouldn't care.

"MATHEMATICS OF LONGEVITY," RUSSELL BURL, *LOS ANGELES Times*, March 26.

The key question about the Ewellers hasn't been raised in our innumerate culture. It is: how fast can they multiply? Does a Eweller female become fertile at age twelve or thirteen? There is no reason to believe otherwise. How long does she remain fertile? This we don't know. A human female's fertility is limited at her birth by a finite number of eggs, but it's a very large number—hundreds of thousands—which is depleted by every menstrual cycle as well as by other factors. If a woman remained "youthful" in other senses for hundreds of years, could she continue to conceive? What we've heard about the Eweller mutants suggests the answer is "yes." If that is the case, the exponential growth of the Eweller population could be catastrophic—particularly if they consider high birth rates important to their influence and survival.

Consider what happens when you combine longevity with even a

330 JOHN C. BOLAND

low number of births. (And don't forget: in parts of the world it remains common for a woman to produce ten or fifteen offspring during her lifetime.) Assume a Eweller woman, beginning at age twenty, produces just ten daughters who live to reproduce. Assume each of the daughters produces ten, and so on. Each does this within the first twenty years of her reproductive life. By the completion of the fourth generation, we would have 11,111 of these women, alive and healthy. In the human species, the first generation would be dying off about now. Not the Ewellers! If the current thinking is correct and their life spans *average* even five hundred years (an estimate that is probably too low), what are we looking at?

If society did a better job of teaching math in our schools, I think we would be very, very worried. Because five generations per century, over five centuries, with each member of each generation multiplying itself ten times, equals 10 to the 24th power. We could express it as a "1" followed by twenty-four zeros. In U.S. usage, that is a septillion. Not that it matters, but it is more than *a hundred trillion times* the current population of the earth. Since all the Ewellers born are presumed to be still alive, the actual figure would be a 1 followed by twenty-four 1's, but why quibble?

So we would have standing room only? We should be so lucky. The land surface of the earth, including Antarctica, equals about 57 million square miles. That's about 1.6 quadrillion square feet (a quadrillion is "1" with fifteen zeros after it). If "standing room" is one square foot per person, the Ewellers would be "standing" 625,000,000 *deep* over every square foot of the land surface of the planet. Assuming they average six feet in height, they would form a second skin on our planet *3.75 billion feet deep.*

If you're curious, that works out to about 710,000 miles. The "new" earth would extend three times past the orbit of the moon, which is only 239,000 miles out. I'm not bothering to factor in the compacting effects of this additional mass's gravity, because such population growth is impossible to begin with. Our ecosystem would collapse long before then—sometime between the tenth and eleventh generations.

We can take some comfort in the thought that this new species apparently doesn't reproduce at anything like ten female children per female. It's been around a while, and we aren't even bumping into them on the subway. But if their hybridization with humanity delivers us the gift of longevity, we ought to look at the gift skeptically. Extend human life even a decade, and our own explosive growth will swamp the planet's ability to accommodate us.

Longevity poses a daunting challenge for public policy-makers going forward, whether the policy-makers are human or hybrid. We've gotten a taste of how the pure Eweller policy-maker would deal with the problem. Whatever their other shortcomings, they clearly grasp the peril.

Russell Burl teaches algebra at Los Angeles City College. He is the author of Numeracy and the Neo-Nativist Movement *(St. Martin's Press).*

MEET THE PRESS, INTERVIEW WITH CARSTEN STARNS, FORMER director, National Institutes of Science, September 19 (partial transcript):

Couric: Professor Wald says he believes Variant genes are being deliberately implanted at fertilization clinics.

Starns: I've seen the same reports.

Couric: If true, what does this tell you?

Starns: Katie, we have a fight on our hands. If the Variants are trying to hybridize the human race by stealth, we have to stop them. The same as we would stop the next frontal assault aimed at destroying our species.

Couric: How do you—

Starns: Shutting down fertilization clinics is a good start. Close monitoring of hospitals is needed. There are many things the government can do.

Couric: Let me show you this quote. Professor Henry Wald (September 18): "The privately funded Variant Study Project believes that official figures on hybrid births underestimate the phenomenon because of poor statistical assumptions. In the third calendar quarter, children with at least one copy of the main Variant gene may account for three percent of the total live births in the District of Columbia and suburban Virginia." Dr. Wald goes on to say—

Starns: I know Henry's views, Katie.

Couric: He goes on to say that the deliberate implantation of the Variant strain may have been going on for at least two years before anyone suspected there was a problem. Two or three years of hybridization, Dr. Starns. What does this translate into in terms of the number of children who carry this trait and will pass it on to their children?

Starns: They won't pass it on unless we allow them to. The public needs to understand that this is a disease that still has a cure. The cure is surgical intervention to render hybrids incapable of reproduction. The Supreme Court ruled more than eighty years ago that compulsory sterilization is permissible under certain circumstances. Feeble-minded persons who were institutionalized were sterilized with court permission into the 1970s. We can—

Couric: If your daughter bore a hybrid child, would you tell her to give it up for sterilization, or hide it?

Starns: I wouldn't have to tell her. She grew up believing in service to her community.

Couric: Dr. Wald estimates there could be five million hybrid Variants worldwide right now. You're saying sterilize five million people.

Starns: They aren't people. Even if some radical geneticists are right and this change is programmed into us, we can eliminate these genes from the reproductive pool for the time being. Set the process back perhaps a thousand years. We can turn this around. It requires maturity and commitment. And faith that our Maker doesn't intend the human race's extinction.

Couric: Wald says three percent of births in D.C. may be hybrid. Do we have a clue what's going in Andean villages or suburbs of Khartoum?

Starns: We need global vigilance, Katie. But if that's the price of self-preservation, I'm confident the human race will pay it.

FROM THE PAPERS OF HENRY WALD (UNDATED):

We like to believe in our virtues. Intelligence, charity: they must be wedded to the natural order. Suppose none of these matters. Art, philosophy, happiness, love, purpose, intelligence, cooperation, progress—all these are human values. Suppose the great genetic drift—this mindless tide with no predetermined shore—picks its survivors from the artless and the stupid? I have my purpose, maybe even a few illusions. Nature has neither. As for virtues— DNA chains don't care. Starns and his ilk are all wrong, but so are the people romanticizing the Ewell Variant. I've said that it's a "new" model but never that it's "improved." Nature doesn't make value judgments. The Ewellers are no more a step "forward" than if they had six hands.

Postcard. May 12. Curacao.

David: Too many blondes, if you can believe it. I hear the redhead is pregnant. Naughty boy? Paolo.

Author's Note

THE DEAD APPARENTLY DON'T LIKE HAVING THEIR REMAINS disturbed, even in the interest of science. There is precedent for the mental anguish suffered by the archaeologists on Ewell Island. In 1993, Natalia Polusmak's team in Southern Siberia's Altai Mountains reported ferociously bad dreams as they excavated Fifth Century Scythian burial sites and recovered the remarkably preserved "Ice Maiden." Jeanne Smoot said, "Some of us thought the place was testing us." All sorts of bad luck, including a helicopter failure, was attributed to the malevolence of that remote area. Like some of the people in this novel, the group derided their superstitious susceptibilities even while experiencing the effects.

Science moves ahead, building and destroying theories. Efforts to extract DNA from Jurassic bones and fossilized plant leaves have been proved entertaining failures. Instead of yielding ancient genetic codes, the relics have shown contamination from the laboratory and other sources. It isn't clear how long these fragile strands of genetic information can persist even under ideal conditions. But bioarchaeologists are steadily pushing back the clock. It's well within the current competence to recover Margaret Wakelyn's DNA. Svante Pääbo, director of the Max Planck Institute for Evolutionary Anthropology in Munich, succeeded in replicating several hundred base pairs of Neanderthal DNA in the 1990s and proposed in 2006 to sequence the entire Neanderthal genome.

The founder effect described here is also well recognized. A new gene is much more likely to meet itself, and be perpetuated, within a small, insular community. This is bad news for island populations, even those living in socially defined "islands." The genetically transmitted diseases of the Amish, the French-Canadian Chicoutimi, and other insular groups are well described in medical literature. For the same reasons, if you're searching for the next "human" species, an isolated island such as Ewell would be a good place to look.

Research in longevity proceeds. The mention of Cynthia Kenyon's success in extending the lives of small roundworms called nematodes by gene manipulation is based on fact. Her work at the University of California, San Francisco, helped spur other scientists into related pursuits; they have achieved some success in extending the lives of laboratory mice. It isn't a stretch to suggest that extended human life spans are possible. But if you're hoping for a "longevity" gene, the question posed in this novel comes into play: would a longer life span be a survival advantage for the species? If the answer is "no," then a longevity gene, if it ever existed, may have been flushed from the human genome as a loser.

Current scientific theory holds that human evolution has been rapid—and continues at a lively pace. The findings attributed in the novel to Dr. Jonathan Pritchard, of the University of Chicago, are real. Pritchard led a study that developed evidence of ongoing evolutionary selection in seven hundred areas of the human genome during the last five to fifteen thousand years. "There is ample evidence that selection has been a major driving point in our evolution during the last ten thousand years, and there is no reason to suppose it has stopped," Pritchard told *The New York Times* in April 2006. Selection of five skin genes in versions existing only in Europeans traced to as recently as 6,000 years ago. Pritchard also reported selection in genes affecting human brain size. "The time scale for a strongly favored mutation to sweep through a population is about five thousand years," he told *Wired* magazine. "It's hard to get an exact estimate for rates of change, but we know the lactase gene [which enables adults to metabolize dairy products] is evolving the fastest in humans. It was new five thousand years ago and now it's in virtually everybody in Europe."

The fictional article about the rapid evolution of European

mice on the island of Madeira is based on fact. Janice Britton-Davidian is a real person, and her findings—that six separate species evolved in five hundred years, accompanied by massive chromosomal fusions—have been widely reported.

Mankind appears to be very much an ongoing process. I avoid saying a "work in progress," because there is no sign of a workman. So far no one has come up with DNA evidence to suggest a dramatic split in the modern human line. But imagining such an event has been fun.

The unsavory history of a noted scientific research center, the Cold Spring Harbor Laboratory, mentioned in this work of fiction is unfortunately true. Harvard-trained Charles B. Davenport, who became Cold Spring's director in 1898, established the Eugenics Record Office, which provided the American eugenics movement with scientific credibility in its pursuit of racial improvement. Davenport's protégé Harry H. Laughlin testified before Congress on immigration issues, citing the danger of admitting genetic "misfits," and authored a model law adopted by a number of states authorizing forced sterilizations. Helen Calder's thoughts on the widespread acceptance of eugenics in the United States in the 1920s barely scratch the surface of this miscegenation between science and politics. In *Buck v. Bell* in 1927, Justice Oliver Wendell Holmes Jr. wrote for the Supreme Court, upholding Virginia's forced sterilization of a feeble-minded woman: "It is better for all the world, if instead of waiting to execute degenerate offspring for crime, or let them starve for their imbecility, society can prevent those who are manifestly unfit from breeding their kind. The principle that sustains compulsory vaccination is broad enough to cover cutting Fallopian tubes. . . . Three generations of imbeciles are enough." The eugenics movement had many champions among the notables of its day, including Theodore Roosevelt, Margaret Sanger, Irving Fisher, and prominent academics at a number of universities.

A final note, with a word of apology. Ewell Island, used so harshly in this novel, has roots in reality. But in imagining Ewell, the writer has scandalously disregarded fact in pursuit of entertainment. Both Smith and Tangier islands, which lie in the

Chesapeake Bay, have retained many of their Colonial family names and shades of dialect that are distinct in a world of mass communication. The populations, however, bear none of the negative traits assigned to the fictional islanders in this novel.

Finally, a note of thanks to Hank Ratrie, who took time from his schedule as a lecturer and jogger to check the manuscript for scientific blunders. Whatever of those remain are the fault of the author.

Suggested Reading

GENE SCIENCE MOVES FASTER THAN PRINTING PRESSES. THE following books treat their subjects with clarity, grace and—generally—a modest appreciation of how much is yet to be learned:

The Blind Watchmaker, Richard Dawkins (Norton, 1986)

The Greatest Show on Earth, Richard Dawkins (Free Press, 2009)

The Molecule Hunt, Martin Jones (Arcade, 2001)

Signs of Life, Robert Pollack (Houghton Mifflin, 1994)

The Neanderthal Enigma, James Shreeve (Avon, 1995)

The Journey of Man, Spencer Wells (Random House, 2002)

The Seven Daughters of Eve, Bryan Sykes (Norton, 2001)

DNA: The Secret of Life, James D. Watson with Andrew Berry (Knopf, 2003)

Mutants, Armand Marie Leroi (Viking, 2003)

The Code of Codes, Daniel J. Kevles and Leroy Hood, eds. (Harvard 1992)

The Book of Man, Walter Bodmer and Robin McKie (Oxford 1994)

Genes and Human Self-Knowledge, Robert F Weir, Susan C. Lawrence, Evans Fales, eds. (Iowa 1994)

Abusing Science: The Case Against Creationism, Philip Kitcher (MIT, 1982)

Adaptive Individuals in Evolving Populations, Richard K. Belew and Melanie Mitchell, eds. (Addison-Wesley, 1996)

The Biology of Race (Revised), James C. King (U. of California, 1981)

The Fossil Trail, Ian Tattersall (Oxford, 1995)

About the Author

JOHN C. BOLAND'S SHORT STORIES HAVE APPEARED IN NATIONAL magazines since 1976. His "Last Island South" from 2008 was nominated by both the International Thriller Writers Association and the Private Eye Writers for best short story. He is the author, since 1991, of about a dozen novels under his own name and pseudonyms, published by St. Martin's Press, Pocket Books, and Perfect Crime. His nonfiction has appeared in *The Wall Street Journal*, *The New York Times*, *Barron's*, and other magazines and newspapers. The author's website is www.JohnCBoland.com.

CPSIA information can be obtained at www.ICGtesting.com
Printed in the USA
LVOW091852081111

254076LV00002B/71/P